One Delicious Bite . . .

"The chocolate cake is good," Jake said suddenly.

Blinking, Nicole glanced down at her cake. She hadn't even tried it yet.

"But you taste better," Jake added.

Nicole stilled, then slowly raised her head to peer at him. Oh yeah, his eyes were on fire now . . . and so was she. How the hell did that happen so fast? No kissing, touching, nothing. Just a couple of words and she was ready to go.

Jake picked up his plate and coffee and carried them to the island, then returned to stand beside her. Nicole tipped her head back, expecting him to kiss her, but instead he caught her chair and turned it so she faced him. He then scooped her up and set her on the table where his cake had been moments ago.

"These have to go," Jake announced, reaching for the button of her jeans. "You should wear skirts and dresses," he added conversationally as he slid the button free and started on the zipper. "It would make things much easier."

"I'll have to buy some," Nicole said breathlessly as he slid the zipper down.

By Lynsay Sands

LYNSAY SANDS

ONE LUCKY VAMPIRE

AN ARGENEAU NOVEL

AVON

An Imprint of HarperCollinsPublishers

AVON BOOKS
An Imprint of HarperCollins*Publishers*
10 East 53rd Street
New York, New York 10022-5299

Copyright © 2013 by Lynsay Sands
Excerpt from *The Switch* copyright © 1999 by Lynsay Sands
ISBN 978-0-06-207814-8
www.avonromance.com

First Avon Books mass market printing: October 2013

Avon Trademark Reg. U.S. Pat. Off. and in Other Countries, Marca Registrada, Hecho en U.S.A.
HarperCollins® is a registered trademark of HarperCollins Publishers.

Printed in the U.S.A.

10 9 8 7 6 5 4 3 2 1

ONE LUCKY
VAMPIRE

One

"Last day of this assignment."

Jake nodded silently, but didn't look at Dan Shephard, the blond man at his side and his partner for this job. Instead, Jake's eyes were busily sliding over the crowd that had gathered around the hotel entrance where their client stood answering questions. It was supposed to look like a spur of the moment thing, their client stopping to answer a few of the many questions shot at him by the press who always followed him on visits like this. It was supposed to make him seem more accessible and less the dangerous dictator he was. But it wasn't spur of the moment. Jake, Dan, and the rest of the security team had been told that he was going to stop and answer questions and that they weren't to rush him into his vehicle and whisk him away as would be the norm. Instead they were to let him "do his thing" and just keep an eye out for trouble.

Jake was doing just that, keeping an eye out, looking for any possible threat.

"Damn good thing it's almost over too," Dan added grimly. "One more day of watching out for this arrogant, demanding prick and I might be tempted to kill him myself."

That comment made Jake's mouth twitch with amusement. Their client was definitely an annoying, arrogant, and demanding bastard. But then, what else could you expect from a foreign dictator? Besides, working as professional protection in Ottawa meant that a lot of the people they were sent to guard were arrogant, demanding, or annoying. At least on the outside. Some were a different case inside and just acting up out of fear or stress, but not all. This client was as arrogant, demanding, and annoying inside as he acted on the outside. But, they were hired to do a job and you couldn't like every client, he thought philosophically.

"He flies out at eight, right? Then we're done?" Dan asked.

Jake nodded, but his eyes had narrowed on a man in the crowd. The fellow wore a baseball cap and jean jacket. He was also eyeballing their client. Of course, most people there were, but there was just something about Ball-Cap Boy that was raising alarms in Jake's head.

"Four more hours then," Dan muttered, glancing at his wristwatch. "Four more hours . . . and counting," he added dryly. "Want to go for a drink afterward? I know I need one after a week with this bast— Where are you going?"

Jake heard the question, but didn't stop to answer. He was hurrying through the crowd toward Ball-

Cap Boy, every muscle in his body straining to get there in time as the man pulled a gun from the waistband at the back of his jeans and began to level it at their client.

"That was one hell of a catch," Dan said, slapping Jake on the back six hours later as they headed out of Protection One's swanky offices and approached the elevators. Their four hours of work had turned into six thanks to Jake's stopping and apprehending the assassin in the baseball cap. First there had been the police and all their questions to deal with and then they'd had to fill in their boss, Hank Latham, on what had taken place.

Now, they were finally leaving work, two hours later than expected.

"I don't know how you did it," Dan continued, shaking his head as the elevator doors opened and they stepped on board. "Hell, I didn't even track the guy as a problem, but I sure as hell couldn't have moved as fast as you did. You flew through that crowd."

"Adrenaline," Jake muttered, glancing at his watch.

"You gotta love adrenaline," Dan commented, slapping him again as Jake pushed the button for the main floor. As the doors closed, he commented, "So we get a couple of play days before the next assignment. Want to go for a drink to celebrate?"

"Can't. I'm meeting someone for dinner and I'm already late," Jake said, leaning back against the elevator wall and crossing his arms. He wasn't really sorry he had to decline. He liked Dan, he was a good guy, but Jake wasn't much of a drinker. Alcohol did little for him.

"Someone? Like a lady?" Dan asked with a grin.

"Someone, like sort of family," Jake said evasively.

"Sort of family?" Dan prodded.

Jake hesitated, and then said, "Yeah. You know, that older lady who isn't really a relation but your parents make you call aunt."

"Ah," Dan grimaced. "Yeah. I have one of those myself, a lifelong friend of my mom's. She and her hubby hang with my parents all the time and she's been 'Aunt Betty' most of my life. Dotty old biddy now, but good-hearted."

"Yeah, this is the same deal," Jake said, ignoring the twinge of guilt the words caused. The lady in question was old as hell, but "dotty old biddy" didn't exactly fit her.

"Well . . ." Dan eyed him silently, and then smiled wryly and said, "I'm kind of glad to hear about this aunt who's not an aunt. You never mention family. I was beginning to think you were hatched or something."

"Nah. There just isn't much to talk about," Jake said quietly. "Most of my family live on the West Coast or out of the country. Haven't seen much of them the last few years or so."

"Ah." Dan nodded. "So . . . ? Siblings? Parents still alive? Kissing cousins around?"

Much to Jake's relief he was saved from answering the probing questions when they reached the main floor and the doors began to open. Moving forward, he said, "See you in a couple days," over his shoulder.

"Yeah." Dan said, following him off the elevator.

Jake hurried for the building's exit, but his expression was tight. He knew damned right well that wouldn't be the end of the questions. Dan would repeat them at the first opportunity, and have a dozen more.

Putting away that worry for now, Jake pushed through the front doors and turned right, moving quickly. He was supposed to have been at the restaurant ten minutes ago. Fortunately, the Protection One offices were downtown, just around the corner and down the street from where he was headed. A three- or four-minute walk if he moved fast.

Of course, it was possible he was rushing for nothing. His dinner companion may already have given up and left. He couldn't say he'd be sorry if she had. He wasn't looking forward to this meeting. He had no doubt his "aunt" was trying to arrange a family reunion, and while it may have been more than half a dozen years since he'd left the bosom of his family, he wasn't ready to return. Not yet anyway.

Worrying about how to politely say as much, Jake reached the restaurant and hurried inside, only to pause abruptly, his gaze searching the patrons.

"Hi. Did you want a table or are you meeting someone?"

Jake glanced to the young woman who had spoken. Dressed all in black, she was blond, beaming, and perky as hell. She waited wide-eyed and head tilted for his answer.

"Meeting someone," he assured her, and then turned his attention back to the room, his eye

immediately caught by the auburn-haired beauty
waving at him from a table in the back corner. She
hadn't left. Damn, he thought wearily and headed
for the table. She was on her feet by the time he
reached her, and immediately stepped forward to
hug him.

"Sorry I'm late," Jake apologized as he self-
consciously returned the embrace. "I just got out
of work."

"No need to apologize, Stephano. I'm just glad
you agreed to meet me," Marguerite Argeneau
said, leaning back in his arms to smile at him
warmly. "It's good to see you."

"You too," Jake said stiffly as he released her.
Voice gentle, he added, "I don't go by Stephano
anymore."

"Oh, yes, of course, I'm sorry," she said apologetically. "You go by your second name now.
Jacob."

"Call me Jake," he suggested, urging her back to
her seat, before settling in the one across from her
as another woman all in black approached with
menus in hand. This one was a brunette, but she
wore a beaming smile as perky as the blonde's at
the door as she stopped at the table.

"Good evening!" she said gaily as she set a menu
in front of each of them. "Would you like something to drink while you look at the menu?"

"Water," Jake said quietly.

Nodding, the girl then turned to Marguerite.
"How is your tea? Would you like fresh tea, or
something else to drink?"

"Another tea, please, and a glass of water," Marguerite said, her smile just as wide as the girl's.

Nodding, their waitress beamed again and rushed off.

Marguerite immediately turned to him with a more natural smile. "Jake. The name suits you. And I understand now you use Colson, your father's last name, rather than Notte?"

He shifted uncomfortably as he nodded, and then waited for her to give him hell for being an ungrateful wretch and dropping the name of the man who had been a father to him since he was five.

Instead, Marguerite smiled with understanding and said, "A new name for a new life."

Jake's surprise at her comment must have shown on his face, because she smiled and shrugged.

"I know you didn't want to be immortal, Steph— Jake," She grimaced apologetically for the slip and Jake shrugged it away. No he hadn't wanted to be immortal. His mother had explained everything to him and offered to turn him on his eighteenth birthday, but he'd refused. He was born mortal and had wanted to stay that way. But then some skinny little bitch immortal had stabbed him in the chest while pursuing a vendetta against his boss, Vincent Argeneau, Marguerite's nephew. Vincent had found him dying on the office floor and had used his one turn to make Jake an immortal. It had been the only way Vincent could save him and Jake understood why he'd done it. He even knew intellectually that he should be grateful for it. But he wasn't. Or maybe he was. He just didn't know it. Mostly he'd spent his time since then trying to ignore it and pretend it hadn't happened, that he was normal and not a freak who had to feed on blood to survive.

"I know you've been struggling with the change," Marguerite continued. "And I respect that. I haven't come here to judge you, or try to get you to see your mother, or guilt you with comments about her loving and worrying about you."

Jake's mouth twitched with amusement at the words. Just saying them was enough to inspire some guilt . . . and Marguerite knew that, but he suspected she just couldn't resist. She was a mother too, after all. But he let her get away with it and simply asked, "So how long has everyone known where I was and what I was doing?"

Jake had responded to waking up to find himself a vampire much like a wounded animal, crawling away to a corner to lick his wounds. Only his corner was Ottawa, which was hell and gone from California, where he'd lived at the time. And rather than lick his wounds, he did his best to pretend there wasn't anything different. Other than sending his mother and brother short notes in birthday and Christmas e-cards, he'd broken all contact with the family while he dealt with it. But since he wasn't really dealing with it, this had gone on for seven years. But then, what the hell? Time was irrelevant now. He could take as long as he wanted to deal with it.

"No one else knows," Marguerite assured him, and when he arched one dubious eyebrow, she added, "Well, aside from myself and Bastien, of course."

Jake's mouth tightened. He'd had to let Bastien, the president of Argeneau Enterprises, know. He needed blood to survive and while he might now be a fricking vampire, he'd be damned if he was going to go around attacking and biting mortals to survive. Which meant he needed blood delivered, and Argeneau Enterprises had a blood bank that supplied blood to immortals. Jake was sure there were other suppliers with similar setups, but Argeneau was the only one he knew about, and it wasn't like vampire blood banks advertised in the damned yellow pages. So, he'd had to arrange for delivery of a steady supply. But he'd called Bastien personally, asking him to keep his whereabouts and new name a secret. It seemed he'd trusted the wrong person.

"Bastien didn't tell me," Marguerite assured him solemnly. "He has kept your secret as he promised."

"Then how—?"

"I'm his mother," she said simply. "I can read all my children as easily as reading a book. He can't keep secrets from me. Although he tries," she added with a grin.

Jake smiled wryly and sank back in his seat. He should have suspected as much. His own mother was the same way and had been since she'd met Roberto Conti Notte and been turned when Jake was a boy. He had never been able to keep a secret from her after that, which was damned dismaying to a teenage boy full of hormones. Knowing your mother would know what you were doing was pretty inhibiting sexually.

"I've known from the beginning where you were and respected your need for privacy while you adjusted."

"Until now," he said quietly.

"Until now," Marguerite agreed solemnly. "Because I need you."

That brought him upright in his seat, his eyebrows high. "You need me?"

"Yes." She nodded solemnly, but then sat back and peered past him.

Jake wasn't surprised to look around and see the waitress returning with their drinks.

"Are you ready to order, or do you need a few more minutes?" the girl asked as she set down their drinks.

Jake glanced at Marguerite as she looked down at her menu. She had opened it, but he didn't think she'd really got a chance to check it out before this. On the other hand, he hadn't even opened his, but didn't need to. He had eaten here many times. The workers were always annoyingly perky, but the food was also always great. It was why he'd suggested it as the meeting spot.

"I know what I want," Jake said now, "but Marguerite might need—"

"Ooh, the quail sounds lovely," Marguerite interrupted.

The waitress chuckled and nodded as she took her menu, and then turned to Jake in question. "The grilled hanger steak for you?"

Jake blinked in surprise. "I—yes," he said slowly, a little concerned that she knew that.

"It's what you've ordered the last three times you've come here," the waitress said gently as she took his menu. "At least the last three times I've been working."

"Right," Jake said, and felt a moment's guilt that he hadn't recognized the girl. Before the turn he'd always made sure to remember details like that, making note of people who served him, showing his appreciation for good service. He'd changed since the turn though. His thoughts now were usually turned inward, and he rarely paid attention to his surroundings or even the people around him unless he was at work, where that was a necessary part of the job.

Clearing his throat, he offered her an apologetic smile and nod. "Thank you . . . Melanie," he added, glancing to her name tag. He would make sure to remember her in future.

"My pleasure," she assured him, beaming again before whirling away.

"She likes you and thinks you're attractive," Marguerite said with a grin the moment the girl was out of earshot.

"Yeah, that happens a lot since the turn," he said dryly. "I'm guessing this immortal business includes some kind of chick magnet deal or something?"

"Not exactly," she said solemnly. "Although the scientists at Argeneau Enterprises have noted that we secrete higher levels of certain hormones and pheromones that might affect mortals, both male and female."

"Of course," he said bitterly. "It would make us better hunters."

Marguerite raised her tea for a sip. As she swallowed and set the cup down, she said carefully, "You must have a lot of questions about how you are different now."

"No," he said gruffly, and then pointed out, "While mother and Roberto made sure I was in the dark as a child, I've known about immortals since I was eighteen. I learned a lot in the thirty-some years before I left California. I know most things, I think. I just never realized that my brother, Neil, was such a chick magnet because of what he was, not because of his natural charm and wit."

"Well, see, there's one benefit at least," she said cheerfully. "You're a chick magnet now."

Jake didn't argue the point, but simply said, "You said you need my help?"

Marguerite looked like she wanted to say more on the benefits he'd gained when he'd been turned, but she let it go with a sigh and then asked, "I understand you work as a bodyguard now?"

Jake nodded. Before being turned he'd been a vice president at V.A. Inc. in California, a company with diversified interests. Vincent Argeneau had been the president, but the man had been little more than a figurehead, leaving the actual running of the company to Jake and his younger brother, Neil. Jake had been the daytime president. Neil had taken over at night. But after the turn . . . well, Neil already had the nighttime gig, and most companies didn't need day and night V.P.s. It was only immortal-owned companies that did that, catering to both mortals by day and immortals by night. But Jake hadn't wanted to deal with immortals at that point. If anything, he'd wanted to get as far away from them as possible, but a similar position in a mortal company was impossible. Vampires didn't work days.

Jake had needed a new career to go with his name change, one he could do at night and one that needed minimal training. He'd always been interested in martial arts and had trained at it since he was six. The bodyguard shtick had seemed a good deal: interesting, exciting even. Boy, had he got that wrong. Mostly it was standing around, eyeballing crowds for hours on end. But it was a reason to get up every morning.

Night, he corrected himself. It was a reason to get up every night. After seven years he still had trouble with a lot of the changes to his life. He had never been a night person. Now he was whether he wanted to be or not.

"Well, I have someone who needs guarding."

Jake was pulled from his thoughts by that announcement. He stared at Marguerite with surprise. "Surely Lucian would arrange for Rogue Hunters to protect any immortal who needs—"

"No," Marguerite interrupted. "This situation has nothing to do with immortals. She's mortal and so is the person who is a threat to her."

Jake sat back in his seat and merely quirked an eyebrow, inviting her to explain. Marguerite was an immortal, and an old one. At least seven hundred or something, he thought, though he wasn't positive. He was pretty sure she'd been born in medieval days. As far as he knew, everyone she knew was immortal. He couldn't think what mortal she would be concerning herself with.

"Her name is Nicole Phillips. Her mother, Zaira, is the sister of my housekeeper, Maria," Marguerite said and then explained, "Zaira married and moved north with her husband just before Maria started working for me. But her husband had a heart attack when Nicole was fifteen and they moved back this way to be closer to family. From fifteen until she finished university, Nicole, and Maria's daughter, Pierina, used to help out Maria with spring cleaning of my home, and preparing the house for the rare big parties I threw." She smiled. "They were both good girls, very polite and hardworking."

Jake could hear the affection in her voice, and when she paused, he nodded, encouraging her to continue.

"The two girls grew to be very close, more like sisters than cousins. Pierina really enjoyed cooking. She was also the little organizer, deciding where things should be and who should do what." Marguerite's mouth curved up with affectionate amusement. "Nicole, though, was more interested in artistic endeavors. She grew up to be an amazing artist, and she's now a very successful portraitist. Her work is well respected and much sought after."

Jake couldn't help noticing the pride and affection in her voice. It was obvious she had taken great interest in and had a lot of affection for both girls. He found himself smiling faintly in return.

"And then a couple years back she met a charming Italian while on vacation in Europe. By all accounts, he seemed to adore her. It was very romantic, a whirlwind affair. He was suave, promising to show her the world and proclaiming his love in the most passionate terms . . . and she was smitten. Then they married."

Jake's mouth quirked at her change of tone on those last three words. They sounded flat and grim. "I gather things changed once they were married?"

"Oh yes," she said on a sigh. "Nicole tried to hide it, but—"

"There is no hiding it from you," Jake suggested quietly.

"It wasn't me who figured it out first," she corrected. "As I mentioned, Nicole was always very close to Pierina, but she moved to Italy briefly to be with Rodolfo—"

"That's the suave Italian?"

"Yes, Rodolfo Rossi. She lived with him in Italy for a bit and then they married and moved back to Canada, but to Ottawa rather than the Toronto area where her family is . . . at his insistence," she added grimly. "He claimed he could better find a job in his field in Ottawa. But I realize now that he wanted to isolate her from her family."

Jake nodded silently. That was usually what happened with an abusive mate: lasso the woman and move her away from family and friends and any kind of support or interference they might offer.

"Fortunately, Pierina came out to Ottawa to visit Nicole," Marguerite continued. "She wasn't happy with what she found. At first, Pierina just thought Nicole was working herself too hard, working her way into the grave in fact. She insisted Nicole come to Toronto for a girls' weekend to relax and I invited the two of them and their mothers for dinner. I wanted to ask Nicole about doing a portrait of my son, Christian, and his fiancée, Carolyn, for me," she explained.

"And you read her mind and quickly realized work wasn't the problem," Jake suggested.

"I realized it wasn't the *only* problem." Marguerite corrected. "She *was* taking on too many commissions and working too hard . . . at Rodolfo's insistence. She's much sought after with clients from all over the world. She usually has to refuse a good many of them, or book them years in advance she is so busy, but Rodolfo was insisting she could do more and should accept them all. He insisted she should "strike while the iron was hot"; the commissions might dry up one day and she should make all the money she could before that happened. He had her working around the clock . . . and all the while he wasn't working at all."

"Nice," Jake murmured.

"Yes, well, while that was helping to sap her energy, the real problem, and what she was trying to hide was that he was terribly controlling and hypercritical. While he was insisting she should do all these commissions, he would then complain that she spent no time with him. He was also tearing at her self-esteem and independence and basically making her miserable. By the time she came to Toronto, he had demoralized her to the point that I don't think she could have left him on her own, so . . ." She paused and avoided his gaze briefly, and then admitted, "I gave her a mental nudge to make her leave him."

"Ah," Jake murmured. It was all he could say. He'd never thought much of the way immortals tended to control the minds of mortals and make them do things they might not otherwise have done. The truth was, he didn't like it. But in this instance, Marguerite's heart had been in the right place at least.

"Here we are."

Jake glanced to the side and sat back to get out of the way as their waitress arrived with their meals.

"Thank you," he murmured as she set his plate in front of him.

"You're more than welcome," she said brightly, beamed at him, and then slipped away.

They were both silent for a moment as they tasted their food. As Jake had expected, his steak was amazing. But then it always was. It was the first thing he'd tried here and the last. He tended to stick with things when he liked them. Although, glancing at Marguerite's quail, he now wondered if he shouldn't try some of the other dishes here. It looked delicious too.

"It *is* delicious," she assured him, and Jake grimaced, aware that she was reading his mind. While he too was immortal now, it was a new state for him and he knew most older immortals could read him as easily as if he were mortal.

"Sorry," she muttered.

He shrugged with a wry smile. Swallowing the steak in his mouth, he asked, "So you prodded this Nicole and she left her Rodolfo?"

Marguerite nodded as she took a sip of her water, and then said, "It all seemed good at first. She left him and started divorce proceedings. She also started to see a counselor to try to undo the damage he'd done." Marguerite smiled. "It's working. Nicole's becoming the happy, strong young woman she was before the marriage again."

"But?" Jake prompted. If everything were going so rosy, Marguerite wouldn't need his help.

"But there have been some incidents," Marguerite said on a sigh, cutting viciously into her quail.

"Incidents?" Jake queried.

"Three gas explosions narrowly avoided."

His eyebrows rose. "You think Rodolfo's trying to kill her?"

Marguerite's mouth tightened and rather than answer outright, she said, "He's going after her money, hard. He's claiming he left his country, friends, family, et cetera, to marry her and move to Canada and she is now abandoning him. No one's buying it," she added grimly. "He was actually let go before the marriage and suggested the move back to Canada himself. Besides, Nicole had arranged interviews for him with companies in his field here before he even landed in Canada. He refused to go though, claiming he wanted a career change. But then he didn't look for work in any field, but lived off of her."

Marguerite shook her head with disgust. "Her lawyer doesn't think he'll get much at all. However, if she dies before the divorce is final . . ."

"He gets it all," Jake finished for her and she nodded solemnly. "And you think he's thinking that way?"

"Yes," Marguerite said on a sigh.

Jake nodded, but asked, "So, why doesn't she have a will made up leaving everything to someone else?"

"Because she doesn't believe he would do anything like that," Marguerite said unhappily.

He was silent for a moment and then guessed, "And you feel guilty because you are the one who nudged her into leaving him."

She nodded again and then said firmly, "I am not sorry I did it. As I say, she's regaining her self-esteem and returning to the cheerful, strong woman she was before the marriage. She's much happier. But—"

"But she's also under threat now, which she

wouldn't have been had you not interfered," he suggested quietly and Marguerite sighed and nodded again.

Jake considered her briefly as she took a bite of her quail and then said, "I'm surprised you haven't just taken care of the husband yourself. Wiped his mind and sent him back to Europe or something."

Marguerite bit her lip and then grimaced and admitted, "That's why I'm in Ottawa. Julius thinks I came to go over photos for the portrait Nicole's doing of Christian and Carolyn, and so does she, but really I intended to take care of Rodolfo and send him back to Europe. Unfortunately, I can't locate him. Nicole moved out and left him the house at first, the understanding being that she pay the bills and he live there and act as caretaker until it sold . . . at which point they would split the proceeds. But he was apparently enjoying the free rent and making sure it wouldn't sell, so she had to buy him out of the house. Nicole has no idea where he moved to after that."

Marguerite scowled and shook her head. "I thought, no problem, I'd get Rodolfo's address from his divorce lawyer. So I got his name from Nicole and then paid him a visit, but even his divorce lawyer doesn't know Rodolfo's actual address. His contact with him is a P.O. box and a cell-phone number that is still registered to the marital house address." She scowled. "It's like he's hiding out. Nicole says when she asked him where he'd moved to, he refused to say, joking that she might send a hit man after him."

Jake's eyebrows rose. He was a firm believer in that old saying, a skunk smells its own hole first.

In this case, Rodolfo's thinking she might try to bump him off suggested he was thinking that way himself. He probably *was* trying to inherit rather than divorce, but . . . "Why me?"

Marguerite paused with a forkful of rutabaga halfway to her mouth, and cast him an uncertain look. "I don't know what you mean."

"I mean, why me?" he repeated. "Why has Nicole not hired a company for protection? And why are you coming to me? I work for an agency, I don't run it, Marguerite."

"Oh, yes, I see."

She slid the rutabaga into her mouth and chewed, her expression thoughtful, and Jake guessed she was gathering her thoughts, so turned his attention to his own meal, surprised to find that he'd eaten half of it while they'd talked. That was a damned shame. The steak was good enough it should be savored, not eaten absently and without really tasting it while you were distracted by conversation. He took a bite of steak now, savoring the delicious flavors.

"Well," Marguerite said finally, "The problem is that Nicole is in total denial and refuses to believe she's under threat."

His eyebrows rose and he swallowed before saying, "This doesn't sound like something easy to deny. You did say there were three narrowly escaped explosions."

"Yes." She set her fork down, obviously preparing for a long explanation, and said, "Nicole bought Rodolfo out of the house last month and moved back in herself. Pierina came up to help her unpack. She says they were sitting talking after the move, exhausted and achy and Pierina suggested a glass of wine and a dip in the hot tub would be nice. So, they went to open the sliding glass doors to check and be sure that the hot tub was on, but couldn't get the door open. Wood was jammed in the door, which was keeping it from opening."

"Many people do that to prevent thieves breaking in," Jake commented with a shrug.

"The house is about twenty-five years old, and so are the sliding glass doors. They're a reverse set. The glass door that opens is outside the screen, and the wood was jammed in the track *outside*," Marguerite said dryly. "A thief could have plucked it out. It was stopping the door from opening from the inside."

"Oh," he said quietly.

Marguerite nodded. "So they went around to her studio to go out that way and it was the same thing. Every sliding glass door on the main floor of the house was blocked shut from the outside."

"Interesting," Jake murmured.

Marguerite nodded. "Pierina says they just thought Rodolfo was an idiot at that point and actually laughed about it."

"But something changed their minds?" Jake guessed.

"The next morning they woke up to find the furnace had died. There was no heat, and the house was going cold fast. Nicole called in a heating guy and apparently something had been removed from the furnace. Pierina explained it, but—" Marguerite shrugged. "I can't recall what it was. However, it was preventing the pilot light from relighting. Well, remembering the doors being blocked shut, Pierina got suspicious and asked if that missing piece could have caused a buildup of gas in the house and a possible explosion. The man assured her that, no, it couldn't because newer furnaces have an automatic shutoff, but if it had been an older furnace it could have caused a gas fire if the gas had been ignited, or anyone in the house could have been overcome by gas and died. Still, he was bewildered that someone had removed the piece. He said it had to have been physically removed. It couldn't just fall out, and, even had that been possible, the piece had been taken away. It wasn't lying there anywhere as if it had fallen out."

Jake was silent for a moment, and then said, "I don't see—"

"Someone removed that piece," Marguerite pointed out. "Why? Apparently the furnace in Rodolfo's home back in Europe was old and probably wouldn't have had that new automatic shutoff. An explosion would have been more than possible with his furnace back in Europe had the same thing happened there and Pierina suspects he thought this would act the same way . . . And the doors were blocked," she reminded him. "Nicole would have been trapped in the house if a fire had ignited, or if she'd been overcome by gas."

"Surely there are other doors in the house," Jake said with a frown. "They aren't all sliding glass doors. Her front door for instance—"

"It's a keyed entrance. There are three proper doors on the ground floor and all three are keyed entrances. There is no way to unlock them from the outside or the inside without a key. If the house had burst into flames in the middle of the night, she wouldn't have crawled out of bed with her keys in hand. She would have stumbled downstairs through the smoke, only to find she couldn't open the doors without keys and then tried the sliding doors to find those were blocked. Then she would have had to find her way back upstairs in the smoke and find her keys, and then make her way back down to use a door."

"I see," Jake murmured, and he did. In that situation, chances were the smoke would have overcome Nicole before she got out. "And the other two near misses?"

"There's an indoor gas grill in the kitchen. Nicole planned to make grilled steak for dinner on the second day of Pierina's visit, but when she turned it on, instead of the grill lighting up, flames exploded out of the base by the dials and shot right up into her face. It took her eyebrows off. Fortunately, she was quick to shut it off, and that was all that happened.

"They called in another gas guy to see what was wrong. Apparently there was a layer of foil between where the flames come out and the grill on top. He asked why it was there. Nicole shrugged. She hadn't put it there. When she saw it, she'd thought her ex had done it to catch any drippings so he didn't have to clean the base of the grill. She hadn't thought anything of it.

"But the flames wouldn't have been able to get to the food through the foil," Jake said with a frown.

"Exactly," Marguerite said grimly. "That didn't occur to her though until he pointed it out. Apparently, Rodolfo had always put foil in the oven under the elements, and she hadn't really noticed that the foil would hamper the flames."

Jake nodded. He supposed if she'd been distracted, chatting with Pierina, that wouldn't have occurred to her.

Marguerite took a sip of tea, and then continued, "The gas man removed the foil and right away saw the problem. The gas tubing had been pulled out of its housing, the gas was coming out of the pipe itself, lit up by the pilot and shooting straight up through the dials. He said they were lucky. It could have been much worse than her losing her eyebrows. Pierina says he then asked Nicole if there was anyone who didn't like her. Pierina told him Nicole was in the middle of a divorce. He apparently nodded slowly, and then said it was a two-minute fix, just put the tubing back where it belonged, but he thought he should check anything else gas-related in the house."

"And he found something else," Jake said quietly, beginning to agree that Rodolfo wanted his wife dead. He didn't know if the guy was inept, or Nicole was just lucky, but this was two "accidents" that could have been deadly.

"The gas fireplace in the master bedroom," Marguerite said on a sigh. "Pierina didn't know what the issue there was, but he took one look, muttered under his breath, and then started telling Nicole she needed to get a state-of-the-art security system with cameras. He said people went a little crazy in divorce and she needed cameras, lots of security, maybe a couple of guard dogs too, et cetera, and the whole time he was taking her fireplace apart and then putting it back together, so Pierina thinks there was something wrong with it."

"Nicole didn't ask what it was?" Jake asked with a frown.

Marguerite shook her head. "Pierina was the one who was suspicious, but even though she was so shocked, she didn't ask. Nicole was just dead silent, a troubled look on her face. Besides, Pierina said he was really lecturing the whole time. But she knew he was serious when he refused to charge Nicole for the visit after being there all day. I mean who does that?" she asked, eyebrows raised. "And she says he kept giving Nicole these worried, pitying looks, and repeating she should get security right away. He actually hugged Nicole on the way out. Pierina said it was like he thought it would be the last time he saw her alive."

"So the fireplace was probably rigged somehow and was the third narrow escape," Jake murmured thoughtfully.

Marguerite nodded unhappily. "But Nicole laughed it off. She's sure it's all just coincidence or accidents, and the closest she'll come to admitting that Rodolfo might prefer inheriting everything to getting half the money in the divorce, is to say that if he did do any of those things, then he was terribly inept and she isn't worried."

"Major denial," Jake said dryly.

Marguerite grimaced and then sighed and said, "I supposed it's hard enough to have to admit that you made a mistake in your marriage. But it would be positively humiliating to have to acknowledge that not only was your husband not the man you thought, but he's just a gold-digging bastard who cares so little he'd kill you for the money he was really after all along."

She was silent for a moment and then added sadly, "But those thoughts are there under the surface. That he never loved her. That she's so worthless that her only value is money. That he is willing to kill her to get it. But she won't admit it consciously. She can't. Her self-esteem was almost completely demolished by his actions during the marriage. Admitting this now would undo all the work the counselor has done and destroy her."

"And hiring protection would be admitting all of that, which she can't do," Jake said with understanding.

"Exactly," Marguerite nodded firmly. "So, I can't hire a company and send them over there. She'd just send them away, saying she didn't need it."

Jake nodded, but asked, "So what do you expect me to do? She'll do the same with me."

"Not if you didn't tell her you were a body-guard," she pointed out.

Jake sat back and frowned. "If her husband is trying to kill her, and I will agree that it sounds like he is—"

"I'm sure he is," Marguerite said firmly. "And now that the accidents he set up have failed, he'll have to try something else."

"Then she needs around-the-clock protection until the divorce is finalized. Once it's done, there should be no reason for him to continue to go after her," Jake pointed out.

"The divorce will be final in two weeks," Marguerite said at once.

"Two weeks, huh?" he muttered, but frowned and shook his head. "Still, if she won't accept a bodyguard, what do you expect me to do?"

"She won't accept a bodyguard, but she does need a cook/housekeeper and yard guy . . . well, snow guy this time of year," she added wryly, and then said, "And I told her I knew just the man who could do all three jobs for the price of one."

Jake's jaw dropped. He took a moment to absorb that stunning news and then closed his mouth, shook his head and said, "Cook/housekeeper?"

"Your mother brags about you, Steph—Jake. I know you're a very good cook."

"I'm her son. My mother is biased," he said dryly. "I can make spaghetti, and that's just frying up some hamburger, throwing in a can of sauce and boiling noodles. To her that's amazing. But that's not actually cooking."

"You're smart, you can read a cookbook and wing it, at least enough to get by for two weeks," Marguerite said determinedly and then added, "I'd never forgive myself for not interfering if Rodolfo killed her, Jake. She's a very sweet, genuinely nice person. There are few enough of those in the world. And it's only two weeks."

Jake slumped back in his seat again, knowing he'd already lost this argument. Finally, he sighed and said, "I suppose I could take a couple weeks off. They owe me about five weeks vacation now anyway and have been nagging at me to take it."

"I'll pay you what a company would demand for your time," she said firmly and then added brightly, "It will be a working vacation. You can putter around the kitchen, try new recipes—"

"Shovel snow, clean house, and watch out for murder attempts," he added dryly.

"I really appreciate this," Marguerite said solemnly, digging through her purse on the table and retrieving her checkbook.

Jake rolled his eyes and put his hand on hers to stop her. "You don't have to pay me, Marguerite," he said dryly. "I got a hell of a severance package from Vincent when I left, and that's on top of making a lot of money there for a lot of years that I invested successfully. I don't need money. I really don't even need to work anymore, but it's better than staying home and twiddling my thumbs."

"No, I insist on paying," Marguerite said firmly, slipping her hands out from under his and setting the checkbook on the table. "I already did my homework and found out how much companies charge for two weeks of around-the-clock protection and this is a service I appreciate."

Jake just shrugged and sat back, leaving her to it. She could write it if she wanted. It didn't mean he had to cash it. He accepted the check when she handed it over, slipped it in his pocket, and then crossed his arms and said, "All right, tell me everything you know about Nicole and Rodolfo."

Two

Nicole was carrying an armful of dirty dishes, dirty clothes, and various other items upstairs when the phone began to ring. Cursing under her breath, she rushed up the last few steps to the open-loft living room and then hurried to the phone on the marble counter on the far side of the room. Once there, she twisted and bent slightly to see around the items she was carrying, and then groaned as she saw the number and name on the ID screen. She'd been rather hoping it would be one of those 1–800 or 1–888 numbers that she could ignore but it was Pierina. She couldn't ignore Pierina.

Getting one hand free by using the wall and counter to help hold up the pile in her arms, Nicole quickly snatched up the phone and pressed it to her ear: "Hi Pierina."

"Nicole?" Pierina asked uncertainly.

"Yeah. It's me," she said lightly, catching the receiver between ear and shoulder so that she could free her hand to stabilize the pile she was holding when it began to wobble. Sighing her relief as she got her hand there in time, she asked, "How are things?"

"Well, they're—are you okay? You sound funny."

"Yeah, yeah," Nicole assured her quickly. "I'm just—my hands are full at the moment so I'm holding the phone between neck and shoulder. Maybe it's making my voice funny."

"Well, for heaven's sake, set down whatever you're carrying. I'll wait," Pierina said with amused exasperation.

"Uh . . ." Nicole grimaced and then shifted her hand to better hold her pile and turned to walk into her bedroom, taking the phone with her. Thank God for wireless phones, she thought as she carried everything into her walk-in closet and to the hamper waiting there. In the next moment, she was frowning at the hamper, thinking that she really should have taken the dirty dishes to the kitchen first. They were all piled on top of the dirty clothes.

"Nicole?"

"Yeah, one sec," she said into the phone, then moved up to the dryer and leaned forward a bit to let the dishes slide from her pile to the hard surface. She leaned a bit too much, though, and winced at the clang as a bowl sailed off the pile and nearly shattered a glass that she'd just set down.

"What was that? Did you break something?" Pierina asked with concern.

"No," Nicole said with relief, dropping the dirty clothes and other items on to the dryer top beside the dishes. Opening the washer lid, she began to throw clothes into it as she took the phone in her other hand and said, "Okay. Hands free now."

"What on earth are you doing?" Pierina asked on a laugh. "I heard glass clanging, and I can hear you doing *something* now. There's rustling, or—"

"I'm throwing clothes in the washer," Nicole explained.

"And the clanging?" Pierina asked.

"Dirty dishes, my makeup bag, curling iron and other stuff I brought up from the studio," Nicole explained. "Marguerite's found a cook/housekeeper for me and I'm tidying up a bit before they get here."

"You're cleaning up before your new cook/housekeeper gets there?" Pierina asked slowly. "You do realize that's kind of like pulling your tooth before you go to the dentist, right?"

"It is not," Nicole protested with a laugh.

"Yeah, it is . . . and it's so you," she teased, and then she said gently, "Sweetie, just leave the mess. You work hard. That's why you need a cook/housekeeper. I'm sure Marguerite has explained all that to the woman."

"Guy," Nicole corrected, reaching for the laundry detergent and dumping some in.

"What? Guy? Guy what?" Pierina asked with confusion.

"The cook/housekeeper Marguerite's bringing is a guy, not a woman," Nicole explained.

"No way!" Pierina squealed. "Ooooh, you're going to have some hot, young guy pawing through your panties."

Nicole froze, and then slowly set the detergent back, and returned to throwing clothes in the washer.

"Nicki?"

Nicole sighed and shook her head. "I think he's an old guy, not a hot, young guy," she said finally, but really that didn't make her feel any better. She didn't want an old guy pawing through her panties either. Grimacing, she said, "I can do the laundry myself."

"Nicole," Pierina said, drawing her name out in complaint. "That's ridiculous. You don't hire someone and then do the work yourself. And I was just teasing. I mean, I'm sure he won't really be pawing through them. If this is what the old guy does, he's done loads of laundry for tons of people and will hardly be interested in your undies."

"Right," Nicole murmured, but thought she was still doing at least her whites herself. Most of her panties and bras were plain white cotton now. Pretty boring, she supposed, but then she'd dumped all the lacy naughties when she'd left Rodolfo. Sex was how he'd caught her—great sex, sweet words, and empty promises spoken in a sexy accent. She kind of had a thing against all that stuff now. The next man she hooked up with, if she ever bothered again, would be a nice, normal, down-to-earth Canadian boy. No accent, no exotic locales to aid in his romancing of her, no sexy negligees and no crazy monkey sex that blew her head off and left her a brainless twit and easy target.

Nicole emphasized that silent point by closing the washing machine door with a flourish. Unfortunately, thanks to that flourish, her elbow hit several of the dishes on the dryer next to the washer and sent them flying off onto the floor in a clattering crash of broken glass.

"Crap," she muttered, as Pierina began squawking in her ear.

"What was that? Are you okay? What happened?"

"I'm fine," she assured her on a sigh and then added dryly, "My glassware . . . not so much. I knocked two bowls and three glasses onto the floor. They shattered."

"Oh, sweetie. See! If you'd left it for the housekeeper this wouldn't have happened."

"Yeah," she agreed, but thought it also wouldn't have happened if she'd dropped them off in the kitchen before coming in here, or if the phone hadn't rung, or if she'd taken more care. Basically, if she'd used her head. The last point came shooting out of her mind, not in her voice, but a deep one with an Italian accent. Nice, she thought. A year of counseling and Rodolfo's criticisms were still in her head.

Grinding her teeth, Nicole grabbed the garbage can beside the dryer, knelt in front of the mess, put the phone on speaker and set it on the floor to free her hands to clean up the mess.

"So, to what do I owe this call?" Nicole asked as she began carefully picking up the larger pieces of glass.

"I was just thinking of you . . . and Mom mentioned Marguerite went up there to sort through pictures of Christian and Carolyn to decide which one to use for the portrait and was staying overnight, so I thought I'd see how that is going.

Nicole smiled faintly. "It's good. We picked a picture and I did a rough sketch," she said, and then added, "Marguerite's still trying to convince me I don't need to stick to the timeline and do Christian and Carolyn right away, but I'd rather get it done and off my list of jobs to do."

"She knows how busy you are, hon. She's trying to ease your burden a little," Pierina said gently.

"Yeah, but working keeps me from thinking too much and that's a good thing right now. So I don't mind the crazy schedule I have at the moment. However," she added quickly as she sensed Pierina winding up for a lecture, "I am refusing a lot of future jobs so that I can get back to a more manageable schedule next year. I figure by then the divorce will be done, I should be over the worst of it, and socializing might come back into view as something I should do at least with female friends."

"You should move back this way," Pierina said solemnly. "I miss you and I could be dragging you out to movies and—"

"I might in the future, Pierina," Nicole interrupted quietly. "But I need at least a year to get my head straight before I make any big decisions."

"I understand," Pierina said reluctantly.

"Besides, we should take advantage of my living here," Nicole suggested. "You could come visit and we can . . ." She grimaced, unsure what they could do. She didn't have a clue what there was to do in Ottawa. Her life had been pretty sheltered during her marriage. She'd worked and that was about it. "Well, I know there's skating on the river in the winter," she said finally, and then rushed on, "But we could do girls' weekends. We could even have our mothers up for one. And invite Marguerite too, she's really a sweetie."

"Yeah, she is," Pierina agreed. "I always liked

Marguerite. She was always so nice to us when we were growing up and Mom brought us to her place."

"She still is," Nicole assured her. Finished with the larger pieces of glass, she started carefully on the smaller ones that she thought were still too big for the vacuum. "Marguerite was going to stay at a hotel tonight, but I said that was silly and she should stay here, and then I apologized for the mess and muttered that I need a cook/ housekeeper, and—*voila!*—Marguerite was on the job, saying she thought she knew the perfect person, but would have to see if he was available on such short notice."

"But he was, right?" Pierina asked.

"Yeah. She called half an hour ago and said she'd met with him, and his previous job ended today and he could start right away. He's agreed to a two-week trial."

"His previous job ended today?" Pierina asked with a laugh. "That makes it sound like he does short-term gigs here and there. I thought house-keepers were long term. Mom's worked for Marguerite for . . . like . . . ever."

"Yeah, I kind of wondered about that too," Nicole admitted and said, "But I trust Marguerite. Maybe his last client died of old age or something and he's been doing temp work while he waits to find a good situation. I don't know. I'm sure Marguerite will explain."

"Or I could."

Nicole blinked at that deep voice and then glanced sharply over her shoulder, eyes widening as she stared at the man standing behind her. He was gorgeous, with sandy brown hair cut short, a well-trimmed and short beard and mustache, and the most amazing eyes. Perhaps it was just the lighting in the room and the angle she was seeing them from, but from where she knelt, his eyes were a beautiful teal color shot through with silver. Beautiful. He was also muscular and extremely tall . . . although the tall part might just be because he was standing and she was kneeling on the floor. It—

Dear God, she'd had her rump in the air a minute ago as she'd leaned down to pick up the glass, Nicole realized with dismay, and that had been his first view of her.

"Nicki? Who was that? Are you okay? What's going on?"

Nicole's gaze dropped to the phone at Pierina's concerned squawks. It was only then that she realized she had no idea who the man was . . . or what he was doing in her home. Before she could panic, the man turned his head and called out, "I've found her, Marguerite. We're in the walk-in closet."

Nicole relaxed and answered Pierina with, "Uh, I think he might be the cook/housekeeper."

"He doesn't sound old," Pierina said, interest in her voice.

"No, he's not," Nicole agreed, staring up at the man's profile as he waited for Marguerite to respond or show up.

"He sounds hunky," Pierina added.

"He is," Nicole admitted and then realized what she'd said and flushed when he turned sharply to peer at her, eyebrows raised.

"Thanks," he drawled with a slow grin and offered her his hand.

Nicole just blushed harder, but she accepted the offered hand and got to her feet, avoiding his eyes as she muttered an embarrassed, "Thank you."

"Ohhhh," Pierina chortled. "Leave it to Marguerite to find you a cook/housekeeper who's eye candy too," Her voice, squawking up from the floor, reminded Nicole that she'd left the phone there.

"Sorry," Nicole said to the man on her friend's behalf and quickly bent to snatch up the phone. Taking it off speakerphone, she chastised, "That's sexual harassment, Pierina. The man isn't eye candy, he's—" She paused as her gaze slid back to him, and then Nicole turned and moved quickly to the opposite end of the seventeen-foot-long walk-in closet and whispered, "Okay, he's eye candy, but you don't say stuff like that so he can hear."

A deep chuckle made her frown over her shoulder. Surely he hadn't heard her from there, had he? She would have thought not, but the amusement on his face made her think he could. Turning back to the phone, Nicole muttered, "I'll call you back later."

"No, wait—" Pierina protested, but Nicole just hit the off button to end the call, took a deep breath to try to regain at least a little composure, and turned to offer a polite smile to the man. She started back to him then, her hand out, ready to shake his as she said, "Hi, I'm Nicole Phillips. You must be the cook/housekeeper Marguerite was—Ouch, ouch, ouch!"

Nicole recalled the glass on the floor just as his hand closed around hers. It was the pain radiating up from her foot that reminded her. She'd stepped in the damned glass and was now hopping around on her uninjured foot, the injured foot pulled up like a stork. His hold on her hand was the only thing keeping her from toppling over. At least it was until he suddenly scooped her up in his arms.

"Oh," Nicole breathed, feeling her face pinken. The phone began to ring again, and she was surprised to spot it on the floor.

"You dropped it when you stepped on the glass," the man holding her said, and then suddenly bent over with her in his arms so that she could grab it up off the floor.

"Oh my, you're strong," Nicole said faintly as she snatched up the phone. Glancing at the display screen as he straightened again, she murmured, "It's Pierina. Again."

Even as she pushed the button to answer the call, someone gasped, "What on earth!" behind them.

The man holding her swung to face Marguerite at once and Nicole wasn't surprised to see that the woman stood in the doorway to the walk-in closet, gaping at Nicole in the cook/housekeeper's arms. At least Nicole thought he was the cook/housekeeper. He hadn't really verified that yet, but that was who Marguerite had claimed she was bringing back.

"What's happened?" Pierina squawked from the phone, reminding Nicole that she'd answered it. "Is that Marguerite? Why does she sound so shocked? What's going on?"

"Put the phone to my face," the man holding her said.

Nicole hesitated, but then did as he requested and placed the receiver so he could take the call.

"Pierina, this is Jake Colson," he announced in his deep sexy voice. "Marguerite has asked me to take on the job of Nicole's cook/housekeeper and snow-shovel guy on a two-week trial basis. Marguerite and I are both here. Nicole is fine, but she stepped on some glass and I have to get it out for her now, so she'll call you back later with all the juicy details. But I'm handing you over to Marguerite so she can add her reassurance since you don't know me. Nice talking to you," he added, and then pulled his head away from the phone and nodded toward Marguerite.

Nicole shifted the phone in that direction and Marguerite took it with a smile and headed out of the room, saying, "Pierina darling, how are you? I never thought of it at the time, but you should have come with me to Ottawa. I know Nicole would have loved that and the company on the flight here and back would have been nice."

Marguerite continued talking, but that was all Nicole caught. Alone again with the man she now knew was Jake, she lifted her eyes self-consciously to his. "You can set me down now."

"So you can hop around on one foot?" he asked with amusement and turned to carry her out of the room as if she weighed nothing, which she knew from her bathroom scales, and her soon to be ex-husband's criticisms, wasn't true. If she wasn't so uncomfortable at being in a stranger's arms, Nicole would have enjoyed the experience.

Jake didn't pause in the bathroom that connected the walk-in closet to the bedroom as she expected, but continued out through the dining/living room and then into the kitchen. He set her on the island there, said a firm "Stay," and walked out of the room.

Nicole stared after him wide-eyed. He was very commanding for a cook. He also smelled really good, and he was superstrong. She was not some skinny, model type chick. Nicole was full figured and always had been. Actually, she was more full figured now than she'd ever been. Apparently she didn't take constant criticism well. She'd gained weight during her marriage, which had just led to more criticism. Nicole hadn't yet taken the trouble to lose that weight. She had too many other things to worry about first, or so she'd been thinking. Now she was thinking she really should start a diet . . . and the gorgeous, yummy-smelling man who had just left her kitchen had nothing to do with that decision, Nicole assured herself firmly.

She almost believed that . . . right up until Gorgeous Jake walked back into the kitchen and she found herself sitting up straight and sucking in her stomach.

"Alcohol, tweezers, a needle, antiseptic, and a bandage," Jake rattled off as he set down the items he'd collected, obviously from her bathroom. "I think that's everything we'll need."

"Oh, you don't have to—" Nicole's words ended on a gasp as he suddenly squatted in front of her and grabbed her foot to take a look. Any further protest was prevented by her need to bite her lip to keep from squawking as he began to poke at her foot.

"Does this hurt?" he asked, pressing gently.

"No," Nicole said, but even she didn't think it sounded believable. Her voice was about three octaves higher than normal.

Jake gave her a reproving look. "You have to tell me if it hurts, it's how I'll know where the glass is. You have several pieces in your foot that I can see, and a couple I don't think I'm seeing. So, stoic, no, and honesty, yes, okay?"

Nicole nodded silently, her lower lip caught between her teeth.

He went back to work then, starting with the glass he could see, she supposed, since he didn't ask her if it hurt anymore. However, it did hurt when he dug out the bits of glass and Nicole was clenching her hands and trying not to cry out when he began to ask questions, distracting her.

"Marguerite says you're an artist?"

"Yes. I paint portraits," she answered, looking away in the hopes that not watching would make it less painful.

"You're good," he complimented, and the words made her smile crookedly.

"How would you know? You haven't seen my work," she said with amusement.

"I did," he countered. "When we found the front door unlocked and got no answer when we called out, Marguerite and I searched the house starting on the ground floor . . . including your studio."

"Oh," Nicole murmured, but she was frowning. "The front door was locked. I locked it myself behind Marguerite when she left."

Jake raised his head and peered at her, then glanced to the door. Nicole followed his gaze to see Marguerite in the doorway between the kitchen and living room, the phone in her hand at her side. Apparently she'd finished talking to Pierina. Now she was exchanging a solemn look with Jake.

"It was unlocked when we got here," Marguerite said quietly, as if verifying that he hadn't remembered wrong.

"Well, that's just—" Nicole shook her head. "I know I locked it."

"Marguerite, if you'll finish here, I'll check the house again," Jake said quietly, straightening.

Nicole frowned. "I'm sure that's not necessary."

"You locked it, and it was unlocked when we got here," he pointed out simply. "Better to be safe than sorry."

"Yes, but no one has keys but me. Well, and Marguerite," she said, and then frowned and added reluctantly, "Maybe I just thought I locked it. Or maybe I accidentally unlocked it when I went to take the key out."

"Rodolfo doesn't still have a key, does he?" Marguerite asked with concern.

"No. He gave it back when I bought him out of the house," Nicole assured her.

"Did you have the locks changed after you bought your husband out of the house?" Jake asked.

Her eyes widened. Nicole was surprised he even knew there was a husband, soon to be ex-husband. Apparently, Marguerite had told him about her life . . . which was more than she'd done for Nicole. She didn't know a thing about her new cook/housekeeper. "No, I didn't have the locks changed. There was no need. Rodolfo gave me his key."

Marguerite and Jake exchanged another glance and then Marguerite moved forward and took the tweezers from Jake as he straightened.

"I'll be right back," he murmured, and slipped from the room.

"There's really no need to search the house," Nicole said wearily as Marguerite moved one of the kitchen chairs over to sit in front of her and began to work on removing the glass from her foot. "I probably messed up about locking the door. Besides, Jake just said you guys searched when you got here."

"Better safe than sorry, dear," Marguerite said with unconcern. "Besides, it makes men feel good to do stuff like this. Let him be all manly and protect us womenfolk," she said lightly with a grin, then added more seriously, "Now brace yourself, some of these glass slivers went pretty deep."

Nicole braced herself, but it didn't help much. It took all she had not to howl like a two-year-old as Marguerite set to work on removing the glass from her foot.

Jake checked the upper floor first, looking into the master bedroom, en suite bathroom, and walk-in closet again, just to be thorough. He then checked the sliding glass doors in the master bedroom to be sure they were locked before moving on to the guest bedroom next to the master and its bathroom.

Marguerite and Nicole were in the kitchen, so he didn't need to check there, but couldn't resist glancing that way as he passed the door on the way back through the living room/dining room, headed for the stairs. Nicole Phillips wasn't what he'd expected. After everything Marguerite had told him this evening, he'd expected to find a rather pathetic creature on his hands. She didn't strike him as pathetic.

Certainly, the sweet round derriere he'd come

upon on entering the walk-in closet hadn't looked pathetic, and she just didn't have a pathetic air about her. Actually, while Jake hadn't known her for more than minutes and hadn't really spoken much to her, the overall impression he had so far was a light and cheery one. Nicole's home had lots of large windows, stretching eighteen or twenty feet to the cathedral ceilings. The rooms were decorated in cream, with splashes of red and the occasional black accents. Her studio was a menagerie of color, and the clothes in her closet had been colorful as well.

Nothing he'd seen so far spoke of a depressed woman, crawling out from the wreckage of an abusive marriage. But then, Marguerite had said at the beginning of their conversation that Nicole had sought out counseling right away to deal with the damage from her marriage. It appeared to be working. But he'd have to wait and see to know for sure.

Jake went through every room on the main floor, checking closets, and ensuring doors were locked. He left the front door for last because he'd locked it himself when he and Marguerite had arrived, using the key Nicole had given Marguerite during her stay to do it. So, it was with some surprise that he found that door unlocked again. He opened it and peered out at the driveway, then along the road in both directions. There was nothing to see, but then he hadn't expected there to be.

Expression grim, Jake closed the door and re-locked it, then pulled out his cell phone and called a local locksmith he had dealt with in the past. He was having every lock in the house rekeyed tonight.

It was the fastest and easiest way to handle the situation. Nicole's husband may have given back his key, but he'd obviously had a copy made before doing so. She said she'd locked the door, and while she may claim that perhaps she had only meant to and hadn't actually done it, he knew damned right well he'd locked it when he and Marguerite had entered. It being unlocked again suggested someone had come into the house after Nicole had locked it, and then left again after he'd locked it.

The question was, what had they come in for? His money was on it being Rodolfo who had entered. If they were lucky, Rodolfo had entered, intending to do something nefarious, but had been forced to scrap the plan when Marguerite and Jake had returned. He'd obviously slipped out while they were searching the house. But he couldn't count on the man not having had time to do something, and since the guy liked to set up things that looked like accidents . . .

Turning on his heel, he started through the house again.

Three

"There you are! We were starting to worry you'd got lost."

Nicole looked around at Marguerite's light words and saw Jake entering the kitchen. She smiled at him a little nervously, and then turned back to the cupboard and pulled out a third cup as Marguerite said, "We finished a few minutes ago and Nicole put coffee on. It should be ready soon."

"Oh."

Nicole turned uncertainly at that one word. It sounded a little taken aback and she frowned and asked, "Don't you like coffee? I can make something else for you. Tea, or . . . cocoa? Or maybe you'd rather have something cold to drink?"

"No, coffee's fine," he said slowly, then moved toward her, holding out his closed hand. When he reached her, he opened his hand, revealing three keys.

Nicole took them, her forehead furrowing. "What are these?"

"Keys."

"Well, I know that," she said on a half laugh. "To what?"

"To the house," Jake said, and then explained. "There was something wrong with the front lock. We locked it when we came in, but it was unlocked again when I went to search the house. So I called a friend of mine and he replaced the front door lock and then rekeyed all the others so that one key is all you need to unlock all of them."

"Oh," she said with surprise. "I didn't even realize anyone was here. I didn't hear the doorbell."

"He knocked, and I believe you were screeching in pain at the time," Jake said gently.

"Oh," Nicole repeated, flushing this time. She was not good with pain. She tried to be stoic, but stoic just didn't seem doable for her and she'd screamed like a baby at one point when Marguerite had had to dig out a piece of glass that broke off under the skin when she took out the larger end.

"I had him make six copies," Jake continued. "There is a key in each door now so that if you need to get out in a hurry, you don't have to search for your keys. These three are so that you have one yourself, I get another, or any cook/housekeeper after me gets it, and the third is for you to give to guests when they stay as you did with Marguerite."

"Oh," Nicole said again, unsure what else to say. She was glad to hear the lock was faulty. It was better than thinking her memory was faulty or someone else had a key to the house. But she wasn't sure how she felt about Jake just having someone come in and change her locks without at least asking her about it.

"I told you he was a marvelous cook/housekeeper," Marguerite said beaming. "Just like Maria, he'll take care of what needs taking care of, relieving you of the burden. Your life is going to be so much simpler with him here."

Nicole felt herself relax under those words. She'd never had a cook/housekeeper before and had no idea what all they were expected to do, but if Marguerite thought this was normal . . . well, great. She guessed.

The coffeepot beeped then, announcing it was ready, and Nicole slid the keys into her pocket and quickly moved over to pour three cups. Jake was immediately there to take two of them and carry them to the island where Marguerite had settled on one of the four bar chairs that wrapped around the end and up one side. Nicole followed with the third cup, and climbed awkwardly onto the seat beside Marguerite, a little kerfluffled by his gentlemanly behavior when Jake pulled out the chair.

"Well, this is nice," Marguerite decided as they sipped their coffee.

Nicole nodded, but she was searching her mind for how she should proceed here. Jake had already taken on the responsibility of the door as if his working here was a certainty, and Marguerite was acting the same, but she really felt like she should ask at least a couple questions of the man who would be given a key to her home. In fact, that was why the keys presently rested in her pocket. The coffee being ready had given her an excuse for putting off the distribution of the keys, but the truth was, she was leery of doing so with a complete stranger.

"I know I mentioned to you both about a two-week trial run with Jake working here," Marguerite said suddenly, and then turned her gaze on Nicole and added, "But I'm sure you'd like to know more about Jake, dear, since the man will be living in your house."

"Uh . . ." Nicole grimaced. She hadn't realized that he would be living here, but supposed that was often the case with housekeepers. Aunt Maria and her husband lived in a guesthouse on Marguerite's property, but Nicole didn't have a guesthouse. She supposed he'd have to take the room downstairs. It would at least give him a little privacy . . . and herself. Geez, she hadn't thought this out at all. She'd simply mentioned that she needed a cook/housekeeper to tend things while she worked and the next thing she knew—her gaze slid to Jake—she had one, thanks to her fairy godmother, Marguerite.

"Yes, I suppose I would like to know more about Jake," she admitted finally.

"Right." Marguerite smiled, unperturbed. "Well, first off, Ste—" She paused and grimaced, shook her head, and tried again. "First off, Jake is family."

"Is he?" Nicole asked with surprise.

Marguerite nodded. "His mother is married to my Julius's brother-in-law, Roberto. So he's my step-nephew, although I just think of him as a nephew."

"Oh." Nicole watched as Jake calmly sipped his coffee, seeming to ignore the recitation.

"He used to be vice president of V.A. Inc., a large corporation with its home base in California."

"Vice president?" Nicole asked with a start. Jake didn't look more than twenty-five, which seemed kind of young for such a responsible position to her, but Marguerite nodded again.

"I know he looks young, but he's very responsible," Marguerite assured her. "And he was very good at his job, but a health scare seven years ago made him decide to pursue a more relaxing career, and he's always loved to cook, so . . ." She shrugged. "Here he is."

Nicole stared from Marguerite to Jake. That was it? He was related, used to be V.P. of some big business, had a health scare, and now was happy to be her cook/housekeeper for a pittance of what he must have made as a V.P.? She noted the way Marguerite was scowling at Jake and wondered what that was about. She didn't have long to wonder. Marguerite suddenly blew out her breath with exasperation.

"Look at her expression, Jake. I told you it would sound dubious, but you insisted on the truth," the woman complained, as if to say "and look where that has got us. She doesn't believe a word of it."

"The truth is always the best way to go," Jake responded with a shrug of unconcern, and that was when Nicole decided she knew enough. It wasn't that she didn't still have a lot of questions, but after all the lies Rodolfo had told her, the one most important thing to her now was honesty and Jake was apparently an honest man. There were few enough of those in the world. But Nicole wanted an honest person, man or woman, for the position.

She was trusting him in her home, her sanctuary. Honesty was the most important thing to her. Later she could find out all the other things she was curious about like what the man had done these last three years. Had he been a cook/housekeeper that whole time? Did he really enjoy puttering around the house, cooking, and cleaning for others? Did he not miss the power and excitement inherent in a position like vice president? And why had he moved here to Ottawa when he'd left the job in California?

There were loads of questions Nicole could ask. However, she would learn those answers later if necessary. Right now, she knew enough about the man to go forward with the two-week trial. If he worked out, Nicole could ask her questions. If not . . . then she supposed the answers to those questions didn't really matter.

"Okay, here's your key," she said, digging out two of the three keys she'd shoved in her pocket. She handed Jake one and then turned to Marguerite.

"No need to give me one again," Marguerite said, waving away the key Nicole offered her. "I don't need it. I won't be leaving again until I head home tomorrow and you guys will see me out then."

"Are you sure?" Nicole asked, and when the woman nodded, she slid it back into her pocket with a shrug.

"Well, this was lovely, but I find I'm a little weary tonight. I think I'll take my coffee with me and go read in bed for a bit before I sleep," Marguerite announced, slipping off her seat before smiling at Nicole and adding, "That way I won't have to feel guilty for keeping you from your work."

Nicole had started to get anxious at Marguerite's first words, but the last comment made her relax. She wasn't being abandoned to entertain Jake alone. He was an employee. She could go to work and leave him to settle in and enjoy a free night before he started work in the morning.

"Yes, I suppose I should get back to work," Nicole said with relief, standing herself. "What time is your flight tomorrow, Marguerite?"

"Two thirty. I'll be leaving here at noon to be sure I get through security with plenty of time, so give me a hug now, my dear, in case you're still sleeping when I go."

Nicole moved to give her a hug, but said, "I'll make sure to set my alarm so I'm up to have coffee with you before you go. But thank you for everything, Marguerite. It's always a pleasure to see you."

"It's always a pleasure for me too," Marguerite assured her, hugging her tightly. "And you're more than welcome."

Nicole smiled and stepped back when she released her, then watched her leave the room before turning to Jake. "I guess you don't need a tour?"

"No." He smiled faintly. "I pretty much know my way around after the two searches of the house. I'll just get my bag from the car and settle myself in. I'll probably read for a bit myself tonight."

Nicole nodded, and moved to pour herself another coffee to take down to the studio with her. She had a coffeepot there, as well as a cappuccino machine, a small refrigerator with cold beverages, and a microwave, but the coffee was already made here so she might as well drink it.

"You can take the room down—" Nicole paused as she turned to see that Jake had already left the room. Nicole gave a little shrug and headed for her studio, her mind already on the portrait she was working on and the colors she wanted to use to add contrast to the painting that was furthest along.

While Nicole almost always finished her portraits by having the customer pose for her, that was just to get the final details down. The majority of the picture was done from photos of the subject and she almost always put in her own background in the portraits unless the customer specified a certain one. Sometimes she made the backgrounds whimsical settings, sometimes more dramatic. It depended on the subjects themselves. The main painting she was presently working on was for an actress of some fame, who was also a wife and mother . . . and from what she'd seen, a very loving wife and mother. Nicole wanted to show the contrasts in the woman's life by making the background a whirl of contrasts, soft and hard, light and dark, earth mother and diva. So far it was working well.

Jake made sure to lock the front door as he came back in, double-checked it, and then carried his duffel bag upstairs to the guest room next to the master bedroom. He needed to be close to his client to keep her safe, and right next door was as close as he could get unless he wanted to sleep with her . . . which he actually wouldn't mind. Nicole was a luscious lovely he wouldn't mind tasting, but he suspected Nicole wouldn't feel the same way about him. She thought he was her cook/housekeeper after all, and she was just coming out of a bad relationship, and on the tail end of a nasty divorce. He doubted she was ready to welcome anyone into her bed.

"Nicole's going to be surprised that you're in here."

Jake set his bag on the bed before reacting to Marguerite's comment. He took in the way she leaned casually against the doorjamb and then asked, "Why is that?"

"Because I put my stuff in here when I first arrived, and only moved it downstairs when I left to meet you. I knew you'd need to be close to her."

Jake nodded, not surprised Marguerite had worked that out. She was a smart woman.

"There was nothing wrong with the front door lock," Marguerite commented, pushing away from the door and walking over to sit on the side of the bed as he unzipped his bag.

"There could have been, but I doubt it," Jake said with a shrug, turning to open the top drawer of the dresser against the wall beside the bed. He nodded with satisfaction when he found it empty, and said, "The locksmith didn't find anything wrong with the lock."

"So Rodolfo was in the house when we got here?" Marguerite asked grimly.

"Someone probably was," Jake said carefully, unwilling to jump to conclusions. Rodolfo had been his first thought too, but he had no proof.

"I can't believe she didn't even think to have her locks changed," Marguerite said on a sigh. "Especially after all that business with the furnace and the grill."

"As you said, she's in denial," Jake said mildly as

he began transferring his clothes from the bag to the drawer.

"Yes, but still . . ."

"She loved him, Marguerite," he said quietly. "You can see it in the photos hanging all over this house. The way she looked at him, it's obvious she loved him. She probably still loves him or she'd have taken down the photos." His mouth tightened as he said that. It bothered him that Nicole still seemed to love the man after all he'd done, but it was none of his business and he continued, "You yourself said it would be hard to admit that the man you married was only interested in your money. Well, as you said, it would be harder still to admit that the man you love thought so little of you he wants you dead for profit."

"I suppose," Marguerite agreed quietly. She was silent for a moment, watching him unpack and then suddenly asked, "Have you tried to read her yet?"

He paused, his head lifting with surprise. "No. Should I have?"

"Have you learned to control or read the minds of mortals?" she asked instead of answering.

Jake returned to his unpacking with a grimace. He had sworn he wouldn't do things like that when he became an immortal. But the skill seemed to come naturally to him, and when lives were on the line, it was a handy skill to have. It was how he'd known the guy in the baseball cap was there to shoot the dictator earlier that day, and that he was about to pull a gun. It was why Jake had burst forward to stop him, and had he not managed to reach him in time, he would have controlled and stopped him from aiming and pulling the trigger. But all he said was, "Yes, I've learned."

"Good. You may need to use it on Nicole."

"Why?" he asked with surprise.

"Well with her being in denial, she may do something dangerous or risky, and you'll need to stop her," Marguerite pointed out. "Besides, there are some things you should know about her that you can only learn from reading her."

"Like what?" Jake asked with a frown.

Marguerite shook her head and stood up. "It's not my place to say. Besides, I find I really am tired. I think I'll go to my room. Good night, Jake." She walked over to kiss him on the cheek, and then turned and left the room, leaving him frowning and wondering what the devil he should know about Nicole that Marguerite wouldn't explain.

Jake had thought Marguerite had told him everything about the woman earlier at the restaurant. She'd certainly seemed to, telling him things like Nicole was good in school, but more interested in art than her other courses. That she'd been shy and more reserved through high school and university, preferring to stay home and paint to partying much. That she'd hung out with the artsy crowd, rather than date around, but that Pierina had always been her best friend. That Rodolfo was the wildest, riskiest thing that had happened in her life so she would no doubt be reluctant to take a chance like that again.

The woman had given him some pretty personal details, and she'd known a surprising bit about Nicole for a girl who he understood had merely popped up in her home several times a year.

Shaking his head, Jake returned to his unpacking, but his mind was now firmly on Nicole and what secrets she kept. So much so that he almost stopped packing to go down to her studio and read her. However, he didn't want to disturb her. Another fact that Marguerite had passed along was that Nicole was trying to keep to a ridiculous schedule at the moment and working herself to the point of exhaustion. Tomorrow was soon enough to learn her secrets, he supposed, as he finished putting his things away.

Jake closed the drawer, stowed his bag in the closet and then headed back out to the kitchen. It was after midnight now, but he worked nights as a rule and slept days, so this was still early to him. That coffee hadn't helped. Immortals were sensitive to caffeine, some more than others, and he usually avoided it because of that. Now he was feeling a little jittery and thirsty. He supposed the thirst was the nanos working to remove the caffeine from his system. Water would help, but blood would be better.

However, that thought brought a problem to the forefront of his mind. He needed a way to keep blood close at hand and cold. The best solution was to go out and pick up a small bar fridge and put it in his room somewhere. But he wasn't happy at the prospect of leaving Marguerite and Nicole alone after the business with the unlocked door earlier. Jake had checked the furnace and looked around the house, not finding anything amiss, but that didn't mean that something hadn't been done. It just meant he hadn't found it. He'd rather stick close tonight just in case he'd missed something.

So . . . the blood and refrigerator would have to wait. He could always call Bastien and ask him to send both out to him if he couldn't find a way to manage the task himself. A refrigerator wasn't usually an item Argeneau Enterprises supplied, at least he didn't think it was, but he suspected Bastien would make an exception. Especially when he found out Jake was here at his mother's behest. Besides, he'd be happy to pay for the extra service.

Jake quickly tidied the kitchen. There wasn't much to do there. Marguerite had returned her coffee cup and he put that and his own in the dishwasher, along with the couple of spoons they'd used. He then put the milk and sugar away, wiped up the counter and he was done. He was crazy restless though, and after a hesitation, he went downstairs, donned his coat and boots, and unlocked the front door to go outside.

It was snowing out, the front steps already covered with a thin layer of new-fallen snow. Jake supposed he'd have to take care of that before Marguerite left tomorrow. But he'd leave it till morning, or at least until the snow stopped, he decided, as he turned to lock the front door with his key. As he started walking along the front of the house, he added arranging for the installation of a security system for the house to his list of things to do the next day. With any luck, he could get someone out right away and have it done first thing in the morning while Nicole slept. Then he just had to tell her after the fact as if it were a typical chore he was expected to do . . . and he would in his capacity as bodyguard. Jake suspected few cook/housekeepers were ever called upon to manage the task though.

Smiling at the thought, he walked around the house. It was a full moon tonight, the snow showing up in gray relief with moonshadows cast by the many trees in the yard. Jake automatically scanned the area as he walked, looking for footprints in the snow or moonshadows that might be someone who shouldn't be there. He didn't see anything.

Jake's eye was drawn to a large puddle of light splashing across the snow-covered yard when he turned the corner to the back of the house. He knew the light was coming from Nicole's studio windows, but he was surprised they were uncurtained at night. He was also surprised to find himself drawn forward like a moth to a flame.

Pausing on the edge of the light where he wouldn't be visible, Jake peered into the studio, amusement tugging at his lips when he saw Nicole with headphones on, dancing around as she dabbed at a stretch of canvas with a paintbrush. There were three canvases set up, each at a different stage of completion. One looked to be barely started, a pencil sketch of what appeared to be a couple. It was too faint and he was too far away to be able to see the features, but Jake suspected it was Marguerite's son, Christian, and his fiancée, Carolyn. She'd mentioned that she'd come with photos for Nicole to use for the portrait. He guessed that Nicole must have set to work that evening on the initial sketch for the portrait. The next canvas held a half-done portrait of a rather stern-looking older man against a dark and dramatic background. The last was a rather lovely woman who looked vaguely familiar. That one looked nearly done.

Nicole did a little whirl in front of the woman's

portrait, and then suddenly shifted to the half-finished stern-faced man, and Jake watched with fascination as she began to dab at the background there with the same brush. It seemed she was working on the three canvases at once, he thought with surprise, his gaze dropping to her behind as she paused in her painting to do a little bump and grind to whatever music she was listening to.

It took about two minutes for it to occur to Jake that his behavior was kind of creepy. He was sort of acting like a peeping Tom. Or, really, he supposed he *was* being a peeping Tom, standing there staring in at an unsuspecting Nicole.

Grimacing at his own behavior, Jake forced himself to continue walking. He made his way around the outside of the splash of light on the lawn, determinedly not looking in the window again. He then continued around the side of the building and back to the front of the house again.

There were no footprints but his own in the new-fallen snow, Jake noted as he walked to the front door and unlocked it. But he hadn't expected any. Whoever had unlocked the door twice that day now knew Nicole had company. They'd wait until she was alone to try again, he was sure . . . unless they'd already done something none of them yet knew of. The thought was a troubling one. There were so many options in every house. Poison could have been put in anything from food and drink to perfume or lotion. The electrical could have been messed with, a stair rail could have been loosened, or the chandelier that hung in the curve of the stairwell . . .

Jake grimaced as he walked under the large ten-foot chandelier hanging from the cathedral ceiling some twenty feet up. Having that suddenly crash on to a mortal would definitely kill them. On the other hand, that wasn't even a possibility. The culprit would have needed something to get him up to the cathedral ceiling to mess with it. But there were tons of other possibilities, and Jake simply couldn't check them all. He could check a lot of them though, he decided in the next moment. It wasn't like he had anything better to do, and he wasn't going to be sleeping tonight.

Four

Nicole groaned when the alarm went off and rolled over to slap at it unhappily until it shut off. Her eyes then drifted closed on a little sigh, only to pop open again as she recalled that she'd set it for a reason. What had that been? Oh, right, she'd promised to see Marguerite off, Nicole recalled, snuggling sleepily into her pillow and wondering if it was really necessary.

Painting had gone amazingly well last night and she'd worked until nearly 7 A.M. Nicole hadn't realized that would happen when she'd made that promise last night. Maybe she could just go back to sleep.

The woman was her aunt's boss, Nicole reminded herself and considered that fact, but really, just because she was Aunt Maria's boss didn't mean Nicole had to get up to see her off, did it?

On the other hand, her mind argued, Marguerite was also kind of her boss too. At least she was a client. Although, surely the lady would be glad to know Nicole had worked so hard and would want her to get her sleep so that she could work that hard again tonight, right?

Except that she was also a really nice woman, who had always been kind to Nicole and who had even gone to all the trouble of finding her a hunky cook/housekeeper when Nicole mentioned she needed one.

Her eyes popped open again at that point and Nicole was suddenly rolling out of bed. Though, truth be told it was the thought of her hunky cook/housekeeper that had her suddenly wide awake and eager to head out to the kitchen rather than any sense of responsibility for seeing off her houseguest, which she should be ashamed of and would be . . . later, Nicole promised herself. Marguerite was a lovely woman, and Nicole had been raised to always be kind and polite. Seeing the woman off was what a good hostess would do, and Nicole would feel guilty for even hesitating over the matter. Later . . . when she'd had more sleep. For now, she wanted a shower, some coffee, and to see if her housekeeper was still here.

Her shower was a fast one. Nicole followed it up with brushing her hair, pulling it back into a ponytail, and then sitting down at her makeup table to put on some face powder and blush. That was something she rarely did first thing in the morning. She usually had her coffee before doing anything the least little bit ambitious. Nicole was not a morning person.

She headed into her walk-in closet next, stopping short at the door as she recalled the glass on the floor and the painful efforts Marguerite had made to get the glass out of her foot last night. However, one glance showed that the glass was gone.

Nicole stared at the spot for one perplexed moment, slow to conclude that someone had gone to the trouble of cleaning it up last night while she was painting. The fact that it took any time at all for her to realize that was pretty pitiful considering that was the only explanation, but then she really wasn't at her best in the morning . . . especially after only four hours of sleep.

Sighing at how distressingly slow her brain was in the mornings, Nicole pulled out jeans and a T-shirt and began to struggle into them as she considered who might have done the job. There were only two options: Marguerite and Jake. She couldn't imagine Marguerite doing it after bringing home a cook/housekeeper for her. On the other hand, Jake shouldn't have started work until this morning. But one of them must have taken care of it.

Nicole had her clothes on and was heading out of the closet before she realized that she'd forgotten to don panties and a bra. She swung back toward the closet, grimacing at what a pain it was going to be to tug the jeans off, and just as quickly swung away, only to swing back. She might be able to do without panties, but going braless was not an option. She was full figured everywhere.

Muttering under her breath, she moved to her underwear drawer, dragged out a bra, pulled off her T-shirt and quickly donned the torturous contraption that squeezed her breasts in and up. At least it seemed torturous this morning, but then she was exhausted and so not a morning person, something that kept ringing through her head. To her mind, vampires had the right idea. The world was quiet at night. No one called at 2 A.M., or dropped in for coffee and a chat then. She could and did work undisturbed during the wee hours. It was bliss.

Once she had the bra on, and had replaced the T-shirt, Nicole made her way out of her room. She was crossing the combined living room/dining room, headed for the kitchen, when the upstairs guest bedroom door opened. Her head swung toward it, a smile of greeting claiming her lips for Marguerite. But it faded, replaced by surprise when she saw Jake coming out of the room.

"Morning," he said before ducking into the washroom.

"Morning," Nicole murmured, but doubted he'd heard it. He was already closing the bathroom door. Frowning slightly now, she continued on into the kitchen, eyes widening in surprise when she saw Marguerite seated at the island, perusing the paper. The woman beamed a smile when she spotted Nicole.

"Oh, good morning, dear," Marguerite greeted. "You're just in time, Jake made coffee and a lovely brunch for us. It's in the oven staying warm, but he'll be back in a minute and probably serve it right up. He just ducked into his room to change his shirt. I bumped into him as he was whipping the eggs and some of it slopped on him."

"His room?" Nicole said uncertainly. "He was coming out of your room when I—"

"Oh," Marguerite waved that away with a laugh. "I moved my things downstairs and told him to take the upper guest room. It seemed sensible for him to be on this floor since this is where he'll be doing most of his work, and it would have been silly to make him sleep downstairs last night and then have to move all of his things upstairs today."

"Oh, of course," Nicole said slowly and turned to find a cup and pour herself a coffee. She was in desperate need of one now as she considered that the man had slept a wall away last night . . . close enough to hear her snore. Well, if she did snore. Or what if she talked or mumbled in her sleep? Or tossed and turned a lot? How much could he hear through the wall?

"I hope you like omelets."

Nicole gave a start at that question in a deep male voice. Jake had returned. She offered him a weak smile as he pulled on oven mitts and moved to the stove.

"I had to work with what was available, so I made toast, and an omelet with sausage, onion, potatoes and cheese in it. But if you don't like eggs or something I can make you French toast, or pancakes or—"

"No, the omelet is fine," Nicole interrupted, her mouth watering when he opened the oven door and a lovely scent rolled out on a wave of heat to tempt her nose. "It smells lovely."

"Doesn't it?" Marguerite agreed cheerfully. "I did tell you he was wonderful."

"Yes, you did," Nicole said faintly, following Jake to the kitchen table in the corner. Really she was following the two plates of omelet, not Jake; he just happened to be carrying them.

Her gaze slid over the table, noting the tablecloth,

which she rarely bothered with, and the place mats with perfect place settings. Jake had even set out salt and pepper, ketchup, and A.1. sauce, and milk and sugar . . . which reminded her of the coffee she held in hand that still needed doctoring.

"Sit," Jake ordered and then added, "You too, Marguerite. Dig in before it gets cold and I'll grab mine and the toast."

Nicole sat at the table and quickly added cream and sugar to her coffee, but her gaze was on the omelet. She was not good at making omelets. Hers always came out as messy scrambled eggs, but these looked perfect. Light, fluffy, and oozing with yummy stuff. She actually found herself swallowing repeatedly as saliva built up in her mouth and was glad to be done with the coffee business so that she could try the omelet.

Fortunately, Jake returned to the table just as she set her coffee aside to take up her fork and knife. Nicole had been raised that it was only polite not to eat until the cook had finished and joined the table. The cook being her mom when she was taught this notwithstanding, Nicole would have felt terribly guilty for digging in before Jake was seated. But she would have done it. Now it wasn't an issue.

"Mmmm," Nicole murmured, once she'd popped the first bite into her mouth. It really was good. If the man made omelets for her every morning she'd be happy to get up to eat them, morning person or not. And if all of his cooking was this good, the man deserved a raise, she thought, which reminded her that they hadn't discussed his wages yet. Or anything. She supposed they'd have to sit down and hammer things out after Marguerite left. What pay he expected, what his job description included, and what he expected from her too, because, seriously, he was already looking too good to be true. Nicole didn't want the trial two-week period to end with her wanting him and his culinary skills to stay, and him unhappy with her as a boss and wanting to leave.

"I realized last night after I went to bed that I forgot to tell you what arrangement I'd come to with Jake for you," Marguerite said suddenly.

Nicole swallowed and lifted her head, curious to hear this.

"Jake has agreed to the standard rate for the two-week trial," Marguerite announced.

Nicole tilted her head. She had no clue what that meant. Was there a standard rate for cook/housekeepers? She'd have thought it varied with different employers and their expectations.

"We also worked out what tasks he's willing to take on. But you can worry about that after we eat. I wrote it all up and left it on the dresser in my room. You can look it over and talk to Jake about it later," Marguerite added.

"Oh. Okay." Nicole nodded and began to eat again, but her mind was now on the paper in Marguerite's room and she was curious to read it. She was also curious about the glass in her walk-in closet, and said, "Thank you for cleaning up the glass in my walk-in closet. It was a nice surprise."

She had no idea who she was thanking, so Nicole addressed the comment to her omelet as she cut the next piece.

"You're welcome," Jake answered.

Relaxing, Nicole smiled at him. "I really appreciate it. Especially since you didn't officially start until today."

Jake shrugged. "It was no trouble."

They all fell silent, their attention on their food after that, until Marguerite suddenly popped up off her chair. "My ride's here."

"Oh." Nicole glanced out the window to see a town car pulling into the driveway and stood up. "What about the rental car you had yesterday?"

"I dropped it off last night before returning with Jake," Marguerite said breezily as she headed out of the room. "He followed me and brought me back here. It just seemed easier than fussing today."

"Well, you didn't have to do that. Jake or I could have driven you to the airport today," Nicole said, scraping up her last bite of omelet and popping it in her mouth before chasing after Marguerite with Jake on her heels.

"Don't be silly. I knew you'd both be working today." Marguerite collected her purse off the dining-room table on her way to the stairs. "This is easier all the way around."

Still chewing and swallowing, Nicole merely grunted as she followed her downstairs. She pulled up short though when they reached the entry and Marguerite suddenly paused and turned back. In the next moment, Nicole was enveloped in expensive perfume that smelled really, really good as Marguerite hugged her.

"Thank you, Nicole. You are a dear. I've always thought so. You and Pierina are both sweeties. I appreciate your putting me up last night so I didn't have to fly right back. And thank you for setting right to work on the portrait, but I really wish you'd give yourself a break. We don't mind waiting and I worry about you."

"Nothing to worry about," Nicole said, hugging her back. "Once I get these three portraits finished I can slow down a little. Besides, with Jake here, life should be much easier. Thank you, for that," she added, giving her an extra squeeze. "I was worried about having a stranger in my home. This way, with Jake being family to you, I feel much better."

"Jake is a wonder. He'll take care of everything. It will all work out," Marguerite assured her and Nicole nodded, though she got the feeling Marguerite was referring to more than just her kitchen and home. There was no time to question her on it though, because the doorbell rang then and Marguerite released her.

Leaving Marguerite to say good-bye to Jake, Nicole stepped around her to open the door and smiled in greeting at the suited man waiting patiently on the step.

"Hello," he said politely, his gaze sliding past her to Marguerite and then moving to the suitcase next to the door. "Is that going?"

"Oh, yes," Nicole said recognizing Marguerite's small case on wheels. The woman must have set it by the door before coming upstairs, she realized and grabbed it. But she'd barely slid it a foot closer to the door before the driver stepped in and took it.

"I'll take care of that," he assured her politely. "Is this it?"

"Just that and me," Marguerite said brightly as she stepped away from Jake to move up next to Nicole.

"Very good." The driver smiled at Marguerite and then turned to lead her to the car. He opened the back door and handed her in and then closed it before carrying the case around to set it in the trunk. Nicole was barefoot, so stayed in the doorway and waved when Marguerite finished buckling her seat belt and looked her way. She was aware when Jake stepped up behind her and thought he was probably waving too.

They watched silently as the driver got in and closed the door, but once the vehicle began to head up the driveway, Nicole asked, "How old is Marguerite?"

She was pretty sure Jake stilled behind her. He probably peered down at the top of her head too, but she didn't look around to see. Finally, he said, "What do you mean?"

The question brought a small breathless laugh to her lips and she offered him a crooked smile over her shoulder. "It's kind of a simple question. How old is she?" She tilted her head and added, "She can't be more than thirty or so, though she doesn't look that old even, but I've known her for ten years. She was married to Jean Claude back when I first went with Aunt Maria to help with spring cleaning, so she must have been at least twenty then, which means she has to be in her early thirties now . . . But I swear the woman acts like she's at least twice that in age. She mothers both Pierina and me." Nicole gave an embarrassed laugh and admitted, "I swear, she makes me feel about ten years old every time I'm around her . . . So . . . is she older than she looks? Or just mothering by nature or something?"

"Mothering by nature," he answered, happy to avoid the original question. "She mothers everyone and was probably doing so even as a little girl."

"Yeah, I can just picture her as a five-year-old, fussing over every child and adult in the vicinity," Nicole admitted wryly, and then asked again, "So how old is she?"

When he didn't answer right away, she raised her eyebrows in question, and he murmured, "Let's close the door."

Nicole nodded and moved out of the way as he began to do just that. She watched him lock it, and then turned to lead the way back upstairs to where her coffee waited.

Jake stayed silent as he followed Nicole back upstairs, but his mind was working in overdrive as he tried to figure out what to say in answer to her question . . . and then it came to him.

"She isn't in her thirties," Jake announced as they reached the kitchen.

"What?" Nicole asked with amazement as he moved to pour himself another coffee. "She has to be. She—"

"She was thirteen when she married Jean Claude." Both statements were true. He just didn't mention that the marriage took place back in the thirteenth century, and that she was actually seven hundred and something rather than the thirty-something Nicole had supposed.

"Thirteen?" She sounded as horrified as he would expect as she asked, "Is that even legal?"

Jake shrugged and carried his coffee to the table

as he offered, "The Europeans don't have the same laws we do."

"Yeah, but—holy crap, Jean Claude was worse than I thought," she muttered with disgust as she followed him.

"What do you mean?" he asked curiously.

"Well, you know, he was such a jerk to her," she said on a sigh. "I mean I only saw him maybe a half dozen times over the years before he died, but I remember he would come in and be perfectly awful to her, snapping and growling and ordering her around like she was a dog or something. Even as a teenager I thought, man, she's too pretty and nice to put up with that from anyone."

Jake turned back to his coffee, doctoring it with cream and sugar as he considered what she'd said. He hadn't known that Jean Claude was unkind to Marguerite. The truth was Jake didn't know Marguerite that well, and he hadn't known her when she was married to Jean Claude. He'd heard stories, of course. His boss, Vincent, had been an Argeneau, after all, and was her nephew, which meant there had been talk about his family. But Jake hadn't really got to know Marguerite until the attempt on his life that had resulted in his being turned.

Marguerite had talked to him several times after he'd woken from the turn. That was before he'd run away. And Nicole was right, she was a very nice woman, one who shouldn't have to put up with the kind of behavior Nicole was describing. But then Nicole shouldn't have had to put up with the abuse Rodolfo had dished out either, so all he said was, "I've found in life that the nicest people somehow seem to end up with the most unkind partners. I've never understood that myself. You'd think like would attract like, but it definitely seems like opposites attract when it comes to a lot of couples."

"Yeah," Nicole murmured, her mouth twisting. "I'd agree with that."

"What was your husband like?" Jake asked, taking her empty cup and walking over to pour her a fresh one.

"A jerk," she said, and then smiled wryly as she added, "But then I'm somewhat biased. I'm sure a lot of people think he's great. Certainly, he's the sort who'd give the shirt off his back to friends and acquaintances."

"Just not his wife?" he suggested, pouring coffee into her cup and then carrying it back to the table.

"Me, he wouldn't even have given the time of day," she assured him dryly and doctored her coffee with sugar and cream, before adding, "I suspect he married the artist, and was disappointed when he found himself shackled to the woman."

Jake raised his eyebrows. "Aren't they one and the same person?"

"You'd think so, wouldn't you?" she asked with amusement. Nicole sipped her coffee, swallowed, and then said quietly, "It turns out Rodolfo was all about the surface and appearances. At first he liked going around bragging about marrying a world-renowned artist. *That* was cool. Unfortunately, actually *living* with me was less so." She peered into her coffee and said, "I think he had poor self-esteem, that maybe he thought marrying me would boost it . . . and was terribly disappointed when it didn't." Sighing, she met his gaze and added, "And I suspect he thought that being married to me would mean a life that was one long round of cocktail parties and glad-handing with celebrity clients. Instead, it was day-to-day drudgery, a lot of time spent with him twiddling his thumbs and bored while I worked hard, or his standing by listening to my side of phone calls with those celebrities he longed to connect with, or his having to listen to me being complimented and praised by people who thought of him as 'the husband' who didn't work rather than the charming, dashing fellow who bagged the artist." She breathed out wearily, and shook her head. "But he wouldn't talk about it, so I'm just guessing and with that and ten cents, you still have ten cents."

Jake eyed Nicole silently. She had definitely analyzed her husband and the situation thoroughly. He also suspected she was being kind in her assessment of Rodolfo. The guy had more problems than low self-esteem if he was now trying to kill her for her money. "How long were you married?"

"Two years. I met him at twenty-one, married him at twenty-three, left him at twenty-five and now, a year later . . ." She shrugged.

"The divorce is nearly final," he finished for her.

Nicole nodded and leaned back against the counter with her coffee. "My career was just taking off when we met. I'd just graduated and had my first art show, which was a rousing success . . . thanks to Marguerite."

His eyebrows rose. "Marguerite?"

Nicole smiled. "Yeah. My cousin, Pierina, and I used to help out Aunt Maria at Marguerite's several times a year. I was really into art and during breaks, would usually end up sketching while Pierina and I chatted. Marguerite saw and is the first one who encouraged me to pursue art. Well, the first one to encourage me who wasn't family," she added with a small smile. "But family have to encourage and support you so her compliments carried a little more weight," she explained.

When he nodded in understanding, she continued, "Anyway, Marguerite encouraged me and then kept tabs on me. I did a painting of Julius my last year of high school and gave it to her as a sort of thank-you."

"Her husband, Julius Notte?" Jake asked with surprise. Julius and Marguerite had only reunited and married a few years ago. As far as he knew, Julius hadn't been around when Nicole was a teenager.

"No, her dog, Julius," Nicole said with a laugh. "Weird, huh? That she had a dog named Julius before she ever met her husband Julius?"

Jake didn't comment. Marguerite had caught him up on a lot on their drive here and he knew that while Julius, the man, had only reappeared on the scene recently, he'd been in Marguerite's life long before she'd named her first dog Julius. However, he didn't say that.

"Anyway," Nicole continued, "After I gave her the painting, she asked me to paint a portrait of her daughter, Lissianna, and then one of herself and then her sons: Etienne, Bastien, and Lucern. And when I had my first art show she insisted on making all the arrangements and invited some pretty big names in the art world as well as a lot of people with heavy pockets. The next thing I knew I had commissions coming out of my ears." She smiled faintly in memory and then her smile faded. "That's when I met Rodolfo."

Jake imagined it must have seemed to Nicole like the universe was smiling on her at that point. Her career was taking off and then she met and fell in love with an exotic, foreign man who appeared to love her back. The world had been her oyster, or would have seemed to be. And if she'd met Rodolfo just as her career was taking off, she wouldn't have had the money she had now. There would have been no reason to think he'd someday try to rob her blind in a divorce . . . and when that failed, try to kill her.

"Speaking of commissions, I guess I should get to work," Nicole said suddenly, looking uncomfortable, and he suspected she was embarrassed by how much she'd revealed.

"And I should get to work as well," he said calmly, but when she then headed for the door, he said, "Marguerite mentioned that you were interested in getting a security system for the house. I happen to have a friend who's the best in the business. I can give him a call to come out for a look-see."

Jake wasn't surprised when Nicole grimaced. He knew Marguerite had suggested she needed security and Nicole had most likely reluctantly agreed just to stop the lecturing. But after heaving a sigh, she nodded. "Okay. Thanks."

"No problem," Jake murmured and watched her leave the kitchen, his gaze dropping to her behind and staying there until she was out of sight. Then he realized what he'd done and gave his head a shake. Jake had dated a lot of women both as a mortal and as an immortal, but he never mixed business with pleasure. It was dangerous to get distracted in his line of work, and Nicole would definitely be a distraction. Hell, she was already a distraction. He'd meant to read her after Marguerite left but had forgotten that intention as soon as she'd begun to talk. No, it was better to keep his mind on business and avoid the temptation of Ms. Nicole Phillips's physical attributes . . . but damn, she had a nice round rump and there was nothing he liked better than that.

Grimacing at his own stray thoughts, Jake reached for his cell phone as it began to ring. His eyebrows rose when he saw the call was from Cody, the security guy he'd mentioned. His friend really was the best in the business, and as such, was always busy. He'd talked to his secretary rather than the man himself that morning. She'd said he'd be in at noon and Jake had said he'd call back then. It looked like Cody had decided not to wait. He was expecting the man to tell him he was so busy he couldn't come out for at least a week, but Jake planned to use bribery and calling in favors to get him out earlier than that.

Nicole eyed the covered paintings at the end of her studio, briefly debating whether she really wanted the rest of her coffee and to work, or whether she shouldn't dump the rest of it and go back to bed to sleep for another couple of hours. Nicole was tired and she was never at her best when she was tired. It made her work slow and uninspired, and she often just ended up painting over it again later after she'd rested, which was rather a waste of time. Sleeping for another hour or two or four and then waking up refreshed and excited to paint seemed more sensible. But she didn't want to go to bed. Jake might think she was a slugabed like her ex had always claimed.

The thought of her new cook/housekeeper made Nicole recall the list of Jake's duties that Marguerite had said she'd left on the dresser in her room. Turning away from the paintings, she headed back out through the office and up the hall, intent on fetching the list. She could hear the murmur of Jake's voice as she stepped out into the lower living room and supposed he was making that call to his security buddy. The thought made her sigh, and then she wrinkled her nose at herself.

Nicole had no idea why she was so resistant to getting a security system. She'd actually looked into getting one herself when she'd first moved here with Rodolfo, but then she'd left him instead. When she'd moved back there had been so much to do, and then there had been the problems with the gas grill and furnace and people had begun suggesting her ex was trying to kill her and she should have a security system because of that, and suddenly Nicole had resisted the whole idea.

She would admit Rodolfo hadn't treated her well, and yes he'd tried to go after as much of her money as he could in the divorce, including commissions she'd contracted for before meeting him and a percentage of any commissions she did in the future, which was just ridiculous. But to suggest he was trying to kill her . . .

Shrugging her irritation away, Nicole stepped into the guest room, grabbed the list of tasks Marguerite had left for her and returned to her studio. It looked like an awfully long list. Nicole waited until she was in her studio, cuddled up under the fluffy duvet she kept on the daybed that served double duty as a couch in the corner of the room, before beginning to actually read it . . . and fell asleep doing so.

Nicole shifted sleepily some time later, turning onto her side and tugging down the duvet she'd burrowed under. The action freed her eyes and nose, so when she then blinked her eyes open she had an unobstructed view of the eight-foot-tall silhouetted figure just feet away in her studio and blocking the light from the window.

The shriek that ripped from her throat was high and terrified. The figure reacted to the sound by wobbling and then tumbling off whatever he stood on. Nicole sat up abruptly and stared down at the man now lying on her studio floor.

With the window no longer blocked and light pouring in, she could see the stepladder he'd fallen off of and that he had a screwdriver in his hand. She stared at him with confusion as he sat up and then frowned slightly. The ladder and screwdriver didn't suggest a break-in and he wore a blue shirt with C.C. SECURITY on the pocket. Her gaze shifted to the window and she saw a half-installed small white boxy-looking thing on the edge of the window.

"Man, you scared the crap out of me," the man admitted, turning over and sitting up.

Nicole relaxed as she took in his gangly figure,

red hair, and freckled face. Between that and his open air of chagrin, he wasn't the least bit threatening and he was obviously the security guy Jake had mentioned coming for a look-see. Apparently a look-see had turned into an install, she thought with irritation.

"Are you okay?" she asked, pushing aside her irritation in favor of worry for the man who had taken a tumble. "You didn't hurt yourself, did you?"

"Oh, no, I'm fine. I was only two steps up. I was more startled than anything," he assured her and then they both glanced to the door when it burst open and Jake charged in.

He paused abruptly as he took in the scene, and then turned his concerned gaze to Nicole. "Are you okay?"

When she nodded and began to push her duvet aside, he turned his attention to the man still on her floor and moved forward to offer him a hand up, asking, "What the hell are you doing in here, Cody? I told you not to bother her while she's working."

"I know, but when I was doing the office I looked in and the studio seemed empty, so I thought I'd quickly do it while she was out. She must have been buried under the duvet," he added with chagrin.

"I didn't get much sleep last night. I decided to catch a nap before starting to work," she explained to Jake, feeling guilty that she'd been lazy.

But he just nodded and said, "Good. I was surprised you didn't go back to bed again after Marguerite left. You were working until dawn."

Nicole relaxed a little and stood up, unaccountably

relieved that he was being so understanding rather than glaring at her with disapproval as Rodolfo would have done. "I think I'll make some coffee."

"I set up the pot earlier. You just have to turn it on," Jake said, and then led the way out to the office to do it for her, before adding, "I also made a fruit-and-cheese tray in case you wanted a snack. It's in the fridge."

Nicole moved to the small bar fridge beside the coffee counter and opened it to find a large plate with cheese, crackers, grapes, and a sliced-up apple on it.

"Wow," she murmured, taking it out and peering at it with surprise. Then she smiled at him. "I think I'm going to like having a cook/housekeeper."

Jake smiled crookedly back, and then peered past her, his eyebrows rising. "How much more do you have to do in there, Cody?"

Nicole noted that the man with C.C. SECURITY on his shirt had followed them to the door and was now eyeing the coffeepot with interest. At Jake's question, he forced his eyes away from the dark liquid and answered, "I just have to finish the one window and then do the sliding glass doors. I've already done the keyed door and the other two windows. I'll be done before the coffee is."

When Jake nodded, the man moved back into the room and out of sight.

Nicole raised her eyebrows in question and Jake explained, "He happened to have a cancellation this afternoon. When he got here and took a look around, the quote was so good I told him to go ahead."

"Oh." Nicole frowned, but merely nodded. Despite her resistance to the idea, she would have got a security system eventually if only to stop everyone else from bugging her about it. That or a big dog. She'd been leaning toward the big dog the last little while. It was lonely rattling around in this big house by herself, and a bit nerve wracking. She'd found herself jumping at the littlest thing. Actually, the last couple of days were the first time she hadn't felt edgy in the house and that was because she'd had Marguerite and now Jake here. She supposed he'd worked as well as a big dog in making her feel comfortable in her own house.

"I better get back upstairs," Jake said suddenly. "I was making peppercorn sauce when I heard you scream. I took it off the stove before I came down, but it might curdle."

"Right," Nicole nodded, her mind now on peppercorn sauce. It sounded hot. She wasn't much into hot, but she kept that to herself and turned to her office with her cheese-and-fruit plate. She was wondering now, though, what time it was if he was starting dinner already.

A glance at the clock as Nicole entered her studio told her it was only two in the afternoon. She'd slept an hour and a half. Put that with the four hours from earlier, and it was five and a half. Six would have been better, but five and a half would do. Her gaze slid to Cody now as he stepped off the stepladder and carried it over to the sliding glass doors. She looked at the window now, noting the little white box, and frowned. There were three windows on the back wall of her studio; one large center window and two narrower ones on either side. The center window was the only one that opened though, but there were now boxes on all of them.

"The side windows don't open," she began. "Why—"

"They have glass break detectors," Cody explained. "The center one is fitted with a sensor for breaking glass and opening and closing."

"Oh." Nicole peered at the windows again. She hadn't realized they had sensors for glass breaking. It was clever though, she supposed. Her gaze slid back to Cody and she held out the plate of cheese and fruit. "Cheese?"

Cody grinned and moved forward to take a slice of apple, cheese and a cracker. "Thanks."

Nicole nodded and took a slice of apple herself, then set the plate on a table by her easels. "The coffee should be ready in a minute. Do you want one?"

"Oh, yes please. That would be great," he said, and then popped the fruit, cheese, and cracker in his mouth all at once and headed back to the sliding glass doors.

Knowing she wouldn't be able to get any work done until he finished and left, Nicole settled on the daybed to eat her slice of apple.

"This is a beautiful house," he commented as he began to attach another white box and a magnet sensor on that door.

"Thank you," Nicole murmured, her gaze skimming around her studio. She agreed, she loved this house, and had from the start.

"So your husband must make a load to afford it. What does he do?"

She stiffened briefly with surprise, and then said,

"I'm not married. Or won't be in two weeks," Nicole added reluctantly, because technically she was still married. Though, frankly she'd never really *felt* married. She'd always thought of marriage as a merging of a couple, not just their assets, but their lives, their dreams, their futures. She and Rodolfo hadn't merged anything.

"Ah. I see. Divorcing," Cody said and nodded. "So you got the house in the divorce settlement?"

Nicole stiffened. What was it with people thinking the man was the breadwinner all the time? As if the woman couldn't make it herself. "No. The house is mine. I bought it . . . twice," she added dryly. "Or one and a half times. I paid for it when we moved back to Canada, and then I got to buy my soon-to-be ex out of it as part of the divorce because it was considered a marital asset."

Cody raised his eyebrows with surprise. "*You* bought it?"

"Women can make money too, you know," she said dryly and he flushed guiltily.

"Sorry," he muttered, but his gaze slid to the three covered canvases in the room. "An artist?"

Nicole nodded. She always covered her paintings between sessions. It prevented her looking at them and picking out all the flaws when she wasn't working on them. She was her own worst critic. Turning her gaze back to Cody, she commented, "You seem to know Jake well."

"Oh, yeah. Met him on the job when he first moved out here to Ottawa," Cody said easily. "Being in the same business, we got along well. Went out for a drink after work." He shrugged. "A friendship was born."

"The same business?" Nicole asked with surprise. "You're in security and he's a cook/housekeeper. I wouldn't think that was really the same business."

Cody stilled briefly, but then continued working and said lightly, "House security, housekeeping, it's all about the house."

Nicole eyed him briefly, but his back was to her as he worked and she couldn't see his expression. She stood up. "The coffee should be done. How do you take yours?"

"Just regular, please," Cody said, his gaze now extremely curious as he looked again to the covered canvases on their easels.

She deliberately took her time making the coffees, wanting to avoid any more questions. In the end, she timed it perfectly. Cody was folding up his ladder when she re-entered her studio.

"All done in here," he said cheerfully, crossing the room with the ladder under one arm.

Nicole merely smiled and held out his coffee as he approached.

"Thanks," he said, taking it with his free hand and continuing on out of the room, saying, "I'll let you get back to work now. Sorry for scaring you."

"No problem," Nicole said quietly and followed to close the French doors of the studio behind him as he left. She turned back to the room then with a little sigh. She was still tired and now a little out of sorts as well. Not the best mental state to work in. It was times like this she wished she had a more normal job. She didn't imagine your state of mind affected your work much if you were an accountant or something. One plus one still equaled two no matter your mood. Sadly, it wasn't the same with painting, or probably any of the more artistic jobs like music or writing where your mood could make you more critical. Still, she walked over and removed the covers from the canvases one after another and then stood back to survey what she'd done so far.

Nicole knew at once that this was not going to be a very productive day. Every flaw, real or imagined, immediately jumped out at her. She'd used too much red here, not enough shadow there. Was the actress's nose a touch too big? And the sketch of Christian and his fiancée was all wrong; too stiff, not reflecting the love that seemed to shine from every photo of the couple.

Grimacing, she tossed the covers back over each of the canvases and took her coffee and the cheese plate to the daybed, where she sat down with a depressed sigh. Nicole hated when her work was disrupted. Last night things had really been hopping. She'd been painting quickly and happily, satisfied with what she was doing and how the portraits were working out. Today they all looked like crap to her . . . bleck.

It looked like it was going to be a "to do" day. Those were days she did banking, shopping, and any other chore that she'd neglected while working. Usually there were a lot of tasks to do, cleaning, cooking, shopping, banking, bill paying. Now that she had Jake she could take cooking and cleaning off her list, but that still left some chores.

She had to hit the bank and transfer money from her savings to checking to cover monthly bills that would come out today. She should have done it online yesterday, but now it was too late. It took twenty-four hours for online transfers to go through. Nicole supposed she should find out how much the security system was going to cost and transfer enough to cover that as well. And then she guessed she'd have to go grocery shopping. Jake had mentioned something about only being able to work with what he had, so she supposed she should get him whatever he needed. And she wanted to pick up mousetraps as well. There were always one or two brave mice who tried to move indoors when the cold hit, and while she hadn't seen any yet, she had no doubt there were one or two around. Maybe she could get those sonic things that were supposed to scare them off rather than buy actual mousetraps. Nicole wasn't big on killing things and mice were such cute little fuzzy things. Besides, ever since seeing *Ratatouille* she'd had an aversion to killing the poor little buggers. Although *Ratatouille* had been about a rat, as she recalled. It didn't matter, mice were just smaller rats.

Aware that it was after two and that the bank closed at four or shortly thereafter, Nicole took her coffee with her and headed upstairs to find Jake, passing Cody and several other men installing little white boxes in windows in the living room. She murmured hello in passing, but her mind was on the shopping expedition ahead as she thought that it would be helpful if Jake made a list of what he needed for her to pick up while she was out. She suspected he'd need time to plan his menu to know what he needed, and hoped that wouldn't take too long.

The scent that hit Nicole as she mounted the stairs was amazing. Something yummy was cooking and the air was rich with the aroma of garlic and other spices.

"Something smells delicious," she commented as she entered the kitchen.

Jake glanced around with a start, and then tossed the dish towel he'd been drying his hands with over a book on the counter. It looked like a cookbook and like he was trying to hide it? She had no idea why. She didn't expect him to know how to cook everything without a recipe, but he seemed determined to hide it, so she acted like she didn't see it.

"I have to go into town and do some banking and whatnot, so maybe you could find out how much the security system is going to cost so I can make sure I have the money in the account," Nicole suggested, and then added, "I thought I'd hit the grocery store on the way back too, so do you want to make a list of what I should pick up while I'm out?"

"Oh." Jake frowned, but then turned his attention to the door as Cody came in.

"All done," the other man announced. "The boys are just collecting their equipment and then we'll be out of your hair."

"Perfect timing," Jake said quietly, but she got the sense that he was relieved at this news.

"I need you both to come put in your personal codes," he announced.

"Personal code?" Nicole asked, following when he turned to lead them out of the kitchen. She trailed him to the master bedroom, where a security panel was now installed beside the sliding glass doors.

"That way you know who comes and goes and when by which code is used," he explained. "You need to put one in, and so does Jake. I can put in a third number for guests to use if you like."

"Oh. I see," she murmured and peered at the digital screen briefly before asking, "How many numbers?"

"Four. But you want to make it something that isn't your birthday or anything that someone else can easily guess," he warned.

Nicole nodded, thought briefly, and then quickly punched in four digits while Cody and Jake averted their eyes. Stepping back, she said, "Done."

"Great." Cody worked at the panel briefly, and then stepped away. "Your turn Jake."

"You can watch if you like," Jake said when Nicole started to follow suit and turn away. "It's your system. You should know my number in case you want to remove it later."

Nicole paused and watched as he punched in his own four digits, repeating them in her head a couple of times so that she could remember long enough to write them down somewhere.

"And now . . ." Cody punched a bunch of buttons again and then stepped away for a third time. "The guest number?"

Nicole punched in another number and then stepped away while he finished the setup.

After a moment's work, he stepped back and nodded. "There you are. All done."

"How long have you guys been here?" she asked curiously as he closed the panel.

"My men and I got here at about a quarter after twelve," Cody answered easily, and then added, "When I heard Jake called this morning I didn't think we'd be able to get out here until later in the week. But we had a cancellation this afternoon so here we are."

Nicole didn't comment. They must have arrived just after she'd lain down, but she was more concerned with the fact that Jake had actually called before he'd mentioned it to her, yet he'd made it sound like he was asking for permission to call when he already had. Now she was a bit annoyed. Like with rekeying the locks, she would have liked being consulted before he actually called about the security system the first time.

Actually, she supposed, if the front door lock was broken, that had definitely needed immediate attention so she wasn't annoyed about that too much, but this was a security system, not an emergency. She'd lived here two years without one. She really would have liked to be consulted about this before the first call. What if she'd said no to his calling when he'd brought it up? Cody had already been on the way out by that point. She'd have to talk to Jake about that, Nicole supposed.

Sighing at the thought of the unpleasant task ahead, she asked, "So is a check all right?"

"Yeah. Sure. My office gal will send you a bill and you can send a check in then. Don't worry about it now," Cody said as they started out of her room.

"Can you give me an idea of what it will be?" she asked. "I'm heading to the bank now and can transfer the money while there."

Cody nodded and gave a price, adding, "Give or take. I'm not sure about taxes. And then there's a monthly charge for monitoring."

Nicole nodded but was surprised by the price. It seemed pretty reasonable. She'd expected it to cost more. In fact, she'd priced security systems when she'd first considered getting one, and the price he'd just given was at the low end of the quotes she'd received at the time. He'd definitely given her a break on the price and she supposed she had Jake to thank for that.

"All set?" Jake asked as they entered the kitchen.

"All set," Cody assured him, offering a hand.

"Thank you," Jake said solemnly as they shook hands.

"No problem. Happy to help," Cody assured him, and then nodded at Nicole and said, "Nice to meet you."

"You too," Nicole said politely.

"I'll see you out," Jake said, following when Cody turned to leave.

The moment they were out of the room, Nicole headed for her room to get ready to go. She wanted to brush her hair, her teeth, maybe throw on some makeup and change her clothes for something warmer. Her jeans were all right, but it was cold out and something warmer than a T-shirt was called for. It wouldn't be if she was the kind of person who did up her winter coat, but she tended to take it off in the car and then just tug it on and not bother to do it up just to run into a store.

Nicole didn't know if it was the lack of sleep or what, but she couldn't seem to settle on what to wear. She changed her top three times before settling on a deep purple light knit sweater. She also fussed over her hair, letting it out of the ponytail and using a straightener on it before feeling satisfied. Then she spent longer than normal on makeup, even putting on eye shadow, which she rarely did.

Grimacing when she saw that she'd fussed so long it was now after three, she grabbed her purse and hurried out of the room. Her footsteps slowed, however, when she spotted Jake leaning against the doorjamb between the kitchen and living room, jiggling keys.

"Ready?" he asked straightening.

"Yes," she answered slowly, eyeing his keys. "Are you going somewhere?"

"I thought it would probably be easier if I came shopping with you," he explained, and then added with an apologetic grimace, "I haven't had time to make up a menu plan for the week yet, so I'm going to have to play it by ear. I'm hoping seeing the vegetables that are available this time of year will inspire me."

"Oh." Nicole hesitated, but then sighed and nodded. A moment ago this had been a mostly relaxing, if boring, excursion. No excitement, but no stress either. Now Nicole found herself tensing up as she headed for the stairs with Jake on her heels.

He was jiggling keys, did that mean he expected to drive? Would he have a specific grocery store he wanted to go to? What was he going to do while she was in the bank? Would she have to rush because he was waiting in the car, or—

Nicole stopped abruptly and turned back toward Jake, about to suggest he should go shopping on his own while she took care of the bank and such. But she just as quickly turned forward again as she realized she couldn't expect him to pay for her groceries and she didn't have any money on hand to give him. This would teach her to always have cash handy, Nicole thought grimly.

She was almost to the door to the garage when Nicole realized that she was reacting to the man just as she had to her husband, tensing up and letting him take control. Training, she thought grimly. But this wasn't Rodolfo, this was an employee, and while she understood the need to take him shopping with her, Nicole would be damned if she was letting him drive. She had started out on this excursion alone. He was just along for the shopping. She was driving.

Opening the door to the garage, she walked determinedly to her red Lexus SUV and got straight into the driver's seat. Only after she'd closed the door and slung her purse onto the backseat did she glance around to see how he was taking it. He wasn't there. The door to the house was wide open, but he was nowhere in sight. She was just starting to frown, when he stepped into view wearing his winter coat and carrying hers.

"Oh, crap," Nicole muttered and felt herself flush with embarrassment. Shaking her head, she opened the door and climbed back out to take it from him with a muttered "Thank you."

"No problem," he said easily, turning to lock the door while she donned it. "This is a heated garage, isn't it?"

"Yes," Nicole answered as she pulled on the coat. That was why she hadn't thought of the coat until she'd seen him holding it.

"They don't allow that anymore, I don't think," he commented, checking that the door was locked before turning to face her as he slid his keys into his pocket.

"What? Heated garages?" she asked uncertainly.

Jake nodded. "I think they changed the code and don't allow it anymore. Something about air exchange or something. Obviously it was built when it was allowed though." He shrugged and opened the driver's door, gesturing her in now that she had her coat on.

Nicole climbed back inside and murmured a thank-you as he closed the door. She then pulled on her seat belt and started the engine as he walked around to the passenger's side. She glanced at him curiously as he got in and did up his own seat belt, but he didn't seem the least bit upset that she was driving. In fact, she was getting the distinct impression that he'd only brought his keys to lock the door, as he'd done, and she'd been overreacting.

Shaking her head at herself, Nicole hit the button to open the garage door and then shifted gear and backed the vehicle out onto the icy driveway, hitting the button to close the door as soon as she'd cleared it. They were both silent at first, but once she was out of the driveway and onto the road, Nicole decided she should broach the subject that was bugging her. "Jake?"

"Hmm?" He glanced to her in question.

Nicole hesitated, but then said quietly, "While I appreciate your taking care of the front lock and the security system, I'd appreciate it more if in future you talked to me about things like that first, rather than just going ahead and doing them."

Jake was silent for long enough that Nicole glanced curiously toward him. Her eyebrows rose when she found him staring at her intently, expression focused. She couldn't tell if he was glaring at her, or trying to find Waldo on her face somewhere. Either way, she didn't know how to take this response and arched one eyebrow. "Are you having a mini seizure or something?"

He blinked at the question, and confusion crossed his face, so she glanced toward the road again and explained, "I read somewhere that people can have petit mal seizures where they just stare and aren't really conscious or aware . . . although," she added, glancing toward him again. "You looked aware, just kind of fixated."

"No," Jake turned to peer out the window. But then he cleared his throat, and added, "But my apologies. I understood from Marguerite that you didn't want to be bothered with details, but I will consult you in future."

Nicole relaxed. It was so Marguerite, very sweet, but Nicole was too much of a control freak to allow anyone to take care of her that way. The control thing was a new development. She'd seemed to briefly lose control of everything in her life while married. Now that she had it back, she wasn't letting it go for anyone . . . no matter how good-looking and how nice they smelled.

Damn, she thought as she took a deep breath and her senses were filled with a mixture of a woodsy cologne and what she suspected was just Jake. The man definitely smelled good. The thought made her frown. She had no business noticing that. He was an employee . . . and she was just getting divorced. It was too soon for her to get involved with anyone. Not that he had said or done anything to make her think he wanted to get involved. But she shouldn't even think of him that way, she told herself firmly.

Five

Jake stared out the window and concentrated on his breathing. In one hundred, out one hundred, in one hundred, out one hundred—*damn Marguerite!*—in one hundred, out one hundred—*son of a bitch!*—in one hundred—*dear God what had she got him into?*

He distinctly recalled Marguerite telling him there were some things he should know about Nicole that he could only learn from reading her. Well, now he knew. He couldn't read her, that's what there was to know. She was his bloody life mate. He hadn't even adjusted to being an immortal and now he had a possible life mate. Great.

Closing his eyes, Jake leaned his forehead against the cold glass of the window and tried to just concentrate on breathing again, but he couldn't get that knowledge out of his head. He couldn't read or control Nicole.

When she'd said she wanted him to consult with

her before making decisions, Jake had heard the upset in her tone. He'd thought to get into her thoughts and just ease her annoyance with him. He wasn't surprised by it. In fact, he was surprised she hadn't thrown a fit at his spending her money so freely. But he and Marguerite had decided last night that the security system was necessary. Thanks to her resistance to protecting herself, Jake was on the job alone, and even he, immortal or not, could not stay awake 24–7 for two weeks straight until the divorce was finalized and there was no more reason for her husband to want her dead. A security system would free him up, give him backup of a sort.

However, he'd been startled to find he couldn't seem to get a hold on her thoughts and control, or even read her.

He couldn't read or control Nicole Phillips.

That was what Marguerite thought he should know. The bloody woman was matchmaking again. It made Jake wonder if her ex-husband really was trying to kill her . . . or even if there really was an ex-husband. He wouldn't put it past Marguerite to lie to get life mates together. That thought made him turn sharply to Nicole. "Marguerite said you're on the tail end of a divorce?"

She stiffened at the blunt announcement, her hands tightening on the steering wheel and sending the car swerving the smallest bit before she regained control of herself and steadied it again. Her response was just as blunt as his question. "Yes."

"Amicable?" he asked, watching her. When her mouth tightened, he added, "I'm sorry, I'm not trying to pry, but it occurred to me today that I'm not sure how I should handle the situation if he shows up at the door looking for you."

"He won't come to the door," she said firmly. "And if he does, you can tell him that I'm not in, and that any contact should go through the lawyer."

"Not amicable then," he said wryly.

Nicole was silent for a minute and then let her breath out and seemed to force herself to relax. When she spoke, her voice was softer, less angry. "I tried to handle it amicably, but . . ." She shrugged.

"When will the divorce be final?" he asked. So far everything Marguerite had said was true, but . . .

"Two weeks," Nicole answered stiffly and then corrected herself, saying, "Actually, thirteen days now."

"And counting?" he suggested. "I don't know whether to say congratulations or not. I doubt in your childhood dreams you fantasized that some day you'd marry your prince and divorce his ass as quickly as possible."

His words startled a laugh out of her and Nicole shook her head, her body losing much of its tension for real this time. "No," she agreed. "That was never in my agenda."

Jake nodded and peered out the window again, trying to figure out how to ask about the furnace, the blocked doors, the gas grill and the fireplace. It was trickier to ask about. It wasn't like he could say, "So have any near explosions lately?"

"Have you been married?"

He glanced to her with surprise at the question and shook his head. "No." Jake glanced out the window again and then admitted, "I got close once, though."

"What happened?" she asked curiously.

"My family," he muttered.

"Your family?" she prompted.

"Yeah," he said, thinking back to that time. He almost stopped talking then, but realized that his situation wasn't all that dissimilar to her marriage and admitted: "My family has trouble with boundaries. They were concerned and . . . looked into things." They'd looked into her mind, but he could hardly say that. On the other hand, Jake didn't want to flat-out lie to her if she was a possible life mate. It didn't seem a healthy way to start. Sighing, he said, "And through their looking into her, they found she was more interested in my money than me."

Jake sensed Nicole glancing sharply toward him, but continued to look out the window and simply waited.

"Really?" she asked finally as she braked at a stop sign, and he heard the suspicion in her voice.

"Really," Jake assured her solemnly, turning to meet her gaze. "She'd already taken two men for their money; one in a palimony suit, one in a divorce. I was to be victim three."

"But your family saved you from that," Nicole said quietly and shifted her attention back to the road. As she turned onto the cross street, she said, "You're lucky."

Jake frowned at the soft words and admitted wryly, "I'm afraid I didn't see it that way at the time. I was just pissed at their interference when they confronted her and sent her on her way."

"Why?" she asked with surprise.

Jake shrugged. "I was in love . . . and sure that it was different with me, that she loved me and they misunderstood what had happened in the first two relationships." He grimaced and glanced to her to admit, "I was young and foolish then I guess."

For some reason his words made her laugh. Raising his eyebrows, he asked, "What?"

"Jake," she said on a laugh, "I know Marguerite said you're older than you look, but you look twenty-five. How old were you then when you were so much younger? Sixteen?"

He smiled crookedly, remembering only then that he looked much younger than his fifty-eight years. Well, that was a fly in the ointment, wasn't it? She now probably thought she was older than him. Certainly, she'd addressed him just then with the condescension of someone who thought they were older if only by a year or so.

"Well," Nicole said now. "You're very lucky your family intervened. It saved you a lot of heartache."

"Oh, I still got the heartache," Jake said dryly, recalling that time in his life. He'd been thirty-eight and the advanced age hadn't made the heartache any easier to handle, and he suspected that heartache was the reason he'd never let anyone close again. Shrugging that aside for now, he said, "What they saved was my bank balance."

Nicole smiled slightly and shrugged. "Well at least that insult wasn't added to the injury."

"That sounds like the voice of experience," he said mildly, hoping to get her to tell him about the incidents Marguerite had told him about.

"Yeah. Loads of it," she said, and then shrugged

as if shaking off a bad cloak and said more cheer-fully, "On the bright side, I had enough sense to go for counseling so I don't wind up a nasty and bitter man-hating divorcee."

"True," Jake agreed. "I gather in divorce one partner or the other often goes crazy and does stupid things."

"That's what the gas guy said," she said, her mouth tipping at the edges.

"The gas guy?" he asked.

"Yeah, I had a little trouble with the gas grill when I first moved back." She shrugged and added, "And the furnace, and the fireplace and the doors." Nicole grimaced and waved those worries away. "I had a run of bad luck for a bit, but it's all good now."

"Right," Jake said quietly, pretty sure that Mar-guerite had told him the truth about her near misses after all. So, Nicole was in danger and did need looking out for, and she was a possible life mate for him as well, which was no doubt why Marguerite had put him on the job. Who better to look out for his possible life mate than himself, right?

Jake peered at her solemnly. Short, voluptuous, pretty with a nice smile, big brown eyes and long blond hair. Obviously, her father wasn't Italian. Not with that long golden hair and the last name Phillips. He knew for sure the mother was Italian, though. She was the sister of Marguerite's cook/housekeeper, Maria.

God, more Italians to deal with, he thought with dismay. As if the Nottes weren't enough. Of course, he was a fine one to talk. His grandfather had been full-blooded Italian. It's where his parents had got the name Stephano. His father had been very close to his father and had named him after the old man. His middle name, Jacob, came from his mother's grandfather.

"You're staring at me again."

Jake blinked at that comment from Nicole and glanced away. "Sorry. I wasn't really staring. I mean, I might have been looking at you, but I wasn't really seeing you. I was thinking of my family and that I have Italian in my background too."

"Do you?" she asked with surprise.

"Yes. It's where I got my name."

Nicole raised her eyebrows at that. "Forgive me, but Jake Colson doesn't sound very Italian."

"Oh, no, well, Jacob is my middle name. My full name is Stephano Jacob Colson Notte," he admitted reluctantly.

"Really?" she asked with interest. "So how come you go by your middle names instead of Stephano Notte?"

Jake hesitated and then said, "Rebellion I guess. My family intervened one too many times and I rebelled and rejected any connection with them in response." He frowned and admitted, "I guess it wasn't a very mature response. It wasn't like what happened was their fault, but I blamed them. I also didn't want to be anything like them. Notte was my stepfather's name. I reverted to my father's last name and my middle name and—"

Realizing what he was saying, Jake caught himself and closed his mouth. He had never wanted to be immortal. He'd told himself that he didn't want to be turned because being mortal was better. He could run around in the sun and go swimming in the daylight and attend a normal school with other kids. He'd never wanted to be a bloodsucking, brainwashing vampire. But after finding him dying on the office floor, his boss, Vincent, in a really very selfless move, had given up his one turn to save Jake's life. Four days later he'd woken up an immortal . . . not by his own choice.

Jake hadn't reacted well on finding out he'd been turned. He'd been furious to have his life turned upside down that way. He'd also been furious because suddenly his family was tiptoeing around and gently trying to offer him assistance afterward. Jake hadn't wanted that help, or perhaps it was more correct to say he hadn't wanted to need that help. Jake had always known who he was and what he'd wanted, and suddenly he'd been as lost as a boy, needing to be taught how to feed, how to control his hunger, how to read and control mortals, the best techniques for living with as little exposure to sun as possible, how, how, how. Jake had felt like a cripple, someone with a mental deficit . . . and he hadn't liked it. So, basically he'd reacted like a teenage boy, and—

"Ran away?" Nicole suggested and when he glanced at her sharply, half suspecting she'd read him, she said, "You changed your name and ran away here to Ottawa to punish them, maybe."

She was right, of course. He'd changed his name and run away from his home and his family like a kid. Wow . . . he was such an ass, Jake realized suddenly and shook his head.

"We all act like idiots at times," Nicole said quietly. "We're human. We have emotions and those are sticky and confusing and rarely logical so we do stupid things." She shrugged, and turned off the car. "Welcome to the human race. You'll make many more mistakes before your life is done. Accept it, deal with it, and move on."

Jake stared at her blankly until he realized she was undoing her seat belt.

"What are you doing?" he asked, glancing around with a frown.

"Going into the bank. Do you want me to leave my key here so you can turn the engine back on and have the heat?"

"No." He undid his own seat belt. "I could use a short walk to stretch my legs. I'll come with you."

She shrugged and opened her door to get out and Jake quickly did the same on his side. He scanned the parking lot as he walked around to meet her at the front of the vehicle and walked her inside, but didn't see anyone. Inside, he settled in one of the chairs where he could keep an eye on her as well as the parking lot outside while he waited. A lot of his job was watching and waiting. The bodyguard job, not the cook/housekeeper job. Jake was finding this cover surprisingly challenging. His mother might think he was a good cook, but she was a mother and as such was delusional when it came to her sons. He suspected most mothers were.

As far as Elaine Notte was concerned, he and Neil practically walked on water, or could if they wished. However, if today had done anything, it had proved to Jake that he couldn't cook worth a damn. He'd stayed up all night, silently prowling the house and repeatedly checking on Nicole as she worked. When she'd moved through the dark house to seek out her bed just before seven that morning, Jake had retreated to the shadows, seeing her but not being seen. Once she was safely in her room he'd then gone to the kitchen to consider what to make for brunch for the two ladies when they got up.

Jake had made pancakes, intending to keep them warming in the oven until the gals got up, only to throw them out when they came out looking like Cajun pancakes. He had never been served pancakes as black as the ones he'd produced. And he'd destroyed one of Nicole's frying pans in the effort.

He'd followed up that effort with French toast . . . with the same results.

Omelets had been his third effort, but they had been a sort of congealed mess: half raw, half blackened, and wholly crunchy from the eggshells that had somehow made their way into the mix.

Marguerite had come out as he was inspecting that effort, his clothes covered with everything from flour to eggs, and his face wreathed with disappointment, and had taken pity on him. She was the real person behind the lovely, fluffy, perfect omelets they'd had that morning. She'd called a local restaurant and had them delivered. Marguerite apparently couldn't cook worth a damn either. But then the last time she'd cooked had been in medieval days. She'd only recently returned to eating and had a cook/housekeeper to manage the cooking.

Five minutes after Marguerite had left for the airport and Nicole had gone down to her studio, the doorbell had rung. Jake had rushed to answer it, expecting it to be Cody and his boys to handle the security system, but instead it had been a courier with a delivery. Jake had signed for it, surprised to find his name on the package. He'd taken it upstairs to find that it contained three cookbooks. *Cooking for Dummies* was the first book. The titles did not get more encouraging after that.

After greeting Cody and his men and showing them around, Jake had left them to work with the admonition not to bother Nicole in the studio and had retired to the kitchen to go through the books looking for something to make for supper. Something easy that he couldn't burn or completely destroy. He'd been on his third and most successful effort, the peppercorn steak sauce, when Nicole's scream had drawn him downstairs. He'd been just finishing it off when she'd come up and announced she was going out.

As her bodyguard Jake had to go with her, but there was another reason. He'd pretty much emptied her refrigerator and freezer with his failed attempts at cooking that morning and afternoon. He had to replace the food, or explain where it had all gone. But that was going to be tricky shopping with her. How the devil was he supposed to explain that he was picking up a carton of eggs when she'd had a full carton that morning? Never mind the onions, cheese, and various other foods he'd run through.

Jake contemplated the matter briefly as he watched Nicole slowly make her way toward the front of the bank line, and then suddenly pulled out his phone and punched in a number.

"Dan?" he said a minute later when his call was answered.

"Yeah buddy. This you, Jake?"

"Yeah, listen, Hank gave you a couple days off, right?"

"Of course. He always gives us time off between gigs."

"Yes, he does," Jake agreed, and then asked, "How would you like to make a couple hundred bucks for an hour or two of easy work? Maybe only an hour," he added.

"I'm listening," Dan said with interest.

Jake glanced toward the line to see that Nicole still had a long wait ahead of her. For once in his life he was grateful rather than annoyed that banks never had enough tellers. Turning his attention back to the phone, he said, "Okay, here's the situation . . ."

Nicole gazed over the pest control section with pursed lips. Her choice was catch-and-release traps or sonar. There were other options, but she just couldn't bring herself to deal with killing the poor little buggers. On the other hand, catching and releasing them outside so that they could run back into her house the first time she opened the garage door didn't seem that sensible, so the only real option appeared to be the sonar repellent thingies. She peered at the containers, reading the promises on them and then tossed several in the shopping cart with a shrug. She hoped they worked. She didn't want Jake quitting because of mice in her house.

That thought made her think of the man and she smiled faintly as she recalled his suggesting she go get her other tasks done and perhaps have a cup of coffee while he managed the shopping. Nicole had been trying to think of a way to make the same suggestion so that she could come get mousetraps without him. His suggesting it had worked even better. She'd handed him the cash she'd taken out at the bank and left him at the grocery store to come next door to the Canadian Tire.

Nicole tossed several more of the sonar things in the cart and then wheeled away to explore the rest of the store. She didn't really need anything, but she had time to kill after all, so rolled up and down the aisles, looking at this and that and buying things she didn't really need but that looked interesting or useful. When she got to the till and watched the items rolling up the conveyor belt toward the cashier, she had to wonder if they didn't have some sort of subliminal persuasion on some of the signs in the store. Certainly, she seemed to have a lot of stuff there and she wasn't sure why she'd grabbed half of it.

Once through the checkout, Nicole returned her cart and headed outside with her bags, surprised to find it was dark again. She glanced at her wristwatch, grimacing when she saw that she'd been in the store browsing for an hour. It was just after 4:30, but the sun set early in late November. Nicole hated that. It had just been making an appearance when she'd gone to bed just before seven that morning and now it was already setting. It felt like there was no daylight at all this time of year. But then she supposed it would help if she didn't sleep through it.

Nicole didn't at first see the car. It seemed to

come out of nowhere as she crossed the parking lot. One moment there was nothing, and the next, bright lights were glaring at her from a car roaring toward her. She never would have got out of the way in time. Even as she realized that, something hit her from behind and nearly knocked her right out of her boots.

Nicole landed several feet away on the snowy pavement, grunting when something heavy landed on her back, and then gasping when she was pulled into a bumpy roll, her back riding over something bulky before she was rolled facedown on the ground again with that bulkiness covering her once more. The move got her a good distance away from the car that swept past without slowing.

"Are you okay?"

She heard the question, but was so stunned by the speed and violence of what had happened that Nicole was slow to respond. In the end, all she could manage was a weak nod as she tried to catch the breath that had been knocked out of her. The warm body above and behind her moved away and Nicole eased to her hands and knees on the cold hard pavement, realizing that her wrists were still through shopping bag handles when the action dragged them across the cold ground. She wheezed a breathless thank-you when someone caught her under the arms and lifted her to her feet like a child.

"Deep breaths," the unfamiliar voice said. "I probably knocked the wind out of you. Sorry."

Nicole released a breathless laugh and shook her head. He was apologizing for saving her life.

"Thank you," she gasped finally, managing to

straighten fully. She glanced to the man who had helped her, noting fair hair and a concerned smile. She managed a crooked smile in response and said, "Really. Thank you. I thought I was a goner."

"You nearly were," he said, his smile fading. His gaze shifted to search the parking lot.

Still struggling for breath, Nicole followed his gaze. The lot was as empty and still as it had been when she'd come out of the store. They were the only two people in the parking lot at the moment. There wasn't even a car light to be seen, and the car that had nearly mown her down was either gone, or had parked and shut its lights off to blend in with the others.

Nicole had no idea where that last thought had come from, but it made her shift uncomfortably.

"Here. Allow me to walk you to your car," her rescuer said, relieving her of her bags.

"Oh, thanks," Nicole forced a smile and started to move when he shifted her bags to one hand and took her arm with the other, to urge her to move. She glanced at him curiously as they walked. He was tall, and well built like Jake, but that was where the resemblance ended. This man was fair-haired as she'd noted, but he also had a boy-next-door look rather than the more rugged good looks Jake had. Which she supposed was kind of ironic, considering Jake was a cook/housekeeper and this man had acted like a commando when he'd tackled and then rolled her to save her life. He was also older than Jake by a good ten years, by her guess.

"Ex-army?" she asked suddenly as they paused at the back of her SUV.

He had been scanning the parking lot as they'd walked, but now glanced to her with surprise. "How did you know?"

"It was that or an ex-football player," Nicole said with amusement. "You have a heck of a tackle-and-roll thing going on there."

His mouth widened into a smile, losing the grimness it had held since she'd first seen him. "Well, I did play football in high school," he admitted with amusement. "But the tackle-and-roll thing is a more recent skill."

Nicole nodded and opened the back of the SUV for him to set her bags inside. She then reached to close it and winced as pain shot down her side.

"I really did you in," he said with concern, closing the back of the vehicle himself.

"A couple bumps and bruises," she said waving away his concern. "Much better than the beating I would have taken from the car if you hadn't been there."

"Hmm." He squinted at her through the dark, trying to get a better look at how much damage had been done, she supposed, and then said, "Maybe we should call the police and take you to the hospital."

Her eyebrows rose with surprise. "On that's not necessary. I mean, what would we tell the police? I almost got run over? I didn't catch the license plate, did you?"

"No," he said with an expression that made her suspect he was kicking himself for not getting it. "Still, I don't want to just leave you here like this. In this light I can't tell if you have a head wound or something else serious. If you pass out from blood loss or a head wound on the road and crash, I'd never forgive myself." He glanced around briefly, and then said, "There's a Moxie's restaurant just past the grocery store next door. Let me buy you a coffee so I can be sure you're okay."

Nicole hesitated. She thought she was probably all right, but was aware she was trembling. A result of the adrenaline in her system she suspected, but truth be told she wasn't sure herself if she wasn't wounded somewhere. She'd hit the ground hard and was hurting pretty much everywhere. Moxie's, she thought. It was right beside Loblaws, where she was supposed to pick up Jake.

Nicole nodded. "Okay."

"Great." He smiled and held out his hand. "My name's Dan Sh— Peters, by the way."

"Nicole Phillips," she said, smiling crookedly as she placed her hand in his. Much to her surprise his smile quickly faded then.

"You're shaking," he said grimly, and asked, "Are you going to be okay to drive?"

"Yeah," she said, and heard the uncertainty in her voice, but while she didn't mind having coffee with the complete stranger who had saved her life, she wasn't willing to let him drive her there. Stiffening her spine, she assured him, "I'm fine, and it's just next door."

"Okay," Dan said, but didn't release her hand, instead squeezing it before saying, "I'll follow. Flash your lights and pull over if you start to feel sick or anything."

Nicole nodded, relieved when he released her hand. But he just took her arm to usher her to the driver's seat, saying, "I'm that pickup there." He gestured to a dark pickup parked two cars down from hers. "Pull out and pass me and I'll follow."

"Okay," Nicole murmured as he opened her door and ushered her in.

"See you there," he said and closed the door for her.

Nicole pushed the button to start the engine and then just sat there for a minute, trying to concentrate on her breathing and calm her body. Her hands were trembling and she felt shaky and not quite all there. It was hard to describe, but she felt sweaty and a bit foggy. An overflow of adrenaline she supposed.

Impatient with herself, Nicole did up her seat belt and shifted into reverse.

Six

"What?" Jake stilled, one hand on a can of tomatoes, and the other tightening on the phone pressed to his ear. Releasing the tomatoes, he turned toward his cart demanding, "What do you mean there was an incident? What incident? Is Nicole all right?"

"I think so," Dan responded and he could hear the frown in his voice.

"What do you mean you think so? Dammit, Dan, I—"

"Shut up and listen, buddy. I don't have long," he said and then started right into explanations. "Someone tried to run her down when she came out of Canadian Tire. They came up slow and quiet, lights off and then just when I spotted them, flashed the lights on and raced the engine to charge her like a bloody bull. I barely knocked her out of the way in time and the car was gone when I looked up to try to see the license plate. But don't worry, she doesn't know I was watching out for her. She thinks I was just Johnny-on-the-spot. I even gave her the name Dan Peters instead of Shepherd in case you'd mentioned me as your partner."

Jake cursed under his breath, and left his cart where it was to head for the exit. "I'm on my way."

"No need. I'm following her to Moxie's for coffee."

Jake stopped walking and stiffened at mention of the bar restaurant. "In case I didn't make it clear earlier, Dan. Nicole is off limits. She's mine. Don't mess with her."

"You wound me," Dan said, and Jake could hear the amusement in the other man's voice. "I love women. I would never mess with them."

"You mess with them all the time," Jake growled. "You're a fricking Romeo with a different Juliet every weekend. Nicole is not a Juliet."

"Relax," Dan said soothingly. "I just want to look her over in better light, make sure she wasn't injured. I couldn't tell in the parking lot, but she was pretty shaken up."

"If you wanted to look her over you should have taken her inside the store or to the Tim Hortons coffee shop," Jake said grimly. "The light in Moxie's isn't much better than the parking lot."

"True, but it is more soothing than the harsh glare of a coffee shop's bright lights would have been, and I think she's in serious need of soothing right now."

"Then I'll do the damned soothing. Send her back to the grocery store," he barked, starting to walk again.

"Too late. We're at Moxie's now. She's parked

and I'm parking. Finish your shopping, buddy. I'll behave and follow at a discreet distance when you text that you're done and she heads over to pick you up."

"You—" Jake paused. Dan had hung up. He slid his phone back into his pocket and then stood there for a minute debating what to do. He couldn't just show up at Moxie's. How would he explain knowing she was there? And how would he explain not having the groceries he was supposed to be getting?

Cursing under his breath, Jake turned and hurried back to his cart. He'd taken his time and was only halfway through the grocery store. He'd finish shopping, but much more quickly than he had been doing . . . and he wasn't leaving Nicole's side again between now and the finalization of the divorce. Jake was quite sure the driver of the car had been Nicole's soon to be ex-husband. The bit about turning the lights on just before revving the engine was what made him think that. Why turn on the lights first? It had acted as a warning. But it had also no doubt blinded Nicole and the only reason to blind her before revving the engine was to ensure she didn't glance over at the sound and see the driver . . . and recognize him.

With two weeks—or thirteen days and counting—Rodolfo was obviously getting desperate. Accidental explosions were one thing, but running her down in public was the act of a desperate man.

It was time to find out more about Rodolfo Rossi, he decided, and knew just who to call to put on the case. Pulling out his phone, he searched his contacts and pushed a button, then placed the phone to his ear and listened to it ring as he tossed the canned tomatoes he still held into the cart.

"Hello." The word was said on a laugh and was followed by, "Cut it out, woman. I'm on the phone here."

"Vincent?" Jake asked uncertainly.

"Yeah. Who—Stephano?" Vincent asked, suddenly serious.

"Hello, boss," Jake said quietly, not correcting him on the name.

"I'm not your boss anymore," Vincent pointed out solemnly. "You quit on me."

"You didn't need me anymore. I couldn't be your daytime V.P. and you already had a nighttime one."

"We could have worked something out, Stephano. Besides, you can work during the day, you just need to take in more blood."

"Yeah. Like that was going to happen," Jake said wryly, but frowned as he realized he hadn't fed since meeting with Marguerite yesterday. He'd intended to have a refrigerator and blood delivered to the house to keep in his room while on this case, but hadn't got to that yet . . . and he was kind of hungry.

Pushing that worry away for now, he said, "Look, I'm sorry to call out of the blue, but I need Jackie's help."

"Jackie?" Vincent asked with surprise.

"Who is it?" Jackie asked in the background. "Is it for me?"

"Hang on, babe," Vincent said, his muffled voice suggesting he'd covered the phone with his hand. Voice clear again, he asked Jake, "What's up?"

"I'm a bodyguard now," Jake said in case Vincent wasn't as well informed as Marguerite.

"Yeah?" Vincent asked with interest. "That sounds cool. How do you like it?"

"It's a lot less exciting than it sounds," Jake said wryly.

"Yeah. So is detective work," Vincent said on a disappointed sigh. "Bloody boring most of the time. A lot of sitting around, watching and waiting."

"So is being a bodyguard," Jake assured him.

"Man, what's up with that?" Vincent asked with disgust. "I watched a lot of shows to train for helping Jackie with her cases; *Castle*, *The Closer*, *Criminal Minds*, even old *Magnum P.I.* Not one of them had the hero sitting around twiddling his thumbs and— hey, cut it out, I'm on the phone here, woman." There were the muffled sounds of what might have been a short wrestling session and then Vincent said, "Sorry, Steph. So what can we do for you?"

"I'm guarding a woman in Ottawa and I need you guys to look into her soon to be ex-husband, find out what he's into," Jake explained, turning his cart into the next aisle and moving to examine the different pastas. Why did they make them in so many shapes and sizes? Was one size or shape tastier than another? He frowned over the problem.

"Right. What's his name?" Vincent asked.

"Rodolfo Rossi," Jake answered, tossing several types of pasta into the cart with his free hand. Better to be safe than sorry. He wouldn't want to buy spaghetti and have a recipe call for those little bow tie type things.

"Rodolfo Rossi," Vincent repeated. "Jackie's writing it down. How do you spell it?"

Jake rattled off the spelling as he pushed the cart up to the sauces, adding, "He's presently married to Nicole Phillips, but the divorce will be final in less than two weeks."

"Okay. We'll look into him," Vincent assured him, and then paused briefly before asking, "You okay?"

Now it was Jake's turn to pause. He considered the question seriously. He'd been pretty messed up after the turn, and definitely less than grateful to Vincent for saving his life and using his one turn to do it. He didn't think he'd ever even thanked the man for what he'd done. Sighing, he stopped walking and said solemnly, "Much better. Thank you. And thank you for what you did, Vincent. I do appreciate it and I'm sorry I was such an ungrateful prick at the time."

"Yeah, you were kind of a prick," Vincent agreed with amusement and then gave a startled, "Ow! Hey, that's husband beating!" that suggested Jackie had smacked him for the prick comment. Heaving a sigh, Vincent said, "Look, no problem. I understood it wasn't your choice and that you needed time to deal with it. I'm just glad you're doing better now."

"Thanks," Jake said smiling faintly. "I'll let you two go now. I need to get back to work anyway."

"Okay. Is this the number we can reach you at?" Vincent asked.

"Yeah," Jake said.

"Okay. Later, Stephano."

"Bye Stephano!" Jackie called.

"Bye guys," Jake said, not correcting them on the Stephano bit. It was his name after all.

"Oh," Nicole said, glancing down at her phone when it dinged to announce she had a text message. Jake was at the checkout. "I have to go."

"Nancy's done his shopping, is he?" Dan asked with obvious amusement.

"Jake," she corrected dryly, though she knew he knew the name wasn't Nancy. Dan had seemed to find the whole male cook/housekeeper thing a real hoot from the moment she'd explained about Jake.

"Jake," he said dutifully as he threw money on the table to cover their coffees and stood up to walk her out. "So what's he like, this Jake? A real mama's boy? Gay maybe? Or what?"

"Oh, I don't think he's gay," Nicole said at once, and she didn't. She hadn't really considered it before now, and couldn't claim to have the best "gaydar," as they called it, but she was pretty sure Jake wasn't gay. At least she hoped not, she'd be terribly disappointed if he was . . . and had absolutely no desire to examine why that would be. The guy was younger than her, and an employee. She had no business thinking about him in that way at all. The last thing she needed right now was to think of any man in that way. Nicole had promised herself at least a full year of counseling before she would even consider dating again. But once that date had arrived, she'd decided maybe another six months of counseling was in order. She really did not want to jump back into the dating pool too early and land herself in another abusive relationship.

"Not gay, huh? So just a mama's boy?" Dan said lightly as he walked her out of the restaurant.

Nicole just shook her head. Dan really seemed to have issues with her cook/housekeeper . . . and he didn't even know him. As they neared her car, she teased, "Is someone feeling threatened? What's wrong? Can't cook?"

"Oh, I can cook," he assured her. "I'm the best barbecuer around. Housekeeping, on the other hand . . ." He grimaced and shook his head. "I'm one of those guys who leave a trail of clothes from the front door to the shower. Drove my wife crazy . . . which, I suppose, is why she's an ex-wife now."

Nicole chuckled softly at the comment as he opened her door. She started to climb in, then paused and turned back. Holding out her hand, she said, "Thank you, Dan. For the coffee and for saving my life."

He glanced at her hand, then accepted it and shook firmly. "You're more than welcome, ma'am. All in a day's work for us superheroes."

Laughing, Nicole retrieved her hand and got into the SUV.

"I have your number," Dan said as she settled in the driver's seat. "I'll call you later in the week and see how you are. Find out if you've recovered, had any more problems, or if Jakey boy is driving you wild," he teased. "You might need an emergency coffee date to recover."

"I just might," she said on a laugh, pulling on her seatbelt. "Thanks again."

"My pleasure," Dan assured her and closed the door, gave her a little wave, and backed up.

Nicole started the engine, still smiling. She felt much better than she had right after the near miss. Her nerves were settled again, and while she was a little stiff and bruised, coffee with Dan had cheered her up. The man had flirted, but not seriously, just enough to make her feel good. He was a nice guy. He definitely had issues with men in nonconformist positions, but he was nice.

Nicole shifted into reverse, waved at Dan, then backed out of her parking spot to drive around to the grocery store to meet Jake.

"Do you recognize that car?" Jake asked, eyes narrowing on the little sports car waiting in the driveway when Nicole turned into it.

"It's Joey. My brother," Nicole added as she eased up the driveway and hit the button to open the garage door. She smiled slightly, and said, "He's . . . well, you'll either love him or hate him. There's no middle ground with Joey."

Jake raised his eyebrows at the comment. Marguerite had mentioned Joey while giving him the details about Nicole and her husband, but he'd understood that while the man had made millions in land development here in Ottawa, he'd got out of the rat race and retired down to the Southern states. Marguerite hadn't been sure if it was Florida or Hawaii. Other than that, all he knew about the man was that he was thirty-eight, Nicole's half brother from their father's first marriage. That his birth mother had died when he was young, he accepted Nicole's mom, Zaira, as his mother now, and that he adored Nicole as much as she adored him.

Jake peered at the man curiously as they drove slowly past him, and then Nicole steered into the garage and stopped the SUV. Once she'd put it in park, he opened the door and slid out.

"Yo! What's going on? I come out to see my shut-in, workaholic sister who never leaves home and she's not here."

Jake glanced to the man walking up to the garage just as Nicole closed her door and hurried to the back of the vehicle to greet her brother.

"Sorry, sorry, sorry," she laughed as she hugged him. "I had to go to the bank and then do some shopping. What are you doing here anyway? I thought you had headed for warmer climates?"

"I did. But Mom called and did the Jewish mother guilt thing so I came back," he said with exasperation.

"Mom isn't Jewish," Nicole pointed out with amusement as she pulled out of the man's arms.

"Tell *her* that," Joey said dryly and then glanced to Jake with raised eyebrows. "Replaced Rodolfo already, have we, Nicki? Nice."

"No!" Nicole flushed with embarrassment and gave Jake an apologetic look as she made the introductions. "Joey, this is my new cook/housekeeper, Jake."

"Cook/housekeeper," Joey repeated, eyebrows askance as he looked Jake over again. Despite that he moved forward, offering his hand. "Is that a euphemism or are you really a cook/housekeeper?"

"I really work for your sister," Jake assured

him solemnly, looking the other man over as well. Joey was a good-looking guy: golden hair and eyes, a nicely chiseled face, tight black jeans, a black leather jacket, expensive watch, and a confident swagger Jake suspected women swooned over. He looked a lot like his sister in the face and hair, but otherwise not so much. Nicole was short and curvaceous to his tall and lanky, and a jeans and T-shirt type gal compared to his more stylish dress. She also did not have a confident swagger. She was more like a hummingbird, rushing here and there with an anxious air.

"Well, cool then," Joey said, shaking his hand firmly and then added, "No offense, but Nicki's had a rough time of it and the last thing she needs is to be hooking up with someone right now."

"So I understand," Jake said with a nod, and then glanced to the SUV as Nicole opened the back.

"Good God, girl!" Joey exclaimed, moving to help take bags. "What did you do? Buy out all of downtown Ottawa?"

"I'm only responsible for the Canadian Tire bags," Nicole assured him. "The rest is Jake's fault. I think he thinks he's feeding a small army . . . or a big one," she added with a frown as she looked over the bags. "Geez, Jake, you did get an awful lot."

"Don't worry about the groceries, I'll get those," Jake said quickly, moving up to shoo them away from the vehicle. "Why don't you two go in and visit. I'll bring these up and make coffee for you, then start on dinner. I'm guessing you'll be staying for dinner, Joey?"

"Thank you, I think I will," Joey said, walking

Nicole to the door. As they went inside, Jake heard him say, "This cook/housekeeper thing was a good idea. Whose was it? I know you didn't come up with it by yourself."

"Marguerite," Nicole answered. "She suggested a cook/housekeeper would ease my burden quite a bit so I could concentrate on work. She even found me Jake. He's a family member of hers so I know he's trustworthy."

"Ah, yes. Clever Marguerite," Joey responded as the door closed behind them.

"Clever Marguerite," Jake agreed dryly as he began to gather grocery bags, and wondering what the hell he was going to do about supper. He'd made several attempts at dinner, the last and only successful one being the peppercorn steak sauce that was to be poured over the steaks after they were grilled, but the recipe had been for two steaks. Of course, he could feed that to them and make himself something else to eat. It wasn't like they'd welcome the housekeeper at the dinner table anyway.

Shaking his head, he turned his attention to the groceries.

"This one's almost done."

Nicole glanced up from the bags she and Joey had just carried into her studio to see that Joey had lifted the cover to peer at the portrait of the actress. Turning her attention back to searching the bags, she said distractedly, "Yeah. I'll probably finish it tonight."

"And this one?" Joey asked, peering under the cover over the stern older man.

"By the end of the week," she said, barely sparing the painting a glance before returning to her search. She was looking for the mouse sonar. She wanted to plug them all in while she was thinking of it.

"Who's this?"

Nicole glanced up again. Joey had uncovered the sketch of the couple. "Marguerite's stepson, Christian, and his fiancée, Carolyn."

"Geez, she must have married an old guy if he has a kid this old," Joey commented. "I bet this Christian hates having a stepmom so young."

"No." Nicole smiled. "He seems to really like Marguerite. He calls her Mom and she calls him her son rather than her stepson. If they weren't so close in age, I wouldn't know they were steps. It's really very sweet."

"Hmm," Joey said. "I'm not buying that they get along that well. He's probably got the hots for her and hoping to slip in there when the old man dies . . . and I wouldn't blame him. Marguerite's a hottie. How old is she anyway?"

"I don't know. Jake says she isn't forty yet and that she married Jean Claude when she was thirteen." Pausing, she glanced at the picture with a frown. "But Christian doesn't look any older than Lucern, Etienne or Bastien." She tilted her head. "I wonder if they were Jean Claude's kids and not hers."

"They have to be," Joey decided. "She just isn't old enough to have kids that age."

"No, she isn't," Nicole agreed and then shrugged. "Still, even if she was thirteen when she married Jean Claude, she's got to be thirty-five or something."

"She doesn't look a day over twenty-five," Joey said firmly.

"I know. Nice huh?" Nicole said enviously. She'd probably look forty when she was thirty-five.

"Yeah, that's what money does for you," Joey said wistfully. "Enough money and you can look young forever."

"Or you can look like a fan tester," Nicole said dryly.

"A fan tester?" Joey asked with confusion.

Nicole nodded. "You know, the whole too many face-lifts thing where they look like they're staring into a high-powered fan." She pulled the sides of her face back with her hands so that her mouth and eyes were pulled into wide slits.

Joey chuckled, but then asked, "Do you think she's had face-lifts?"

"Marguerite?" Nicole asked, letting go of her face. She shook her head and turned back to her search. "Nah. I think she just has some amazing fricking genes."

"Hmm." Joey covered the paintings again and wandered back to her. "What are you looking for?"

"I bought these sonar mouse-repellent things," she muttered, giving up on the bag in front of her and grabbing another.

"You have mice?" Joey asked with a grimace.

"No. At least I don't think so," she added. "But I'd like to keep it that way."

"Oh." He grabbed the bag nearest him and began to help look through it. "Are these them?"

Nicole had just found two of them in the bottom of the bag she was searching, but glanced up and nodded when she saw that Joey was holding up half a dozen more. "Yeah. Thanks."

As she got to her feet, he moved over to the rolling table she kept her paint brushes and other paraphernalia on and grabbed a pair of scissors to begin cutting open the packages. "So where are we plugging these in?"

Nicole smiled faintly at the "we" and leaned up to kiss his cheek as she reached his side. "You're a star, Joey. Thank you for helping me."

"Geez, sis. I'm just opening the containers and plugging them in. It's not that big a deal," he assured her.

"But I appreciate it," she said simply.

Joey snorted and shook his head. "God, how did you end up so pathetic?"

"Nice," Nicole said, smacking him in the back of the head when he set down the scissors to pull out two of the little white repellent gizmos.

Joey grinned and said, "You spent too much time around Pierina growing up. She encouraged that nice gene from Mom to bloom and grow. You should have spent more time around me. I got Dad's selfish asshole gene, I could have encouraged that in you."

The words surprised a laugh from Nicole and she ruffled his hair affectionately. "The very fact that you think you're a selfish asshole means you aren't."

"Ha! Got you fooled," he said with amusement, and then concern entered his gaze and he caught her arm.

"What?" she asked, and glanced down. She'd pushed up her sweater sleeves while searching, revealing the bottom of a large, dark bruise on her arm.

"What happened here?" he asked, pushing the sleeve further up.

Nicole blew her breath out and grimaced. "I took a bit of a spill coming out of Canadian Tire earlier tonight."

"That's more than a spill," he said quietly.

"It's just a bruise, Joey. I'm pretty sure I have several more of those. My hip and knee are both sore as heck and feel stiff, and I think I must have wrenched my neck as well. But at least I didn't break anything." Nicole shrugged and tugged her arm free. "I'll take a dip in the hot tub before bed tonight and tomorrow it will all just be a good story to tell."

"Hmm." He didn't look impressed. "Well if you don't feel better tomorrow, you should go see the doctor. Maybe he can give you something . . . for clumsiness."

"Ha, ha," Nicole said dryly. "Come on, smart boy. Let's go plug these in."

"Where are we putting them?" Joey asked, gathering the little items in his hand.

"One in every room," she answered, stopping to plug one into the socket by the door. "We'll do the kitchen last. You can distract Jake while I plug one in there. I don't want him to think I have mice. He might quit."

"We wouldn't want that," Joey said with amusement.

"No, we wouldn't," she assured him. "He makes the yummiest omelets ever . . . and his coffee's good too."

"Can't wait to try it," Joey said as he followed her out of the studio.

Seven

"So, Joey, what do you do?" Jake asked quietly as he cut into his steak. He'd bought more steak today at the grocery store and when Nicole had insisted he join her and her brother for dinner, had quickly cooked one up for himself. He used to like his medium rare, now he ate it rare, so it hadn't taken long to cook. There had already been enough salad and he'd bought those frozen hot and spicy potato wedges to have with the steak. As for the sauce, while the recipe had only been for two, there had been more than enough for three.

"I'm retired. Used to be in land development though," Joey answered lightly as he dug into his peppercorn steak.

Nicole and Joey had both assured him the peppercorn sauce on the steak was very good, which was a relief. He'd worried about it while out shopping. It had seemed to be his first possible success-ful attempt at cooking before they'd left the house, but he'd feared it might dry out or curdle while they were out. It hadn't, and when he'd warmed it up it had actually tasted better than when they'd left.

Thank God, Jake thought with an inner sigh. He'd developed a headache shortly after returning to the house . . . which was something new. He hadn't had a headache, or a sniffle, or any other ailment since being turned, and was glad he hadn't. His head was throbbing and aching so bad he could hardly think. Even his teeth were beginning to ache with it.

"Joey's being modest. He started with nothing, and built an empire," Nicole said proudly. "He had a hand in building some of the biggest malls and complexes in the Toronto area. In fact," she added with a proud grin at her brother. "He's done so well he retired last year and now travels and lives a life of leisure."

"Impressive," Jake said quietly, rubbing at his forehead. He'd already known that, but it seemed better to pretend he didn't. There was no reason Marguerite would have told him that in the normal course of events if he was just a cook/housekeeper. At least he didn't think so. He could be wrong though. This damned headache was really messing with his thinking.

"Jake's pretty impressive himself," Nicole told her brother. "He was vice president of a company called V.A. Incorporated up until a couple years ago."

Joey peered at Jake dubiously. "V.P. huh? You're pretty young for a V.P. Was it a family position?"

"I'm loosely related to the owner now via marriage. However, I wasn't at the time I worked for him," Jake said stiffly, wondering if it was his headache that made the question seem like an insult.

"So, was it a small company then?" Joey asked.

"No," Jake said simply. His head hurt too much to bother describing all of V.A.'s holdings. If the guy wanted to know about the company he could Google it.

"Are you all right, Jake?" Nicole asked suddenly, concern puckering her forehead. "You look pale."

"Actually, I don't feel well," Jake admitted, staring down at his meal with a frown. He loved steak, but his headache was bad enough that he was starting to feel nauseous. This was just bizarre. Immortals weren't supposed to get sick.

"Would you like an aspirin or ibuprofen?" Nicole asked, getting up and heading for the cupboard beside the door where she presumably kept such things.

"No, no, I'm fine," Jake said at once, frowning after her. There was no use taking the painkillers: drugs and alcohol weren't supposed to affect immortals.

"Here, in case you change your mind," Nicole said returning to set a bottle of ibuprofen on the table beside his plate.

"Thank you," Jake murmured, tempted to take the pills anyway. They weren't supposed to affect his kind, but then his kind weren't supposed to get sick either, and he was feeling pretty sick. Sighing, he glanced up and found both Nicole and Joey peering at him; Nicole with concern, Joey with curiosity. As much to distract himself as them, he asked, "So what do you do now, Joey?"

"Oh," Joey blinked and sat back with a wry smile. "This and that and nothing at all. I travel, mostly. See the sights and play."

"Is Ottawa still your home base?" Jake asked, hoping to get the man talking again.

"Toronto was his home base, not Ottawa," Nicole explained, and then added, "He has a house in Florida now, but pops around for a visit on occasion." Turning to her brother, she asked, "How long are you staying this time?"

Jake glanced to the man with interest. Nicole's question seemed to suggest Joey would be staying, which could be good. With the other man there, he'd have help keeping an eye on Nicole.

"Actually, I'm not staying with you this time, Nicki," Joey announced and popped a potato wedge in his mouth.

"What?" Nicole seemed surprised. "But where will you stay then? Not a hotel?"

"Yes. I booked a hotel . . . I thought Melly would be more comfortable there than being thrust on family for the first meeting."

"Melly?" Nicole asked, smiling faintly. "A new girlfriend? And one who's lasted more than a week and that you're actually willing to travel with?"

"She's lasted six months," Joey informed her, and then grinned and added, "And I asked her to marry me."

"What?" Nicole's eyes nearly popped out of her head. "Seriously?"

"Seriously," Joey said with a grin.

"That's marvelous!" Nicole cried, jumping up to hug her brother. "Congratulations, bro."

"Thank you," he murmured, hugging her back.

Moving back to her chair once they'd finished hugging, Nicole asked, "So who is she? How did you meet? When do I get to meet her?"

Joey chuckled and reached for his wine. He took a sip and then set down the glass and said, "I met her in Florida. Her name is Melanie, and she's a model from Toronto."

"A model?" Nicole asked, appearing impressed. "And from Toronto?"

Joey nodded. "She has an apartment in New York too, but lives here in Ontario when she's not working. But she was on vacation in Florida when I met her."

Nicole sat back with a laugh. "That is so you."

"What?" her brother asked, smiling uncertainly.

"You move all the way to Florida to meet a gal from your hometown," she pointed out.

He smiled wryly and nodded. "Yeah. What are the odds, huh?"

"With you? Pretty good. Things like that always happen to you," Nicole said with a smile, and then repeated, "So when do I get to meet her?"

"How about tomorrow? A late lunch?" he suggested. "Or breakfast for you, I suppose. But late lunch for Melly and I."

Nicole hesitated the briefest moment and Jake suspected she was thinking of all the work she had to do, but then she nodded and breathed out with resignation. "Of course."

"Well then, I should let you get back to work now," Joey said, apparently having understood the hesitation as well.

When the other man pushed back his chair and stood up, Jake glanced to his plate, surprised to see that Joey had finished his meal. So had Nicole, he noted, glancing to her plate next. Apparently, he was the only one with most of his food still on his plate.

"Yeah, I guess so," Nicole agreed apologetically, getting up as well. "I'll see you out." Turning to Jake then, she said, "I'll be back in a minute."

Jake nodded and remained seated as they left the room, but then stood up and began gathering plates. He put the empty plates in the dishwasher, but covered his and put it in the refrigerator. If his headache cleared up, he would finish it later, he thought as he quickly finished clearing the table.

When Nicole hadn't returned by the time he finished, Jake moved into the living room and up to the railing overlooking the lower living room to listen, relaxing when he heard the murmur of voices from below. When silence fell and he heard the door close and the click as it was locked, he continued on to his room. His head was killing him and since immortals weren't supposed to get sick, it had to be a tension headache. Perhaps lying down would help. He hoped it would. Jake didn't know if seven years of pain-free living had made him less tolerant to pain or what, but this headache was killing him.

Jake didn't bother turning the lights on in his room; he didn't really need them anyway. The moonlight coming through the window was enough for him to be able to navigate his way to the bed. He lay down on top of the blankets and tried to relax, but the pounding in his head made that impossible. He closed his eyes, opened his eyes, turned on one side and then the other before returning to his back, and finally gave up. Lying there he had nothing to think about but how much his head hurt. It just seemed to make it worse.

Getting up, he headed back to the kitchen. It was empty. Nicole had no doubt gone back to work. Perhaps cooking would distract him from the pain. Jake opened the refrigerator and considered the contents. He could get a start on the next day's dinner. Or maybe he should be cooking Nicole another meal for today. Technically, what he had served as dinner had really only been Nicole's second meal of the day. It might have been her lunch. It was his lunch. He normally didn't have dinner until much later in the day, himself, and he kept hours similar to hers.

Frowning, Jake closed the refrigerator and headed downstairs to ask her if she wanted another meal later and what time that would be.

As usual, the blinds were up on the French doors to the studio and Jake could see her hard at work. She wasn't wearing her headphones yet, so he tapped lightly at the door. Nicole glanced around with surprise and then smiled and waved him in.

"How are you feeling?" she asked with concern as she set her paintbrush down. Frowning, she added, "You're really pale, Jake. Are you coming down with something?"

"No. I never get sick. It's just a headache," he assured her, and then quickly changed the subject. "You've only eaten twice today, and I wondered if you wanted another meal tonight?"

Nicole tilted her head briefly, considering the question, and then said, "Maybe a sandwich or salad or something. I can grab it myself though. You aren't feeling well."

"It's okay, I can make it," he assured her. "This is just a tension headache. It will go away eventually."

"If it's a tension headache, why don't you try a dip in the hot tub?" she suggested. "It might help."

Jake blinked at the suggestion. He was surprised he hadn't thought of it himself and he was willing to try anything to rid himself of the damned pulsing in his head. "Yeah, I think I will," he said finally. "Is there anything you want before I do?"

"No. I'm good," Nicole assured him.

Jake nodded and headed for the door, saying, "I'll let you get back to work then."

"Okay. Feel better."

Jake closed the door and headed back upstairs. He was in his room before he realized he didn't know what time Nicole wanted to eat. He'd ask after his dip in the hot tub, Jake decided, pausing in front of the dresser and then frowning as he realized he hadn't brought his swimsuit.

Shrugging, he stripped out of his clothes and pulled on his bathrobe, then went to grab a large towel out of the bathroom. The hot tub was outside the sliding glass doors of Nicole's studio, but he'd noticed while in her studio that while she left the blinds open on the windows along the back of her studio, the blinds for the door were closed. The sun rose on that side, and no doubt shone right in through the sliding glass doors in the morning. He supposed she kept them closed to avoid it heating up the room and glaring on her work. Whatever the case, with the blinds closed it should be okay if he went without a swimsuit.

Nicole was bebopping between paintings, headphones on and tunes cranked. The first song she'd put on was her present favorite, Pink's latest, but it was near the end of the playlist. There were only three songs following it, so it seemed like she'd barely put it on when the playlist ended and silence filled her ears. Silence always seemed worse to Nicole when she had earphones on, it seemed to crowd into her head, blocking out everything else.

Grimacing, she shifted her headphones off her ears and crossed to the computer to start the playlist from the beginning. She'd just grabbed the mouse when muffled sounds from outside made her hesitate.

Leaving her headphones around her neck, Nicole turned her head so that one ear was to the window and listened. She'd opened the window a crack when she'd come in earlier. Unless it was an especially cold or windy night, she always had a window open. Nicole didn't mind the smell of paint, it was her stock and trade after all, but it could get a bit strong if she didn't open a window to let fresh air in to dilute it.

Frowning as she recognized the sounds as those of someone being sick, she took her headphones off altogether and walked over to the sliding glass doors. The blinds were closed and she didn't open them right away, but tugged one of the slides aside to look out. In the next moment, she shoved them aside to unlock the door, tugged it open and rushed out.

"Jake?" she hurried to the hot tub, hardly aware of the cold snow under her bare feet as she rushed to aid the man. Jake was half upright and hunched over the far side of the hot tub, vomiting into the snow. If that was not enough to concern her, when she reached that side of the tub the white snow was splashed red in the overhead light. The man was vomiting blood . . . and a lot of it.

"Oh God," Nicole gasped in dismay, and froze, gaping at it briefly. But when Jake sagged against the side of the hot tub and began to slide back into it, she snapped out of her shock. Careful to avoid the bloodstained snow, she moved up to the side of the hot tub and tried to grab his arm to help him keep his head above water, but he waved her away.

"I'm okay," Jake muttered.

"No, you're not," Nicole said grimly. Since he wouldn't let her help that way, she turned and looked around for his robe or a towel. Spotting his robe hanging from the hook on the light post, she stepped away to grab it. By the time she turned back, Jake was stepping onto the hot tub seat in that corner and heaving himself out of the water to sit on the edge of the hot tub.

This made Nicole pause and gape again. The man was completely nude. Completely. Like, not a stitch on. A moan from Jake managed to distract her from this realization, at least enough that she gave first her head, then his robe a shake and wrapped it around his bare shoulders, making sure that the robe hung down along his hip and didn't fall into the water. In the next moment, she was jumping back to avoid getting splashed as he suddenly hunched forward and began vomiting again.

The deep red blood on the snow in the stark light was rather shocking. For a moment, Nicole merely watched helplessly, but when Jake slid off the hot tub and dropped to his knees in the snow as he retched, she moved to his side again, trying to offer support if only with her presence. It was all she could do until he stopped retching. Then she dropped to her haunches beside him and pulled one robe-covered arm over her shoulder.

"Come on, let's get you inside," she said quietly, pushing hard with her legs to get them both upright. Despite his getting himself out of the tub, Nicole had expected him to have to lean on her, but not to the extent he did, and they both staggered to the side once he was on his feet. Nicole reached for the lamp pole to catch herself and him both, letting out a small relieved breath when it prevented their toppling over.

She took a moment to shift her stance to counterbalance his weight on her and then started forward. Fortunately, while he was leaning on her heavily, Jake was still able to walk, slowly and in a stumbling manner, but they were moving.

Nicole steered him toward the sliding doors into the lower living room. It was obviously the way he'd come and it was a couple steps closer. It also didn't have a bunch of easels in the way, which they were likely to bump into, send crashing to the ground, and then stumble over. By some miracle they made it inside and to the couch before Jake collapsed.

"It's all right. You're going to be all right," Nicole

said anxiously as she covered him with a throw. "I'll call an ambulance. We'll get you to a hospital—"

She broke off with amazement when Jake suddenly surged up, grabbing her arm. "No! No ambulance. No hospital. I'm fine."

"You're not fine," she said, trying to break his hold on her. His grip was desperately hard and she knew bruises were probably popping up under her shirtsleeve. "You're throwing up blood. You need to go to the hospital."

"The hospital won't know what to do," he said wearily, falling back on the couch, but still grasping her arm.

"Well, they'll have a better idea than I do," Nicole said. He was pale and sweating, but the blood in the snow outside was what worried her most. That was a very bad sign.

He shook his head. "No hospital."

"Jake, I need to get you help. You're sick. I—"

"Call Marguerite," he interrupted.

"Marguerite?" Nicole stared at him with amazement. "What can she—?"

"She'll know what to do. Call Marguerite," Jake insisted, his eyes closing.

"Okay," she said slowly, thinking she'd call Marguerite as he asked and *then* call an ambulance. Much to her relief he started to release her, but then tightened his hold again and opened his eyes.

"Promise me," he insisted. "You'll call Marguerite and not an ambulance."

Nicole stared at him silently. His eyes appeared to be glowing, the silvery teal they'd been before now almost completely silver, and the whites around it bloodshot and sparkling with silver as if someone had dropped glitter in his eyes. It had to be a trick of the light, of course.

"Promise," Jake insisted, his fingers tightening painfully on her arm.

"I promise," she said at once.

Jake stared into her eyes for a moment and then gave the slightest nod and released her to drop back on the couch, murmuring, "Marguerite will know what to do."

Nicole frowned slightly, but turned away and moved to grab the phone off the end table, only to set it back as she realized she didn't know Marguerite's number. It was in her cell phone contact list though, she recalled and moved quickly around the couch and end table to the door to the hall leading to the office and studio. "I'll be right back, I have to get my cell phone."

Jake closed his eyes and tried to concentrate on breathing. He knew Nicole was in a panic, but so was he. He didn't understand what was happening. He'd gone out to the hot tub in the hopes of ridding himself of the headache, and it had seemed to work. The pain had begun to ease almost before he'd got into the hot tub, the cold air seeming to ease his tension and clear his thinking. The pain had been completely gone within moments of stepping into the hot tub, only to be replaced by nausea instead. That had caught him completely by surprise. He hadn't felt nausea in seven years. It was a most unpleasant sensation . . . and it had built so quickly. Within moments of getting in the hot tub, Jake had been leaning over the side, retching and throwing up blood, his body weak and shaking. Honestly, if Nicole hadn't come out, he wasn't sure he would have been able to get out of the hot tub on his own.

Jake didn't understand what was happening. He was an immortal. This wasn't supposed to happen. He wasn't supposed to be able to get sick, yet he seemed to have the immortal version of the fricking flu. Vampire flu. Great. And a serious case of it. He was hot, feverish, weak, and throwing up blood . . . and his head was pounding like crazy again.

He was also crazy thirsty . . . and not for water. Jake supposed it was all the blood he'd thrown up, on top of already being low. He really should have taken care of the blood and fridge thing right away. That had been driven home when Nicole had helped him inside and bent over him on the couch. It wasn't her sweet, spicy perfume he'd smelled, but her blood, and he'd been hard-pressed not to bite into her neck. Truthfully, if he'd had more strength and hadn't felt so nauseous, Jake might not have been able to keep from chomping into the woman's throat and sucking her dry, life mate or no life mate.

Another wave of nausea rolled over him and Jake reared up desperately from the couch. He knew he wouldn't make it to the bathroom only ten feet away, but he had to try. He managed to get half upright before collapsing to his hands and knees on the floor. His back bowed as his stomach heaved and he stared at the cream-colored carpet with horror, and then a large red and black bowl was suddenly on the floor under his face. He caught a glimpse of Nicole's hand before she released the bowl, and glanced to her as she straightened and moved away.

She was punching buttons on her cell phone he saw. Jake didn't bother to try to listen, but turned his attention back to the bowl, recognizing it as the one that sat on the coffee table. It had held large frosted glass balls when he'd seen it earlier. They were gone now, which was a good thing, he decided, as blood poured out of his mouth and splashed into the bowl.

Halfway through this bout of heaving, Jake heard Nicole talking in quick anxious tones. He tried to stop and listen, but it was impossible. The blood was coming out whether he liked it or not. He had just given up the effort when he heard her say Marguerite's name. Jake felt a moment's relief knowing the woman would know what to say to keep Nicole from calling an ambulance. She would also know what to do in this situation . . . he hoped, and then gave up worrying about it as he began to heave again.

Eight

Nicole paced around the couch one more time and leaned to check the cold cloth she'd placed on Jake's forehead. Once she felt that it was still cool to the touch, she quickly backed away and paced around the couch again, eyeing her patient from a relatively safe distance. Marguerite was the one who had suggested that. She hadn't explained why she should keep her distance. Nicole was guessing the woman was worried that Jake was contagious. But if he had something contagious, then why were they both insisting she not take him to the hospital?

Nicole fretted over that for about the hundredth time since calling Marguerite, which was—half an hour ago, she saw, glancing at her wristwatch as she paced around the couch again. Marguerite had said help was on the way. Nicole presumed that meant a doctor or something, but how long was this help going to take? For cripes sake, Jake seemed to be dying on her here. He'd finally stopped throwing up blood about ten minutes ago, but not before tossing up a hell of a lot of it. She'd emptied the bowl four times, and that wasn't counting what he'd lost outside. It was a big bowl. How much blood did a body hold? And how much did he have left inside him?

Her worried gaze slid over Jake again. He'd lain moaning and writhing after his last bout with the bowl. It had looked like he was in agony. She'd thought that was scary . . . until he'd stopped moving and gone silent about five minutes ago. This was scarier. If his chest weren't moving up and down—

Nicole stopped pacing and peered at Jake worriedly. His chest didn't seem to be moving anymore. He'd been breathless when he'd first gone still, as if his thrashing and writhing had worn him out. While he'd lain still, his chest had been heaving with his effort to catch his breath. Now it didn't seem to be moving at all. She took an instinctive step toward him and then paused, Marguerite's words running through her mind.

No matter what happens, keep your distance. He will not die. He will be fine, but you need to stay away from him. You are the one who could be in danger, Nicole. Don't get too close, and if he becomes active again and gets up and comes at you, you have to lock yourself in the bathroom or even leave the house. He could be a danger to you right now.

"Jake?" she said, shifting where she stood. "Jake, wake up."

He didn't react at all.

Biting her lip, Nicole took a step toward him and said a little more loudly, "Jake! Wake up!

There was still no reaction and she took another step closer, and then stepped back again, Marguerite's words making her afraid. But she couldn't just stand there. Marguerite had assured her he would be all right, but what if she was wrong? What if he needed CPR? She couldn't stand it, she had to see if he was breathing, but she tried to be careful about it. The couch was three feet from the wall, leaving a walkway to the sliding glass doors. Nicole walked around into that space and leaned over the back of the couch so that it was a bit of a barrier as she gave his shoulder a shake.

"Jake, are you—"

He grabbed her so swiftly Nicole nearly bit her tongue with surprise. One moment Jake was as still as the dead and the next he'd snatched her arm and was trying to draw her wrist toward his mouth. She didn't understand what was happening at first. She had no idea why he'd grabbed her, and then she saw his mouth opening and realized he was going to bite her.

Nicole immediately began to jerk her arm back. Weak as Jake was, she nearly broke free, and would have had she not glanced back to his mouth and spotted the fangs sliding down into view.

Fangs. Literally. Like a dog . . . or a vampire. Nicole didn't just freeze like a deer in headlights, she went momentarily weak. Jake gave a sharp tug at the same moment and she went over the side of the couch. The action snapped her out of her shock and she was struggling again even before she landed on top of his blanket-covered form.

Screaming now, Nicole thrashed and kicked with her legs, pushed with her free arm and pulled on the one he was trying to get to his mouth, trying to break loose. She threw herself back and to the side, rolling off of him and onto the floor, hoping to break his hold on her, but he just followed, crashing down on top of her on the floor, her arm still gripped firmly in his hold. Now she was in a really bad situation. His weight was pinning her and preventing her from offering any real resistance. Nicole couldn't retreat, all she could do was try to hold him off, pushing at his chest with her free hand and tugging at the arm he held, all the while screaming at the top of her lungs.

Nicole was so caught up in the struggle that she didn't at first realize that Jake was being pulled away from her and that other voices had joined hers in shouting. But while she was just screaming in terror, these were calmer voices, barking Jake's name as if they thought they could get through the madness presently clouding his mind and snap him back to his senses. Jake was fully off of her now, but he was still holding her and she was being pulled upward, but then someone reached around and pulled his fingers and thumb apart, freeing her, and Nicole fell back. She immediately scrambled backward several feet on her butt on the carpet, stopping when she bumped into something. Tipping her head back, she peered up at the woman behind her.

"Who—?"

"It's all right, Nicole. My name is Nina and we're here to help." The words poured over her as warm and soothing as heated honey down a sore throat and Nicole felt herself immediately relax.

"Oh," she murmured and then was suddenly caught under the arms by the woman and lifted to her feet.

"Why don't we go make some tea?" Nina suggested, slipping an arm around her waist to steer her across the room.

"Oh, but Jake . . ." Nicole's voice trailed off as she glanced around to see two men now kneeling on either side of Jake, holding him down on the cream carpet while a third man set up an IV of blood beside him.

"He'll be fine," Nina assured her, ushering her toward the stairs. "I'm more concerned with you. Is any of this blood yours?"

Nicole glanced down at herself and frowned as she noted the blood smeared on her shirt, but shook her head. She must have got it on herself when she'd fallen on Jake. "No. I don't think so."

"Then he didn't hurt you?" Nina asked.

"No. I don't think so," Nicole repeated and then stopped on the stairs. "He was trying to bite me . . . and he had fangs. At least I think he did. I'm sure I saw fangs," she muttered vaguely as Nina urged her to move again. It was the oddest thing, her upset and even her recollections were becoming a bit fuzzy.

"Everything is going to be fine," Nina said quietly. "Marguerite is on the way and she's bringing Danielle with her. Do you know Danielle?"

"Danielle?" Nicole frowned. The name sounded vaguely familiar. She was sure she'd heard it mentioned before, but couldn't recall in what context.

"She's married to Marguerite's nephew Decker. I think she goes by Dani, and she's a doctor. Marguerite's bringing the two of them, her husband and some others. They'll be here in forty-five minutes or so. Everything is going to be fine."

Nicole nodded and allowed herself to be led to the kitchen, her worry fading. Once in the room, she automatically put water on to boil, and then turned to the coffeepot.

"Can you tell me what happened before Jake started to get sick?" Nina asked as Nicole took the old filter out of the coffeepot and replaced it with a new one.

Nicole frowned at the question as she began to scoop coffee into the pot, but answered, "He seemed quiet and a bit pale at dinner, and then he complained of a headache," she said slowly. "I suggested he take a dip in the hot tub to get rid of the headache, and he did, but then he started to vomit up blood."

"And how are you feeling?" Nina asked.

"Me?" she asked with surprise. "I'm fine."

Nina nodded. "Did he eat something different than you?"

Nicole shook her head. "No. We had the same thing for dinner, although he didn't eat all of his. It's probably in the fridge."

Nina immediately moved to the refrigerator. A moment later she had Jake's half-eaten plate in hand. Removing the cellophane covering it, she lifted it close to her face and inhaled slowly. Nicole had no idea what she was sniffing for, but apparently she didn't find it. Nina was frowning as she returned the cover to the plate and set it on the counter.

Her gaze slid to Nicole then, and seeing that she'd

stopped working on the coffee, the other woman joined her at the pot and took the coffee carafe. Carrying it to the sink, she turned on the tap and began to fill the carafe as she asked, "So he didn't eat anything different than you before dinner?"

Nicole shook her head and turned back to the coffee pot to continue scooping coffee grounds into the filter. "I don't think so. We had omelets with Marguerite for breakfast."

"Did he drink anything different at dinner?"

"No. We all had water and then Joey and I had wine but he didn't," Nicole recollected, dropping the scoop into the coffee can and closing it.

"So you and your brother had something he didn't, but Jake didn't have anything you didn't," Nina murmured as she turned off the water.

"How did you know Joey was my brother?" Nicole asked, eyebrows drawing together.

"You mentioned it," Nina answered calmly as she carried the carafe of water back to her.

"No, I don't think I did," Nicole countered with a frown.

"Yes, you did," Nina assured her and Nicole nodded. Yes, she had.

"I'm going to just go down and check on the boys while you pour the water in, set the carafe on the base, and turn on the coffeepot. I'd like you to sit at the table and wait for me after that. All right?"

Nicole nodded. She would pour the water in the machine, set the carafe on the base, and sit at the table and wait.

"Nicki?"

Nicole glanced around with surprise at the sound of her name. She felt like she was waking from a dream, but she knew she hadn't been sleeping. She'd simply been sitting at the table waiting . . . for a very long time. She wasn't sure what she'd been waiting for though.

"Marguerite," Nicole said uncertainly as she spotted the woman crossing the kitchen toward her, and then she frowned. "How did you get here so fast?"

"It wasn't that fast, dear," Marguerite said grimly, moving toward her. "It's been two and a half hours since you called, but it took some time to arrange for one of the company planes to bring us here."

"Us?" Nicole peered past Marguerite to the people following her. A woman and four men, none of them the people who had dragged Jake off of her.

"You remember my husband, Julius," Marguerite said, pausing beside her seat and turning back to gesture toward the tall, swarthy man she'd married.

Nicole nodded and smiled uncertainly at the man with short raven-black hair.

"And these are my nephews from his side of the family, Tomasso and Dante," she introduced, waving to two men who were carbon copies of each other. The pair were pretty imposing. It may have been because she was sitting, but Nicole didn't think so. Really, they were two of the biggest men she'd ever seen. Both were tall and muscular, with long black hair, and both of them were dressed in black leather from head to toe. Nicole stared at them wide-eyed, but then forced a smile and nod of greeting.

"And our nephew from my side, Decker, and his wife, Dani."

Nicole drew her gaze from the two mountains to the smaller, but still large, man named Decker, and the pretty woman who stood with him. She offered them both a smile of greeting and then her mother's training made her stand and move toward the coffeepot. "You're probably all thirsty after your flight. I'll make fresh coffee."

"I'll do that, dear," Marguerite murmured, reaching past her for the coffee carafe before she could pick it up. "Why don't you sit down? Dani has some questions for you."

"Er . . . Marguerite," Dani murmured as Marguerite carried the coffeepot to the sink. "I actually could do with a coffee, and no offense, but I've tasted yours," she added apologetically. "Why don't I make the coffee?"

Far from being offended, Marguerite chuckled at the words and handed over the carafe. "Thank you, dear. I know I make lousy coffee and I could do with one myself."

"You'll both be wired for hours," Julius warned.

"Bouncing off the walls," Decker agreed, and then said, "Make a full pot, honey. I think I'll have one too."

"And me," the twins said in stereo.

"Can I get you something else?" Nicole asked Julius when he just shook his head with amusement and settled at the table. "Tea, perhaps? Or soda?"

He considered the offer and then asked, "You do not happen to have mint tea, do you?"

"I do," Nicole said and moved to turn on the teakettle. She collected cream from the refrigerator, pausing to consider the contents. Somewhere under her calm demeanor, she knew there was a part of her that was almost frantic with worry, but Nicole couldn't seem to connect to it. Instead, she felt calm but kind of empty and at a loss. In that state, old training kicked in and she asked, "Is anyone hungry?"

Several minutes later the coffee was ready, tea had been made and the table was laden with everything from coffee cake to sandwich fixings. As everyone settled at the table and began to doctor their drinks or serve themselves food, Marguerite said, "Nicole . . . Nina assured me Jake didn't bite you. Is that true?"

"Yes," Nicole answered at once, startled by the question.

"Yes, he bit you?" Marguerite asked with concern.

"No, I mean yes, it's true that he didn't bite me," she explained.

"Good, good," Marguerite smiled and patted her hand before commenting, "Nina said you were wrestling with Jake when they arrived."

Nicole nodded. "I know you said not to get near him, but I wasn't sure he was breathing, and I just wanted to check—"

"Of course, I understand," Marguerite interrupted, patting her hand again before she was distracted by Julius setting a slice of coffee cake before her.

"How is he?" Nicole asked as concern suddenly rushed upward inside of her on an unexpected wave. It was as if a curtain had been tugged aside, allowing her to connect with her emotions again. "He's really sick, Marguerite. He really needs to go to the hospital."

Marguerite immediately turned her attention back to her and the worry inside of Nicole quickly receded.

"Yes, he is sick," Marguerite agreed, her tone, or perhaps her words having an immediate soothing effect on Nicole. "But it is not as bad as it may seem. He will recover. We simply have to sort out what the problem is . . . and a hospital can't help with that."

"Are you sure?" Nicole asked with a frown.

"Quite sure," Marguerite said firmly. "We will help him. In fact, Nina and the boys have already made a good start. They moved him to his room after Nina brought you up here and have been giving him blood. Apparently, he's still vomiting it up as fast as they can give it to him, though, so we need to figure out what's causing it."

"Of course," Nicole agreed and then frowned as she recalled the fangs that had slid down from his upper jaw. Troubled, she leaned forward to whisper for only Marguerite to hear, "He had fangs."

"I know, dear. It's fine," Marguerite assured her and Nicole immediately relaxed. It was fine.

"Tell me what happened," Marguerite suggested quietly. "Nina said he complained of a headache?"

"Yes."

"We don't get headaches," Dani said with certainty, a forkful of coffee cake coming to a halt halfway to her lips.

Nicole glanced to the doctor with confusion. Everyone got headaches, some more than others, but everyone could get them.

"Actually, Dani, yes we can," Marguerite countered quietly and the doctor looked almost shocked at the admission, and then understanding crossed her face.

"When we're dehydrated and need blo—"

"Yes, then," Marguerite agreed, cutting Dani off with a glance toward Nicole. "But there are more reasons for headaches than just physical ailments or such."

"It is rare, but can happen," Julius agreed. "Emotional stress, frustration, annoying sounds, certain strong smells . . . all of this can cause them."

Marguerite smiled at her husband and then paused to take a bite of cake. It was Dani who then asked Nicole, "So, it started with a headache?"

Nicole nodded.

"And then he got in the hot tub and started vomiting blood?" she asked. When Nicole nodded again, she considered this news with a frown and then heaved a sigh and said unhappily, "Marguerite, I know you're counting on me to help Jake, but I'm not sure I can. This isn't like treating a mortal and—" Pausing, she shifted and then said with frustration, "And I thought immortals couldn't get sick. Have you ever seen anything like this?"

Marguerite frowned and shook her head. "No. I've never heard of an immortal vomiting up blood."

"I have," Julius said quietly, and when everyone

turned to him curiously, he explained, "During the Renaissance one of my sisters received a dress as a gift from a mortal whom she thought was a friend. It was coated inside with a type of poison that can be absorbed through the skin. Had she been mortal, my sister would have died. Instead, she began vomiting up blood."

"That makes sense," Dani said slowly. "The nanos must try to surround or somehow bond with the poison and then purge it from the system. Blood is their vehicle, so the more poison absorbed, the more blood is purged."

"And nanos with it," Decker said.

Nicole found the whole conversation confusing. Nanos? A poison dress? The Renaissance? That word stuck in her foggy mind and she turned to Marguerite and asked in a whisper, "Did Julius say during the Renaissance?"

Marguerite smiled reassuringly and patted her hand. "Yes, dear. I'll explain in a bit, I promise. But for now, everything is fine."

"Right. Everything is fine," Nicole murmured, relaxing.

"Did your sister suffer a headache first too?" Dani asked.

"No." Julius shook his head. "But I believe I'm developing one."

"So am I," Tomasso announced.

"And me," Dante acknowledged.

"Me too," Dani said, and glanced to her husband, who nodded solemnly.

"Just the beginnings of one," Marguerite said when the group then turned her way in question.

Realizing their attention had turned to her,

Nicole shook her head quickly. She was finding a lot of this confusing, but every time she started to feel panic growing in her at something that was said, Marguerite would murmur, "Everything's fine," and her panic would recede. That being the case, the best thing to do seemed to be to simply sit and wait for the explanations Marguerite promised her. She was sure everything would be fine until then.

"And there's a buzzing in my ear," Julius said suddenly. "Very faint, but there, like an annoying insect, constantly buzz buzz buzzing."

Nicole peered at the man curiously. He sounded extremely annoyed about the buzzing.

"I don't hear anything," the twins said together.

"I do . . . now that you mention it," Decker announced, head tilted and frowning. "I didn't notice it until now, but it is rather annoying, isn't it?"

Marguerite stood and moved around the kitchen slowly, her head tilted as if listening for something. "Yes. I hear it now. It—"

Nicole watched curiously when the woman paused suddenly and moved toward the wall socket beside the water cooler. Her eyebrows rose though when Marguerite bent and unplugged the little white unit Nicole had plugged in there earlier that night.

"It's gone," Julius announced.

Decker nodded. "That was it."

"That can't be it," Nicole protested with a frown. "It's an ultrasonic rodent repellent. It's for mice. They're the only ones who can hear it."

"Mice and other rodents . . . like bats," Dani said dryly.

"Dani, love, I've told you, we are in no way connected to bats. That's all just myth," Decker said in pained tones.

"Yes," Dani agreed. "But apparently when it comes to sounds you're on the same wavelength."

"*We* are on the same wavelength, dear," Marguerite corrected, moving back to the table again and tossing the repellent on its surface as she reclaimed her seat next to Nicole. "You're one of us too now."

"Sort of," Dani said quietly. "Besides, I couldn't hear it."

"Yes, you could. You were getting a headache," Julius pointed out. "But you're young like the twins, so while it was affecting you, you couldn't register the sound."

"Hmm." Dani grimaced, but didn't argue the point and simply said, "Well the headache is easing now."

"Yes," Marguerite murmured. "Mine's receding quickly too."

Everyone but Nicole nodded or murmured in agreement.

"Then that's probably what caused the headache," Dani concluded.

Everyone nodded again but Nicole. She just thought they were all a bit crazy . . . but everything was all right. The words drifted through her head and she relaxed.

"What did you do about your sister's poisoning?" Dani asked Julius.

"We didn't realize it was poisoning until afterward, and we only realized it then because she had a natural aversion to the dress after that. She gave it to one of her servants . . . who was mortal. The poor girl died in terrible agony and distress," Julius said quietly, and then sighed and added, "Before that we had no idea what was wrong with Adriana. We just kept giving her blood until it passed."

"Right. Then I guess that's what we'll do here," Dani said solemnly. "Nina brought a cooler of it, and we brought two. Hopefully that will be enough." She glanced to Julius. "I don't suppose you remember how much blood your sister went through?"

Julius shook his head apologetically. "We did not have blood banks back then. It was donors, and we needed a lot of them. We had to take her from village to village in a wagon until it ended and she began to recover."

"I'll call Bastien and tell him to have more delivered here," Decker said, standing and withdrawing a phone from his pocket as he moved out of the room.

"Nicole," Dani said, drawing her gaze. "How are you feeling? Did you eat the same things Jake did? Or did he—?"

"She isn't poisoned," Julius interrupted. "Something that affects Jake like this would have killed her in a heartbeat. Besides, this isn't from ingested poison. That usually doesn't cause vomiting in an immortal, and if it does, it would just be a one-round deal. But not anything like this. This is full-body exposure, the poison has to be all through Jake's system for the nanos to react like this."

"The robe he's wearing?" Decker suggested.

"It started in the hot tub," Marguerite reminded them quietly.

"True, but he probably wore the robe to go down and get in the tub," Decker pointed out.

"But Nicole wouldn't wear Jake's robe and no one wants him dead," Marguerite countered.

"What?" Nicole asked with surprise.

"Everything's fine, dear," Marguerite murmured, and then glanced to Dani to ask, "Do you think the hot tub being poisoned with a drug that can be absorbed through the skin would have the same affect as a poisoned dress?"

"Yes, I imagine it would," Dani said slowly, her expression thoughtful. She was silent for a minute and then said, "I'll have to take a sample and have it analyzed to be sure, but I don't suggest anyone even stick a finger in the hot tub until we find out."

"So? What's the verdict?"

Nicole glanced to the door at that question to find the woman who had introduced herself as Nina standing there, a grim expression on her face.

"What happened to him?" Nina added. "And can it happen to us? Because all four of us have headaches right now."

Dani glanced to Nicole. "You put the mouse repellents in every room?"

Nicole nodded. "Not in Jake's room, though. I didn't want to intrude. But I put it in the plug socket directly across from his door in the hall, so if the door is open . . ."

"We had it closed until you arrived, but you left it open after you stopped to talk to us on your arrival and none of us bothered to close it," Nina said. "But what's this about mouse repellents? Why would it cause headaches in us?"

"Our hearing is apparently sensitive enough to

pick up the sound they emit and it's causing headaches," Marguerite explained.

Nina nodded. "What do the little buggers look like? I'll take out every one of them. I haven't ever had headaches before this and I'm not enjoying this one."

"Dante, Tomasso," Julius said, turning to the twins. "Go around the house and remove all the ultrasonic mouse repellents."

Nodding, the two men moved out of the room.

"So that's the headache," Nina said. "But what's causing Jake's vomiting?"

"We think it's poisoning," Dani answered.

"Poisoning?" Nina asked with surprise and then narrowed her eyes. "In food?"

"Right now the hot tub is the most likely culprit, but we don't know for sure, so just be careful of what you touch or consume."

"I don't consume anything but blood anymore," Nina assured her. "I'll warn the others, though. I don't think Mark and Gill eat food anymore either, but Tybo does."

Dani nodded. "Is Jake still throwing up?"

"No. He's stopped finally, but he's in a lot of pain. With him throwing up, we had to give him the blood intravenously. It was the only way to ensure he didn't just toss it back up right away. But the intravenous is slow and he was losing blood faster than he was getting it. He's suffering. The nanos are definitely attacking his organs in search of blood."

"Well let's try giving it to him orally now. It might stay down," Dani suggested, ushering her out of the kitchen.

Nicole watched them leave and then leaned to Marguerite and asked, "How did they get in?" When Marguerite turned to her in question, she explained, "The front door was locked and I didn't let them in."

"Ah." She nodded solemnly. "Yes, I asked the same thing when Nina came down to unlock the front door and let us in. Apparently, the door was locked when they got here too, but they could hear you screaming and hurried around the house checking doors and windows. I guess the sliding doors to the living room were unlocked and they came in that way."

"Oh, yes," Nicole murmured. The sliding doors to her studio and the living room made an inverted L around the hot tub. Jake must have used the living-room sliding doors to get to the hot tub, because they had been unlocked when she'd helped him inside . . . and she hadn't locked them behind them. Heck, she'd been so upset at the time, she wasn't even sure she'd closed them. But she knew she'd left her studio door unlocked too and said so now. "I'm pretty sure the sliding doors to my studio are unlocked too. They might even be open."

Decker had just started back into the room, done with his call. But hearing this, he turned around at once, saying, "I'll take care of it."

Nicole turned to Marguerite then, a lot of questions bubbling in her mind. Before she could ask even one, Marguerite smiled at her apologetically and said, "I'm sorry, dear. I know you have a lot of questions, but the answers aren't really mine to give. Jake will have to answer them when he's recovered. I think the best thing for you to do is to go back to work while we do what we can to help Jake. So, I want you to relax, empty your mind of all worries, and simply go to your studio and work."

Nine

Jake opened his eyes to find sunlight creeping around the edges of his blinds. He stared at the light and shadow it caused in the room, and then pushed his blankets aside and sat up, surprised to find he was buck naked. He normally slept naked at home, but he'd brought pajama bottoms to wear here. It was always good to be prepared and if an emergency struck in the middle of the night . . . Well, having the family jewels hanging out was never good at times like that.

Standing up, he opened the top drawer of the dresser and pulled out a T-shirt and a pair of loose, cotton pajama bottoms in a black, white, and gray plaid. He'd dress properly after he made coffee . . . and brushed his teeth. God, his mouth tasted like a sewer. What was up with that?

And what time was it? He glanced around to the alarm clock, frowning when he saw that it was two in the afternoon. What—?

Jake stilled as memory washed over him like a ten-gallon barrel of water. It left him just as stunned as a sudden dunking would have done. In the next moment, he was hopping around, pulling his pajama bottoms onto first one leg and then the other. Once he had them on, Jake headed out the door, tugging his T-shirt on as he went.

Nicole's bedroom door was open, he saw as he passed. The bed was made, which meant she was up. He checked the kitchen for her first, and came to an abrupt halt when he spotted the stranger seated at the table, an iPad on the table before her. The woman had fair hair like Nicole, but did not have her generous curves. She was dressed casually in faded jeans and a cobalt sweater, and she was an immortal. Jake didn't know how he knew that, he just did. Since being turned, he always recognized one of their kind when in their presence. It was like a low-key awareness that went through him, as if all his nanos were sensing and saluting hers.

The blonde glanced over now. Spotting him, she leaned back in her seat to give him the once-over.

"You're up," she commented, pushing her long, wavy blond hair behind one ear. "How are you feeling?"

"Good," Jake said slowly, his gaze narrowing on her eyes. They were a bright silver green. Not an Argeneau or a Notte then. Argeneaus were known for their silver-blue eyes, and Nottes for their dark metallic eyes. "Who are you?"

"Nina Viridis," she announced, standing up. "I'm an Enforcer."

Jake nodded, relaxing now that he knew she was a Rogue Hunter. "So Nicole did call Marguerite?"

Nina nodded, and leaned back against the table, arms crossing over her chest. She hadn't stood to approach and shake his hand in greeting as he'd first expected, but so that she wasn't at a disadvantage. As a Rogue Hunter, it would be second nature to ensure she was never at a disadvantage, he supposed.

"She called Marguerite, who called Lucian, who sent us over to look after things until Marguerite and the others could get here."

"Marguerite's here?" he asked, instinctively glancing over his shoulder as if expecting the woman to come walking across the upper living room from the stairs.

"She was," Nina said, drawing his attention again. "And she brought Julius, Decker, and his wife, Dani, as well as Dante and Tomasso. They're gone now though. Everyone but the twins left once you were resting quietly and obviously on the mend."

"Dante and Tomasso are still here?" he asked with a frown.

Nina nodded. "They remained behind to help babysit the mortal."

Jake shifted uncomfortably at this news. He hadn't seen anyone from the Notte family since moving to Ottawa and wasn't sure he was ready to see his cousins now. "I'm sure with you here I don't need Tomasso and Dante to—"

"My team's not going to be here," she said at once. "Mark and Gill already left. Tybo's leaving after he finishes clearing the drive of snow, and I was only waiting for you to wake up." She smiled wryly. "Marguerite suggested it. I gather Dante and Tomasso aren't the most talkative duo on the planet and she wanted to be sure someone told you what happened."

Jake sighed at this news. It seemed he was going to deal with family now, ready or not. Shrugging that worry away for now, he asked, "So what did happen? Was it vampire flu or something? Because between the headache and vomiting, it sure as hell felt like flu, but I thought we couldn't get sick."

"We can't," she assured him. "It wasn't flu. The headache was caused by some sonar mouse repellents Nicole had bought. We removed them and have wiped them from her memory. Several times," she added dryly. "She keeps remembering them and wondering where they are and one of the twins or myself wipes her memory . . . again. We thought it best not to get into explanations like that until you could talk to her."

Jake merely grunted at this news and then asked, "So that was the cause of the headache. What about the vomiting up blood?"

"Poison," Nina said grimly.

Jake's head went back at this news, and then he immediately began shaking it. "I was weak, puking, and had a fever. It was flu."

"You were weak from lack of blood, puking up the poison thanks to the nanos, and what you thought was a fever was the nanos working in overdrive to save you. They heat up in your blood, so your blood heats up," she said simply. "It was poison, not flu."

"But I couldn't have been poisoned," he argued. "I cooked supper. I did the shopping too, and I replaced anything in the house that had been opened on that shopping trip, just in case poison had been slipped into something. There is no way—"

"It was the hot tub," she interrupted. "Dani took a sample and had it tested at a lab here in Ottawa and there were high concentrations of some poison that can be absorbed through the skin, nicotine and dimethyl sulfate—" She paused and frowned. "Or was it sulfide?" She shook her head. "No, it had fox in it somewhere. Sulfoxy maybe?"

"Whatever. It was poisoned," Jake said grimly. He didn't care about the specific substances. The hot tub had been poisoned.

"Yeah." Nina nodded. "Apparently, Nicole got lucky she put the robe on you before helping you inside. Dani thinks she might have got enough poison from just skin to skin contact to kill or at least make her sick. I guess the concentration was super high."

Jake's mouth tightened at this news as he distinctly recalled Nicole reaching out to help him while he was still in the hot tub. Fortunately, he'd felt sick and cranky and had waved her away, refusing her help. If she had touched his bare arm then, would she have been poisoned from just that small contact? Nina was suggesting she may have been. "So the vomiting was from the poison?"

"It was the nanos getting the poison out of your system, which is why it went on so long. I mean you got a full body dunk in poison soup, my friend. It would have been in your skin, blood, organs . . . well, if it got that far. The nanos probably went after it as soon as it soaked into your skin, but we humans have a hell of a lot of skin."

Jake nodded and sighed. He had no doubt that

particular poison soup had been meant for Nicole, and as unpleasant as it had been, he was glad he'd taken that dunk in it rather than her. He survived. She wouldn't have. Raising an eyebrow, he asked, "Where is Nicole?"

"Down in her studio, working. Dante and Tomasso are with her," Nina added as if he'd worry about that.

"Why? She should be safe in her studio," he said with a frown. "I had a security system installed and as long as she keeps her sliding door locked she's fine on her own down there."

"Yeah, as long as she leaves the door locked. But while we got a lot of snow dumped on us last night, it's mild today and she had her studio door unlocked and cracked open to let the paint fumes out," Nina announced dryly. "I gather she has no clue she's the target of someone who wants her dead?"

"No," Jake admitted. "She's in denial. She thinks the things that have happened are just accidents and such."

"Yeah, well, someone needs to kick her ass out of denial," Nina said grimly. "This was no accident. She would have died if she'd got in that hot tub, and she wouldn't have gone pleasantly. Someone's playing hard ball."

Jake nodded. "What did she say when Marguerite told her the hot tub was poisoned?"

"Marguerite didn't tell her anything," Nina said with amusement. "She said it wasn't her place."

Jake frowned. "What? Well, how did you guys explain what happened to me?"

"We didn't. Marguerite slipped into her little

mortal head, made sure she felt everything was okay, and that she was relaxed, and sent her back to work, and Dante and Tomasso have been keeping her in that headspace. Actually," Nina added wryly, "It may have been the best thing she could have done for her. Apparently, Nicole has painted up a storm since. In fact, she was painting until well after dawn this morning, and then went right back to it after little more than four hours of sleep. I gather she's finished two portraits, is almost done with a third and is going gangbusters on two new ones."

"She only got four hours of sleep?" Jake asked, picking on the one thing that had bothered him.

"She worked late and then had an appointment this morning with some old guy in one of the portraits," Nina explained. "I guess she does the final details with the subject there posing and he was available this morning when she called last night. It didn't take her long, but afterward she wanted to keep working." Nina shrugged. "I suppose she'll sleep when she gets tired."

"Hmm." Jake turned toward the door, intending to go down and talk to her.

"I wouldn't if I were you," Nina said, stopping him.

"You wouldn't what?" he asked, turning back.

"She's working well right now, probably faster than she ever has. I suspect that's thanks to a suggestion Marguerite put in her head," Nina added wryly, and then pointed out, "No doubt that's going to come to a shuddering halt the minute you tell her how things are. Why don't you let her get as much done as she can, while she can? Eat, shower, shave, and just take it easy for a bit. The boys will bring her up for dinner and you can bring her world crashing down around her ears then."

"Dinner," Jake muttered. After yesterday, eating was the last thing he was interested in, but he had to cook dinner.

"Marguerite arranged for meals to be delivered for the next couple of days," Nina informed him, turning to her iPad and shutting it down. "She thought you'd appreciate the break."

"Yeah," Jake muttered, relaxing. After dinner was soon enough to talk to Nicole, mostly because he very much feared Nina had it right and this conversation was going to bring Nicole's world down around her ears. She was so resistant to acknowledging that her ex-husband might wish her actual physical harm . . . She wasn't going to take this well.

"Just a heads-up," Nina said, closing the cover of her iPad and picking it up to walk toward him. "You have more than the hot tub poisoning to deal with here. You tried to bite her and flashed your fangs while you were out of your head," she announced as she slid past him to exit the room. "Marguerite fiddled with her memory to keep her from freaking about it, and Dante and Tomasso have been reinforcing it while you were asleep. But it won't last long once she's in your presence again. You're going to have to tell her everything."

"What?" Jake asked weakly, turning to stare after the woman.

"You can handle it," Nina said quietly, pausing to retrieve a brown leather jacket that had lain on the end of the couch. She tugged it on, shifting her iPad from hand to hand to do it, and then pulled her hair out of the neckline and moved toward the stairs with a solemn, "Good luck."

Jake stared after Nina, wanting to call her back. He wanted to ask her to do the talking for him. Or to tell him what to say. This was not a conversation he was ready for. He'd only just learned Nicole was his life mate, and he hadn't yet accepted and handled that; how could he expect her to accept not only that she might be a perfect mate for him, but also that there were such things as vampires and he was one?

Yeah, this was definitely a conversation that could wait until after supper. It would give him some time to figure out what the hell he was going to say.

"That's good. It looks just like Christian and Caro. It looks live, like they could walk right off the canvas and into the room."

Nicole smiled at that compliment from Tomasso as she shifted away from the portrait of Marguerite's son and soon to be daughter-in-law to the next painting and began to work on it. It was the perfect compliment and exactly what she was trying to achieve. She loved it when work went well, and it was definitely going well. She was on a roll. The last two days since Jake had got sick she'd been on fire and had got more done than she normally did in a week. It was a real high for her, better than drugs. She was jazzed.

"Yeah," Dante agreed. "But why do you work on more than one painting at a time?"

"It keeps it interesting," Nicole said with a shrug as she played with the skin color on the portrait of the local politician. She was trying to get just the right shade to emulate the rough, somewhat florid color of the man's face in life.

"Hmmm," Dante muttered.

Nicole smiled faintly, and shook her head. "You guys must be bored to tears. I don't know why you aren't off doing something more interesting than watching me paint." Frowning now, she added, "What are you doing here anyway?"

"We're Jake's cousins. We're visiting," Dante said.

"Jake said he ran away from his family," Nicole told them.

"Yeah," Tomasso said. "Some people don't handle things so well, and some people need time to handle things. Stephano needed time."

"Stephano," she murmured and shook her head as she shifted to the next painting. "I know that's his first name, but it's still weird to hear him called that. I know him as Jake."

"Jake's a good name," Dante commented.

"Yeah." Nicole smiled. She liked the name. She guessed she liked Jake too. He seemed like a nice guy. He was certainly easy on the eyes. Not that she was looking at him a lot or anything, but he was handsome . . . and a good cook, and thoughtful. Like that cheese-and-fruit tray. That had been a nice surprise and she didn't think it was really part of the job of a cook to supply snacks. Or was it? She had no idea. She'd never had one before, and he didn't exactly fit what she would have imagined a cook/housekeeper to look like. The only housekeeper she knew was her Aunt Maria, a sweet, grandmotherly type woman who bustled around in black dresses and orthopedic shoes.

Jake was nothing like her aunt, Nicole thought, recalling him sitting on the edge of the hot tub, buck naked. With a flat stomach, and muscular arms and legs, the man was built. He could be a Chippendale, or a male model.

Nicole frowned as she recalled the blood staining his face and chest. The man had been vomiting blood. That had scared the hell out of her. He was better now, though, some part of her mind reminded her. He was apparently sleeping well and recovering. Everything would be fine.

Those familiar words soothed her. Everything would be fine, but her stomach kept gnawing at her.

"I'm hungry," Dante announced in his deep growl.

"Me too," Tomasso agreed.

Nicole grinned at that. "You two are always hungry."

"Yeah, but I'm really hungry. And it's after six."

Nicole straightened from the portrait and glanced around to the clock with surprise. It was indeed after six . . . and that was no doubt the reason for the continued gnawing in her stomach. Clucking under her tongue, she quickly gathered her paintbrushes to wash and moved to the sink, saying, "I'm surprised Nina didn't come and bark at us to get upstairs for supper like she did at lunch."

"Nina's gone," Tomasso rumbled.

"What?" Nicole glanced around with amazement at that. The woman had been standing guard over Jake like a German drill sergeant since arriving. She hadn't even allowed Nicole to peek into his room just to see for herself that Jake was alive and well. "Then who's watching over Jake?"

"Pinocchio doesn't need watching. He's not sick anymore," Dante informed her.

"Yeah, he's walking and talking like a real boy now," Tomasso added dryly.

Nicole frowned. They'd been calling him Pinocchio since she'd met them. She didn't understand the reason for it and they refused to explain.

"Well, he shouldn't be on his own," she muttered, working a little more swiftly to clean the brushes. "The man was at death's door just yesterday." She paused and frowned. "Or was it the day before?"

"The day before," Dante confirmed.

She scowled. "Right, so he was on his deathbed the day before yesterday and now he's up and moving around?" She shook her head. "What if he passes out or just falls down and hits his head?"

"It's okay, it couldn't hurt anything," Tomasso assured her.

"Of course it could," she snapped. "People have been known to die from head wounds."

"People have," Dante agreed. "But not Pinocchio. His head is full of wood."

Nicole shook her head and set her brushes aside to dry, then slid out of the white smock she'd been wearing to keep from getting paint on her clothes and headed for the door.

The two men were on her heels as Nicole scurried out of the studio and up the hall. The door into the living room was open and she hurried out and took a sharp left right into a very tall, very hard body.

"Jake," she gasped, grabbing at his shirt to keep from tumbling back. Their closeness and position caused a flash in her mind of his being on top of her and her struggling with him, which she didn't recall or understand. But even as that flash slid through her head, she was gasping in surprise as one of the twins crashed into her from behind, squishing her against Jake's chest.

"Sor—" Dante ended the apology on a grunt as Tomasso apparently bumped into him, squishing him against her a little harder.

When Nicole tipped her head up and back to peer at the man behind her, he smiled wryly and muttered, "Choo choo."

Nicole gave a breathless laugh at the train sound and then slid out from between the two men, leaving them inches apart. She hardly noticed, however; she was busy trying to sort out what had just happened and what those memories in her head were. Had that really happened? Were they fragments of a dream?

Fragments of a dream. Everything is fine. Relax. The thoughts wafted through her head and she found herself relaxing.

"I was coming to fetch you for supper," Jake said, stepping back from Dante.

"And we were just coming for supper," Nicole said, looking him over now that those flashes were no longer an issue. His color was back and he seemed fine. Better than fine. He had more color now than he had since she'd met him. He almost glowed with good health, and certainly had he still been suffering even the least bit of weakness, she was sure he would have toppled over when she'd crashed into him. Instead, he'd stood strong and caught her arms to keep her up. Still, he'd been seriously ill, and she couldn't resist asking, "How are you feeling?"

"Good." His gaze slid to the twins and back and then he turned abruptly. "Let's go before dinner gets cold."

Nicole glanced to the twins herself, noting their hard, expressionless faces. It seemed there were bad feelings between the three men, which was a shame in her opinion. She and her own cousin, Pierina, were as close as sisters. But Nicole didn't know what the situation was with Jake and his cousins. She knew they were cousins through his stepfather, but if they'd grown up together . . .

Whatever the case, their relationship definitely wasn't good right now, she thought as she followed Jake to the stairs.

"I set the table in the kitchen rather than the dining room. I hope that's okay," Jake commented as he crossed the upper living room to the kitchen.

"Of course," Nicole murmured. The dining room was the left half of the large upper room in the loft off the stairs. There was no wall separating it from the living area to the right and the entire area was carpeted in cream. The house obviously had not been built for children, she thought as she glanced to the large, dark oak dining-room table with ten chairs. She had never used the more formal dining space yet. It would be handy for large family functions, but she hadn't had anything like that so far. Maybe she should consider having the family up for Christmas, she thought now.

"Would you like wine, water, pop, coffee . . . ?"

Nicole turned her attention to Jake's back at that question as he led them into the kitchen. "Wine sounds nice."

She'd worked hard and a glass of wine sounded relaxing, something she suspected she would need, considering the tension building in the air around her. Geez, there were definitely bad feelings between the trio of men in whose company she found herself. Dante and Tomasso obviously resented Jake for running away from the family. They also obviously wanted to bring him back to the fold, or they wouldn't be here. The question was whether Jake would be willing to rejoin his family.

"Dinner is some kind of chicken, so is Creekside okay?" Jake asked, pulling a bottle of white wine out of the refrigerator. He or someone else had obviously put it in to chill. Nicole didn't drink much and only put white wine in the refrigerator when she was expecting company. Rodolfo had wanted to put in a wine fridge, but they hadn't got around to it before they'd split.

"Sounds good," she murmured, moving to the table and hesitating before taking the end seat backing the front window. It meant the three men would have to take the other end and the sides. They'd have to deal with each other. She wasn't surprised when Dante and Tomasso each took a side, leaving the other end of the small bar-height table for Jake. He would now have one man on either side of him. There was no way to ignore their presence.

Nicole's gaze shifted to the table as she settled on her high seat. Aside from the four place settings there were several covered dishes on the table, and even as she took note of them, Dante and Tomasso began lifting covers to look underneath. The smells that wafted out were amazing and she felt her stomach rumble with interest.

"It's chicken with a creamy mustard sauce, dilled potatoes, asparagus with butter and lemon, and a light cranberry salad," Jake read off a piece of paper held to the refrigerator door by a magnet as he opened the wine in front of the door.

"You didn't cook, did you?" she asked with a frown.

"Not me. Marguerite apparently ordered catering for a couple of days," Jake said quietly. "I just warmed it up."

"Good," Nicole said relaxing. She didn't care how much better he seemed, or the fact that Dante and Tomasso claimed he was back to normal. The man had nearly died. She didn't want him doing anything for a day or so while he recovered . . . which she supposed was ironic. She was paying the man to work, he'd worked one day and then got sick and spent two days down. Now she didn't want him working for a couple more. Go figure.

"It must be from the same place the last two dinners were from," Dante said with a blissful sigh as he surveyed the chicken.

Tomasso nodded in agreement. "It smells as heavenly as those meals were."

"Two dinners?" Jake asked with a frown as he set a glass of wine in front of Nicole. "You mean one."

"Two," Tomasso said.

"Two," Dante echoed.

When Jake glanced to her with a questioning frown, she nodded. "Two. You started throwing up Friday night, were unconscious all day Saturday and Sunday. This is Monday."

"Oh," he said weakly and turned away to move around to his seat. As he sat down, he muttered, "Sorry."

"There's nothing to be sorry for. You can't help it if you got sick," Nicole said firmly and frowned when she caught the looks the twins exchanged. Jake had a funny expression on his face too, she noted, but simply reached for her wine. She paused with it halfway to her lips, though, when she noted that she was the only one with wine. Glancing from man to man, she asked, "Doesn't anyone else want wine?"

All three men shook their heads as one. Nicole stared at them, but they were all busy removing the lids on the food and beginning to serve themselves, so she took a sip and set the glass down, suddenly self-conscious about having it.

The meal was as amazing as it smelled and Nicole made a note to call Marguerite and ask which restaurant she'd had cater the meal. It would be a number she would keep right beside the phone in future.

Dinner was a mostly silent affair. Nicole made several efforts to try to start conversation, but none of the men were biting. They weren't even looking at each other. Well, Dante and Tomasso exchanged glances that she was sure held whole conversations, but neither twin was looking at Jake and Jake was staring at his plate, his forehead knitted through the entire meal. The atmosphere was enough to put Nicole off her food, and she was relieved when she was done eating.

"I guess I should get back to work," she murmured, picking up her plate and starting to stand.

"Actually, I need to talk to you," Jake said quietly.

"Oh." Nicole started to sit back down, but then changed her mind and finished getting up. She carried her plate and silverware to the sink to rinse off before putting them in the dishwasher and then returned to her seat.

A moment later Dante and Tomasso both did the same, carrying their dishes over to rinse and set them in the dishwasher.

"Would you like coffee?" Jake asked as he stood up with his own plate.

"Sure. I'll get it," Nicole said, starting to stand.

"We've got it," Dante announced, picking up the coffeepot as Tomasso gathered four cups from the cupboard.

"Oh, thanks," Nicole said, settling back in her seat, but she wasn't used to being waited on and found it a bit discomfiting.

"Thank you," Jake murmured as he moved over to rinse his own plate and silverware. By the time he finished, Dante and Tomasso were carrying the coffees back to the table.

"Thank you," Nicole repeated as Dante set a cup in front of her. She then reached for the cream and poured some in, passing it on to Dante as she reached for the sugar.

They fell silent then as the twins fixed their own coffees. They were all sipping their hot drinks when Jake returned to the table. He sat down, fixed his own coffee and then frowned from Dante to Tomasso.

"Guys, I need to talk to Nicole," he said finally.

Dante and Tomasso both nodded silently and relaxed back in their seats. For some reason their attitude made Nicole want to smile and she had to bite it back, especially since Jake appeared frustrated by their attitude.

"Could you give us some space?" he asked finally.

"No," Dante said bluntly.

"We're here to help," Tomasso added.

Nicole bit her lip. She could see that Jake was getting annoyed, and when he opened his mouth to say something else, said quickly, "It's fine if they stay, Jake."

He frowned at her for the comment, which kind of confused Nicole. He was her cook/housekeeper. That was all. It wasn't like he would have anything private to say. At least she didn't think he did. On the other hand, she had no idea what he wanted to say. Maybe he didn't want to stick to the two-week trial, maybe he'd made up his mind already and didn't want to work for her anymore. Maybe this latest health crisis was making him want to run again.

"Like Tomasso said, we're here to help," Dante said solemnly. "Marguerite seemed to think you might need it."

Nicole felt her eyebrows rise at this claim. What

were they supposed to help with? And why would Marguerite think their help would be needed? It was like there was something everyone knew . . . except her . . . and that was starting to make her anxious.

Turning to Jake, she said, "Just tell me whatever it is you need to tell me. I'm sure it will be fine."

Ten

Jake let his breath out on a sigh and sat back in his seat. It seemed he was going to have to do this with Dante and Tomasso there. He hadn't factored that into the equation when figuring out how to broach this. Now he didn't know how the hell to go about telling Nicole everything he had to say.

"Jake?" Nicole prodded when the silence drew out.

He forced a smile for her and sat up. He'd just have to go with what he'd planned anyway, he decided. Resting his elbows on the table, he pressed his fingertips together and tried to gather his thoughts. He'd come up with a good opening line earlier, but couldn't seem to recall it now. Giving up on it after a moment, he lowered his hands and glanced up to see that not just Nicole, but Dante and Tomasso too were peering at him expectantly. Obviously it was time to shit or get off the pot, he decided, and just launched into it. "You're my life mate."

Jake heard the words that left his mouth, but wasn't sure how the hell that had happened. He'd meant to work up to that part. He'd intended to start with the fact that her hot tub had been poisoned. That he would have died had he been mortal, but he wasn't. Then work into the fact that he was an immortal and explain what that was, and what he, as an immortal could do, and finally end with the whole, "I can't read or control you" and "that suggests you are a life mate to me" bit. All of which would have ended either with her throwing herself into his arms and saying, "Oh, Jake, that's wonderful! Take me as your life mate now," which was what he'd fantasized about and hoped for . . . or her grabbing a cross and stake, not necessarily in that order, and then chasing him out of her house.

"What?"

Jake glanced to Nicole to see that she was staring at him with complete and utter incomprehension. Jake opened his mouth, closed it, and then glanced to his cousins, muttering, "Some of that help would be good about now."

"Oh, no, Pinocchio," Dante said on a laugh. "You're on your own here."

Jake scowled at the man and ground out, "I thought you said you were here to help?"

"Not if you're going to lead with that," Tomasso said with amusement.

Cursing under his breath, Jake glanced back to Nicole, and forced another smile. "I'm sorry. Forget I said that. That was a mistake. What I meant to say was that—Nicole, I wasn't sick. I was poisoned."

Nicole blinked several times and shook her head with confusion. "What?"

Yeah, she wasn't taking that any better than the life-mate bit, and he wasn't surprised. Nina had said Marguerite had played with Nicole's memories and that Dante and Tomasso were reinforcing it so that she would relax and work. He knew what that meant. Marguerite must have pretty much erased most of her memory of the night he'd started puking up blood in the hot tub.

Jake was trying to figure out how to handle that when Dante stepped in with some of that help he'd promised and said, "Nicole, think back to the night Jake got sick. You were in the studio, heard him vomiting, went out to check on him, and . . ."

Nicole sat back abruptly as if Dante had physically hit her with the memories, and Jake didn't doubt that it felt like that to her. Dante had led her to the memory and then finally let her recall what had happened. He watched with concern as she paled and then flushed and paled again.

"Fangs," Nicole breathed, her thoughts obviously turned inward as she recalled that night.

Jake winced, guilt pinching at him as he had his own flash of memory of trying to bite her.

"You tried to bite me," she recalled with horror.

"I'm sorry," Jake said at once, almost drowning in guilt now. He'd never bitten anyone in the seven years since he'd been turned, but he'd been out of his head with both blood loss and bloodlust, and she'd smelled so good. The scent and sound of the life-giving fluid pounding through her veins had tempted him beyond reason. "I would never hurt you. I swear."

"But you tried to," she pointed out. "You tried to bite me."

Jake grimaced. There was no getting around that.

"Pitiful," Tomasso said, shaking his head sorrowfully, and Jake glanced to him with confusion.

"What?" he asked.

"You don't seem to handle emotional situations well, Pinocchio," Dante said for his brother. "You're kind of pitiful."

Jake scowled with frustration. "Well, if you're so damned smart, why don't you tell me how I should be handling this?"

Dante exchanged a glance with Tomasso, and then turned to Nicole. "You trust Marguerite?"

"Yes." She drew the word out slowly.

"You don't think she'd put you in a dangerous situation, or put dangerous people in your home?" Tomasso asked.

"No, of course not," Nicole said more certainly. "Marguerite has always been kind and supportive of me and my family. She's almost like family herself."

"So you know you're safe with the three of us," Dante said simply and then added, "No matter how crazy Jake sounds, you're safe with him."

Nicole let her breath out on a slow sigh and relaxed a little in her seat with a nod. "Yes. I believe I must be."

Dante nodded, and then warned her, "You're

going to remember and learn some things now that will freak you out."

"Some of it will sound crazy," Tomasso added.

"But you need to just listen and stay calm and remember you're safe."

Jake stared from one twin to the other. This was the most he'd heard the pair speak in all the time he'd known them, and he'd known them since he was four years old. Roberto Conti Notte had business interests in Italy and after he married Jake's mother, the family had spent the summers, Christmas, and most every other school holiday in Italy. Dante and Tomasso had often come around with Christian to visit and Jake had looked up to the three of them with a boy's hero worship. He'd wanted to grow up to be just like them . . . at least until he was eighteen and "the family" had decided he was old enough to know the truth about them . . . that they were different. That he was different from them . . . and could never be like them, not without becoming something he'd always thought was evil and bad.

Jake had grown up on vampire movies, and in those movies the vampires were always the bad guys. Finding out about "the family" had been like waking up to find himself in the middle of a horror movie. It had been even worse to find out that his mother had been turned and that his little brother, who he had adored from birth, had been born one. But the unforgivable bit had been learning that they all, including his little brother, had used their abilities to control him to keep him from realizing what they were before he was old enough to decide if he wished to join them.

Jake had avoided the rest of the family after that, but he couldn't do the same with his little brother. It wasn't Neil's fault that he was born the way he was, so Jake's interaction with the family had been limited mostly to his brother and mother. He'd avoided the rest of them as much as he could, but it was pretty much impossible to avoid a Notte who didn't want to be avoided . . . unless you ran away and disappeared, which he hadn't done until he was turned and became one of the "bad guys."

"There you go," Dante said and Jake peered at him blankly.

"What?"

Dante and Tomasso exchanged a glance, shook their heads in unison and then Tomasso said, "Nicole is willing to listen. Tell her."

"Tell her what?" he asked with alarm. He'd rather hoped the two of them were going to do that for him. It had certainly seemed like they were going to.

"We are here to help, not do it for you," Dante said dryly.

"Besides, maybe in the explaining, you'll understand better," Tomasso said quietly.

Jake peered at the man silently for a moment and then glanced to Nicole. She was eyeing the three of them uncertainly, prepared to listen, but obviously not sure she was going to like what was coming. The problem was, he wasn't sure either. Breathing out unhappily, he said, "I—you see—it's—"

He turned to Dante helplessly and the man clucked with exasperation and turned to Nicole to announce, "We're vampires."

"We're not!" Jake denied at once, smiling reassuringly at Nicole.

"Yes, we are," Tomasso argued.

Jake scowled at him and then assured Nicole, "We aren't. We're immortals. Vampires are cursed, soulless dead people. We are not cursed, soulless, or dead. In fact, I was turned seven years ago to *save* my life."

"Yeah, but we're still bloodsucking neck biters," Dante told Nicole. "And that's what everyone thinks of when they think *vampire* so you might as well just call us vampires."

"We are not bloodsucking neck biters!" Jake snapped, eyeing Nicole with alarm, afraid they were going to scare her off. Smiling reassuringly, he said, "I have never, ever bitten anyone. And these guys only did it before blood banks, because they had to, to survive. We consume bagged blood from blood banks, like transfusions, like hemophiliacs do. I have never ever bitten anyone," he repeated.

"You tried to bite her," Tomasso reminded him.

"Like some Stoker monster," Dante added.

Jake jerked his head to the man and nearly snarled with frustration. "I was sick and in agony and out of my head with blood loss. I'm not a monster."

"Neither are we," Dante said quietly.

Jake sat back as if he'd been slapped. Ever since finding out about what his mother had become and what the Notte family were, Jake had thought of them as monsters. The kind who acted all friendly and lured you in with candy and cookies like you were Hansel or Gretel. Only once they got you back to their little cottage in the woods, instead of revealing themselves to be a witch, they sprouted fangs and swept you up in a dark embrace so they could suck your blood.

He'd been afraid of them, Jake acknowledged. He'd seen all those horror movies as a boy, labeled these people he'd known all his life as vampires, and had been terrified of them. And then, once he was turned, he'd feared that now that he was one of them, he too was a monster. But while he'd tried to bite Nicole the night he was so sick, he *had* been out of his head, and he'd felt guilty as hell ever since waking up to the recollection. Monsters did not feel guilty.

Being turned had not changed who he was, Jake realized. He was still the same man inside, with the same values and beliefs. He was just healthier, looked younger, was a hell of a lot stronger, and was likely to enjoy a much longer life.

Jake glanced from Dante to Tomasso. These two men had been nothing but kind to him since he'd first met them as a boy. Even when he'd found out what they, and all the others were, they'd remained kind, responding to his attempt to shun them and shut them out of his life with patience and kindness. They'd just been waiting for him to get over his fears and realize that carrying the nanos that made them immortals did not make him, or them, less than human. That he *was* still a real boy.

"I'm sorry," he said solemnly and it was all he had to say. Dante and Tomasso had been sitting still and expectant, waiting for the breakthrough they hoped had come, but no doubt fearing disappointment. Now they both relaxed back in their seats and grinned.

"No problem," Tomasso rumbled.

"Took you long enough to come around though," Dante said dryly. "But then you always were a stubborn cuss, kiddo."

Jake didn't miss the fact that the annoying "Pinocchio" he'd been plagued with since being turned had reverted back to the "kiddo" they'd called him before that. And he liked it, which was kind of strange since he'd hated it before this. He'd been in his early fifties when he was turned, and being fifty-one and called "kiddo" by two guys who looked twenty-five had irritated him no end. Now he took the nickname as a sign that he was forgiven for being such an ass . . . and he was grateful for it.

"I—" Jake began, intent on telling them how much he appreciated it, but Tomasso interrupted him.

"Don't go getting all sappy on us, kiddo. You're forgiven. You're family. Enough said."

"Besides, there are other issues now," Dante added, nodding his head toward Nicole.

Jake glanced to her quickly, noting that she was eyeballing them all with trepidation. But at least she wasn't running. Her trust in Marguerite was keeping her there, willing to listen to them. That or Dante or Tomasso, or both, were keeping her there.

Swallowing, Jake smiled at her reassuringly. "Right, I suppose you'd like to know about this vampire deal first?"

Nicole nodded silently.

Jake nodded as well and briefly debated how to do it. In the end he decided that— like ripping off a bandage—it was best to just get it done quickly. "Okay, here's the deal, while we do have some things in common with vampires, we are not vampires," he assured her quietly. "We are humans who have been infused with bio-engineered nanos that have been programmed to repair wounds and fight illness and infections. The nanos are kind of like supercharged robotic white blood cells."

"Nanos that heal wounds and fight illness," Nicole said slowly, relaxing a little. It was only then that he realized while her trust in Marguerite had made her willing to listen, she'd still been pretty anxious about it all.

"Exactly," Jake said with a nod and then added, "Scientifically designed nanos, and they're great." He paused briefly to offer an apologetic smile to Dante and Tomasso, silently acknowledging that he'd changed his tune and this was the first time he'd ever said anything good about the nanos now traveling through his blood. He then glanced back to Nicole and added, "They've saved my life twice now. They *are* good. But while there are a lot of benefits to the nanos, they use more blood to carry out their work than any human body can create, and so we have to get that extra blood from an outside source. Our kind evolved and gained fangs, and at one time did have to bite people to get the blood they needed. But now that there are blood banks we have laws that don't allow us to bite necks and suck blood, as Dante put it. We use blood from blood banks to get the blood we need."

"Your kind bit people *before* blood banks?" Nicole asked with a frown. "How long ago were these nanos developed?"

"Quite a while," he admitted with a grimace. "They were developed in Atlantis before the fall.

Atlantis was quite isolated from the rest of the world by its geography and it advanced both socially and technologically much more swiftly than the rest of the world."

"It must have been advances if they were creating nanos there while the rest of the world was sitting around fires with spears," Nicole said dryly.

"Yes," Jake agreed quietly. "And that world with fire and spears was the world the Atlanteans with nanos found themselves in after their homeland fell. They'd received blood transfusions to get the extra blood in Atlantis, but suddenly had no access to such things. They might have died, but the nanos had been programmed to ensure their hosts' survival, so the nanos forced an evolution on their carriers: the fangs, increased night vision, even mind reading and mind control," he listed off. "All of it meant to aid in their getting the blood they needed to survive."

"I see," Nicole murmured.

Jake hesitated, she seemed to be handling it okay so far, but this was a lot to accept. Deciding to hope for the best, he skipped on to the present. He could explain the rest of their special skills and such later. "Those nanos are the only reason I survived my dip in the poisoned hot tub the other night."

"You're sure it was poisoned?" Nicole asked with a frown.

"Yes. Dani—" He hesitated and then asked, "You do remember Marguerite showing up here with Julius and Dani and those guys?" Jake asked, unsure how much Marguerite had removed of her memory and how much she recalled.

"Yes. Marguerite, Julius, Dante, Tomasso, and Marguerite's nephew Decker, as well as his wife, Dani, were here," she said and then her expression turned troubled. "I think I remember them talking about the hot tub . . . and that it might be poisoned."

"Yes," Jake said, relieved that she was remembering. He had no doubt Marguerite had veiled those memories to keep Nicole calm until he could talk to her, but they were coming back now that Dante and Tomasso weren't reinforcing Marguerite's efforts.

"Dani took a sample for analysis," he told her now. "And the water in the hot tub has a high concentration of nicotine and DMSO. Enough to kill quickly. If you had got in the hot tub instead of me, you would be dead."

"And you think someone was deliberately trying to poison me," she said quietly.

Jake frowned. "Well, it didn't get in there by accident, Nicole. And it wasn't put there for my benefit. It had to be put in with the intent of killing you."

"Right," she said unhappily.

"I know it's hard to accept that the man you love would try to kill you," he said gently. "But Rodolfo—"

"I don't love Rodolfo," she protested with amazement. "I'm divorcing him, for heaven's sake. I'd hardly do that if I loved him."

Jake glanced away with a sigh. He didn't really want to tell her that she was divorcing her husband because of Marguerite's controlling her mind and nudging her in that direction. Marguerite had Nicole's best interests at heart when she'd done it, so instead of telling her that, he pointed out gently, "You still have pictures of him all over the house, Nicole. That suggests you still have feelings—"

"I still have pictures of him all over the house because the egotistical idiot went and superglued them to the fricking wall," Nicole interrupted grimly.

"What?" Jake gasped even as Tomasso and Dante spat the word.

Nicole sighed and shook her head. "Rodolfo is a spiteful, nasty, selfish creep. I don't know what he was thinking. If he thought it was a good way to make me have to think of him even after he was gone, or if he just doesn't know how to wield a damned hammer, but every single picture is super-glued or spackled to the wall. Pierina and I tried to take them down while she was here. We managed to pry one off the wall, but it left a great gaping hole. I'm going to have to have professionals in to remove them, but I don't know who to call about something like that and I've been too busy with all these commissioned portraits to call around, so I've just done my best to ignore them."

She scowled and glanced to one of the half dozen pictures affixed to the kitchen wall and added, "I considered buying a glass cutter and removing the glass from each frame so I could at least remove the pictures, but then I'd be left with empty frames everywhere. Besides, it seemed like I was giving it too much energy that way. Like he'd somehow have succeeded at whatever he was trying to do, so I decided to just ignore them until I could get people in to fix it. And mostly I *have* managed to ignore them."

"Until someone points them out," Jake said quietly. It was pretty obvious she was pissed right now just thinking about it.

"Yeah. Then I get annoyed all over again," Nicole admitted with a grimace, and added, "But that isn't because I love him. It's because he's taken control from me again. He's decided what will be on my walls and made sure I had to live with it for at least a while. And it's because it reminds of all the damned, stupid annoying and petty little things he did when I bought him out of the house."

"Like what?" Dante asked with interest.

"The agreement was he take half of the furniture and whatnot as marital assets . . . Forget that I paid for every damned thing." Nicole grimaced with disgust, and then continued, "Fine. So he took half of everything, but he also did his damnedest to mess with anything left behind."

"Mess with them?" Jake asked curiously. "How."

"Well, the stereo, for instance," she said. "It was here and in working condition, but he took the power plugs as well as the connecting wires to the speakers. He did that with the PlayStation, the mosquito catcher, and anything else that had a removable cord. So I had them all here, but couldn't use them until I replaced the wires . . . and then there was the dishwasher, it was missing its silverware holder. There were shelves missing from the refrigerator, and the dining-room set? It was a twelve-chair set, but he took the end chairs. You know, the chairs with the arms?" Nicole said, and when they nodded, continued, "I called him on it, of course, through our lawyers, and he had an answer for everything. He didn't know what I was talking about. He hadn't taken any cords or shelves. And the chairs? Those had suffered an unfortunate accident during the year he lived here. Hadn't he mentioned it to me when we were agreeing on what would go and what would stay? He was sure he had."

"As for loving him," Nicole continued quietly. "Not only do I not still love him, in truth, I don't think I ever did. It turns out I didn't even know the real him. I suspect I was in love with love, with the whole romance of the relationship, the exotic foreigner, sexy accent, seeing the world thing . . . I was a fool."

"That's kind of harsh," Jake said quietly.

"Yeah," Tomasso agreed. "Besides, we're all fools for love."

"She didn't love him," Dante reminded him.

"Oh, right," Tomasso muttered, then peered at her hard. Jake knew at once that he was reading Nicole's mind, and wondered what he was finding. His eyebrows rose when Tomasso added, "Well, we're often fools for sex too."

Nicole flushed and demanded, "You're doing that mind reading thing Jake mentioned, aren't you?"

Tomasso grimaced.

"Stop it," she said firmly and stood up. Her gaze shifted to Jake. "If you're done explaining things, I'd like to get back to work."

Jake hesitated. He hadn't got to the part about their being life mates, but he'd dumped a lot on her already. Besides, he'd rather discuss that part with her alone without his cousins there to hear.

Still, he eyed her briefly. She seemed to be handling everything pretty well so far. He didn't think
he had to worry that she'd slip out of the house
and run away, freaked out about everything she'd
learned. But he wasn't positive. It wasn't every day
you learned you were hosting vampires in your
home . . . and she hadn't asked any questions yet.
He didn't know if that was because she needed to
process what she'd learned, or what, but he hoped
so, he wanted to trust her. That was a hard thing
for Jake. His experiences in life had left him with
some trust issues and it wasn't just because of the
woman he'd nearly married who had been intent
on robbing him blind. His family had aided in
those trust issues too, with their deep dark secret
and by keeping him in the dark for so many years.
But he had to learn to trust Nicole eventually for
them to be life mates.

Sighing, Jake sat back and nodded. "Of course."

Nicole slipped away at once, leaving the table
and the room without another word.

Jake watched her go and then glanced from
Dante to Tomasso. "Well?"

Dante pursed his lips and then said, "Give her
twenty minutes and then take her coffee."

"And jump her bones," Tomasso added.

"What?" Jake asked on a half laugh of disbelief.

Dante shrugged. "You've rocked her world."

"Not in the good way," Tomasso added, in case
he'd misunderstood.

"Nicole's spinning right now," Dante added.

"You need to anchor her," Tomasso said.

Jake arched one eyebrow and said, "You want me to anchor her with my cock? Seriously? We barely know each other."

"Sometimes it's incredibly obvious you were born in the Leave It to Beaver era," Dante said dryly.

Jake stiffened and scowled. "Excuse me, you two are older than I am."

"Yeah, but we're Italian," Dante said with a shrug.

"And that means what?" Jake asked dryly.

"The Brits are known for bad food, the French for good food, and the Italians for being the best lovers," Dante explained.

Jake gave a disbelieving laugh. "You're delusional."

"Casanova." Tomasso rumbled, and then added, "Enough said."

"One man does not—Ah hell, never mind," he muttered standing up. "I'm going downstairs . . . to *talk* to Nicole."

"I'm telling you, sex is the way to go," Dante assured him as he headed for the doorway. "It will bond her to you."

Tomasso added. "One taste of life-mate sex and she'll be hooked like a heroin addict."

Jake halted in the door and turned back. "Life-mate sex?"

Dante raised his eyebrows. "No one's told you about life mates?"

"Well, I know about life mates. Can't read 'em, can't control 'em, a perfect mate."

"And crazy, blow your mind, so intense it leaves you unconscious, sex," Tomasso added.

"It leaves you unconscious?" Jake asked with a frown.

"And blows your mind," Tommaso repeated.

Jake narrowed his gaze on the pair. "You're pulling my leg, right?"

The twins merely shook their heads solemnly.

"Hmm," he said dubiously, but then merely turned away and headed for the stairs. He wasn't sure he believed Dante and Tomasso. After all, surely someone would have mentioned that to him prior to this?

Even as he mentally asked himself that question, Jake realized how ridiculous it was. No one would have told him that before he was turned. It wouldn't have meant anything to him as a mortal. As for after the turn, he hadn't given them much of a chance to tell him anything then. Anytime his mother had tried to point out the benefits of being an immortal to him, he'd shut her down. His brother, Neil, hadn't tried to coddle or convince him his being turned was a good thing. He'd simply stood by him, silent and supportive, but Jake hadn't wanted support. He'd wanted to be mortal again . . . a real boy, just like Pinocchio. But he wasn't Pinocchio anymore. He wasn't exactly happy to be immortal, but he was grateful to be alive. Vincent's turning him had saved him the first time, and being immortal had saved him from the poisoned hot tub . . . and now he might have a life mate.

Jake considered that without the bitterness of being an immortal that had plagued him on first realizing he couldn't read or control Nicole. He didn't really recall his birth father. The only father he recalled was Roberto, and his memories of his childhood were very happy ones filled with love.

Love between his mother and Roberto, and the love they'd showered on him and Neil. He supposed the reason he'd reached fifty-one years as a mortal without marrying and having children of his own was because no relationship he'd ever had, had ever come close to the love, friendship, and joy that his mother and Roberto had shared . . . and he'd wanted that. Now, he might be able to have it.

Jake knew how lucky that made him. He also knew he was extremely lucky to find it so soon after being turned. Most immortals waited centuries, even millennia to find a life mate. The twins were over a hundred years old, his cousin Christian was over five centuries, and while Marguerite had found Julius centuries ago, they were only reunited and able to enjoy each other now, and Marguerite was over seven hundred years old. His finding a life mate so young was a gift, and it was one he didn't want to mess up.

Eleven

Jake paused outside the studio's French doors and peered through the window. He wasn't surprised to see that Nicole was not working. He'd expected the information she'd been given would disrupt her ability to concentrate. He was concerned though to find her simply standing in the middle of her studio, staring at her uncovered paintings. He suspected she wasn't really seeing the portraits. Her shoulders were hunched and Jake was quite sure he knew exactly how she was feeling. It was the same way he'd felt when he was eighteen and had been told about immortals. Betrayed, confused, as if the world wasn't the place he'd thought it was.

Jake didn't knock, but simply opened the door. Nicole didn't turn, but he could tell by the way she stiffened that she knew he was there.

"I came to see if you were all right," he said quietly. "I know this is a lot to take in."

She gave a little snort and Jake smiled wryly.

"Yeah, I guess that's an understatement, huh? Believe me, I know. Been there, done that, and have a whole wardrobe full of T-shirts to prove it," he said quietly.

"You said you were turned when you were attacked?" Nicole asked quietly.

Jake nodded, and then realized she couldn't see him so cleared his throat and said, "Yes."

"When was that?"

"Seven years ago, give or take six months," he answered and wondered what she was thinking when she nodded. He wished he could see her face, but she still had her back to him.

"Was that the health crisis that made you run away?"

Jake sighed and pushed the door closed. He walked over to the nearest of the half dozen swiveling stools she had in the room and sat on it, before saying, "Yes, but it was just the last straw of many."

Nicole was silent for a minute and then asked, "What was the first straw?"

The question surprised him and he took a moment before saying, "The first one was more of a tree than a straw."

"Which was?" she prompted.

"It was when I was eighteen and my mother and stepfather sat me down and told me about immortals and that they, my brother, and every Notte I had ever met, which was all the family I knew, belonged to that select party."

"All the family you knew?" Nicole asked, turning to peer at him curiously. "The Nottes are your stepfather's family. What about your mother and father's family?"

"My mother had a brother, sister, and parents, and my father had two brothers and parents. Apparently there were cousins and grandparents too, on both sides."

"But you don't know them?" she asked.

Jake shook his head. "They didn't approve of my parents' marriage. On my mother's side it was because they were Jewish and my father was Catholic. On my father's side it was a combination of that and the fact that as far as they were concerned my mother came from the wrong side of the tracks. My father's family had money, my mother's didn't. Dad's parents expected him to marry a nice girl from a comparatively rich, Catholic family, not a poor Jewish girl whose family didn't even own their own home. So . . ." He shrugged. "After Dad died, Mom was pretty much on her own with me."

Jake paused briefly, but when she didn't comment, he said, "I guess she was struggling something fierce when she met Roberto, working two jobs to try to support us and taking night courses at university in the hopes of getting a better job, to better support us. I gather she had no time for romance and made Roberto work hard to win her."

"He was immortal?"

Jake nodded. "And he turned her."

"But not you?" Nicole asked with a frown.

"I was a child," Jake said with a shrug. "I gather they frown on turning children."

"But when they told you at eighteen, why didn't she turn you then?" she asked.

"I gather that was the plan," Jake admitted with a grimace, and then explained, "They told me on my eighteenth birthday. My mother thought it would be a grand gift to tell me all about immortals, and then offer to use her one turn to turn me into one."

"But she didn't," Nicole said with certainty and then arched an eyebrow and asked, "You wouldn't let her?"

Jake shifted uncomfortably, and then sighed and said, "You have to understand, I was a horror buff. I watched every monster movie ever made. They scared the crap out of me and I slept with a nightlight until I was twelve, but I had to watch them. I was crazy for horrors." He shook his head slightly at the memory. He'd lost his taste for horror since then, but he'd been addicted to them then and that hadn't really helped the situation. "Back when I was a kid, they didn't have your Twilights and True Bloods. In every movie where vampires made an appearance, the vampire was the bad guy and the Van Helsing types were the good guys running around staking them and ridding the world of their evil."

Jake grimaced. "So, essentially, on my eighteenth birthday, my mother told me that not only was my stepfather and his entire clan a bunch of blood-sucking fiends, but that she'd allowed him to turn her into one, and that the half brother I adored and looked out for was one too . . . and I'd been living with them all, unsuspecting all that time."

"Seriously?" Nicole asked with suspicion. "Before they told you what they were, you didn't have a clue?"

"They made sure I didn't," Jake said quietly. "I suspect they used some mind control to keep me unaware while they fed, or fudged my memory a bit here and there, not erasing anything, but adding things here or there to explain inconsistencies." He shrugged. "I didn't have a clue before then that I lived with what I thought were monsters."

"And you didn't agree to the change at that point," Nicole said quietly.

It wasn't a question, but he treated it as one. "No. I was shocked, horrified, repulsed. They were all suddenly monsters to me, and I didn't want to be a monster too."

"It must have been hard for you," Nicole said quietly, moving to sit on the stool next to his.

Jake hesitated and then swung the seat slightly toward her and said judiciously, "Probably no harder than it is now for you."

Nicole smiled wryly, but shook her head. Swinging her stool to the side and back with one foot, she said, "It's a bit of a shock for me to find out such things exist. But for you . . ." She frowned and stopped swiveling to peer at him solemnly. "It was your family. You must have felt—I don't know, alone?"

Jake nodded. He *had* felt alone. He'd also felt betrayed, abandoned, lost. "I guess at that point I felt like I was just finding out that I'd really been orphaned at four and had been living in a fantasy world all the years since Roberto came into our lives. In truth, I suppose I ran away emotionally that day, and my actual leaving seven years ago was just me physically following up on what happened emotionally years earlier."

"Why didn't you run away back then, at eighteen?" she asked curiously. "I mean if you felt they were monsters . . ."

"My brother," Jake said quietly. "I was angry at my mother for letting Roberto turn her, but I was close to my little brother, Neil, and it wasn't his fault he was born immortal. Besides, logically, after she explained everything, I understood that they weren't monsters."

"But there was still a part of your mind that thought of them as monsters," Nicole guessed.

Jake nodded. "Eighteen years of training via horror movies can't be eradicated that easily."

"And then you were turned to save your life?" Nicole commented.

"Yes." Jake's mouth twisted at the memory. "My boss, Vincent Argeneau, who also happens to be Marguerite's nephew, was being plagued by someone who was trying to ruin his life. They attacked me, and stabbed me just to the side of the heart. When Vincent found me I was dying and he turned me to save my life. I woke up an immortal . . . and didn't handle it well."

"Why?" Nicole asked quietly. "Surely it's better to be an immortal than to be dead?"

"You'd think so, wouldn't you?" Jake said with dry amusement, and then glanced down. After a moment, he sighed and admitted, "I was fifty-one years old, miserable, and bitter." He smiled wryly and lifted his head again, meeting her gaze. She was silent, waiting, wanting to understand, so he had to explain. "I was in a pretty dark place at that time. I'd had a happy childhood, but after finding out about everything, it felt like that childhood had all been a house of mirrors. After that I went through life feeling like an orphan. On top of that, nothing had turned out as I'd intended. I had no wife or kids, no one but my family and they were monsters as far as I was concerned. By the time I was attacked, I felt alone and tired and, frankly, I guess I was at a place where I was just killing time and waiting for the end . . . and then I got attacked. I remember lying there on the office floor, thinking, this is it, the end of my story. No more loneliness, no more disappointment, no more betrayal . . . and, instead, I woke up a vampire."

"You keep saying *vampire*, but you told me you guys aren't vampires," Nicole pointed out quietly.

"Yeah," Jake smiled faintly. "But I've been thinking of them as vampires so long . . ." He shrugged. "Old habits die hard, I guess."

Nicole was silent for a minute, and then tilted her head to peer at him, a frown growing on her face. "Fifty-one?"

Jake smiled wryly. "When I was turned yes. I'm fifty-eight now."

"You do not look fifty-eight," she said firmly and then asked, "Is that something to do with the nanos?"

He nodded. "They were programmed to keep their host at their peak condition. I don't think the developers intended that to include age, but the nanos are basically fancy, hybrid computers, and computers are pretty literal. Every immortal looks somewhere between twenty-five and thirty."

Nicole considered that and then said, "So Marguerite . . . ?"

"I'm not sure of her exact age, but I know it's over seven hundred."

"Oh cripes." Nicole sagged on her stool.

Jake eyed her worriedly, but waited, and then

she suddenly straightened and peered at him accusingly.

"You said she wasn't even in her forties."

"I said she wasn't in her thirties," he corrected. "And she isn't. I haven't lied to you about anything, Nicole. I knew almost from the start that we were life mates and didn't want to lie." Jake grimaced and added, "I have kind of a thing about lying anyway . . . ever since finding out I was lied to for so long while growing up . . ." He shrugged.

Nicole was silent for a few more minutes, and then sat up straight again and asked, "So what is this life-mate business anyway?"

"Well . . ." Jake paused and swallowed. This was the tricky part, or perhaps it was just the most important part so felt tricky. If she didn't accept that they were life mates, and agree to be his, or at least agree to consider it, then it could very well be decided that she should have her memory wiped and be left as ignorant of their existence as she'd been before he'd explained things. It would be necessary to ensure the safety of their kind. But if that happened, he wouldn't be allowed to be around her again. None of them could, in case their presence made the memories return.

It was an odd thing. Jake *felt* odd and somewhat confused. While he knew that she was a life mate, or could be if she agreed, he hadn't really known her long. Jake liked Nicole, or at least he liked everything he knew about her so far. He also found her attractive. But he wasn't experiencing any mad, passionate desire to have her or anything, and he was wondering about this life-mate business himself. Shouldn't he feel more? Want her more?

Shouldn't his every waking thought be about her?

That last question made him pause, because Jake suddenly realized that his every waking thought had included her in one form or another since meeting her. Still, he supposed he'd expected more.

"Jake?" Nicole prodded.

"Oh, sorry," he murmured, and then blew his breath out and tried to gather his thoughts to answer her question. Finally, he said, "Well, I mentioned that the nanos didn't just give immortals fangs, but other skills to help with survival."

"You said mind reading and mind control," she recalled and didn't look pleased. He understood that. He hadn't been too pleased himself to know that his mother and everyone else could read his private thoughts. It had been pretty inhibiting to an eighteen-year-old full of raging hormones. Made aware that they might all be reading his thoughts, Jake had suddenly become aware that sex played a huge role in most of his thoughts at that age. And forget about masturbation in the same house with them. Dear God, what if they all knew? Or read it in his head in the morning? Even thinking about that now made him shudder.

"It's not just mind reading and control," he said when Nicole shifted restlessly on her stool. "We're faster, stronger, have better hearing, sight, night vision, et cetera."

"Okay," she said patiently.

"But, the mind reading, that isn't just of mortals. We can read each other's minds too. Usually it's only older immortals able to read younger ones, but it can go the other way too if the older immortal is distracted or not blocking their thoughts,"

Jake explained. "So, it means when we're around each other we have to constantly guard our thoughts, and of course mortals can't really guard their thoughts from us. It can make relationships tricky."

"I would think so," Nicole said dryly.

Jake nodded, but added, "Any relationship. I mean, you can't imagine what it's like to be eighteen and know your mother can read your thoughts."

"I think I know," she said grimly. "Perhaps not what it's like to have a mother reading your thoughts or control you, but if you, Dante and To-masso can read and control me—"

"I can't," Jake interrupted.

Nicole tilted her head and peered at him uncertainly. "Why? Is it because you were only turned seven years ago?"

"No. I have gained the skill, and can read most mortals," he assured her, and then grimaced and added, "I resisted it at first. I didn't want to be like my family. But in my job it's a handy skill and so I eventually gave in and have used it pretty regularly . . . on the job," Jake added to ensure she didn't think he ran around reading and controlling people willy-nilly.

"Okay," she said slowly.

"However, I can't read or control you," he added.

"So you said," Nicole reminded him.

Jake grimaced and nodded. "And that is the sign of a life mate."

Her eyes narrowed. "Which is what?"

"It's—" He frowned, wanting to get it right, to find the perfect words to make her understand and at least be open to the idea of being his life mate. "A relationship wouldn't work if both parties could read each other, or even if one could read and control the other."

"You said that," Nicole pointed out quietly.

"Yeah, I guess I'm struggling here," Jake admitted on a sigh, and then shook his head and said, "Forgive me, this is the first time I've had to explain any of this."

"Right. Sorry, I'll keep that in mind," she said wryly.

"Thanks," he muttered, and then said, "Look, basically a true life mate is someone that an immortal can't read and control. It's the one person they can relax around and not constantly guard their thoughts."

"Surely you don't have to guard your thoughts around mortals?" Nicole asked. "We can't read you."

"No, but some mortals think really loud and we have to put up guards against that too. Otherwise it would drive you crazy. People are always thinking, and sometimes just the stupidest, most nonsensical things. We have to keep our guards up against that as well, filter it out, basically."

"I see." She tilted her head again. "But you don't have to do that around a life mate?"

"No. We can relax around them," he said. Jake gave her a moment to consider that and then added, "Of course there are other things that are special about a life mate."

"Like what?"

"Well, actually, nobody's ever explained it to me and I'm not sure what they all are," he admitted on a wry laugh. "But I know from watching my mother and Roberto that . . . well, it's a special relationship. They seemed to have mostly the same tastes and values. Like the same things, enjoy each other's company. They still had disagreements and such, but much less often than I think most couples do, and they seemed to get over them really quickly. They just seem so bonded . . . and apparently, if Dante and Tomasso are to be believed, the physical relationship is much more intense."

Nicole was silent, which made him worry that she wasn't getting how important a life mate was, but then he wasn't sure he fully understood himself.

"It's also very rare, or hard to find," Jake added. "Some immortals wait centuries to find one, and some never find one at all."

She was still silent.

"I've heard that the nanos have something to do with selecting a life mate, that they recognize them as a good mate for the immortal and are the reason the immortal can't read that particular mortal or something. So that it works, I guess." The conversation where he'd been told that had been a while ago and he hadn't paid much attention.

Nicole stared at him.

Jake stared back, his mind racing around in search of something to say to help convince her that being a life mate was a good thing, or at least not reject it out of hand. But he feared he had an uphill battle ahead of him. Nicole had just come out of a terrible relationship. She wouldn't be interested in getting involved again so soon. This was really bad timing.

"I don't—" Nicole began and Jake was sure she

was going to tell him she wasn't interested, and if she did, he was screwed. He'd lose her. Jake didn't want that. He wanted what his mother and Roberto had. He'd always wanted that. It was why he'd still been alone at fifty-one. There had been women he'd cared about, and even maybe loved somewhat in his life, but having watched his mother and Roberto together all those years, nothing less than that kind of relationship would do. So when she started to say, "I don't," he flat-out panicked and resorted to Dante and Tomasso's advice. He stood up, stepped forward and bent his head to kiss her.

It was very effective. Not just at silencing her either. Certainly, it did that, but that wasn't all. Had he wondered and worried about the fact that while he found her attractive he had no great desire for her? Had he really thought that? The question ran through Jake's head, free-floating around the passion that exploded up within him the moment his lips touched hers. Honestly, it felt like it slammed up from the ground, through his feet, up his legs and straight to the groin. Talk about your instant erection, Jake was very aware that the loose joggers he had pulled on before dinner were now a pup tent that had sprung out from between his legs and, damn, but it felt good.

Nicole had stilled when he first covered her mouth with his, but the moment she relaxed, allowing her lips to slip open with a little moan, Jake moved one hand up to catch her hair in his hand. Using that hold to tilt her head to where he wanted it, he thrust his tongue into her mouth even as his other hand slid around her back and urged her closer against his chest.

Now that she'd given in to the kiss, Nicole wasn't still either. He felt her arms slide around him, to dig into his back and grasp at him, and then she scooted forward on the stool, her legs sliding along the outside of his thighs until she bumped into the pup tent in his drawers. She hesitated then, but Jake reached down and shifted himself as he moved right up so that his legs pressed against the stool and his erection was pressed flat against his stomach between them.

That brought another moan from Nicole and he felt her legs close around him, her heels pressing into the backs of his calves. Encouraged, Jake pressed himself more firmly against her, his right hand now moving around to her back and down to clasp her behind and urge her closer still as his hips ground against her.

"Jake," she gasped, tearing her mouth from his, and the excited plea incited him further. Turning his lips to her neck, he nibbled and sucked and licked there as his hands shifted to her top and began to work at the buttons, slipping them quickly from their eyelets until he could pull it open and get to what was underneath.

Urging her backward, one arm under her back for support, Jake closed his other hand over one generous silky cup of her bra and moved his mouth down to run his tongue along the top of it. When Nicole groaned and shifted her hips against him in excited reaction, he caught the edge of the bra and pulled it down until her breast was free. He then lavished the hard, rosy nipple with attention; licking and suckling at it with feverish excitement . . . and then he suddenly froze.

"Jake?" she said uncertainly, her voice shaking, and he raised his head, letting her nipple slip from his mouth to peer at her with confusion.

"I'm sorry, I just . . . never mind," he murmured, sure he was wrong. But rather than bend his head to her breast again, he covered it with his hand, squeezing and kneading and then plucking at it. Nicole groaned, her eyes dropping closed, her body shifting against his again and he almost closed his eyes too as pleasure shot through him as well.

This wasn't the first time Jake had done this. He loved women's bodies and had enjoyed many lovers in his life, but it had never been this intense for him in the past, and he had certainly never enjoyed the sensation this way, not as if he himself were experiencing the pleasure he was giving her . . . but now he was. Earlier while he'd been suckling, and now, every time he plucked at her nipple, it sent a shaft of pleasure shooting through him that just ratcheted up his own pleasure.

Fascinated, he released her breast and slid his hand down between them to cup her between the legs through her jeans. Nicole cried out, and Jake sucked in a startled breath at the sharp excitement and need that shot straight through his groin. Was it the nanos? Were they somehow communicating her pleasure to his body? Jake had no idea, but this was . . . Hell, he didn't even know how to describe it. It was incredible, amazing, fricking awesome! And he wanted to explore it fully.

Nicole gasped with surprise when Jake suddenly picked her up with one hand behind her back and one between her legs and under her bottom. She grabbed at his shoulders nervously as she was lifted off the stool, and then glanced around with surprise when he set her on the edge of her desk and used one arm to swipe the papers, stapler and other odds and ends out of the way, before shifting her to sit on it more fully.

Her gaze slid back to Jake then, but before she could say or even think anything, he kissed her again. Nicole kissed him back at once, with all the passion and need he'd stirred in her. Her own tongue tangled with his briefly before she withdrew it to suck at his, and then Jake broke the kiss and stepped back to pull at her jeans. It was only as they began to slide off of her that Nicole realized that he'd undone the button and zipper while he'd kissed her.

He made quick work of removing them, which was probably a good thing. She didn't get a chance to protest that way, and didn't really want to, but if she'd had time to think, Nicole might have felt she should.

Tossing her jeans aside, Jake stepped back between her legs to kiss her again, his arms slipping around her and hands dropping to cup her behind through her panties to squeeze and knead her cheeks as he pressed her against him again. The sensation was even more exciting without her jeans there buffering it somewhat, and Nicole gasped and shifted eagerly against him as much as she could. Her own hands slipped down to cup his behind and urge him on briefly, before she began to work at the top of his jogging pants, first tugging, then pushing them down off his hips in the back until his bottom was bare.

Nicole squeezed hard, pressing him tightly forward until it was almost painful and then jumped in his hands and gasped when one of his hands slid far enough under her to press between her legs through her panties.

"Oh God," she groaned, and then released a small disappointed sigh when he stopped doing that and eased his hips back from hers. In the next moment, she cried out with surprise and pleasure when his hand slid between them again. This time he didn't just cup her, but tugged her panties to the side and slid his fingers beneath the thin material to caress her hot, damp skin.

"Oh-please-yes-God-Jake." The words were gasped in one long slurred sound and almost unintelligible, but then Nicole didn't really have a clue what she was saying. Didn't care either. The only thing she knew was that what he was doing felt so damned good. It was instinct alone rather than any conscious thought that made her slip one of her own hands around to find his hardness through the joggers. They had been trapped between them in the front when she'd pulled them down in the back, but had ridden down somewhat when Jake had put space between them. He was still covered by the cloth, but barely.

The moment her hand closed on him through the material, Jake sucked in sharply through his teeth and stilled. Nicole hardly noticed what he was doing, however. She herself had gone stock-still at the sudden sharp stab of excitement that shot through her.

Confusion hard on the heels of that excitement, she hesitated, and then jerked his joggers down so that he sprang free and closed her hand over the velvety skin of his erection. That sent an even more powerful wave of passion shooting through her, but Jake was no longer caressing her.

"What . . . ?" Nicole raised her head to look at his face. "I feel—It's like—"

"I know," Jake ground out when she faltered. "So do I when I touch you." He slid his fingers over her again as if to prove it, and groaned out loud, but it was the way his erection jerked in her hands that told her he was experiencing her pleasure along with her. Though it was rather amazing that she was aware of his body's reaction with her own body reacting to his touch.

"But how?" she asked breathlessly.

"I don't know," he panted and began to caress her again. "And right now I don't care. I'll ask Dante and Tomasso later."

With her mind already losing its grip on her attention, Nicole thought that was fine. Later they could find out why this was happening. Right now—she slid her hand along his shaft again. Dear God, right now all she knew was that she wanted more of this.

Jake gave a grunt of surprise when Nicole suddenly released him and gave him a push away from her. Before he could ask what she was doing, she'd slid off the desktop and dropped to her knees before him. She'd always wondered how she was as a lover, and now she could find out.

"Nic—" Jake cut himself off with a curse as she closed her mouth over his erection.

Nicole moaned at the sensation she sent rifling through them both. She was aware when his legs began to shake, and wasn't surprised when he bent over her to grab for the desk behind her to steady himself. However, she was caught completely by surprise when Jake suddenly jerked himself free of her, caught her under the arms and drew her to her feet even as he headed for the daybed. He swung her around as he reached it, almost tossing her on top of it and then he was on her, kissing her almost violently before starting to slide down her body.

Suspecting what he was up to, Nicole caught him by surprise and rolled, shifting him on to his back on the daybed. She had started this and wanted to continue. Not giving him the chance to roll her back, she shifted quickly off of him and turned to take his erection in hand again. Jake had started to rise up, no doubt to grab her again, but fell back with a gasped protest as she closed her mouth over him again. He was as stubborn as she was though, and she wasn't surprised when he grabbed her upper leg and tugged her hips toward his head.

For one moment, Nicole had to stop what she was doing and balance herself with her hands as he shifted her knees to either side of his head. She nearly toppled over when Jake suddenly ripped her panties off, tearing the sides away to get the thin cloth out of the way. Nicole was glad he did that rather than shifting her about to remove them properly. In fact, it kind of turned her on . . . and then he pulled her hips down and buried his face between her legs and she forgot her poor panties.

Groaning, Nicole dropped her head briefly, her hair trailing over his upper thighs as his tongue rasped over her sensitive skin. With the second rasp, her nose bumped against his erection, and—recalled to what she'd been doing—she returned to it, taking him in her mouth and helping to drive them both crazy.

What followed was quite the most amazing, mind-blowing thirty seconds of her life. If it was thirty seconds. Nicole couldn't be sure. It went so fast, passion crashing down over her in wave after hard wave, making the tension building and growing in her body expand exponentially until every nerve in her body was strained and tingling and her brain was a pile of worthless mush.

The release when it came was like a nuclear explosion in her body. White lights went off in her head, blinding her to everything but the pleasure blowing through her. She was vaguely aware that someone was screaming their head off and thought it must be Jake, but while some of the sound was a man's deep timbre, she recognized a woman's higher pitch in there too. Just as she realized it was herself, the white light dimmed quickly to black.

Twelve

Nicole opened her eyes and peered at the ceiling of her studio with a completely blank mind. There wasn't a thought in her head for at least a full minute, and then her brain kicked in and began to ask questions.

Why was she asleep in her studio? What time was it? Where were her pants?

That last question only occurred to her as she started to sit up and noted they were missing. It also brought a wave of memories washing over her, which made the tingling increase.

"Damn," she breathed, scrambling to get off the daybed and look for her pants. When she didn't see them anywhere, Nicole dropped back on the bed. Her body was still tingling everywhere. How long had it been since they—

Had she really fainted? She wondered suddenly.

Good God, she'd never ever before in her life experienced anything like that. Nicole had thought her ex was good in bed, but what she'd just experienced was transcendental. Life altering. Mind-blowing. Fricking amazing! And where the hell was Jake? How could he just leave her there like that after what they'd experienced?

Scowling now, Nicole stood up and looked for her pants again. She distinctly recalled Jake tugging them off and tossing them, but her jeans were nowhere to be seen. Neither were the panties he'd torn off of her. After a hesitation, she decided there was nothing else to do and quickly grabbed the throw off the daybed to wrap around herself. Her shirt was still unbuttoned, her bra askew with one breast out and while she quickly tucked her breast back in, she didn't bother with doing up the shirt, but wrapped the throw around her chest so it covered her from above her breasts to just above her ankles. Then she headed upstairs.

There were sounds coming from the kitchen when Nicole stepped off the stairs at the top. She turned her feet in that direction, her thoughts so focused on Jake and what had happened in her studio that it didn't even occur to her that it could be Dante or Tomasso making the sounds and she might have to explain her state of undress.

"Oh, shoot. I was hoping to get back before you woke up."

About six steps into the kitchen, Nicole glanced to the right at that comment to see Jake standing by the counter in just his jogging pants, a knife in hand and a tray of various foods before him. His words made her relax. He hadn't abandoned her after what they'd done. Well, he'd left, but had planned to come back.

Her gaze slid over his bare chest and she wondered briefly where his T-shirt had gone. Neither of them had removed their tops downstairs. But then Nicole noticed that his hair was wet and she realized that he must have taken a shower before starting on the tray.

"I thought you might be hungry when you woke up, so I was getting us a snack," Jake said quietly.

Her gaze slid to the tray. There was cheese, crackers, olives, wine . . . and a can of whipped cream and container of chocolate syrup? Her eyebrows rose. There was no ice cream or any other dessert-type food that might need whipped cream and or chocolate sauce. That had to be for something else, and it didn't take much thought to figure out what that something else was. The answer popped into her head at once, along with images of drizzling the chocolate over his body and licking it off.

Turning abruptly, Nicole hurried out of the room. She was moving so fast she was nearly running as she crossed the living/dining room to her bedroom. She didn't stop there but continued on to the en suite bathroom, straight to the shower. Cranking it on with one hand, she let the throw drop and then quickly shrugged out of her top. She was struggling to undo her bra when she heard a sound behind her. Nicole glanced over her shoulder. She'd left the door open and Jake now stood in the doorway, staring at her wide-eyed, concern on his face.

"Are you okay?" he asked uncertainly.

"No. I can't get my bra undone and want to take a shower," she answered.

He hesitated and then offered, "I can undo it for you if you like."

"Please," she murmured, turning her face forward again and simply waiting.

Nicole heard the rustle as he crossed the room and then he set to work, but said quietly, "When you rushed out I was worried that you were upset about what had happened."

Nicole was silent for a minute, and then said, "I will be. Later."

"Later?" Jake echoed. "And right now?"

She hesitated, but the tingling that she'd woken with had increased, first with memory, further at the sight of his bare chest, and even more with the realization of what he no doubt planned to do— and she could definitely do—with the whipped cream and chocolate sauce. Now, with his fingers brushing against her back, she was positively shivering with excitement and emboldened to say, "Right now I just want to shower and then spread whipped cream and chocolate sauce all over you and lick it off."

Jake's fingers stilled against her and then her bra snapped open and went loose in the front. Even as she realized that, his hands slid around her sides to slip beneath the cups and squeeze.

"The things I want to do with you," he growled, kneading the round globes and pressing his groin against her from behind.

"Tell me," Nicole breathed, reaching back to find the hardness pressing up against her.

Bending slightly, Jake pulled her hair to one side and nibbled at her earlobe before saying, "I want to lay you out on the kitchen table and make a meal out of you. I want to cover you with whipped cream and lick and suck my way across every inch of your body." He paused then to lick, nip and suck at her neck briefly as his hand slid down across her stomach to dip between her legs.

Nicole groaned as he began to caress her there, his fingers firm and knowing as he circled the hard center of her excitement. When he slid a finger inside of her, Nicole gasped with pleasure and grabbed for the shower door to keep her balance.

"I want to take you in the shower, position you with your hands on the wall and legs spread and take you from behind while the warm water pours over us."

"Oh, yes," Nicole gasped, pushing against the shower door and hips moving as she rode his hand.

"Then I want to take you in every position, in every room of this house," Jake slid a second finger inside of her, his thumb still playing with her as he moved his fingers in and out, in and out.

"I want to fuck you until neither of us can stand up," he growled, his finger thrusts becoming harder and swifter. "I want to be drenched in your pleasure, drown in it. I want . . ." He broke off abruptly and Nicole didn't need to ask why. Her whole body was convulsing with pleasure as release crashed over her and she knew it had hit him too.

This time Nicole knew the screaming in her ears was herself as well as Jake, but it was just a brief awareness before the darkness began to claim her. She saw the floor coming up to meet her, realized she was falling forward into the shower, but couldn't do a damn thing about it and didn't particularly care at that moment. She never felt the blow when she landed.

Nicole woke up in her bed. For one moment she thought Jake must have woken first again and carried her there, but then she shifted her arm and her hand bumped up against something solid and warm in bed next to her. She turned her head swiftly. Jake was beside her, dead to the world. Apparently, he'd woken up long enough to carry her here, but this time hadn't left.

Nicole stared at him silently. Dawn's early light was coming through the open blinds and splashing across them both. He was a handsome man. She'd noted that from the first, of course, but now, with him unconscious and unaware, she could look her fill. Until now she'd only taken quick glances here and there, not wanting to get caught gawking at the man. But now she could gawk to her heart's content and did. Jake had such a nice face . . . and those lips . . . A little shiver went through her as she recalled the various things his lips had done to her. The man hadn't just been gifted with a pretty face and nice body, he knew how to use the gifts he'd been given.

That, or the fact that they both seemed to experience the other's pleasure had transformed him into an amazing lover.

The thought made her consider that aspect briefly. It was pretty amazing. Seriously . . . it rocked. But it was over so damned fast. It was like having to gobble down chocolate cake when you wanted to savor it. And it was so overwhelming that they hadn't yet even actually had sex.

Nicole considered that fact briefly, wondering if they would ever get past the foreplay. The passion came on so hard and fast, she suspected they wouldn't at this rate.

Her gaze traveled down his body to where the sheet lay across his groin and she eyed it briefly, aware that she hadn't really got much of a look at it. She'd had two mind-blowing orgasms and hadn't really seen much other than his chest. The first time . . . well, it was hard to look at something when it was in your mouth, and the second time he'd been behind her.

Nicole's gaze slid back to his face, but he was still dead to the world so her gaze dropped again and she contemplated the situation. She wanted to peek. She also wanted to feel him inside her. She wanted to be facing him, connected to him as they rode the wild wave of passion that rose up in them both, but she suspected Jake was too considerate for that to happen. Judging by his actions so far in prepping the coffee for her and making her snacks, Nicole suspected Jake was the type to always start with foreplay and as long as he did that, she wasn't likely to get to the main attraction anytime soon . . . unless she took the situation in hand.

"And I don't mean that literally," Nicole murmured to herself and sat up. The action pulled the sheet away from his upper chest, and she tugged it the rest of the way clear of his body, then released a little sigh as she peered at him. Damn, the man looked good everywhere. Nice chest, flat stomach, nice legs and nice in between. Those nanos definitely kept their host at their peak. The man could have posed for Michelangelo or Rodin. He was almost as pale as marble too, she noted, and slid her fingers lightly along his hip.

Jake might be asleep, but his body reacted immediately to the touch, his penis growing and hardening. Nicole watched, eyes widening, and then brushed her fingers lightly over him again so that he continued to grow.

A sleepy murmur drew her gaze to Jake's face. When his eyes started to open, Nicole quickly shifted and threw one leg over to mount his hips. She didn't take him inside her right away, but glanced to his face and waited as he woke up.

Jake blinked sleepily at her and then confusion covered his face. It passed quickly though, his eyes growing wide as he noted her position.

"Your eyes," Nicole breathed with surprise. "The silver is growing and they're glowing.

"The nanos," he said simply, his voice sleep-roughened. His hands rose to clasp her hips briefly, and then he slid one around and down to slip it between her legs. "Good morning."

Nicole moaned, and promptly lowered herself onto him, only to moan again as he filled her. It had been more than a year since Nicole had left her husband and she hadn't had sex since then, but that wasn't the only reason he felt so big. She had noted that while Jake didn't seem unusually long, he had girth and that girth filled her completely, even stretching her a bit. God, it felt good.

"Damn you feel good," Jake muttered through his teeth, both hands at her hips again.

Since that was exactly what she'd been thinking, Nicole gave a breathless laugh and then began to move.

Much to Nicole's surprise, she was the first to wake up again. This time, strong winter sunlight was glaring in through the sliding glass doors and onto them. Nicole automatically got up to close the blinds and then turned to peer at the now shadowed bed.

She eyed Jake curiously, as she realized that the light earlier and this time hadn't seemed to disturb him . . . and he'd gone shopping with her in daylight. Obviously, that was another difference between vampires and immortals; sunlight didn't bother immortals.

Nicole crossed the two feet to the bed, intending to climb back in, but she wasn't really tired now. She was thirsty though . . . and her throat was a bit sore. It wasn't the only place she was sore. It seemed that all this caressing and having sex after a year of abstinence was causing some tenderness. Interesting, she thought and then walked around the bed and through the en suite to the walk in closet. Her gaze slid to the shower as she passed through the en suite and Nicole briefly considered taking a shower, but suspected if Jake woke up to find her naked in the shower, she wouldn't be leaving the room for another little while.

The idea held more than a little appeal, but Nicole was tender enough that she feared another round with Jake right now would just make it worse. Besides, she was thirsty . . . and hungry now too.

In the closet, Nicole pulled out a pair of plaid pajama bottoms and a bra and T-shirt to don, deliberately avoiding underwear this time to give her lower half a break. She dressed in the walk-in closet, her gaze slipping over the seventeen-foot-long and seven-foot-wide room. Built-in drawers were at either side of the far end of the room and a washer and dryer sat against the wall behind her on the other side of the door from the bathroom. But the rest of the room was lined with both upper and lower hanging rods, each side partitioned into two parts along each wall . . . except directly beside her, where there was only an upper rod to allow for robes and dresses to hang.

Nicole grimaced as she peered at the mostly empty rods. It had been stuffed to brimming when Rodolfo had been there. The man was a clothes horse, with so many shirts and pants he'd had a whole selection that still had the tags on. He'd taken up all of one side and almost half of the other with his clothes when they'd lived together, but now her own clothes barely filled half of one side . . . and that was with the clothes spread out to prevent wrinkling. That had never bothered her before, but now Nicole was thinking maybe she should buy herself some nice outfits to wear out on dates and such and perhaps some nice nightgowns and sexy underwear and—

Nicole stilled. What the heck was she thinking? She'd just got out of a relationship. She was not ready to get into another one. And she'd promised herself another six months before she'd even consider dating, but here she was, a couple of rounds of bouncy bed with Jake and she was ready to go out and buy clothes? Including sexy underwear? God, she was such an idiot. And a ho' too, Nicole told herself viciously. She'd slept with her cook/

housekeeper after barely knowing him a couple days. What was the matter with her?

Nicole knew that was harsh. She knew too that lots of women saw nothing wrong with sleeping with someone they'd just met in a bar and didn't know from Adam. And she'd agree . . . for others. But Nicole knew herself well enough to know that she couldn't just have sex. She would get emotionally involved, and the last thing she needed right now was to get emotionally involved with anyone.

Angry at herself and grumpy now, Nicole finished dressing and slipped out of the closet. She practically tiptoed through the bedroom in an effort not to wake Jake. She wasn't ready to see him just now. She needed some time to sort herself out and decide how to handle this situation with him.

That might include firing him as her cook/housekeeper, Nicole admitted to herself unhappily. But she knew it was the smartest thing to do . . . because she very much feared that as long as he was around, she wouldn't be able to resist playing more bouncy bed with the man. The sex had been that good. Hell, if she weren't sore, Nicole would probably be crawling on the man right now.

"Jake isn't here to be a cook/housekeeper."

Nicole nearly leapt out of her skin at that deep rumble as she entered the kitchen. Whirling, she stared at Dante Notte. The man stood two steps behind her, apparently having followed her from . . . well, somewhere. The living room, probably, she thought, but hadn't noticed him.

"You were busy thinking about bouncy bed with Jake and how to avoid it," he offered helpfully.

"To avoid getting involved with him," Tomasso added, stepping into view behind his twin.

Nicole flushed and turned sharply away to walk to the refrigerator. "Please stop reading me."

"It's hard not to. New life mates are often rather loud with their thoughts," Dante explained.

"And in other ways," Tomasso muttered, and Nicole felt her blush deepen as she recalled screaming her head off with pleasure, not once, but three times now. She supposed that explained why her throat was sore.

"My apologies," she said stiffly as she opened the refrigerator door in search of something to drink. A bare second later though, she frowned and glanced to the men. "What do you mean, Jake isn't here to be my cook/housekeeper? That's his job."

"That's what you think," Tomasso said with amusement.

"What do you mean, that's what I think?" Nicole asked, scowling.

"Well, you think he's here to be your cook/housekeeper, while he thinks he's here to be your bodyguard," Dante said with amusement.

Nicole's eyes narrowed. "And which is true? Why did Marguerite bring him here?"

"Because you're his life mate," Tomasso said as if that should be obvious.

"You're telling me that Marguerite thought I would be a life mate to Jake and—" Nicole began.

"She *knew* you would be a life mate to Stephano," Tomasso corrected.

"Marguerite has a certain gift about such things," Dante informed her quietly. "She has put together several life mates over the last few years."

"Well, I'm pretty sure she has it wrong this time. I—" Nicole began but Dante interrupted.

"Please try to remember that we can read your mind and know when you're lying . . . even to yourself," he said solemnly.

Nicole slammed the refrigerator door closed with more violence than was necessary and walked over to sit at the table. Propping her elbows on the table, she dropped her face into her hands and scrubbed her eyes almost painfully with the heels of her hands. She did it hard enough that she almost saw stars.

"You know Marguerite is not wrong," Dante said quietly, settling at the table on one side of her as Tomasso claimed the chair on the other side. "Jake told you that he cannot read or control you and that the lack of those abilities is a sign of a life mate. But that aside, you enjoyed the life-mate shared pleasure, and even if you didn't know that was another symptom, you knew it was special enough to mean something."

Nicole grimaced. Yeah, she'd known that was pretty special. Not only had she never experienced anything like it before, she suspected it wasn't even possible, at least between two mortals. Still, she shook her head. "I—"

"You're afraid," Tomasso interrupted before she could spout whatever lie she'd been about to spout to both herself and them.

"Fear is to be expected after what you've been through," Dante said quietly, placing one hand on her arm. "But Jake is not Rodolfo . . . and this is not a normal situation."

"Maybe, but . . . I don't want to make another

mistake," she burst out, flopping back in her chair to escape the support he offered with his touch.

"The nanos got it right," Tomasso said with amusement. "She resists help and support just like Stephano did when he went all Pinocchio on us. They're alike."

"Yes, they are," Dante agreed dryly, but said to Nicole, "If you don't want to make another mistake, then trust the nanos. They don't make mistakes. Neither does Marguerite. The couples the nanos put together last. Centuries."

"Millennia even," Tomasso put in.

Nicole glanced to him with surprise, but it was Dante who said, "Our grandparents have been together for millennia."

"Pretty much forever," Tomasso said dryly. "And they're still going strong."

Nicole stared at them uncertainly. "But I hardly know Jake."

"You haven't known him long," Tomasso agreed.

"But we know him," Dante said quietly. "We've known him all his life and he's a good man."

"A little stubborn and bullheaded at times," Tomasso said.

"But he's always honest," Dante added.

Tomasso nodded. "He doesn't drink, or take drugs either."

"He's honest and fair," Dante assured her, and then added, "He's considerate too. He was always trying to help out with whatever was going on while growing up, whether that was clearing the table after a big family dinner, or reroofing a neighbor's house."

Both men fell silent briefly, allowing her to think

that over, and then Dante said, "Nicole, I promise you, the only mistake to be made here is not giving him a chance."

"If you don't trust your own judgment, trust the nanos," Tomasso added.

Both men stood and headed out of the room then, but when Dante paused at the door and glanced back, Tomasso, who was behind him, was forced to stop as well, as the other man said, "But the two of you need to be more careful in future. You could have drowned in the shower if you'd fallen with your face up and mouth open. As it is, you have a nice bruise on your cheek."

Nicole instinctively reached for her cheek, wincing when she touched the swelling there.

"Try to keep the bouncy bed to a bed," Tomasso added with amusement.

"But at least avoid any water bouncy, whether it's tub or shower. And definitely no outside bouncy this time of year," Dante said grimly. "You'd freeze to death before you ever regained consciousness."

"Definitely no outside bouncy," Tomasso agreed.

Groaning, Nicole crossed her arms on the table and dropped her head to rest it on them, hiding her face, which she knew was now bright red. It didn't stop her from hearing the men chuckle gently as they left the room.

At first, Jake thought it was night when he woke up, but then he noticed the sliver of light creeping around the edges of the blind and readjusted his thinking. By the looks of the light it was late afternoon on the day after his waking from being poisoned. He hoped. It was possible it was the day after that. It was hard to tell. He and Nicole had made love and passed out three times. It could be one day after telling her about immortals or two. All he knew for sure was that he was alone in the bed.

That realization immediately made worry rear inside him. He didn't mind that Nicole had left him alone in the bed, so much. But he was worried about how she was taking what had happened between them. Had it anchored her as Dante and Tomasso had suggested? Or was she now freaking out and wishing she'd never set eyes on him?

Tossing the sheet aside, Jake got quickly out of bed and looked around for his jogging pants, only to recall that he'd shed them in the bathroom during the little episode outside the shower. As he'd kissed and sucked at her neck while caressing her, she'd moved so deliciously against him, he'd wanted to feel Nicole's bare flesh against his erection and had quickly pushed the joggers off his hips. That was all he'd had to do. They'd fallen to the floor on their own from there . . . and then he'd woken up in bed without them.

That memory made him frown. Jake didn't recall getting to bed after passing out in the bathroom. In fact, he was sure he hadn't got there under his own steam. But Nicole couldn't have carried him there. Which left Dante and Tomasso. They'd probably heard the shower running and when it continued for a protracted period, had no doubt come to investigate.

Surprisingly, the idea bothered him. Jake didn't care that they'd seen him in that state, but he didn't like the idea of them seeing Nicole like that. She'd been completely naked when he finished removing her bra. Naked, unconscious and under him. He didn't like that they'd seen her like that at all.

Scowling now, he got up and walked into the bathroom, freezing and instinctively turning his head quickly away when he saw Nicole standing in front of the shower, drying herself off.

"Sorry," he muttered, quickly pulling the door closed again. He then stood there uncertainly, unsure if he should feel stupid or not. After everything they'd done, seeing her naked shouldn't be an issue, and it wasn't for him. Jake had averted his eyes and closed the door for her sake. She might still be shy and want her privacy.

Well, if she thought he was being silly by offering her privacy to tend her personal hygiene, Jake was sure she'd let him know. In the meantime, he had some personal needs to tend to as well.

Jake slipped out of the master bedroom and headed along the dining-room table for the guest bath outside his own room, completely unselfconscious about his nakedness. There were only Dante and Tomasso there after all, or so he thought until Joey said, "Jesus, Jake. This isn't a nudist colony. Get some clothes on."

Jake's head whipped around to see Nicole's brother standing by the couch on the living room side of the loft, a pretty, petite redhead at his side. Joey was scowling at him, but the redhead was ogling him with a small smile. Jake was so surprised that he almost stopped, but the woman's leer decided him and he continued on to his room instead of the bathroom. As much as he needed to relieve himself, grabbing some clothes first seemed like a good idea.

He wasn't terribly surprised when moments after he closed it, someone knocked at his door. Nor was he surprised when after he called out, "Come in," Joey stepped into the room.

"What the hell are you doing coming out of my sister's bedroom bare-ass naked?" Joey demanded grimly.

"That's really none of your business," Jake said calmly, stepping into clean jogging pants and quickly tying the tie at the waist. "It's between myself and your sister."

"Well, where the hell is she?" he demanded at once. "That Dante character who let me in said she was in the shower and should be right out."

"She is out of the shower. I'm sure she'll be out shortly."

"Well, what the hell's been going on?" Joey barked. "I've been calling for three days trying to talk to Nicole, and one or the other of those behemoths downstairs kept telling me that she was sick and that's why she didn't meet me for lunch and couldn't talk to me on the phone."

Jake stilled, briefly concerned that Nicole had been sick while he was down from the poisoning, but then he realized that Dante and Tomasso had simply used that with Joey as an excuse to keep Nicole and her brother apart while he was recovering. No doubt they'd wiped her memory of the appointed lunch with her brother too. Seeing him might have led to memories cropping up, and if that had happened without at least one of the twins there to prevent it, all the blocking they'd done would have fallen like a string of dominoes. Nicole would have recalled everything before they were ready for her to recall it.

"And then," Joey continued furiously, "I come out to see what the hell is happening and it turns out those guys are your cousins? You've moved your family in while Nicole was too sick to protest?"

"Of course not," Jake said calmly, tugging his T-shirt on next and heading for the door. "They are visiting briefly and helping me."

"Helping you with what?" Joey demanded, following him out of the room.

"I'll explain in a minute. But right now I really need to use the facilities," Jake said politely. He slipped into the bathroom and closed the door. He then locked it as well, just in case the irate man decided to follow. Jake understood Joey's upset. He'd have been upset in his place as well, but he really needed to relieve himself, so explanations would just have to wait a few minutes.

Thirteen

"Joey?" Nicole said uncertainly as she spotted the man fuming outside of the guest bathroom. After Jake's brief interruption, she'd dressed quickly, put her hair up in a ponytail and rushed out to find him, only to find her brother instead. "What are you doing here?"

Joey jerked around to peer at her. "There you are!"

Her eyebrows rose at his tone, and the way he rushed to her side. Grabbing her arm, he started to pull her across the room toward the stairs.

"Come on. I'm getting you out of this mad-house," he said determinedly.

"What?" she asked on a startled laugh. "What are you talking about? What madhouse?"

"Nicole." Joey paused and turned to face her with exasperation. "You missed our lunch with-out warning or even a courtesy call, which is com-pletely unlike you. And then when I repeatedly call to speak to you, I get some woman and then these strange men answering and telling me you're ill and couldn't make it and don't want to see me. Finally, I've had enough and come out here to check on you and you have two mob goons downstairs and your supposed cook/housekeeper is coming out of your bedroom as naked as the day he was born. Something weird is going on here. You need looking after and I'm taking you to our hotel until I sort it all out."

Nicole stared at her brother weakly as his words poured over her. In all the excitement the last few days, she'd quite forgotten about her lunch with Joey. In fact, she'd forgotten all about him, and his being in town, and . . . well, just everything.

Or someone had helped her forget, she thought suddenly, but let that go. If Dante and Tomasso had blocked her brother from her memory, she knew exactly why they'd done it . . . and she understood. But she couldn't explain it to Joey. He was a bit of a blabbermouth. Nicole didn't think there was a secret the man had ever actually kept.

She also couldn't explain Jake's coming out of her bedroom buck naked. Or she didn't want to, so Nicole settled on the one thing she could say in response to his long diatribe and assured him, "Dante and Tomasso are not mob goons."

Apparently, it was the wrong approach to take. Joey's mouth dropped open, snapped closed, and then he reached for his phone. "I'm calling Mom."

"Joey," she said on a sigh. "There's no need for that. Look, just come have a cup of coffee and—" Nicole paused abruptly and peered around her brother toward Jake when the bathroom door opened and he came out. He wore baggy gray jogging pants and a T-shirt that was pretty tight. He also had bed-head and a day's worth of growth on his face . . . and damn, but didn't he look fine, Nicole thought, her knees going weak and mouth actually salivating as Jake met her glance.

In the next moment, he had crossed the room toward her like a moth to flame, and—completely ignoring, or oblivious to Joey's presence—slid his arms around her and drew her against his chest as he laid one hell of a hot, wet kiss on her lips. Nicole was on the verge of wrapping her legs around the man and climbing him like a telephone pole when he broke the kiss and eased back to peer down at her.

It was only then that Nicole became aware of her brother's protesting squawks.

"What the hell? Stop that! Get your hands off my sister! Nicole! Get away from him! I'm dialing Mom now!"

Nicole grimaced apologetically at Jake, then swiveled her head to peer at her brother. "I'm fine, Joey. There's no need to call Mom."

Joey glared at her, phone at the ready and breathing heavily. He then stepped closer and hissed by her ear, "We need to talk. Something isn't right here. I want you to come with Melly and me. You can stay at our hotel with us until we get this straightened out."

"Melly?" Nicole asked, glancing around. "Is she here?"

Even as she asked the question, Nicole spotted the beautiful redhead standing by the couch. It wasn't hard to believe she was a model, Melly was gorgeous; large exotic eyes, a straight nose, full, pouty lips, flowing red hair and stick thin. The woman looked like she was born to walk the runways of Europe and grace magazine covers.

Nicole was suddenly very aware that she was dressed like a bum, completely makeup free, and that her hair was a damp mess stuffed into a ponytail. Damn, she thought, life could be so unfair at times. Pushing that thought away, she produced a perfectly sincere smile and crossed the room to greet the woman her brother loved.

"Hello, Melly. It's so nice to meet you," she said, taking the woman's cold hand in her own and shaking it warmly.

"It's Melanie," the woman said, with a cool smile as she retrieved her hand. "Only Joey calls me Melly."

"Oh." Nicole smiled uncertainly, glanced toward the men and then turned to head for the kitchen. "I'll put coffee on."

"I don't drink coffee," Melly announced. "It ages you prematurely."

"Well then I'll put water on for tea," Nicole said, moving a little more quickly.

"Tea is as bad as coffee," Melly announced as if she should know that and added, "Just hot water with lemon for me."

"Right," Nicole said through her teeth as she escaped into the kitchen.

She only realized that Jake had followed her when he said, "I'll make the coffee and put the kettle on. You go visit with your brother and Melly."

Nicole grimaced. "I'll just get out some of that cake I saw in the refrigerator earlier."

"Cake?" Jake asked with surprise.

"Mmm-hmm. I think Marguerite bought it while she was here." Grinning, she added, "She has a sweet tooth."

"What kind of cake is it?" Jake asked with interest, moving over to peer into the fridge over her shoulder. "And why the hell didn't I see it when I was making our snack?"

"It's double chocolate," Nicole answered, pulling out a large carton of orange juice, another of milk, and a couple of creamers to reveal the covered cake at the back of the refrigerator. "Because I hid it so the boys wouldn't gobble it down. They have a tendency to inhale everything."

"Yeah, they do. They were always like that," Jake commented, stepping back to get out of the way as she pulled the cake out and turned to set it on the counter.

Nicole started to take the lid off, and then paused and frowned. "I suppose if she won't drink coffee, Melly probably doesn't eat sweets either."

"Yeah, she does," Jake assured her absently, his attention on the cake. "She plans to puke it back up afterward."

"What?" Nicole turned to him with surprise.

"I read her mind," he explained, glancing to her and then smiled crookedly and added, "She doesn't know you're serving chocolate cake, of course. But when you said you were putting on coffee, she hoped you would serve a sweet too. She's starved, wants to gorge on two or three pieces, and then slip away to the bathroom and purge it to avoid the calories."

"Geez," Nicole muttered, peering at the cake. It seemed a terrible waste to feed it to Melly just to have her puke it up afterward. "Maybe I won't put it out."

"Good. Save it for later. We can watch a movie and eat cake," Jake said with a grin.

Nicole smiled faintly, but then her expression turned serious and she said, "Please don't read Joey and Melly while they're here, Jake. It's kind of rude."

His grin died slowly and he nodded. "You're right. I hated it when my mother and the others read me. I shouldn't do it. I'll try not to."

"Thank you," she murmured, reaching out to place a hand on his chest to balance herself as she leaned up to press a kiss to his cheek. At least, she meant to kiss his cheek, but he turned his head at the last moment so that her lips landed on his.

"Is that chocolate cake?" Joey said behind them just as their lips brushed across each other's.

It was probably a good thing, Nicole admitted as she turned to smile and nod at her brother. The way Jake affected her, she very well might have tried to climb him right here in the kitchen.

"Good," Joey said grimly. "Chocolate is Melly's favorite."

"Oh, that's nice," Nicole murmured with a sigh. It looked like she was serving it after all. Forcing a smile, she suggested, "Go sit down and relax, Joey. We'll be out in just a minute with coffee and cake . . . and water and lemon," she added quickly when he frowned. Truly, it had just slipped her mind.

"You're right. We shouldn't leave Melly alone. It's rude," Joey said with forced cheer. "Besides, you should get to know her. She's going to be your sister-in-law someday."

"Oh—" Nicole glanced to Jake.

"Jake will bring out the coffee and cake when it's ready," Joey added grimly and then arched an eyebrow and added, "That's what he's here for, isn't it?"

Annoyance slid through Nicole at the comment. Jake was more than just a cook/housekeeper to her now, but she wasn't sure just what that more included yet. However, Dante and Tomasso's talk had convinced her to give this . . . whatever this was, a chance.

"Then he can come back in the kitchen and cook or clean or whatever while we visit," Joey added firmly and Nicole felt herself stiffen.

"Actually, then he can *visit* with us so that *you* can get to know *him*," she said sharply, and then mimicked him, adding, "You never know, he might be your brother-in-law some day."

The minute the words were out of her mouth, Nicole wanted to pull them back in. Jake had stiffened behind her, and Joey looked horrified, but no more than herself. She'd said them out of anger . . . but they were too much. She'd agreed to give Jake a chance, not accept him as a life mate. She wasn't ready for—

"Go visit with your brother," Jake said quietly, his hand landing on her shoulder and squeezing gently before he urged her forward. "I'll bring everything out when it's ready."

When Nicole glanced over her shoulder to him uncertainly, he smiled reassuringly and nodded her on. Letting her breath out on a sigh, Nicole followed when her brother turned sharply and strode out of the kitchen.

Melly was lounging on the couch, and lounging was the only description; she looked like she was posing for an ad for some exotic tropical resort. Nicole smiled at the girl, but before she could say anything, Joey caught her arm and pulled her close.

"What's going on, Nicole?" he asked in a low, worried voice. "When I arrived just a couple days ago, Jake had just started on as your cook/housekeeper and you hardly knew him. Now he might be my new brother-in-law? What's going on? Has he drugged you? Hypnotized you? Are they holding you hostage and forcing you to say this stuff?"

Nicole sighed and shook her head. "I didn't mean that, Joey. I was just annoyed that you were treating him so badly."

"He was naked and coming out of your room," he pointed out grimly. "You aren't the type to sleep with someone you barely know. And they haven't been letting me speak to you. Something isn't right here, and I'm *worried*. Please tell me what's going on. I'm your big brother. I want to help you."

Nicole relaxed and gave him a hug. "And I appreciate that. Thank you." Pulling back she added, "But really, everything's fine." When he didn't look convinced, she added, "There are some weird things going on, and Jake, Dante and Tomasso are trying to help me."

"And Jake's coming out of your room naked?" he asked.

Nicole opened her mouth, closed it, and then shook her head, aware that she was blushing. She also couldn't help noticing that he hadn't asked what weird things were going on . . . which she found a bit weird.

"You *are* sleeping with him," Jake accused with amazement.

"Look, this is—really, I—we're being rude to Melly," she said desperately.

"Nicki, this isn't good. You haven't fully got over Rodolfo. I don't want to see you hurt again," Joey said quietly.

Nicole shook her head. She really didn't want to get hurt again either, but after getting over her humiliation at knowing that Dante and Tomasso were the ones who had put her and Jake to bed after they'd passed out in the shower, Nicole had sought the men out and asked them to tell her about life mates. They'd said that life mates were made for each other. That Jake would never cheat on her, never hurt her, and never abuse her because he couldn't risk losing her. That losing her could very well mean losing his sanity and humanity and going rogue. She didn't understand how that could be the case, but those promises were tempting and—

"Nicki?" Joey said with a frown. "I really—"

"We're being rude to Melly," Nicole interrupted, and this time followed it up by moving away and settling on the couch to offer the other woman a smile. She didn't want to discuss this with Joey. She didn't want to think about it at all. She was giving Jake a chance and that was that. The only other thing she could do was pray that Dante and Tomasso were right, everything would work out, and she wouldn't get hurt again.

"Well," she said with forced cheer, smiling at Melly. "Joey tells me you're a model, Melanie."

"Yes."

Nicole hesitated, but when she didn't add anything else, said, "That must be exciting?"

"Yes."

Again, the girl didn't follow up with any experiences or how it was exciting. She didn't seem to grasp the concept of a conversation. Person A spoke and then person B responded . . . with more than a flat "yes." Or she just couldn't be bothered, Nicole supposed, and glanced to her brother for help.

That was a mistake. Rather than help get his girlfriend talking, he went right back to the conversation they'd been having, and hissed, "I'm worried about you."

"I'm fine, Joey, really," she assured him with a touch of exasperation. He was like a dog with a bone.

"But they said you were sick when I called," Joey said with a frown. "Were you? Or were they just not letting me talk to you? If they're making you do something you don't want, or are here against your wishes, Nicki, we can leave now and—"

"No, no," Nicole assured him quickly. "It's nothing like that. They—I—" She blew her breath out on a sigh. Either she told him that Dante and Tomasso and whoever the woman was who'd answered one of his calls had lied, which would just freak him out further, or she lied to him now. As much as she hated to do it, her lying now seemed the best option to calm him down. Joey was already freaked out and suspicious, unreasonably so and she had to wonder what Dante or Tomasso had said or done to cause it.

"I'm fine now, but I wasn't . . . myself the last few

days." Nicole smiled as she finished that, proud of herself. She hadn't had to lie, after all. She really hadn't been fully herself while Marguerite, Dante and Tomasso had been playing with her head.

Joey frowned. "Well, what was wrong? Was it the flu, or what?"

"Oh, just some—" she waved vaguely, and finished, "thing. I'm fine now though."

"And these men who are here?" Joey asked.

"You know who Jake is, and Dante and Tomasso are his cousins. They're visiting from out of town. Jake was very sick for several days and they came to make sure he was all right."

"He was sick too?" Joey asked with surprise.

"He was very sick," she assured him.

"With what?" Joey asked suspiciously.

"He had a bad reaction to the chemicals in the hot tub," she said, and then frowned and murmured, "Which reminds me, I need to get someone in to empty, clean, and refill it."

"I'm bored."

Nicole glanced to Melly with a start at that announcement.

"I want to leave," she added, and Nicole was sure her jaw dropped to the floor. The woman made the announcement like she was some royal princess and expected everyone to start jumping to please her . . . which Joey did. Much to Nicole's amazement, her sometimes selfish and annoying brother was immediately on his feet, and moving to take her hand to help her up.

"Okay, we'll go, baby," he said soothingly.

Nicole stood uncertainly, eyes wide. "But Jake is making coffee and—"

"I don't drink coffee," Melly reminded her.

"Well, he's boiling water for you," Nicole said grimly.

"I don't care. I want to leave." Melly said simply and then turned to Joey and demanded imperiously, "Take me shopping, Joey."

"Of course," he said quickly, taking her arm to usher her to the stairs. "I'll buy you something shiny and pretty."

"And expensive. It should be expensive to make up for this," Melly informed him.

"Of course," Joey assured her.

Nicole stared after them with amazement as the couple descended the stairs out of sight. She couldn't believe what she'd just seen and heard. Good God—

"She must give one hell of a blow job."

Nicole jumped and turned at that dry comment from Jake. He stood behind her, hands on hips, a disgusted look on his face. Eyes wide with amazement, Nicole asked, "What?"

He shrugged, his mouth twisting. "Well, it's true. She must be beyond amazing in bed for Joey to put up with that crap. She's a bitch and he grovels and panders to her like a peasant in the presence of a queen."

"Yes," Nicole agreed on a sigh, glancing out the large front window as Joey ushered Melly to his car in the driveway. "She's perfectly horrid."

"Hmm." Jake nodded, watching the couple as well. They both simply stood there, silently watching until Joey had Melly in the car, got in himself, and backed out of the driveway. As the car drove out of sight along the road, Jake announced, "The coffee should be done and the cake is sliced up. Want some?"

"Oh yeah," Nicole said with feeling, turning to lead the way into the kitchen.

"I cut four slices," he commented. "I thought slices rather than bringing the cake out would help prevent Melly from eating three or four slices to purge."

"I guess we'll just have to have two slices each," Nicole said, brightening somewhat. Chocolate always helped, and she suspected it would take two slices to help rid her of the bad taste in her mouth. She couldn't believe Joey was with that horrible woman. Melly was rude, and arrogant and—Really, Nicole couldn't think of a single nice thing to say about the woman . . . except, "She's beautiful."

"She would be if she kept her mouth shut," Jake responded dryly as he fetched two cups and began to pour coffee. Then he added, "Actually, no that's not true. She'd have to stop thinking too. I was trying not to listen, but could hear her thoughts plain as day and not one of them was pleasant. What she actually said was the cream of the crop. That was just selfish stuff. The rest was nasty, critical crap."

Nicole tore her gaze away from the four plates with cake on them that sat on a tray on the kitchen counter, and peered at Jake curiously. "You were trying not to listen? You make it sound like her thoughts are a radio playing. Don't you have to actually read people's thoughts?"

"Sometimes," he said with a shrug. "It's different with different people. It's—" He stopped, frowning as he carried the coffees to the table. Nicole suspected he was trying to figure out how to explain it and waited patiently. As she did, she picked up two of the plates, grabbed a couple of forks and followed Jake. They were seated and fixing their coffees with cream and sugar before he continued.

"Okay, close your eyes and imagine you're in a room full of people. At an art show maybe, a big art show and everyone is standing around talking," he said.

Nicole took her spoon out of her coffee, set it on the edge of her plate and closed her eyes. The scene he suggested immediately sprang up in her mind. A room full of people, drinks in hand, circulating, talking, laughing . . .

"Now, hear their voices. Some are louder than others, right? I mean you can stand in the middle of the room and while most of the talking is just an indistinguishable murmur, you can catch bits of conversation from others more clearly. There's a sudden burst of laughter to your right. Someone to your left is saying in a high, distressed voice, "Oh my God, I can't believe he did that to me." Behind you a sharp angry voice is saying, "What a bitch." Someone else is telling a joke in a too-loud voice that's clear as a bell above the rabble and so on."

"Okay," Nicole murmured when he fell silent. She could picture the whole scene pretty clearly, and imagine the conversations.

"Well, that's what it's like for me with people's thoughts," he explained. "Most of the time, when I'm out in public, there's a constant buzz of people's thoughts and to actually hear a specific person's thoughts I have to focus on them, block out everything else and concentrate on what they are thinking. That's reading them."

Nicole nodded slowly.

"But," he added, "There are other people out there, who think more loudly than others, or whose thoughts are sharp and distinguishable from the general rabble. For them you actually have to try to block their thoughts, but it's like plugging your ears when someone's shouting at you, it usually still gets through."

"And Melly is a shouter with her thoughts?" Nicole asked, finding this information fascinating.

Jake grimaced and nodded. "Her thoughts are deafening. I couldn't even hear the murmur of Joey's thoughts with hers screaming at me."

Nicole picked up her coffee and took a sip, thinking about what he'd said and then she frowned. "It sounds . . . noisy," she finished, but wasn't satisfied with the word. "I mean, you're saying that not only do you hear actual sounds when you're out in the world—and all of them since you say your hearing is superior—but there's also the constant hum of people's thoughts?"

"Unless I'm alone," Jake said, and then added, "Or alone with you."

Right, he couldn't read her, she thought.

"That's one of the reasons why a life mate is so special," he said quietly. "To avoid the constant barrage of sound and thoughts, an unmated immortal has to isolate themselves and too much isolation can lead to an immortal going rogue. But an immortal with a life mate can find peace while still enjoying their company. They don't have to isolate themselves, and the peace they find with that life mate recharges their batteries and allows them to better handle being out in the noisy world. A life mate is soothing."

"I see," Nicole whispered, and she did. She now understood how a life mate would be special. But she grinned suddenly and teased, "So I'm kind of like a tranquilizer for you."

Jake blinked with surprise, whether at the suggestion or because he was surprised to find it true, she didn't know. But then his eyes began to glow and he admitted, "Kind of. But more a cross between a tranquilizer and Viagra."

Nicole felt her face flush. It wasn't with embarrassment. She recognized that silver glow in his eyes. The more passion he experienced, the stronger the silver was in his eyes. She didn't know why that was, but was aware of it and knew his thoughts had shifted to more carnal matters. And that knowledge had her own thoughts heading in that direction as well. Her body was beginning to tingle, her nipples were hardening, and the familiar dampness was growing between her legs.

Damn, all he had to do was look at her and she got wet . . . like some upside-down version of Pavlov's dogs, Nicole thought.

"The chocolate cake is good," Jake said suddenly.

Blinking, Nicole glanced down at her cake. She hadn't even tried it yet.

"But you taste better," Jake added.

Nicole stilled, and then slowly raised her head to peer at him. Oh yeah, his eyes were on fire now . . . and so was she. How the hell did that happen so fast? No kissing, touching, nothing. Just a couple words and she was ready to go.

Jake picked up his plate and coffee and carried them to the island, then returned to stand beside her. Nicole tipped her head back, expecting him to kiss her, but instead he caught her chair and turned it so she faced him. He then scooped her up and set her on the table where his cake had been moments ago.

"These have to go," Jake announced, reaching for the button of her jeans. "You should wear skirts and dresses," he added conversationally as he slid the button free and started on the zipper. "It would make things much easier."

"I'll have to buy some," Nicole said breathlessly as he slid the zipper down.

Jake woke up slumped at the kitchen table, his head in Nicole's lap, exactly where he'd been when he'd passed out. Damn, this life-mate sex was intense, he thought, sitting up and giving his head a shake to try to wake up fully. Pounding and the sound of some power tool caught his attention, and he glanced toward the kitchen door, but the sound seemed to be coming from the main floor.

Wondering what was going on, he started to stand, but then paused as his gaze fell on Nicole again. She was flat on her back on the tabletop, bare from the waist down and legs spread, knees on either side of him and dead to the world. Despite having just woken up from a post-coital fainting spell, the sight was tempting. Although, it hadn't really been coitus, he supposed. Maybe he should move on to that now, Jake thought, his hands sliding up her legs of their own accord.

A smile curved his lips and he began to harden when Nicole shifted on the tabletop and murmured sleepily in response to his touch. The idea of waking her with kisses, pulling her to the edge of the table and sliding into her warm welcoming body grew in his head, and Jake's erection grew with it. Damn, even when unconscious and drooling, the woman was the sexiest thing he'd ever seen.

"Jake?"

Head shooting toward the door, he quickly stepped away from Nicole and rushed to the entry to peer into the living room. Dante was just stepping off the step, heading toward him.

Jake was about to ask him to stop where he was when Dante did so on his own and announced, "Just a heads-up. Those workers you called in to take care of the pictures are done downstairs and ready to start up here."

"Oh." That explained the noise, Jake thought, glancing over his shoulder to Nicole.

"I'll tell them to give you two minutes," Dante said turning back to the stairs before adding, "That way you can wake Nicole and get her dressed before they come up."

Jake's eyes shot back to the man, but he was already out of sight on the stairs.

"And that is why living with immortals who can read you is a pain in the ass," Jake muttered, turning back into the kitchen. His cousin must have read his mind to know Nicole wasn't dressed. That or he'd already been up here before this and had actually seen it, Jake thought and scowled harder. He really needed to remember to make sure they were somewhere private before jumping Nicole.

The problem was, he found it hard to think when she was near. His brain seemed to have one mode right now and that was the "Let's get Nicole naked and . . ." mode. The part after the getting her naked changed with the situation, but it always involved getting her naked. Though he didn't even seem to be able to accomplish that fully, most times. Out of the four interludes so far, she'd been completely naked only once.

Jake didn't wake Nicole, he merely scooped her up and carried her out of the kitchen to the bedroom. But by the time he set her on the bed she was stirring.

"Hi," he said softly when she opened her eyes as he straightened.

"Hi." She smiled uncertainly.

"We had to vacate the kitchen. Workers were about to invade," Jake explained.

"Workers?" Nicole asked, sitting up and peering around with a frown. "Where are my jeans?"

"Oh, crap. Hang on," he muttered and hurried back to the kitchen to retrieve her jeans and panties from the kitchen floor. Men were just coming into sight on the stairs as he hurried back through the living room. Jake slipped back into the master bedroom and then paused. Nicole wasn't on the bed anymore. He relaxed when he heard the water turn on in the bathroom, and then set her jeans and panties on the bed and slid out of the room again to head to the bathroom outside his own room.

Jake quickly relieved himself and washed his face and hands, then headed out to investigate what had been done in the house so far. He nodded in passing at the men working in the loft living room and then hurried down the large, open winding staircase to the main floor. Dante and Tomasso were settled one on each of the couches in this larger living room, working on two large pizzas that lay open on the coffee table between them. An action movie was playing on the big-screen TV at the end of the room.

"Pizza?" Dante offered, lifting the box closest to him for Jake to consider its contents.

"No. Thanks," Jake murmured, his gaze moving to the sliding glass doors next to the big screen. Through it he could see a man standing beside the hot tub, watching a pump spit water out into a large open barrel.

"Did you remind him that the water's poisonous?" Jake asked, eyeing the man. He'd warned him when he'd called, but people sometimes didn't listen.

"Yeah. He's wearing protective gear and that's why it's going in the barrel. He brought several of them to take the water away. He said it probably wasn't a good thing just to pump it out onto the grass and let the ground soak it up," Dante told him and then asked, "When the hell did you call these guys? I thought you were so busy with Nicole you wouldn't think of it. I was going to make the calls myself."

"While I was making coffee when Joey and his girlfriend were here," Jake answered. He'd put the coffee on and quickly made the calls. Quick as he'd been, Jake had barely finished when he'd heard Melly announcing that she wanted to leave. He glanced to Dante and Tomasso now. "She was something else, huh?"

"A bitch," Tomasso rumbled.

"Couldn't get away from her quick enough," Dante said dryly. "Nicole's brother is an idiot to put up with her. She doesn't care about him. All she's thinking about is what he can give her."

"Yeah." Jake grimaced, but then shrugged. "He'll figure it out soon enough.

"You don't think we should give him a heads-up?" Tomasso asked.

"I don't think he'd appreciate it," Jake said mildly, recalling his own resentment when they'd given him much the same message about his fiancée years ago. "Besides, how would you explain knowing?"

Dante and Tomasso both merely nodded, and then glanced past him and smiled.

Glancing over his shoulder, Jake found himself smiling as well. Nicole was coming down the stairs. She'd changed her clothes, put on some makeup, and her hair now flowed in soft golden waves around her shoulders. She was also carrying her purse.

"Where are we going?" he asked with a grin, moving to meet her at the foot of the stairs.

"I'm going shopping," she answered lightly and then blushed and added, "For skirts and dresses."

"Sounds great," Jake said with a grin, and turned to lead the way to the coat closet. And it did sound great. The skirts and dresses had been his suggestion after all and he was thinking about how much easier things would be if she were wearing them instead of jeans. All he'd have to do was lift her skirt and—

"You don't want to come with me," Nicole protested as she followed him to the closet. "You'd be bored to tears."

Pausing, Jake turned to face her and said quietly, "You can't go alone, Nicole. Remember? Your—"

"Oh, right, right," she said with annoyance. "Someone's trying to kill me."

Jake frowned. It seemed while she would now admit someone was out to kill her, Nicole still wouldn't admit it was her soon to be ex-husband. Did that mean she still loved him? She'd claimed she didn't, but then why was she so resistant to acknowledging that he was the only one who would benefit?

"Do you want us to come with you?" Dante asked. "Follow at a distance, maybe, reconnoiter the area and see if anyone follows the two of you?"

"Oh, this is ridiculous," Nicole said with frustration, turning to head for the stairs. "Never mind. I won't go shopping."

"No, wait." Jake hurried after her, grabbing her arm to stop her at the foot of the stairs. "We'll go, just the two of us. It's fine. Besides, I want to help you pick them out . . . and change in and out of them," he added, his voice deepening.

Nicole hesitated, but then smiled crookedly and shook her head. "You're a pervert."

"I am," he acknowledged. "For you."

"Yeah." She sighed. "And the sad thing is, I'm a pervert for you right now too." Shaking her head, she moved past him and back toward the closet again.

Jake grinned at winning the mini battle, and then turned to Dante and Tomasso. Smile fading, he nodded solemnly.

Both men nodded back, equally solemnly, and Jake followed Nicole to the closet to get his coat. The twins would follow at a distance and keep an eye out while ensuring Nicole had no idea. What she didn't know wouldn't hurt her . . . and might just save her life.

Fourteen

"Are you hungry?"

Nicole pulled her gaze from the passing lights going by outside the car window and glanced to Jake as she considered that question. She didn't have to consider it long. Now that he'd asked, she was suddenly aware that her stomach seemed to be trying to eat itself. "Actually, I am."

"Yeah, me too," Jake murmured, his gaze on the road ahead. "We never did get to eat that chocolate cake."

Nicole bit her lip and turned her head out the window again, trying to hide a blush as she recalled why they'd not eaten the cake. They'd had a snack at the food court when they'd first got there, so whether they'd eaten the cake was irrelevant. He'd only brought it up to tease her, she was sure, and she didn't want to give him the reaction he was looking for and let him see she was blushing. With the average guy, Nicole wouldn't have worried he could see her blush in the dark light of dusk, but Jake wasn't your average guy. He'd said immortals had better night vision. How much better, she didn't know.

"Want to order pizza when we get back?" Jake asked now and she could hear the smile in his voice and knew from that, that he was aware that he'd succeeded at making her blush.

"Yes, please," Nicole said sweetly, and when he glanced to her, stuck her tongue out.

Jake burst out laughing at the childish action, and then took one hand off the steering wheel to reach over and squeeze her knee.

"Mmmm," he murmured, as his fingers closed on naked skin. "Or we could eat out."

"You already did," Nicole said, grabbing his hand and removing it when it started to slide up her leg. Damn, just that little touch had fire traveling through her veins. She really shouldn't have agreed to changing into one of the new skirts when he'd suggested it at the mall. They were never going to make it home without stopping at the side of the road at this rate.

"Ms. Phillips!"

She glanced around with surprise at his scandalized tone. "What?"

"Did you just say what you said?" Jake asked, eyes wide and laughing as he glanced from the road to her.

Nicole frowned, not getting it. She— "Oh!" Her eyes widened incredulously as she suddenly understood his play on words. Flushing a brilliant red now, she protested, "I meant at the food court! You ate out at the food court when we first got there." Adding a frustrated "Ohhh," she smacked his arm.

Jake chuckled. "You should have seen your face when you caught on."

"Yeah?" Nicole asked, eyes narrowing. He really was enjoying this, which made her decide that since he so enjoyed tormenting her, she could do a little tormenting of her own. Smiling, she announced, "Well, I think I want dinner out after all."

Jake's eyebrows rose at her change of heart.

"It's probably the only way to ensure I'll get fed within the next several hours," she added dryly.

"Yeah, it is," Jake admitted, mouth spreading wide in an unapologetic smile. He then shrugged. "Sorry. Can't seem to help myself. Every time I touch, smell, or—hell, just look at you—I want to do things that would make a prostitute blush."

Nicole was trying to sort out what those things might be when he asked, "Is there anywhere special you want to go?"

Nicole immediately named a restaurant that she knew had good food, low lighting . . . and booths.

"Okay," Jake turned down the next road to head for Highway 417 and take it across town.

They'd shopped at Bayshore Shopping Centre, a good twenty-minute drive from the restaurant. The drive would give her time to plot her attack. Nicole intended to use the low lighting and privacy of the restaurant booth to drive the man wild, in public, where he couldn't do a thing about it. She suspected it would mean she'd find out what it was like to have sex in the backseat of a car on a dark country road on the way home. But heck, that was an experience she'd missed as a teenager, and new experiences were a good thing. Right?

They'd only been on the highway for a couple of minutes when Nicole was distracted from her plotting by a low curse from Jake. She glanced curiously toward him and then had to grab the overhead grip to steady herself as he suddenly swerved sharply into the outside lane to avoid rear-ending the car in front of them.

"What's wrong?" she asked, noting the frown on his face.

"The brakes aren't working," Jake said through his teeth, hands tightening on the steering wheel.

"Are you sure?" Nicole asked, and then realized how stupid that sounded. Of course, he must be sure. It wasn't like he could be wrong about something like that. Besides, one glance down showed her that he was pumping his foot on the brake, but they weren't slowing at all.

"Yes, honey, I'm sure," he said grimly.

"Sorry, it was a stupid question," she muttered, glancing toward the road ahead. It was clear for a bit, but she could see rear lights in all three lanes about a half mile ahead. "I had the car in for its winterization last week. They checked everything then, including the brakes, and said it was fine."

"Yeah, well they aren't fine now," Jake said quietly. "Worse yet, I've had my foot off the gas pedal for a full minute now and we aren't slowing down."

"Oh, that really isn't good," Nicole said faintly, her eyes shifting back to the road ahead again.

Jake didn't comment. His full attention was apparently on driving . . . or perhaps he was trying to decide what he could do. Sensing movement beside her, she glanced over just in time to see him try the emergency brakes. Nicole instinctively braced herself for an abrupt halt, but nothing happened. Jake didn't look terribly surprised. In fact, he seemed incredibly calm, if extremely grim. Meanwhile, she was having a major panic attack inside.

"What are we going to do?" she asked nervously.

"Downshift," Jake answered, and did just that before hitting the hazard lights.

Nicole bit her lip and glanced out the front window again. They were coming up on the cars quickly and it didn't seem to her that downshifting had worked. Her head swiveled to the window beside her when it started to roll down.

"Wind resistance," Jake shouted over the sudden roar of air rushing into the SUV. "It might help a little."

Nicole nodded, noting that he'd opened all the windows . . . and it was damned cold. But better cold than crashed she supposed, doing up her coat. This really hadn't been the best time to wear a skirt, she decided, regretting changing out of her jeans at the mall.

"I'm going to use the center barrier to try to slow us down," Jake yelled.

Nicole nodded, but didn't bother trying to talk over the wind. Nothing seemed to be working yet. At least, it didn't appear to her that they'd slowed any, but she kept that opinion to herself and let him do what he had to do. Nicole was extremely grateful that Jake was driving though. She'd have tried the emergency brakes, but wouldn't have thought of downshifting, or windows . . . or scraping the car up against the center barrier to try to slow the vehicle. She added that last thought as the tires hit the bottom of the pear-shaped barrier. Nicole had expected the driver's side door to scrape along the concrete, but it was just the tires . . . for now.

She started to bite her lip, and then quickly stopped doing that, afraid that if they crashed, she'd bite it off. Instead, she tightened her hold on the overhead grip and grabbed for the car seat with her other hand and waited.

Nicole was sure what followed only took seconds or a minute or two at the most, but it seemed much longer to her. In fact, the wait seemed interminable, and then they were mere feet behind the three lanes of cars with nowhere to go.

Jake tried hitting the horn repeatedly, but the car in front of them had nowhere to go. There were cars in front of and beside it as well. When the driver of the car beside them apparently saw what was happening and hit the brakes, slowing out of the way and forcing those behind him to do so as well, Jake took a chance and swerved into the middle lane, honking the horn the whole way. Much to Nicole's relief the car in the next lane did the same as the center car had done and slowed quickly.

With a choice between hitting the car in front or veering to the side, Jake was moving into the lane before the car was even fully out of the way. They made it, but barely, and were now in danger of hitting the car in front of them in that lane.

Nicole was panting like a woman in labor as they slid into the opening. If Jake had been a lesser driver, they never would have made it. There was literally a finger's width between them and the car behind them. But they did make it. However, even as he slid fully into the lane, Jake warned, "Hang on," and continued steering to the side, sending the car off the highway altogether.

Nicole held on. She also closed her eyes and began to pray so never saw exactly what happened. She felt it though. The vehicle swerved back toward the highway as if Jake was trying to avoid something and, caught by surprise, Nicole slammed into the side window, her temple bouncing off of it just seconds before they crashed into something. The air bags exploded and the vehicle began to roll even as Nicole lost her hold on consciousness.

Jake tore the empty blood bag from his mouth, and struggled to sit up. "I'm going in."

"No," Tomasso boomed, and forced him back to the van floor with one hand on his shoulder. "You're not ready. Two more bags of blood and fifteen minutes and then you should be okay to go into the hospital."

"I want to see Nicole," Jake growled.

"Dante is with her. She's fine. You need more blood," Tomasso insisted, picking up a full bag. When Jake opened his mouth to argue, he popped the bag on Jake's still extended fangs.

Jake scowled at the large man over the bag at his mouth. It had been seven hours since the accident and he had spent most of that time stuck here in the back of the van, in the hospital parking lot, being fed blood and healing.

Jake hadn't come out of the accident in good shape, although he hadn't known that right away. He'd passed out when the front driver's side had caved in around him, crushing and damned near amputating his left leg. He'd only woken up as Dante and Tomasso were tearing the buckled car door off to get him out of what would have been a metal casket had he been mortal. They'd already got Nicole out and had assured him that other than a head wound she seemed fine. She was lying unconscious in the snow while they worked on getting him out of the crumpled driver's side.

They'd barely managed to get him into their van before the police and ambulance had arrived and had to leave him there while they handled the emergency responders and the gawkers who had stopped. Apparently, they'd smeared some of Jake's blood on Dante's forehead and a little on his clothes and claimed Dante was driving the car, but was fine other than a couple cuts and bruises. Obviously, they'd performed some mind control and memory altering to ensure that tale was believed, because one look at the driver's side of the car would have immediately brought that story into question.

The twins probably would have just wiped memories and sent everybody on their way were it not for the fact that this was obviously another attempt on Nicole's life and they wanted to be sure the police knew about it. She was mortal, and so was her ex-husband. It was better in this instance for the mortal legal system to handle the situation than to step in and take care of it themselves.

Once the police had been seen to, and Nicole was in an ambulance and on her way to the hospital, Dante and Tomasso had returned to their van and followed the ambulance to the hospital. Dante had driven while Tomasso knelt in the back, feeding Jake bag after bag of blood from the van cooler.

At the hospital, Dante had left Tomasso to tend to Jake and went in to answer more police questions and keep tabs on Nicole and how she was doing. She'd hit her head on the side window when Jake had swerved to avoid a head-on collision with a tree. However, his swerving to avoid the one tree had steered the driver's side into another. Jake was okay with that. Better he take the brunt of it than Nicole. But he'd been going so fast the SUV had crumpled on that side, the back end had swung to the right where the land suddenly sloped, and they'd begun to roll just before he passed out from the leg wound.

"That's good enough," Jake said, tearing the latest empty bag away and sitting up. "I want to check on Nicole."

"Dante texted less than ten minutes ago and said she was still resting comfortably," Tomasso pointed out, but didn't force him back to the floor as he had the first time. Instead, he simply reached for another bag.

"But she hasn't regained consciousness yet," Jake said worriedly. "It's been seven hours. I want to see her, make sure she's all right."

"There's nothing you can do for her," Tomasso said with a shrug and held out another bag. When Jake merely scowled at it, Tomasso gave a long-suffering sigh, and then bargained, "One more bag and you can go in."

Jake took the bag and popped it on his fangs, waiting impatiently for it to empty. It didn't take long, but felt like forever to him.

"You can't go like that," Tomasso said as Jake ripped the bag from his mouth and started to scoot along the floor toward the back doors.

Jake glanced down and grimaced at the state of his clothes. The left leg of his jeans was sliced through and hanging from the inside seam, and they were now black all the way through with his blood. His shirt was pretty bloody as well, although Jake suspected that was just transference. The air bags had cocooned his upper body from serious injury.

"Here." Tomasso pulled a shopping bag from the front of the van. "Dante and I did some shopping while we followed you around the mall. There are joggers in there you can borrow."

Jake accepted the bag with relief and quickly sorted through the contents until he found a jogging suit. The twins were built like linebackers and he had no doubt he would be swimming in them, but beggars couldn't be choosers.

He'd thought the worst of his healing was over, but as Jake stripped his jeans and pulled on the jogging pants, it became clear that wasn't the case. While his leg had reknitted where it had been almost amputated, and there was a large healing scab no doubt most of the way around his upper leg, it hurt like the devil to move it. The muscles and tendons and bones were no doubt still reknitting inside the leg. But Jake merely ground his teeth together and kept moving. He had to see Nicole. She should have regained consciousness by now.

The leg buckled under him when Jake opened the van's back door and started to get out. Fortunately, Tomasso immediately grabbed his arm to support him, keeping him from falling. He kept that hold on his arm as he got out behind him, and closed the van door. He then walked him into the hospital, half holding him up. Once inside, Tomasso grabbed a wheelchair, urged Jake into it and wheeled him into the elevators and up to Nicole's room.

Dante was seated in a chair next to the hospital bed when Tomasso wheeled Jake in. Since Dante's chair was on the side closest to the door, Tomasso wheeled Jake around to the far side so that he could get him as close to Nicole's face as possible.

"How is she doing?" Jake asked worriedly, leaning forward to peer at Nicole's pale face as Tomasso moved back around the bed to Dante's side.

Dante hesitated and then simply said, "The nurse keeps coming in and flashing a light in her eyes, but she hasn't stirred yet."

Jake frowned and brushed the hair off of Nicole's forehead. She had an ugly bump and bruise on her right temple and he eyed it unhappily, thinking of about a million things he could have done differently to have avoided her getting hurt.

"You did the best you could," Dante said quietly. "She'll come around."

Jake didn't respond and after several moments of silence had passed, Dante stood up. "I'm going to go find the food court and see what's available. Do you two want anything?"

"I'll come with you," Tomasso said as Jake shook his head.

"We'll be back," Dante assured him and Jake nodded without glancing around as they left.

He seemed to have sat there, repeatedly brushing

his fingers over Nicole's cheek for a long time when someone entered the hospital room. Expecting it to be Dante and Tomasso, or the nurse, Jake glanced toward the door and froze briefly, shock rippling through him when he saw who it was.

"Neil." The name slipped from his lips, barely a breath of sound.

"Why so surprised?" His younger brother smiled crookedly. "You should have known Dante and Tomasso would call and let us know about the accident. We're family."

A breathless laugh slipped from Jake now, some of the tension that had claimed him slipping out with it. "Yeah. I guess I should have known."

Neil nodded and moved forward. "How are you?"

Jake shrugged. "Okay now, but I got banged up pretty good. My side of the SUV was crushed like a stomped-on pop can. I lost a lot of blood and I was trapped, but Dante and Tomasso weren't far behind us and pulled me out." He smiled crookedly. "They peeled the metal away as easily as peeling an orange. My leg was sliced pretty much straight through, but they managed to get me out without it coming off completely, and then they put me in their van while they handled the scene. Fortunately, they've been keeping their blood in the back of their van since arriving at Nicole's, and they started feeding it to me the minute they could get away from the police."

Neil's eyebrows rose. "Hell, I didn't know the accident was that bad. I'm glad you didn't lose the leg."

Now it was Jake's turn to raise his eyebrows.

"Wouldn't it have grown back? I'd think the nanos would feel that two legs were necessary to be at peak condition."

Neil looked surprised at the question. "I don't know. I've never heard of an immortal losing a limb. I know a couple who have suffered a bad enough wound the limb was hanging by a bare thread of skin and it healed. But I don't know if the nanos are capable of actually replacing a whole limb." He smiled wryly, and added, "And since the only way to find out is to cut off a limb and wait, I don't think I really want to know."

"No," Jake agreed.

Neil hesitated, and then said, "Actually, when I asked how you are, I didn't mean physically. I can see you're recovered from the accident."

"Oh," Jake flushed. Neil meant was he over the snit he'd been in since waking up to find he was an immortal . . . or really since he was eighteen and found out about immortals. Had he accepted the turn and emotionally adjusted to it? Was he willing to be welcomed back into the fold of the family and stop shunning them like lepers?

"I'm sorry," Jake said finally. "I realize now that I acted like an ass and you guys deserve better."

Neil tilted his head slightly. "So you're okay with everything?"

"Yeah," Jake said slowly, "I think I am." Smiling apologetically, he admitted, "Having to explain everything to Nicole helped me see things more clearly."

Neil glanced to Nicole at the mention of her name and Jake did as well.

Reaching out, he brushed her cheek. "I've been

running around thinking you all were monsters and that I was too now that I was immortal. But telling Nicole that I hadn't changed inside and that I was still the man I used to be before the change, with the same beliefs and feelings as I had before ... Well, I realized that was true ... and that it was probably true for all immortals. I mean, Mom was still a great mom, and Roberto was a good father to us both and you were a good brother. The only thing that changed when I found out about immortals, and that you were all members of that select group, was me. You didn't change in your attitude to me, but my perspective and how I treated you guys changed. Explaining it to Nicole made me realize that immortals are just people, but with some extraordinary gifts."

"Then thank God for Nicole," Neil said with feeling.

Jake chuckled and reached out to take her hand where it lay on top of the sheets and hospital blanket. "Yeah. Thank God for Nicole."

Neil moved closer to the bed and peered down at her face silently for a moment, and then announced, "She's pretty."

"She's fricking beautiful," Jake corrected and added softly, "The most beautiful woman I've ever met."

"Yeah, you're in love," Neil said with amusement and when Jake glanced to him with surprise, he shrugged and said, "She's pretty bro, but I've seen prettier . . . and so have you. So it must be love that is making her the most beautiful woman you've ever met."

"Love," Jake murmured with a frown as he

peered back at Nicole. He liked and cared about her. Nicole was a good person, with a big heart and an almost naïve trust in the goodness of people. She was also creative, talented, and funny. Jake found he was often smiling or laughing with her. He had fun with Nicole. Hell, he'd even had fun shopping with her today and Jake wasn't a fan of shopping. But in love?

In lust, maybe. He would accept that. The woman was hot. She smiled and he got a semi erection. She touched him, even just a brush of her fingers on his arm, and that semi turned into a full-on nuclear erection. But when she kissed him? Forget about it. His blood immediately went south leaving his brain a bloodless blob incapable of functioning.

"Isn't the combination of all of that what makes up love?" Neil asked quietly, obviously reading his mind.

"Maybe," Jake allowed, and then argued, "But we've only known each other a matter of days. It can't be love already."

"Man," Neil said with disbelief. "You've spent most of your life around immortals, have even been one yourself for seven years now, and yet still think like a mortal."

"I'm not sure—" Jake began.

"Time means little to immortals and absolutely nothing when it comes to life mates," Neil said, interrupting him.

"Ah." Jake smiled crookedly. "So Dante and Tomasso told you about that too?"

"About Nicole being your life mate? Yes." He peered at her and then said quietly, "I'm happy for you . . . envious too," he added with a small smile.

"But mostly happy for you. Especially since her arrival appears to have helped you deal with things."

"Do I need to apologize again?" Jake asked wryly. "I probably should. I haven't been fair with you and Mother, or Roberto and the others."

"We understood you were struggling with it," Neil said quietly. "We wished we could help more, and were sorry you felt you needed to be alone to handle it, but we understood."

"Thank you," Jake said quietly.

"Mind you, you'll pay for it where Mom is concerned," Neil added dryly.

"How?" Jake asked warily.

"Well, after seven years of your absence, she's going to want to spend time with you . . . a lot of it. I suspect she'll show up and plant herself for a while until she's reassured everything is okay and her oldest baby boy is her baby again."

Jake managed not to wince. He loved his mother, always had, even while being afraid of her. But he knew her well enough to know Neil was right. The woman would no doubt head out here from whichever home base—

"Are they coming from Italy?" he asked.

Neil shook his head. "California."

That made Jake's eyebrows rise. "Then I'm surprised she didn't fly out with you."

"I was in Toronto. Business," Neil added. "I would have been here sooner, but I was in the middle of a business meeting when Dante called and didn't call back to find out what was happening until it ended. Then I had to arrange for a flight."

Jake nodded. It was now two o'clock in the

morning. The accident had taken place around five. It was only an hour and a half from Toronto to Ottawa by flight so it must have been an important meeting. That or it had taken quite a while to arrange a plane to bring him here. Either way, Jake had no doubt his brother had got here as quickly as he could.

"I called Mom after I got off the phone with Dante, that was about three hours ago," Neil said, hesitated, and then added, "She and Dad are on a plane right now, headed this way."

Jake stiffened at that news, his eyes shooting to his brother. "No."

Neil nodded, looking almost apologetic.

"Damn," Jake muttered, glancing to Nicole and worrying about what that might mean. He wasn't sure she was ready to meet his parents. Good Lord, they'd only met themselves days ago.

"Look on the bright side, you'll have extra help keeping her safe," Neil pointed out.

Jake nodded. That would be good, he supposed. Once their flight landed, he'd have his parents and Neil there as well as Dante and Tomasso to help keep Nicole safe and they obviously needed the help. Her soon to be ex would be desperate when he knew this latest attempt had failed.

Thoughts halting, Jake glanced at Neil. "Dante told you about Nicole's ex?"

"Marguerite did. I've been in Toronto for almost a week. I was there when the hot tub incident happened. I was going to drop everything and come out here then, but she cautioned against it. She thought it would be better if Dante and Tomasso came alone."

Jake smiled crookedly. "She was probably right. I wasn't really ready to be pulled back into the fold yet, but those two are . . ." He shook his head helplessly. The twins were not generally the talkative sorts to start with, so hadn't bombarded him with arguments for why he was being an ass. They'd just stood by, strong, silent support while he'd figured it out for himself. Neil would have tried to talk him around and Jake hadn't been ready for that.

Marguerite was apparently a brilliant strategist, Jake thought, and then glanced to the door as Dante and Tomasso entered.

"We brought you a coffee," Dante announced, crossing the room and moving around the bed to offer Jake a cup of Tim Horton's coffee, even as he glanced over to take note of Neil's presence.

"Sorry, Neil. We didn't bring you one," Tomasso said. "Didn't know you were here."

"That's all right. I don't drink coffee," Neil said.

"Caffeine makes him bounce off the walls," Jake told them. Some immortals simply couldn't handle coffee. Neil was one of those and that was why Jake had avoided coffee since being turned. He'd been afraid he might react the same way. They were half brothers after all. However, it seemed that sensitivity to caffeine came from Neil's father, because Jake had been drinking coffee since meeting Nicole and hadn't noticed it affecting him much at all.

Dante nodded and then glanced to Nicole. "How's she doing? Any change?"

Jake opened the tab of his coffee lid and shook his head. "She hasn't stirred at all."

"It's probably for the best. She's going to have

one hell of a headache when she wakes up. Better to sleep through it," Dante said.

Jake grunted as he sipped at his coffee. He didn't mind her sleeping through the headache . . . so long as she woke up. He was very aware that Nicole was a fragile mortal, and mortals had been known to die from head wounds. That thought had him peering at her worriedly. "Maybe I should turn her."

"She's fine," Neil said quietly.

"You can't turn her," Tomasso rumbled. "She needs to give permission."

"What if she doesn't wake up to give that permission?" Jake asked grimly.

The twins exchanged a glance and it was Neil who said, "Why don't we just wait and see what happens? You remember how you reacted to being turned without giving permission. You don't want that with Nicole."

Jake grimaced as he realized he was thinking of doing exactly what Vincent had done and which he'd resented so much. He was just so worried that she wasn't waking up . . . that she might never wake up.

"We'll wait and see what the doctors say. If it doesn't look like she's going to come around, then we'll consider turning her," Neil said patiently.

"Do I smell coffee?"

Jake stilled at that weak question, and then turned his head sharply to Nicole. This time her eyes were open. Her nose was also working, sniffing the air with interest, but then she frowned and asked, "Why does my head hurt so much?"

Fifteen

Nicole yawned sleepily and opened her eyes to stare at the ceiling. It took one glance to recall that she was in the hospital. The slightly antiseptic smell helped.

"How is your head, dear?"

Nicole turned to peer blankly at the woman at her bedside. She was young, with short blond hair, and a nice smile. From the way she'd addressed her, Nicole had expected an older woman, but they were about the same age.

"Er . . ." she murmured, uncertainly, wondering where Jake was. He'd been sitting where the woman presently was when Nicole had finally fallen asleep. That was after the doctor had been informed she was awake and had come to see her. He'd quickly examined her and then announced she seemed fine, but he wanted to keep her overnight for observation. Since it was three in the morning by the time he announced that, it hadn't seemed worth arguing over.

Nicole had managed to stay awake for a bit, long enough to learn what had happened after she'd passed out, and that she had Dante's using mind control to thank for the private hospital room she'd woken up in. Those mind-control skills of theirs were really very impressive, she thought. But then there was a lot to be impressed by with these immortals, or at least with Jake. Well, she supposed Dante and Tomasso were impressive too, but Jake was special. The man was smart, which she wasn't sure could be attributed to the nanos, but they probably didn't hurt. Aside from that, though, he was strong and funny and the most amazing lover ever. All the man had to do was kiss her and her toes curled. As for the sex itself, that was mind-blowing . . . and he had a cute ass too. Jake had thought her tendency to slow down and lag behind at the end of their shopping trip was because she was tiring, but the truth was Nicole had just enjoyed looking at his butt in his tight jeans as they walked.

A choked chuckle came from the blond. The unexpected and unwarranted sound made Nicole peer at her warily, suddenly worried that she was a patient who had wandered down from the psychiatric department. Was that possible? They wouldn't just let psychiatric patients wander the hospital, would they?

A startled laugh slipped from the woman now, and she shook her head, "Oh dear, I'm sorry. I should have introduced myself."

When the woman then held out her hand, Nicole eyed it with trepidation.

"My name is Elaine Colton Notte. I'm Stephano's mother."

"You're Jake's mother?" Nicole gasped, sitting up and gaping at her. She also finally took note of the woman's silver-teal eyes. Oh yeah, this was Jake's mom. It was like his eyes were looking back at her out of the woman's face. Good Lord, Jake's mom, she thought. It wasn't the fact that Elaine Notte looked so young that stunned Nicole. It was her being there at all that had her staring at her, tongue-tied and amazed.

"Yes, dear." Elaine reached out and patted her hand reassuringly. She might not look older, but she definitely acted like a mother who could be a grandmother if only her children would cooperate. "We headed out as soon as we heard about the car accident. We would have come after the hot-tub incident had anyone bothered to tell us," she added grimly.

"I'm sorry," Nicole said at once. "I called Marguerite because Jake made me, but I didn't know your number, or I would have—"

"Oh, my dear, please, I wasn't blaming you," Mrs. Notte interrupted quickly, patting her hand again. "I meant my son Neil. He knew and should have called, but didn't."

"And I shall be in the dog house for at least a century for that," a voice said from the door and Nicole glanced over to see two men entering. Both had short jet-black hair, and very Italian features. Both also looked to be in their mid- to late twenties, wore what she guessed were designer suits, and had amazing silver-black eyes. She was guessing the one who had spoken was Neil, but hadn't a clue who the other man was. Jake's stepfather maybe?

"Yes, this is my husband, Roberto Conti Notte," Elaine said proudly, reminding Nicole that these people could read her mind. Turning to Neil, she added in a grim voice, "And yes you will be in the doghouse for a very long time. I should have known if your brother was in trouble."

"Oh, come on, Mom," Neil chided, walking up behind her chair and squeezing her shoulder. "I didn't want to worry you. Besides, you're really just annoyed that you didn't know about Nicole until after everyone else did."

Elaine scowled at him. "I should have known about that right away too."

Bending, he kissed her cheek. "How about I promise you'll be the first one I call when I meet my life mate?"

"I should be anyway," she muttered, glowering over her shoulder at him.

"Don't worry, son," the man who was apparently Jake's stepfather said with amusement. "It won't take your mama a century to get over this. You know how soft a heart she has. A decade at most and she'll stop bringing it up and glaring at you."

"I won't," Elaine assured them. "This upset me very much."

Nicole watched this all wide-eyed, wondering where on earth Jake was. It seemed like his whole family was here, but him . . . and why was his whole family here? In her hospital room? When he wasn't?

Elaine turned apologetically to Nicole. "I'm so sorry, dear. Of course you are wondering where your Jake is." She smiled at her widely as if Nicole's wondering was to be expected and something to be celebrated. "I should have told you at once. I insisted Tomasso and Dante take Jake home to shower and change. His shirt had blood all over it and his borrowed jogging pants kept falling down." She wrinkled her nose and added, "He was beginning to smell a bit rank too."

"Oh," Nicole said weakly, kicking herself for forgetting about the mind reading. Sheesh, she needed to keep that in mind and—Oh good Lord, hadn't she been thinking something about Jake's fine butt earlier?

"Yes, but it's okay," Elaine assured her. "Stephano does have a fine behind. He got that from his father. A good man with a fine mind and an even finer ass."

"Oh God," Nicole breathed weakly.

"Mother!" Neil protested.

"What?" Elaine glanced at her son, her nose in the air. "I've heard much worse from your thoughts over time. Besides, your father already knows about Stephano's father. He loved his first wife as much as I loved my first husband. He understands."

"I do indeed," Roberto said with amusement. "Your mother, she is nothing if not honest. It is part of the reason I love her. Besides, she assures me while I cannot compare with her first husband when it comes to his behind, I kick his fine ass when it comes to the bedding. To be fair though, he *was* a mere mortal."

Neil was squawking with alarm and embarrassment at this, but Nicole was peering at the elder

Notte man curiously. He had a very thick Italian accent, but his speech was . . . well, it sounded kind of . . . antique? It was the only word she could think to describe it. If she closed her eyes, she'd think a television show was on that was set in the Renaissance or something.

"Yes, well, that's understandable, dear. Roberto is very old." Elaine patted her hand again. "He's been around for centuries. I'd tell you how many, but it makes him self-conscious."

Nicole smiled uncertainly. She was feeling rather as if she'd been knocked senseless. Oh wait, I have, she thought wryly and blushed when Elaine, Roberto, and Neil all chuckled. Right, they can hear my thoughts.

"Yes, and it's not fair," Elaine said apologetically.

"What's not fair?"

Nicole glanced to the door, relief flowing through her as Jake walked in with Dante and Tomasso on his heels. He had obviously showered, shaved, changed his clothes and returned without dawdling. While the man's face was clean shaven, his hair was still damp.

"Mom's reading Nicole's mind and seeing that she thinks you have a fine ass," Neil said drolly.

The twins burst out laughing at the announcement, and Jake grinned widely, but Nicole closed her eyes and wished herself anywhere but there. This was really too much. The poisoning, learning about vamp—immortals, she corrected herself silently, the car accident, and now her lover's family had invaded her hospital room.

Dear God, she was meeting the family, Nicole realized with dismay. Already. This was something that usually didn't happen for—well, at least until you had a bloody date. That thought made her realize that she was sleeping with a man that she'd never even gone on a date with.

I'm such a ho', she thought with dismay. What must his mother think of Jake hooking up with such a skanky chick?

"All right, all boys out of the room," Elaine ordered abruptly.

"Ah," Neil complained. "Things were really starting to get interesting."

"Neil," Elaine snapped, and then glanced to her husband. "Roberto, darling, take the boys down to the hospital cafeteria and buy them ice cream."

"Mother, we're not children anymore," Neil muttered as his father caught his arm and pushed him toward the door.

"You'll always be my child," Elaine said with unconcern as Neil and the twins filed out. Glancing at Jake, who hadn't moved, she said, "You too, Stephano."

"But—"

"Now," Elaine ordered. "In fact, go find Nicole's doctor and tell him to sign her out or whatever it is doctors do. We are taking her home."

Jake hesitated briefly, but apparently decided that was a good idea and turned to head out with a nod.

Elaine immediately turned to Nicole. "I'll have to be quick. He won't stay away long, so forgive me if in my attempt to be quick, I'm less than delicate."

When she paused briefly, Nicole nodded that she understood. Apparently that was all she was waiting for; the woman immediately launched into it.

"Fifty-some years ago I was sitting exactly where you are."

"In a hospital bed?" Nicole asked uncertainly.

Elaine gave a breathless laugh. "No dear, I mean that's when Roberto came into my life. I was newly widowed, raising a young son on my own, working two jobs to make ends meet, and taking night courses to try to better myself and make more money. I had no time or interest in men, and then came Roberto." She sighed, her eyes misting as she looked into the past. "I loved my first husband, dearly, Nicole. He was a very good man. He loved Stephano and me more than anything else in the world and treated us like gold."

Her gaze focused on Nicole again, and she said solemnly, "I know that wasn't your experience with your husband, but the end result was the same. I was heartbroken and even angry at him when he went and died on me, just as you are heartbroken and angry over the failure of your marriage."

"How did Jake's father die?" Nicole asked quietly.

"A heart attack." Elaine shook her head, her expression suggesting she was still bewildered by it. "He was only twenty-five years old, and appeared healthy and well on the surface, but apparently there was something wrong with his heart. He had a heart attack at the wheel on the way home from work one night and . . ." She shrugged helplessly.

"I'm sorry," Nicole murmured.

"There is nothing to be sorry for. I was fortunate to have enjoyed the time with him that I did . . . and I like to think a part of him lives on in Stephano."

Nicole nodded, but every time the woman called Jake Stephano, she felt a momentary confusion and disorientation. He just wasn't Stephano to her. He was Jake.

"Anyway, the point is, I was young and mortal once too, nursing a broken heart, afraid to love again and risk yet another heartbreak . . . and I want to tell you, not as Steph—Jake's mother," she corrected herself gently with a smile for Nicole that suggested she'd read how the use of his proper name threw her off. "As a woman, not Jake's mother, I want to tell you that this risk is well worth it."

Elaine let her consider that briefly and then said, "But you need to know that the normal mortal courting rules do not apply with these men. You cannot judge your behavior or theirs by mortal standards. The passion comes hard and fast, as it is meant to. I think it is how the nanos bond you at first, or perhaps how they ensure you do not let your fears make you think your way out of the relationship. Like with cats in heat in nature, the nanos seem to do something similar with life mates, both mortal and immortal. Your hormones are no doubt going crazy. He is probably releasing pheromones at an accelerated pace that you can't resist."

Elaine patted Nicole's hand and stared her in the eyes as she said solemnly, "You are not a "ho'." Grinning then, she added, "Or if you are, than I guess I am too . . . along with every other female who has found themselves in this most enviable position."

"Is it enviable?" Nicole asked quietly.

Elaine nodded solemnly. "It most certainly is. I

have been with Roberto for fifty-some years and every day is as good or better than the one before. My first husband made me as happy as any mortal could, but the happiness I've experienced with Roberto surpasses that a hundredfold. And it will be the same for you and Jake."

"You sound pretty certain about that," Nicole said, wishing she could believe her.

"I am very certain. I have never yet met life mates who are not as happy as Roberto and myself. The nanos are never wrong," she assured her and then squeezed her hand. "Believe me . . . if you allow your fears to convince you to pass this up, you will never again find the happiness you can have with my son."

Nicole stared silently at Elaine Notte. She really wanted to believe her, because—Nicole cut off her own thought there, unwilling to finish it.

"Because you're afraid you're already half in love with my son," Elaine finished for her and then smiled sympathetically and said, "You're wrong."

Nicole blinked in surprise at the words. "I am?"

Elaine nodded. "You're not half in love with him, you just love him, plain and simple," she assured her, and then added, "I can read your mind, dear. I can see that you think you may only be on the way to loving him, but I can also see the veils and subterfuge you have put in place to protect yourself from admitting that you do love him. The logic you're using that claims it's too soon. But it isn't. You love the man you think Jake is, but are afraid he's not that man and is presenting only what he thinks you want him to be. But he isn't playing games. What you see is what you get with Jake and he is every bit the man he seems to you: smart, funny, brave, and considerate. You love the man this time, not the idea."

Nicole let the words resound inside her head briefly, but then glanced toward the door as Jake returned to the room.

"The doctor is signing the release papers right now. We can take her home," he announced with a smile. "I ran into Father and Neil on the way back and they're off finding a wheelchair for her."

"Do Dante and Tomasso know?" Elaine asked, standing up. "Or are they busy trying to eat the cafeteria out of food?"

"They know," Jake said, his smiled fading before he added, "They went down to check the vehicles and be sure they haven't been tampered with before we leave."

Elaine nodded, apparently unsurprised, and then glanced to Nicole. "You don't want to wear that hospital gown home. Where did they put your clothes, dear?"

"Do you want another pillow behind your back? Or maybe another blanket?"

"No," Nicole said on a laugh. "Jake, I'm fine, really. Stop fussing."

"You just got out of the hospital, Nicole. I'm sup-posed to fuss," he said mildly, glancing around the bedroom.

"I only bumped my head. It's fine now. I—what are you looking for?" she interrupted herself to ask.

"The television remote," Jake muttered, moving over to the love seat against the wall beyond the bed and across from the TV. "You can watch television and relax while I get you something to eat and drink."

Nicole frowned. Relaxing in bed watching television sounded delightful . . . and decadent. She hadn't watched TV in what seemed like months. Her workload was too full for that. Reminded of her workload, she immediately felt guilty and began to push aside the sheets and blankets he'd just finished arranging over her. "I should really go down to the studio and—"

"Do not even think about getting up," Jake barked, whirling on her, remote in hand. Striding back, expression grim, he added, "The doctor only agreed on your release if you relaxed today and that's what you're going to do. Tomorrow, if you don't have a headache and everything seems fine, you can go down to the studio. But for one day you will relax. Doctor's orders.

Nicole heaved an irritated sigh and pulled the sheet and blankets back over herself, but she also stuck her tongue out at Jake for being so bossy. However, the truth was, she liked his bossiness right now, and his concern. Rodolfo would have told her to suck it up and get back to work. The world didn't care if she had a little headache, she had deadlines to meet and she should get to it. Rodolfo hadn't been a very sympathetic fellow. During their two-year marriage, he'd urged and even insisted she work while down with a fever of 104 due to pneumonia, and then another time when she had a broken ankle. Painting while delirious was really not very smart, but standing on a broken leg for hours on end had been worse. Incidents like that had made it hard to believe he cared about anything but the money she made for him to spend.

"There." Jake turned away from the television as it came on and carried the remote to her. "Find something you want to watch and we'll cuddle in bed and eat lunch while we watch it when I come back."

"You cuddle?" Nicole asked with interest. That seemed to be something most men avoided like the plague as far as she could tell.

"Oh, baby," he said, dropping the remote in her lap and placing his hands flat on the bed to lean in and growl, "I'm just a big old teddy bear when it comes to cuddling."

He was close enough she felt his breath on her lips as he spoke, and then Jake kissed her. She suspected he'd meant it to be a quick brush of lips before leaving, but it didn't end up that way. Quite simply, it couldn't end up that way. The moment his lips touched hers, the passion that always seemed to lie in waiting roared up between them like a backdraft exploding up a long hallway when a door was opened. In the next moment, Nicole somehow found herself flat on her back in the bed with him crawling on top of her, his hands seeking out all her hot spots through the flannel pajamas she'd changed into on getting home.

Nicole wasn't still under the onslaught; her own hands were pulling at his clothes, tearing at them desperately as she alternately sucked at his tongue and thrust her own out to tangle with it.

"Yo, Stephano!" Dante said from the open door. "Your mom wants you in the kitchen . . . now. And get off that poor girl or I'll find a pail of water to dump on you. Nicki has a concussion."

Jake groaned into her mouth, then slowly disentangled himself and crawled off the bed, saying, "I'll make you grilled cheese and tomato soup . . . and ginger ale and orange juice."

Nicole blinked with surprise. "That's what my mother always made for me when I wasn't feeling well."

"Yeah? So did mine," Jake said with a grin and then he was gone.

Nicole stared after him for a minute, and then glanced to the television. She picked up the remote and pulled up the guide, looking for something interesting, but it was the middle of the afternoon on a weekday. Talk shows seemed to be the only thing on and she wasn't big on talk shows. She continued to click through the guide, but her mind began to wander to wondering what Jake was doing. He was making them lunch, of course, but how far had he got? And did he like his tomato soup made with water or milk? Her mother had always used milk and Nicole did as well. It was too acidy for her taste with just water.

Maybe she should just go out and see if he used water or milk. She could always sit at the island and chat to him while he cooked. That would still be relaxing, wouldn't it?

"Ugh," Nicole muttered as she realized how pathetic she was. The man had just left her and she wanted to follow him like a lost puppy following a kid home from school. How pathetic was that?

It was the nanos' fault, she told herself. Elaine had said so. She wasn't supposed to judge herself by normal—or mortal—standards. This situation was neither normal, nor mortal.

Gad, Nicole realized with a grin. The woman had basically given her permission to just follow her instincts and act like a ho' . . . guilt free.

"Cool," she muttered. Tossing the sheet and blankets aside, Nicole looked around for her robe. She'd donned it over her pajamas after changing out of her street clothes at Jake's insistence on arriving home. Now she couldn't recall what she'd—oh, there it was, she'd laid it over the end of the bed and then tossed the blankets over it to get up.

Pulling it on, Nicole left the room in search of Jake.

"So she now accepts that someone is out to kill her, but still doesn't accept that it's her husband," Elaine Notte murmured thoughtfully and Jake glanced around to where his mother sat at the kitchen table with his brother, stepfather and the twins.

"She doesn't?" he asked with a frown. "Still? After everything that has happened?"

"No, I'm afraid from the thoughts I've read she's completely bewildered as to who could be causing these events, but she's quite sure it's not her husband."

"Ex-husband," Jake growled, turning back to give the soup in the pot a stir and flip the grilled cheese in the frying pan.

"He's not quite yet her ex, dear," his mother said gently.

It made Jake want to growl. He didn't like the

idea that any man had a claim to Nicole, no matter how short term or tenuous.

"Well, it doesn't matter what she thinks, someone is out to kill her and they aren't going to stop now," Neil said quietly. "I suggest the two of you stick close to home until this is resolved."

Jake frowned at the suggestion. "I was thinking of taking her out for dinner and a movie either tomorrow night or the night after . . . if I can drag her away from work," he added wryly.

"Well, that's just not really a good idea right now, bro," Neil said and then pointed out, "She's mortal, which makes her vulnerable, and someone's trying to kill her." When Jake turned a scowl on him for his advice, Neil added, "Although, I suppose if we came with you, we might be able to keep her safe between us all."

"I believe Stephano was thinking more along the lines of a date than a family outing," Roberto said with amusement.

"Oh." Neil frowned.

"Neil wouldn't know about dating," Dante said, sitting back in his chair with a grin. "His head's too full of numbers and quarterly reports to think about such things."

"I date," Neil said defensively.

"When?" Tomasso asked with amusement.

"Last—" He frowned and muttered, "Well it couldn't have been more than—" Shaking his head, he scowled and said, "I have a very busy life now that Stephan—Jake isn't there to carry the daytime burden at V.A. Inc."

Jake glanced around with surprise. "Didn't Vincent hire a replacement for me?"

"Of course he did," Neil muttered. "But the man is mortal and doesn't know about us. I spend more time trying to ensure he doesn't find out about us than I do getting work done. It's frustrating as hell." He scowled briefly, and then sighed and grimaced at Jake. "Sorry. Not your problem."

Jake turned back to the food he was cooking, but he was frowning now. He hadn't thought about how his leaving would affect his brother. Or anyone else for that matter. He'd been pretty wrapped up in his own hurts, real or imagined. Now he kind of felt guilty. He suspected it was a feeling he should get used to. There had no doubt been more fallout than that from his running away.

"Back to the issue at hand," his mother said firmly. "The best way to handle this is to hunt down her husband, read his mind to ensure he is behind all of this, and then take care of the problem."

"And how would you take care of the problem?"

Jake stiffened and then whirled toward the kitchen door to see Nicole standing there in a fluffy white housecoat, and fluffier pink slippers, peering in at them all worriedly.

Sixteen

"You shouldn't be out of bed," Jake said with concern, turning off both burners under the food he was cooking and rushing over to urge Nicole back to the bedroom.

She, however, wouldn't be urged, but stood her ground and said quietly, "I need to know."

"It's nothing as sinister as you're thinking," his mother said.

Jake glanced from one woman to the other, wondering what exactly Nicole was thinking.

"We wouldn't kill him or anything. We'd just perform a mind wipe and check him into a psychiatric hospital where he could spend the rest of his days."

"Where he could spend the rest of his days mindless and drooling on himself," Nicole said dryly. "You think that is better than killing him?"

"If he's the one behind these attacks, he deserves that and more," Jake said grimly.

"Well, at least you added the if," Nicole said stiffly.

Jake peered at her helplessly. "I know you don't want to believe that your ex-husband is trying to kill you, but—"

"It isn't Rodolfo," Nicole said firmly. "I'll admit, someone appears to be trying to kill me . . . or maybe you," she added, and pointed out, "You were the one poisoned in the hot tub, and you were in the SUV with me."

"That's true," his mother said and peered at him with worry. "Have you made enemies since leaving California, son?"

Jake scowled. "No. Besides, no one knows I'm here but you guys, and, while the last two attacks have hit or included me, you're forgetting the car that nearly ran you down in the Canadian Tire parking lot."

Nicole waved that away. "A bad driver."

Jake's mouth tightened. "And the gas issues?"

"The gas issues?" Neil asked with interest.

"The furnace was fiddled with, the doors blocked closed, the gas grill was pulled out of its housing and something was wrong with the fireplace," he listed quickly and then frowned at his brother. "Didn't Marguerite explain that to you?"

"Those were just . . ." Nicole waved her hand impatiently, apparently not sure what to call them. "Look, the furnace thing wasn't deadly. It just knocked the heat out and was an inconvenience." Frowning she added, "I told you he took cords and whatnot from things and removed two chairs. And look at what he did with the pictures. He—"

"The pictures?" Roberto interrupted curiously.

"Her ex-husband crazy glued framed pictures of them to the walls all over the house," Jake explained. "I had to call in some wall guys to remove them and fix the walls where they'd been glued."

"Thank you for that," Nicole said quietly. "I meant to thank you as we were leaving the house to go shopping and then you asked me which car I wanted to take and I got distracted."

Jake nodded stiffly. "You're welcome."

"Anyway," Nicole sighed. "The furnace was just another bit of his trying to bug the hell out of me," she said quietly. "The worst it could have done was let the house go cold and make me call in the furnace guy. All it did was cost me money, just like everything else he's done."

"Are you sure he knew that?" Jake asked. "Marguerite said his furnace in Italy was older, and could have blown up had he done it there," he pointed out and then added, "And he put the wood in the door's tracks *outside*, blocking them from opening. That was obviously an effort to trap you inside when the furnace exploded."

"No, that was Rodolfo being the idiot he is," she responded dryly. "He was always doing stupid things like that. The man was cute, with a sexy accent, but he wasn't the brightest lightbulb in the chandelier."

"Or maybe he's smarter than you think," Jake said grimly. "Your doors are keyed, and you wouldn't have thought to grab them had you woken up to find the house on fire."

"No I wouldn't, but I also wouldn't have run downstairs into the fire. I would have gone out the balcony door off my bedroom, which wasn't blocked," she pointed out impatiently, and then added, "And if I was sleep addled and stupid enough to run downstairs without keys, I would have just gone out through the garage."

Jake frowned at the logic in that. "What about the gas grill?"

Nicole sighed. "Like I said, he wasn't the brightest bulb in the chandelier. He was also lazy and didn't like cleaning. He put foil in the bottom of the oven to catch drippings and I imagine he did the same thing with the grill."

"But the flames couldn't have got through the foil to cook food," Jake pointed out.

"No," she agreed dryly. "I did mention he wasn't bright and if I myself had been thinking at the time, I would have noted the foil, thought of that, and removed it to see that the tubing had been knocked out of its housing . . . probably when he put the foil in. But I was busy yapping with Pierina. I'd also had a couple glasses of wine, so I didn't notice and started it without thinking."

"And the fireplace?" Jake shot out at once. "The gas guy took it apart and put it back together as if there was something wrong with it."

"Yes, he did," Nicole agreed. "But he never said there was anything wrong with it. He was too busy going on about how one partner always goes a little crazy in a divorce and whatnot."

"Well, he seemed to think your ex-husband was trying to kill you. He apparently hugged you on the way out, insisting you should get a good security system. *And* he charged you a pittance for being there most of the day."

"He hugged *both* of us, and I think he only

hugged me so he could hug Pierina and cop a feel," Nicole snapped. "He was crunching on her. I think that's why he took the fireplace apart in the first place, so he had an excuse to hang around, ogle her, and chat her up. He offered to take us out on the town and show us the city while Pierina was here," she added dryly. "And I think his crunching on her is why he agreed with her worries that Rodolfo was trying to kill me."

Jake was aware that everyone had been glancing from him to Nicole as they'd argued, as if watching a tennis match. They were now focused on him again and he shifted uncomfortably, unsure what to say. She seemed to have an answer for everything . . . and Marguerite hadn't mentioned that the gas guy had been crunching on Pierina, but then Pierina probably hadn't mentioned that either.

His thoughts were distracted when the doorbell rang.

"I'll get it," Dante said.

"What is crunching?" Elaine asked with confusion as the twin left the kitchen.

"Hitting on," Tomasso answered. "The gas guy had the hots for Pierina."

"Oh." She nodded with understanding. "Well then it's possible he was exaggerating the dangers to be the hero in Pierina's eyes."

"Mother," Jake complained. He was having enough trouble trying to convince Nicole it was her husband without his mother siding with the woman.

"Well, it's true, dear," she said apologetically. "Men do silly things like that when they want a woman. And these earlier things you're talking about don't sound nearly as deadly, or as well planned as the hot tub and the accident. The poisoning of the hot tub took some knowledge of poisons, and fiddling with the car brakes and accelerator took some skill."

"The police have already found out what was done to the car?" Nicole asked.

"Dante gave them a mental nudge at the accident scene to ensure they had it examined right away," Jake said quietly.

"They called while Jake was settling you in bed when we got home," Elaine added. "And it was no accident, the car had definitely been messed with."

"It must have been while we were in the mall," Jake muttered unhappily. "It was fine on the way out."

Nicole nodded in agreement and then sighed and returned to the original topic. "Look, I know Pierina is convinced that Rodolfo is trying to kill me, but trust me, he isn't. He's greedy, selfish, and a bully. But he's too fond of his own hide to risk landing in jail by getting caught trying to kill me . . . and he would be the first suspect in this instance. If he was going to kill me, he would have done it before I left him. But afterward? No."

"I'm afraid she's right."

Jake glanced sharply past Nicole as she whirled at that announcement. His eyebrows rose as he watched Vincent Argeneau and his wife Jackie greet her.

"You must be Nicole," Jackie was saying, shaking her hand with a smile as Dante slid past the trio to reclaim his chair at the table. "I'm Jackie, and this is my husband, Vincent."

"Hello," Nicole said uncertainly, and then blinked and peered more closely at Jake's old boss and said, "Vincent Argeneau?"

"That's me," Vincent said lightly.

"You saved Jake's life. You turned him when the skinny bitch stabbed him," she said, using Jake's exact words from when he'd told her about the incident.

"He was Stephano then, but yes," Vincent said, eyes sparkling with amusement at her words.

"Not that he was too pleased at the time," Jackie added dryly.

"Well I am now," Jake said quietly, moving forward to greet the pair. He hugged Jackie first, murmuring, "I'm sorry I didn't say it then."

Hugging Vincent next, he added, "But thank you for my life." Stepping back, he added solemnly, "And for giving up your one turn. I realize what a sacrifice it was, especially since you already knew Jackie was your life mate and that you couldn't turn her once you turned me."

Vincent smiled crookedly. "Well, if I'd stopped to think at the time, I might not have done it and risked losing Jackie," he admitted wryly. "But it all worked out in the end, so you're more than welcome."

Jake smiled, understanding exactly what he meant. Each immortal was allowed only one turn in their life. It was meant for, and usually reserved for, a life mate, but Vincent had given up his one turn to save his life seven years ago. Jake didn't know if he could do the same for anyone now that he'd met Nicole. He wanted to turn her, if she was willing. To keep her with him for always.

"Ah, Jackie, Vincent, what a nice surprise to see you," Elaine said with true pleasure, appearing at his side to hug the pair in greeting. Roberto was right behind her, greeting the couple like family.

Jake knew they'd been grateful for what Vincent had done back then, but it appeared obvious from this greeting that Jackie and Vincent were now considered part of the family. There were probably a lot of changes that had taken place since he'd run away, he acknowledged wryly. But he was glad of this one.

"So," Neil said after he and Tomasso had greeted the couple as well. "What was that about Nicole being right?"

"Oh." Jackie grimaced. "Rodolfo isn't behind whatever is happening here."

"At least the last two attempts," Vincent added, and explained, "Dante told us about the hot tub and car accident, and Rodolfo definitely isn't behind those. At least not personally."

"He's in Italy," Jackie added.

"Are you sure?" Jake asked with a frown.

"Positive," Vincent assured him, and then added, "We just came from there. He's bought a house with the money he got from Nicole and is already romancing an heiress with heavy pockets."

"Poor thing," Nicole muttered and when Jake glanced her way, shrugged and said, "Rodolfo can be as charming as hell in the short term. He'll romance her, sweep her off her feet, promise her the world, and then, once he has her, treat her like a dog, go through her money, and hate her for letting him."

"Yeah," Jackie agreed with disgust. "That's

what I got when I read him. He hates women, especially any woman who gives him the time of day. He knows he's worthless, so any woman he fools enough to succeed in making fall in love with him must be even more worthless than he is in his eyes."

"I wouldn't feel sorry for the heiress though," Vincent added with amusement.

"Yeah," Jackie agreed with a grin. "Rodolfo may have bitten into the wrong apple here."

"Why's that?" Nicole asked with interest.

"Because the heiress's uncle is neck deep in the mob and very fond of the niece he's raised since his brother's death when she was "just a bambina," Vincent said with a wicked grin. "I guarantee if he treats her like he did you, he'll wind up with a fine new pair of cement shoes."

"Does he know about the mob ties?" Jake asked with interest, and smiled when the couple grinned and shook their heads. His gaze slid to Nicole to see that she was biting her lip, looking slightly concerned. Jake slid his arm around her waist and murmured, "You reap what you sow in this life, Nicole. Whatever happens, he will have brought on himself . . . and who knows, maybe Uncle will give him a warning to be good to his niece, or else." Jake shrugged. "He may be a better man for it."

"He'll have to be," Dante said with amusement.

Jake nodded, but then frowned as his mind shifted back to the matter at hand. "So . . . Rodolfo isn't behind this, but could he have hired someone?"

Vincent shook his head. "I read his mind pretty thoroughly. He did take something out of the furnace, thinking she'd have to have someone in to fix it. It was a nuisance act. As for the wood in the doors, that was to prevent break-ins."

Jake raised his eyebrows at this news. It seemed the guy really was a moron if he thought putting the wood outside would prevent someone outside from getting in.

"I told you he wasn't bright," Nicole muttered with satisfaction.

"Well, to be fair," Jackie said, "He was aware that he was putting it outside, and that it could be lifted from the outside. His thinking was that they'd never look to see that it was actually there on the outside. He seems to think most people are stupid."

"The kettle calling the pot black," Dante murmured.

"And the grill?" Jake asked. "Did you find anything about that?"

"He put the foil there at the same time as he put the foil in the oven and never used it after that. There were no thoughts about pulling the tubing out of its housing," Jackie said, almost sounding apologetic.

"And there was nothing at all about the fireplace in his thoughts," Vincent added. "It really doesn't seem like he was trying to kill Nicole. That's why we stopped here on our way back to California. We thought we'd be bringing good news."

"But then we got here and Dante told us about the car trying to run Nicole down, and then the hot tub and the car accident, and it seems like you really do have a problem," Jackie said on a sigh.

"So the incidents that made Marguerite concerned enough to hire you to protect Nicole weren't murder attempts at all," Elaine murmured slowly.

"But the hot tub and car accident were," Jake said firmly. "And Rodolfo seemed like the most likely culprit. He had the most to gain from her death."

"No he didn't," Nicole said at once, and Jake glanced at her with surprise.

"Certainly he did," he argued. "He would have got everything instead of just half."

"How stupid do you think I am?" Nicole asked irritably, sliding out from under his arm to go to the cupboard and grab a coffee cup. He noted that she took several deep breaths as she carried it to the coffeepot, as if to calm herself, and then she admitted, "The first thing I did after I left Rodolfo was to change my will and the beneficiaries on my insurance."

So, despite her protests that Rodolfo wasn't trying to kill her, she'd protected herself . . . and she was obviously annoyed that they would think she hadn't. Jake watched her pour herself a coffee and then asked, "Who did you make your beneficiary?"

"Joey and Pierina get everything," Nicole answered and then glanced around. "Do you want a coffee? I—"

Something in his expression must have told her what he was thinking, because she stopped and scowled.

"Oh, come on!" she protested. "You can't be serious?"

"What is he not serious about?" Roberto asked curiously.

"He's thinking Joey must be behind the hot tub

and car accident," Elaine murmured, obviously reading his mind. Jake was only surprised Roberto hadn't.

"Do they know you put them in your will?" Jake asked, ignoring the pair.

Nicole sighed wearily. "Jake—"

"Do they?" he insisted.

"Yes, but Joey has his own money. He made a fortune in land development. That's why he was able to retire."

"And he's running through his retirement like water," Dante said quietly, drawing Nicole's startled gaze.

"What?" she asked with surprise.

"That bitchy beauty of his is expensive," Dante said with a shrug. "He's spent a good bit of his retirement on making her happy."

"And once she's gone through it all, will no doubt move on to a new sucker," Jake said dryly. He really hadn't liked the woman.

"It doesn't matter. Joey wouldn't try to kill me," Nicole said firmly. "He's my brother."

"What is this about Dad's selfish asshole gene?" Elaine asked suddenly.

Jake glanced to his mother uncertainly. "What?"

"Please stop reading my mind," Nicole said stiffly.

"What did you read?" Jake asked with interest.

"Dammit, my brother is not trying to kill me," Nicole snapped before his mother could answer. She then headed for the door, weaving her way through the group to get out of the room. "I'm going to my studio to work."

"You're supposed to be relaxing," Jake growled. "And what about the lunch I was making you?"

"I'm not hungry. And working is a hell of a lot more relaxing than standing here listening to you guys accuse everyone in my life of wanting me dead," Nicole snapped, heading for the stairs.

"Let her go," his mother said gently, catching his arm when he started to go after Nicole.

Jake paused and looked from Nicole to his mother unhappily. "What were you talking about with the asshole gene?"

"It was a conversation Nicole thought of even as she denied her brother would try to kill her. He said she was pathetic and too nice and it was because she'd spent too much time with Pierina who had encouraged that in her. That she should have spent more time with him. He'd got his father's selfish asshole gene and would have nurtured that in her instead," she explained, and then added, "Nicole was surprised and said that his thinking he was selfish meant he wasn't."

"And what did he say to that?" Jake asked when she paused.

"I believe it was, "Ha! Got you fooled," she said solemnly.

"Maybe Vincent and I should go have a chat with Joey," Jackie said slowly. "Do we know where he lives?"

"Florida," Jake answered, and then added, "He's staying at a hotel downtown while here, though."

"Do you know which one?"

Jake nodded. Joey had mentioned it the night they'd had dinner here at the house. He gave them the name now.

Nodding, Jackie glanced to Vincent.

"We shouldn't be long," he said, slipping his arm around his wife to escort her out of the kitchen.

"We'll go with you," Dante announced and he and Tomasso followed them out.

Jake watched them go and then returned to the stove. He'd taken the soup and frying pan of sandwiches off the burner when Nicole had entered. Now he put them back on the burners. He would finish cooking it and take it down to her anyway. She hadn't eaten in twenty-four hours now. Besides, maybe she'd accept his peace offering and some of her anger with him would ease.

"Well, Neil," Roberto said now. "I guess we should take your mother and go check into our hotel."

"Hotel?" Jake asked with surprise, turning to peer at the trio as his mother collected her purse from the table. "I thought you'd stay here."

"It's not your place to make that offer. This is Nicole's home," Neil reminded him with amusement.

"Yeah, but I'm sure Nicole would—"

"There's no need to bother Nicole," his mother said, slipping her purse strap over her shoulder as she walked over to him. Pausing beside Jake, she gave him a hug, kissed his cheek, and then reminded him, "There are only the three bedrooms here, son, Nicole's and the two guest rooms. You and the twins are already using the guest rooms."

"Yeah, but . . ." Jake hesitated. He'd been about to say that he was sure he would be staying in Nicole's room with her from now on, leaving the bedroom for his parents. Neil could sleep on the daybed in the studio, or one of the couches. But

Jake wasn't all that sure he would be welcome in Nicole's bed at the moment. She was pretty upset with him right now . . . and all because he was trying to keep her safe, he thought unhappily. Was it his fault her brother was trying to kill her?"

"We are happy to stay at a hotel," Roberto announced, coming over to give him a hug too. "Your mother and I have got used to not having to be quiet when we go to bed and would not be very good at it now."

Jake couldn't keep the grimace off his face. He understood what the man was saying. The older couple were as passionate and loud in the bedroom as he and Nicole were . . . as most life mates were. Roberto may be saying they had tried to be quiet, but while the pair had slept during the day while he was at school, they would disappear into their bedroom at all hours when he and Neil were younger and still living at home. To be sure, they hadn't bellowed like a couple of mating mooses, but they hadn't exactly been silent either. The sounds that had come from their bedroom had been enough to traumatize him when he was young.

"Oh, stop," his mother said with a combination of amusement and embarrassment. But he didn't understand that she'd caught his thoughts, until she added, "We weren't that bad."

"No," Roberto agreed, and then grinned, eyes sparkling wickedly as he contradicted himself, admitting, "We were that bad."

Jake didn't miss the quick squeeze his stepfather gave his mother's derriere either. The pair was as frisky today as they had been fifty years ago. Oddly enough, he didn't mind. It meant he had a lot of frisky years to look forward to with Nicole.

"Come see us off, son," Elaine said, slipping her arm around her husband.

Nodding, Jake followed the trio out of the kitchen. As they started down the stairs, he said, "Call and let me know what room you're in when you get settled."

"We will, and you call and tell us what happened with Joey when the boys get back," his mother ordered firmly.

"If you get the hotel switchboard telling you we are unavailable, we are probably sleeping," Roberto commented. "It is well past our bedtime now and I am not sure how long we will be up."

Jake nodded. It was just after noon and he wouldn't mind a couple winks himself. He'd wait until the twins were back though and could keep an eye on Nicole for him. She was the only one of them who had slept last night.

"Perhaps later tonight we could meet for dinner," his mother suggested as they stepped off the stairs. "It would be nice to sit down for a meal with you again."

Jake felt guilt pinch at him. His mother sounded so wistful. The last seven years had obviously been hard on her. Probably the last forty had been hard on her, he acknowledged. His pulling away from the family to hang out on the fringes when he'd found out what they were at eighteen had probably hurt her terribly. He wished now that he'd reacted differently. But he couldn't go back and change history.

Pausing at the front door, Jake turned and gave her a big, hard hug. "I'm sorry, Mom. I love you."

"I love you too . . . and always have," she whispered and there were tears in her eyes when he released her and stepped back.

"The past is the past," Roberto said gruffly, hugging Jake now himself, and thumping his back. "We are just glad to have you back. We love you, son."

"Thank you," Jake said solemnly. "I love you too . . . Dad."

Roberto hugged him more tightly and then stepped back, swiping at his eyes. Jake wasn't surprised to find his own eyes misting. Roberto was the only father he'd ever had, or at least the only one he recalled with any clarity. His birth father was just a picture he'd been shown, and stories he'd been told. The only father he remembered was Roberto, and he'd been a good dad. While he'd offered discipline and direction when necessary, he had also given abundant love and affection. But Jake had refused to call him father since his eighteenth birthday.

"Well, now that you have Mom and Dad blubbering away . . ." Neil said dryly, stepping up next to hug him. "I'm glad you're ready to come back into the fold. I've missed my big brother."

"I've missed you too," Jake assured the younger man and knew it was true. Even at his angriest, he'd missed having Neil, his parents, and the rest of the family there in his life . . . and he'd done it to himself. Shaking his head, he gave Neil's back a pat as they parted. "I'll call when I hear anything."

"Call my cell," Neil said. "I'll answer."

"Oh hey," Jake said as that reminded him. "Do you want my cell-phone number?"

"I have it," Neil assured him and when he looked surprised, grinned. "What? You didn't think we'd keep tabs on you? I've known where you were and what you were doing since you left. Jackie is a very good detective."

Jake chuckled and shook his head. "Right."

"Later bro," Neil said smiling, and then turned to follow their parents to the car waiting in the driveway.

Jake watched until the car had started and pulled out onto the road, and then gave a wave and closed and locked the door. He considered going to check on Nicole, but cowardice reared its head and he decided he'd wait until he had her lunch ready first. The smell of it might—

Jake sniffed the air. He thought he'd caught a whiff of something burning, but it was gone now and he couldn't think what—

"Crap!" he muttered and rushed for the stairs as he recalled he'd put the soup and sandwiches back on the burner and then left them there to see his family out.

That whiff came again and stayed this time as he got halfway up the stairs, but it was the smoke he could see billowing out of the kitchen when he reached the top of the stairs that really alarmed him. Hell, he was burning down the bloody house!

Jake charged into the kitchen, relieved to see that there wasn't actually a fire. The grilled cheese was producing all the smoke. Grabbing the pan, he whirled and stuck it in the sink and turned the tap on, and then whirled back to the soup pan, which was boiling over onto the burner. Jake automatically grabbed that as well to throw in the sink, only to curse and drop it when the handle burned his hand. It hit the floor with a loud clang, sending tomato soup flying in every direction.

"Damned metal handles," he muttered, grabbing paper towel off the counter and bending to the mess he'd made. He swiped up a good portion of the orange-red mess, tossed the sopping paper towel in the garbage and started to reach for more, but changed his mind and stood to hurry to the sliding glass doors instead. The air was thick with smoke and the stench of burnt food. His eyes were beginning to burn and water. He needed to air out the room.

God, he hoped Nicole stayed in her studio for a while, Jake thought as he unlocked and opened the sliding glass doors. He hoped he hadn't completely destroyed her pot and pan too. And he guessed he wasn't feeding her tomato soup and grilled cheese.

Grimacing, Jake left the door open and moved back to finish cleaning up the mess. He then picked up the much cooler pan and examined it as he set it in the sink. It was a mess, the soup a blackened mess on the bottom of the pan, but he thought he might be able to clean it off. Maybe. As for the frying pan . . . Jake grimaced as he examined it. The Teflon on the bottom was discolored. He'd put the heat on too high.

Sighing, he set the plug in place in the sink so it would fill with water and dumped some soap in, then caught the floating, blackened sandwiches and tossed those.

He'd have to figure out something else to feed her, Jake thought. But first he needed to change. The soup had splashed all over, catching even his top, but really getting his jeans good. Grimacing, he started out of the kitchen, but then paused and turned back to turn off the tap. Causing a flood on the heels of the first calamity would have been impressive, he thought grimly, and shook his head as he left the kitchen.

Seventeen

Nicole paced to the end of her studio and back, and then did it again . . . and again. She really didn't know what else to do. She was angry, and restless and frustrated. She was mad because it seemed someone *was* out to kill her. While Jake had taken the brunt of the two attacks, no one knew he was here but his family, so she had to be the target. But she didn't have a clue why anyone would want to kill her. Truthfully, Joey *was* the best suspect because he got the bulk of her estate if she died . . . and she was angry about that too. As mad as she wanted to be at Jake and his family for suspecting her brother, he *was* the most likely one . . . and she hated that too. Nicole didn't want to suspect her brother. But the facts were he'd arrived in town the day the hot tub poisoning happened, after she'd told him she planned to take a dip in the hot tub later.

Was that just a coincidence? Or had he poisoned

the hot tub before leaving that night? He might have already planned to poison the hot tub and had the poison with him, or her mentioning planning to use it might have made him run into town when he left here, purchase whatever poisons it was that had been used, and drive back, park up the road and walk to the house in the dark to dump the poison in. There were no streetlights out here and the houses were a good distance apart; each sat on a plot of land of at least two acres. No one would have noticed him.

As for the car, Nicole hadn't mentioned it to Jake, but Joey was pretty handy with cars. He'd bought and restored old ones since he was a teenager. He could have tampered with her SUV.

Sighing, Nicole dropped onto her daybed/couch and closed her eyes briefly. She could hardly be angry at Jake and his family for suspecting her brother when she suspected him too. And she wasn't really angry at them. She was just angry in general, or maybe angry at herself. What was it about her that the men who were supposed to love her, treated her so shabbily? Her husband had professed to love her and then had abused her and screwed her royally financially, and now her brother, who she had always been sure loved her, might be trying to kill her for a couple bucks.

Was it something about *her* that made them react this way? And what if that something eventually made Jake come to loathe her or think her only value was the money she made and he turned on her like her husband and brother?

That was where her true upset lie. Or at least half of it, Nicole corrected, because losing her brother to greed and attempted murder would hurt terribly. But she suspected Jake going the same way would hurt more, and what did that say about her? It would upset her more if Jake, a man she'd only met a week or so ago now, turned on her than the fact that her brother may have.

Elaine had said she could read her mind, see through the subterfuge and knew she loved Jake. Nicole was beginning to think the woman was right. She did love the man despite the short time since she'd met him . . . and she didn't like having these ill feelings between them, but she'd caused them and, therefore, she was the one who needed to apologize for getting so upset about his suspecting her brother when she did too.

Cursing, Nicole stood and headed out of the studio. The house was silent as she walked through it, and a glance out the windows that wrapped around the front stairway showed that the only vehicle left in her driveway was Jake's. It looked like everyone else had left. Including the twins.

The knowledge made her pause on the stairs. They were alone . . . completely and utterly alone. If they were alone, then they could—

Geez. Nicole interrupted her own thoughts with disgust. She finds out they're alone and her thoughts immediately turn to sex. These nanos of theirs were powerful mojo. She was acting like a heroin addict or something, and Jake was the drug. But she needed to stop that. She owed Jake an apology before she could even consider such things.

Nicole heard that lecture from her own brain, but her body was still reacting to the thought of being alone with Jake and the things they could do . . . all over the house. Honestly, Nicole didn't know how many times over the years she'd heard women claim that most men thought with their genitalia, but that affliction obviously wasn't restricted purely to men. Her brain appeared to have dropped into her panties since meeting Jake.

On the other hand, a part of Nicole's mind argued, there was nothing that said she couldn't look nice to apologize. She could put on one of the skirts he'd helped her pick out . . . maybe the short black one that had made his eyes glow silver; pair it with a white blouse and high heels . . . maybe skip the panties. They wouldn't even have to take their clothes off if she did that . . . and then, if they did indulge somewhere other than the bedroom, and someone came home, they could just straighten their clothes and smile innocently. Well, if they weren't unconscious on the floor, she thought wryly, and continued up the stairs.

Much to her relief, Nicole didn't run into Jake as she crossed the loft to the master bedroom. She thought she caught a glimpse of him in the kitchen as she scooted past, but he didn't spot her and come out before she reached and slipped into her room. Nicole eased the door closed to prevent giving away her presence, and then slipped into her walk-in closet.

Nicole had only taken two steps into the long room when she recalled that they'd had the accident after shopping. She had no idea what had happened to her bags, but didn't see any sign of them in her closet.

Nicole walked back out to her bedroom to check and be sure they hadn't been set there, but there was no sign of them there either. It was possible they were still in the SUV . . . or that they'd been ruined in the crash and tossed out. There had been blood everywhere from Jake's injury.

Nicole had been unconscious and hadn't seen Jake get hurt, or how bad it had looked right afterward, but from what she'd been told and the amount of blood on her own clothes, little if any of it from her head wound, the man had lost most of his blood in the accident. A mortal would have died, she was sure. Thank God he wasn't mortal. It would have been a tragedy to lose such a smart, vital, sexy man.

Sighing, Nicole returned to her closet, to search it, hoping she had something pretty and or sexy that would do. But she didn't hold out much hope of finding anything like that. She'd deliberately tossed out everything she'd owned that was even close to sexy when she'd left Rodolfo and sworn off men. Still, she looked.

Nicole started with the hanging clothes and finished with the built-in drawers. She'd only intended on searching the built-in set on the left, which was her side. When that turned up nothing, she started to head out of the closet, thinking she was just plain out of luck. But then Nicole suddenly stopped and peered at the other set of drawers. Rodolfo had always used them, and she hadn't even looked in them since returning.

They were probably empty, she thought, but searched them anyway. The top three wide drawers were empty as she'd expected, but the bottom drawer wasn't. Kneeling on the carpet between the two drawer sets, which were built into the oppo-

site walls and faced each other, she began to sort
through the contents with curiosity. There was a
hand-knitted afghan that her grandmother, her
mother's mother, had knitted for her before dying.
It was old and a bit ratty, but Nicole had kept it
for sentimental reasons and then apparently left
it behind when she'd moved out so abruptly. But
then, she'd moved out in a rush, eager to get out
from under Rodolfo's glowering gaze.

Nicole was surprised Rodolfo hadn't thrown it
out on her. She would have been upset when she
realized she couldn't find it and he seemed to like
to upset her. She folded the afghan neatly and set
it aside, and then stared at the boots that had been
covered by it. Her eyes widened as she recognized
them, thigh-high black boots that were nothing but
crisscrossed lacings in the front and had six inch
heels. They'd had matching gloves and a top that
was mostly crisscrossed lacing in the middle front
from almost nipple to nipple as well. The "top"
had ended just above the belly button, except for
two tails that ran down over the center of the front
of each leg and attached to the thigh high boots
by snaps attached at the end, turning them into
garters of a sort.

Nicole had bought it for her and Rodolfo's first
Halloween together with no intention of wearing it
anywhere but the bedroom. As she recalled, she'd
felt super sexy in it too when she'd tried it on. She'd
intended to greet Rodolfo at the door in it on Halloween. Unfortunately, they'd had a big fight when
she'd got up that day. Rodolfo had taken off in a
snit and hadn't returned until the next day. The
costume had never got worn.

Maybe that was fortunate, Nicole thought as she lifted out one of the boots and found the costume itself tangled in with the lacings. The gloves were caught up in the other boot. Which meant the only thing missing were the tiny black panties. But she had black panties, Nicole thought, and bit her lip, wondering if she had the courage to wear it for Jake.

If she did, she probably wouldn't have to apologize, Nicole thought with amusement. She glanced back to the drawer as she set the second boot on the floor and smiled when she spotted the fedora that went with the costume at the back of the drawer. The fact that it was all here and that Rodolfo hadn't tossed it seemed to her to be a sign that she should wear it. Not that she'd probably wear it long.

Gathering the costume's bits, Nicole stood, retrieved a fresh pair of black panties from her top drawer, then carried everything out to the en suite bathroom. She managed to take a quick shower without getting her hair wet, thanks to a shower cap, and then she dusted herself with baby powder and slipped into the costume.

One look at herself in the mirror and Nicole nearly chickened out. Geez, the costume didn't hide much, and she appeared to have a lot of flesh to show. She shifted briefly, torn, and then muttered "screw it," straightened her shoulders, and headed out of her room.

Nicole spotted Jake disappearing into the kitchen as she opened her door, and was glad she hadn't come out sooner. She would have felt stupid standing around in the kitchen waiting for him, and she definitely wouldn't have wanted to search the house for him in case the twins or one of his other family members returned and caught her like this.

That thought made her realize that her original plan was not going to work here. She would have to walk into the kitchen, smile and then hurry back to the bedroom, hopefully, with him following. There was no way that straightening this outfit and offering an innocent smile would convince anyone she wasn't up to anything. One look at her and they'd know what they'd been up to, or at least what she'd planned.

"Who are you?"

Nicole had been approaching the kitchen door, but paused before reaching it when she heard Jake ask that question.

It was quickly followed by, "Did Nicole let you in?"

"No."

"Then how—" Jake cut himself off and said, "The sliding glass doors."

"Yes. It was kind of you to leave them open for me."

Nicole frowned at the tone of voice, it was mocking and amused.

Moving close to the wall, she eased the last few feet to the kitchen doorway and snuck a quick peak into the room. Jake was standing a couple of feet inside the kitchen, with his back to her. The other man sat at the kitchen table, lounging sideways to the door in one chair, legs stretched out and crossed at the ankles on another. She could see that he wore jeans, and a leather bomber over a T-shirt.

His body looked completely relaxed. She couldn't say what his expression was, though, Jake's body blocked his head from her view.

"It wasn't for you," Jake said grimly. "It was to air out the room."

"Still," the man said, and though Nicole couldn't see him, she was pretty sure he was grinning as he added, "I appreciate it."

Nicole eased back out of sight of the kitchen. She didn't think the man could see her, but if Jake had moved just the smallest amount to the right he would have.

Shifting anxiously from foot to foot, she debated what to do. It seemed obvious to her that the man in the kitchen must be the one behind the hot-tub poisoning and the car accident. Nice, normal people simply didn't saunter into just any open door in homes that weren't theirs. What she didn't understand was why Jake was asking questions instead of taking control of the man's mind.

The obvious answer was that he couldn't, and as far as she knew, that only happened with life mates or older immortals. Had an immortal been trying to kill her? And if so, why? For heaven's sake, she hadn't even known about immortals until this last week, and was pretty sure she hadn't met any besides Marguerite and this crew.

"Who are you?" Jake's voice sounded grim.

"You asked that already," the other man pointed out lightly.

Nicole turned and slid back along the wall to her room. She had to help Jake, but how? She glanced to the sliding doors in her room. They led out to the deck, which wrapped around the back of the house and up the side to the sliding doors in the kitchen. If the doors were still open—

Nicole started toward the doors, but then paused before stepping out. She needed a weapon. Turning, she glanced around the bedroom, looking for something hefty, but it was a bedroom, for heaven's sake, not a weapons locker. Her gaze slid from the bed to the television to the couch. There was nothing she could see that would be useful. There weren't even any lamps in the room; wall sconces were set into the walls on either side of the couch, as well as the bed, to remove the necessity of lamps.

Her mouth tightened with annoyance and then her gaze slid to the bed again and she eyed the pillows. They were rather special; quilted cloth on the outside with a water bladder inside. The user filled them with water to reach the firmness they desired. A couple quarts made a soft pillow, three quarts made it medium, and five quarts made it firm. Nicole liked hers firm. She had five quarts in hers. That was more than a gallon of water. It weighed a good ten pounds, she would guess.

Moving up the bed, Nicole grabbed one of them, and headed out of the room through the sliding glass doors.

"You don't remember me, do you?"

Jake's eyes narrowed on the intruder's wide unpleasant smile. His voice was deep and raspy, as if he spent a lot of time screaming at the top of his lungs. Jake had heard that voice before, but where didn't come to him right away. It was recently though.

"You ruined everything. Stopped me from carrying out what I was put on this earth to do, and yet—barely a week later—you don't even remember me," the man said bitterly.

Jake eyed him warily. He'd been trying to get into the man's thoughts to read and control him since entering the kitchen, but it was like trying to navigate the ocean in a fog with no compass or sonar . . . and there were monsters coming out of that fog, accompanied by agonized shrieks. The man wasn't in his right mind. That was the only explanation. Jake had always heard that it was hard to the point of impossible for an immortal to read or control a crazy person. Now he understood why.

Jake opened his mouth to admit that, no, he didn't recognize him, when he suddenly did.

"Ball-Cap Boy," he murmured, recognizing him as the man who had intended to shoot the client he was suppose to protect, and who he'd tackled his last night on the job before meeting Marguerite for dinner. Tilting his head, he asked, "Why aren't you in jail?"

Ball-Cap Boy gave a short laugh. "For what? I didn't get the chance to do anything. All they could charge me with was the improper transportation of a registered weapon."

"Registered?" Jake asked with a frown.

"Yes. You see, there's a law that if you work in a remote wilderness area, where your life can be under threat by wild animals, you can get a special license to carry weapons, like rifles and handguns."

"And you have one of those special licenses," Jake guessed dryly. He now understood the old saying "crazy like a fox." The bastard might be nuts, but he was smart too.

"Yes, sir, I do," he said with a grin so wide it was almost painful to see. "That and a family with the resources to hire an excellent lawyer who is quick and very good. I was out within hours."

Jake was really beginning to dislike this guy's smile.

"Of course, it helped that the security tape showed you moving toward me before I even reached to adjust my gun so it was no longer digging into my ribs." He smiled and offered, "Well, at least that's what I told them I was doing."

Jake didn't respond to the comment. He was trying to decide what to do. The man had had a gun before and probably did now, no doubt tucked into the arms he presently had crossed. Jake wasn't too concerned about being shot dead, that wasn't a worry unless Ball-Cap Boy blew his head completely off, which would take a sawed-off shotgun or an equally powerful weapon, he was sure, and this man couldn't be hiding one of those on his person. Jake suspected he had his handgun though, and while that wouldn't blow his head off, it could incapacitate him temporarily and leave Nicole alone in the house and at the mercy of this nut. He didn't want to risk that, so had to move carefully.

"It also helped that I told them that I'd run into you before," Ball-Cap Boy continued conversationally. "When I was out on a date with your live-in girlfriend." He grinned widely. "And that you've had it in for me ever since."

Jake didn't react on the outside, but inside he was mentally kicking himself. He often had dealings with the police on the job, and knew a good number of them by name. However, busy feeling sorry for himself as he'd been, and thinking himself a monster, Jake hadn't encouraged any friendships since leaving California. So, while many of the officers had given some personal details about their lives in an offer of friendship, mentioning wives, girlfriends, or kids, Jake hadn't responded in kind. As Dan had said in the elevator the day they'd encountered this man, he didn't know a thing about him and had thought him without family. It would be the same with the police. Had he bothered to befriend the men he worked with and encountered on the job, they'd have known this man was lying about a live-in and hesitated to let him go to cause trouble again.

"How did you find me here?" Jake asked abruptly, turning his attention to the situation at hand. Self-flagellation was really a waste of time and useless in a situation like this. He could kick himself later.

"The angels led me to you."

Jake was aware that his eyelids flickered at this claim, but all he said was, "Oh?"

"Hmmm." The man nodded. "My lawyer wanted to talk after he got me released. He took me to a bar downtown and sat trying to convince me to let my parents help me, which translates to locking me up," he added bitterly and began to rant. "They don't believe the angels talk to me through the radio and that I have a purpose in this life. They think I'm crazy, that I've spent too much time alone up north and it's affected me. That I need to take those stupid pills the doctor gave me again. But I'll show them. They'll understand when I carry out the charge I've been given. You screwed up the first service I was supposed to perform to make this a better world, and for a minute my faith was shaken. How could God allow that when I was doing his work? But when I saw you coming out of that restaurant across the street with that brunette, I knew the angels had led me there. I understood that the devil would, of course, not want me to carry out my mission, and that you and everyone you associate with are in league with him."

Crazy as a loon, Jake thought grimly, but knew the brunette that Ball-Cap Boy had seen him with was Marguerite, when they'd left the restaurant where they'd dined together.

"So you followed us," Jake guessed. It was the only explanation.

Ball-Cap Boy nodded. "I left the lawyer with his mouth wide open and followed you. I had to hire a taxi to do it." He smiled. "I told the taxi driver the brunette was my wife and the two of you were having an affair. He was very sympathetic. It seems his wife 'stepped out' on him, as he put it." He shrugged. "We followed you to that car rental place and while she was returning her car, I rented one, and then I followed you back here."

"And poisoned the hot tub?" Jake asked, and then said with certainty, "No, not then. You didn't have the poison with you in the rental car."

"No," he agreed. "But I saw the hot tub that night. Disgusting things," he added with a shudder. "Only whores and whoresons use those. Poisoning it was the only thing to do."

Jake frowned. He was recalling his first night here when he'd arrived with Marguerite. The door had been unlocked when they'd arrived, he recalled. They'd locked it, and then when he'd checked later it was unlocked again.

"You followed us here, you weren't here before us?" he asked, despite knowing he couldn't have been.

Ball-Cap Boy looked at Jake as if he were the one who was crazy. "I told you I followed you. The angels led me to you, they don't give out addresses."

Jake didn't react to that, his thoughts were on the fact that the door had been unlocked when they'd arrived. Nicole had claimed she'd locked it behind Marguerite when she'd left, but it had been unlocked when they'd arrived. The only answer was either Nicole had only thought she'd locked it, or she'd locked it and then unintentionally unlocked it when she'd turned the key back to take it out of the lock. But he knew Marguerite had locked it when they'd entered. He'd even checked it himself afterward. Yet it had been unlocked again later.

"You were in the house," he said with certainty.

"The studio door was cracked open."

Jake frowned. Marguerite had searched the main floor while he took the upper when their calls hadn't drawn Nicole out. Marguerite must have just stuck her head into the studio, or maybe she even just glanced through the French doors. Whichever the case, she hadn't noticed the sliding glass doors being open.

"I was really impressed with the girl's paintings," Ball-Cap Boy said now, surprise in his voice. "I expected them to be orgy scenes and such, but they were well-done portraits. Of course, I realized then that the angels had left the door open for me so I could see my next targets. Obviously, a servant of Satan would only paint other minions of hell."

"Christ," Jake muttered, thinking of the portrait of Christian and Caro. The man was saying they were now a target too, along with the actress and the politician.

"Don't you dare utter Christ's name in vain," Ball-Cap Boy barked, suddenly on his feet, the gun Jake had been sure he had in view and pointing straight at him. Ball-Cap Boy had held it tucked between his arms and body, hidden until he was ready to reveal it, which was exactly what Jake had suspected.

He eyed the weapon warily, very aware that Nicole, as one of Satan's minions, was also a target now. He definitely couldn't afford to be incapacitated, even for moments. Trying to turn the man's thoughts from his anger and get answers at the same time, Jake asked, "Did the angels lead you out of the house through the front door?"

Ball-Cap Boy looked at him with disgust. "Don't be ridiculous. I decided to go that way myself after the brunette went upstairs and I'd searched the main floor. It was closer and easier than marching through the snow."

"Right," Jake murmured, but at least he knew how the door had got unlocked after Marguerite locked it. "And you tried to run over Nicole in the Canadian Tire parking lot?"

He shrugged. "She's in league with you."

Jake nodded grimly. "And you messed with the SUV's brakes and accelerator?"

"Well, I would have just shot you, but the police

are still suspicious of me, and you aren't my primary target. I can't get caught until I complete my mission and kill all the politicians in the world."

Jake's mouth twitched. As missions went, he couldn't really say that was a bad one. Jake wasn't big on politicians. Politics seemed to be peopled with greedy, larcenous, uncaring morons who couldn't run a corner store let alone a country. Geez, there were at least two mayors of major cities in just this province right now who were in hot water. One was accused of using government funds for the wedding of one of his children, the other of using his position to strong-arm funds for some pet charity of his or something. Charity was good, but using such tactics to get money for it made people think maybe he was getting a percentage of the donations. Why else risk your job?

"Unfortunately, you are turning out to be difficult to kill," Ball-Cap Boy said with a perplexed frown. "I mean, I wouldn't expect the devil to make it easy, but I don't know how you managed to survive the hot tub. I saw you get in, and thought for sure I'd succeeded when you started vomiting blood. I went away thinking I'd come back in a day or so to take care of the girl, but when I returned you were on your feet and those two behemoths were here."

"So you followed us to the mall and messed with the SUV while we were inside shopping," Jake said.

"Yes." He scowled. "But you survived that too."

Jake wondered if the guy expected him to apologize or something, and then movement behind Ball-Cap Boy drew his gaze to the sliding glass doors and the woman easing into view on the deck outside. For a moment, he was so distracted by the outfit that he didn't look at the face. Cripes, talk about a sex trap. The only cover the outfit offered was scraps of almost see-through black material over the three most important bits. They appeared to be held in place by crisscrossing straps or lacing . . . and were those thigh-high boots? There wasn't enough material in them to put together to make a proper shoe. But then there wasn't enough material in the whole outfit to make anything decent. Who the hell—?

His gaze slid upward, finding a fedora perched at a jaunty angle on long, wavy blond hair and then he focused on the face. Nicole! Jake suspected his heart stopped at that moment and he would never know how he managed to control his expression and keep his jaw from dropping to thud on the floor. She looked fricking amazing, hot as hell, sexy as sin . . . and boy was Ball-Cap Boy gonna want to kill her for that outfit. He could imagine him shrieking Jezebel! and shooting her full of holes. This was not good, not good at all.

"So I thought a personal approach was called for," Ball-Cap Boy announced.

Realizing he was staring and likely to draw the man's attention to Nicole, Jake shifted his gaze quickly back to the man as he waved his gun around. He opened his mouth to say something clever, but all that came out was, "Er . . ."

It was the best Jake could come up with, and, really, he thought that was pretty good considering his penis was reacting to Nicole's outfit by trying to form a pup tent in his pants. Jeans are much more resistant to such things than jogging pants, he noted, shifting uncomfortably as his gaze skittered back to Nicole. She had slid through the door and was now raising something she'd been carrying at her side, something big and white and—a pillow.

Seriously? Jake thought with amazement. This wasn't a pillow fight. What kind of person brought a pillow to a gunfight? Cripes, she was dressed for a pillow fight too . . . well, a sexy pillow fight that ended in toppling her onto the bed, ripping her panties off and thrusting—

"What the hell's the matter with you?" Ball-Cap Boy asked suddenly, distracting him from his less than helpful thoughts. "You're panting and your eyes look funny. Are they glowing?" he asked with a frown, taking a step closer.

"I'm possessed," Jake blurted out on inspiration. That inspiration being that he mostly felt possessed . . . by his penis. It seemed to have a mind of its own and didn't particularly care what kind of situation he was in. It wanted Nicole bad, and seemed to be trying to force its way through his jeans in her direction.

"Possessed," Ball-Cap Boy looked alarmed. "But—"

"I didn't want to stop you, the demon possessing me did," Jake added, his gaze skittering from Ball-Cap Boy to Nicole and back. She was only a step behind the man now, and was raising her pillow as if she planned to smack him with it. Was she CRAZY? he wondered, and gave his head a small shake, trying to tell her with the gesture not to do it. You didn't piss off the man with the gun and that was the only thing hitting him with the pillow was going to do. Dear God, when this was over, he was going to have a stern talk with her about self-defense tactics.

"Possessed," the man said and frowned uncertainly, obviously not sure what to do now. "What—?"

The word ended on a surprised "oomph" as Nicole wielded her pillow. Much to Jake's surprise it seemed to pack quite a wallop. She must have stuffed it with rocks or something, he thought as he watched in amazement as Ball-Cap Boy flew sideways under the blow, crashed into and bounced off the table, then slammed his head on the island counter as he stumbled and fell forward.

"I did it!" Nicole squealed, jumping up and down in her ridiculously sexy heels, the heavy pillow held aloft. "I saved you."

Jake rushed forward now, kicking the gun away from Ball-Cap Boy's body, and sparing a moment to be sure he was unconscious. He then turned to catch Nicole in his arms mid-jump and planted his mouth on hers.

She immediately collapsed against him. Her arms slid around his shoulders even as he heard the pillow hit the floor with a loud thud and slosh that made him wonder what the hell was in it. When she opened her mouth to his with a moan, Jake stopped caring about the pillow or anything else and lifted her off the floor with his arms around her waist and started to turn, intending to carry her to the bedroom and do exactly what he'd thought of doing moments ago.

Some very small part of Jake's brain knew he shouldn't, that he should deal with Ball-Cap Boy first, but it was a very small part. There wasn't much blood left in his brain right now. It had all raced south to fill his still-growing erection. Cripes, if he didn't find release soon he was pretty sure his erection would explode like an overfull balloon. *Pop, no more penis*, he thought.

"Don't worry, we'll handle things here."

Jake paused and frowned against Nicole's mouth at that dry announcement. Fortunately, he had enough blood left in his brain to tell him he should stop and see who the hell was yipping at him. Breaking their kiss, he turned with Nicole still held off the ground and peered blankly at Dante and Tomasso.

"How'd you get here?" he asked with surprise.

"A car," Tomasso said drolly.

Dante gave a laugh, but explained, "We pulled up just as Nicole was slipping into the kitchen. Seeing her getup, we almost backed out to give you some privacy, but then Tomasso spotted this guy"—he gestured to the unconscious man on the floor—"through the kitchen window."

"And his gun," Tomasso added.

Dante nodded. "So we thought we'd best come see what we could do."

"Only she handled it while we were crossing the deck," Tomasso added, and then smiled at Nicole and said, "Nice pillow work."

"Yeah," Dante agreed. "What do you have in that thing? Rocks? It sure knocked him for a loop."

"Water," Nicole said, blushing, but didn't get to explain further. Jake didn't give her the chance to. He was turning away with her again, and continuing out of the kitchen.

"Hey," Dante called. "Who is this guy? Is he the one who poisoned the hot tub and messed with the SUV?"

"Yeah, but I don't know who he is," Jake answered, not slowing. "Never got his name. He's just a lunatic who tried to kill one of my clients at work. He thinks angels talk to him and he's supposed to kill politicians and pretty much everyone I know because I stopped him, so we must all be in league with the devil."

"Hmm," Dante said directly behind him and Jake set Nicole down to sit on the side of the bed, then propped his hands on hips and turned to scowl at the man for following them.

"Nicole and I need to talk," Jake said firmly. "Go deal with sicko in the kitchen."

"It's not talking you're thinking of doing," Dante said dryly, his gaze sliding to Nicole and a smile curving his lips as he admitted, "And I don't blame you. Nice outfit, Nicki," he complimented.

"Thanks," she murmured, blushing.

Dante turned his attention back to Jake. "But talking is what you should be doing."

Jake stiffened at the solemn words. "Why? About what?"

"About your situation and whether she's willing to be your life mate," Dante said calmly, and then pointed out, "Lucian will want this whole situation settled at the same time rather than sending people out to do a three on one on sicko in the kitchen, and then possibly having to return to do the same for Nicole if she isn't willing to be turned."

"Lucian has nothing to do with this," Jake said stiffly. "Ball-Cap Boy is a mortal."

"But his target wasn't," Dante pointed out. "Or should I say targets?"

Jake almost asked how he knew that, but then realized the man had read his mind while following him in here. He probably knew everything Jake had seen and heard since finding Ball-Cap Boy in the kitchen. So he knew the man wanted to wipe out him, Nicole, and every other person he'd seen enter this house, most of whom were immortals.

"He's sick," Dante said quietly. "His family know that and haven't done a damned thing about it, but hire lawyers to keep him out of trouble and on the streets. They'll do the same this time and then he'll be a threat again, not just to you and Nicole, but to us, your parents, Neil, Marguerite, Christian and Caro, Tybo—"

"Basically everyone who he's seen me with," Jake interrupted wearily.

Dante nodded silently.

"Right," Jake said stiffly. "I guess I'd better talk with Nicole then. Would you like to leave so I can do it?"

Dante turned away and headed out of the room for answer.

Jake followed him to the door and pulled it closed, then took a deep breath and turned to face Nicole. One glance at her on the bed in that getup though, and he whirled to face the door again. Damn! How the hell was he supposed to just talk to her with her looking like that?

"Honey, can you maybe get out of that outfit or pull on a robe so we can talk?" he asked in a pained tone. He really didn't want her out of it, he wanted to make love to her while she wore it . . .

well, minus the panties. He'd like to rip those off of her . . . maybe with his teeth.

Jake heard Nicole moving around behind him, some rustling, and then she said, "Okay."

Letting out a breath, Jake turned to look at her and felt his knees go weak. She'd taken off the fedora and pulled on a short black silk robe that didn't cover a damned thing in the pose she'd assumed. She was reclining on the bed, one leg bent, the other flat out, resting on her elbows, her hair and the robe hanging down to gather on the bed and cover absolutely nothing.

"Nicole, please," he pleaded weakly. "We have to talk."

"Yes," she said and he blinked in confusion.

"Yes, what?" he asked uncertainly.

"To whatever you want to ask me," Nicole responded at once.

Jake hesitated and then said, "I want to ask if you'd be willing to at least consider being my life mate."

"Yes," she repeated.

Jake frowned. "You will?"

Now she looked uncertain. "Am I not supposed to say yes? Did you want me to say no?"

"No, of course not," he said at once. "But . . . don't you want some time to think about it?"

Sighing with exasperation, Nicole sat up and scooted to the end of the bed, the robe trailing out behind her. "Jake, I just took on a gun-toting sicko with nothing but a pillow to save your life. I'm pretty sure that means my feelings for you are pretty strong."

She tilted her head and smiled crookedly. "You're

smart, I respect you, and . . ." Nicole hesitated and then confessed, "That day in the SUV when the brakes went out, all I kept thinking was, "Thank God it's Jake at the wheel." She eyed him solemnly. "I trust you with my life. I'm pretty sure I love you. But more importantly, I like you."

"That's more important than love?" he asked with amusement.

Nicole nodded solemnly. "I have relatives I love, but don't much respect or like. I couldn't live with them if my life depended on it. But I like and respect you. I enjoy your company and I can imagine a future with you."

Jake simply stared at her in the silence that followed. His heart had felt like it expanded with every word she'd spoken and now it felt so swollen it ached. She liked and respected him. The way she explained it, that was the best thing in the world.

When Nicole stood up suddenly, looking uncertain, and muttered something unintelligible as she turned toward the bathroom, Jake realized he'd been silent too long.

"I like you too," he blurted, catching her arm to stop her leaving.

Nicole hesitated and then turned slowly back, eyes still uncertain. "Really?"

"Oh, yes, really," Jake assured her, pulling her against his chest so he could wrap his arms around her and hold her close. "I love your talent, your brain, your sense of humor, your body"—his hands began to move over her back and bottom as he continued—"your passion"—he slid the robe off her shoulders, leaving her in only the sexy outfit and urged her back to get a better look as he added, "your taste in clothes. Cripes, this is the sexiest damned thing I've ever seen."

"I wanted to apologize for getting short with you about suspecting my brother. He was the best suspect," she admitted.

"But not the culprit," Jake pointed out dryly and then ran his finger lightly down the lacing on the front of the top, brushing along the curve of one breast between each narrow strip of black leather that held the nearly see-through scraps of the top together. "And if this is your idea of an apology, it's a damned fine one and I love that about you too."

Nicole gave a breathless laugh and shivered under his touch, her nipples hardening under the thin cloth. The sight of it made his mouth water, but he asked, "Are you sure you're willing to be my life mate?"

She nodded, and said breathlessly, "If it means you'll make me feel like this for the next century or two, then definitely."

When Jake paused and frowned with concern at the answer, Nicole sighed, and raised her hands to frame his face, saying solemnly, "Jake, I have never been good at choosing men. My husband and every guy I've dated have been jerks. But your mother assures me that the nanos never make mistakes, and that you're a good man. Maybe it's just because I want to, but I believe her and that makes me feel for the first time in my life that my instincts are right and we'll work. That my love has been given to the right man this time. So . . ." She kissed him lightly on the lips. "Yes, I'm sure I want to be your life mate."

"You know it means becoming one of us?" Jake added solemnly.

Nicole glanced up, the first flicker of uncertainty crossing her face, and making him hold his breath, but then she straightened her shoulders and nodded.

Relief rushing through him, Jake picked her up by the waist and tossed her on the bed.

Nicole landed with a squeal and a bounce, and then pushed herself up to watch him rip off his T-shirt and jeans with more haste than grace. He couldn't get them off quick enough. They'd had their talk, she'd agreed, and now he fully intended on accepting her apology and making love to her until she couldn't stand up straight. Well, okay, until they both passed out, which ought to be about two or three seconds. Jake didn't think he'd last much longer than that at this point, and could only be grateful that the nanos would ensure she experienced the same pleasure he did.

"Will it hurt?"

Jake was hopping on one foot, tugging off a sock when Nicole asked that with trepidation. Straightening, the sock in hand, he peered at her uncertainly, and then his brain cleared. With his thoughts on making love to her, he'd thought she was asking if sex would hurt. But they'd had sex before. It was the turning she was talking about, he realized.

Jake hesitated, thinking back to his own turning.

He'd been stabbed in the chest, which had hurt like crazy, and then had passed out and woken up several days later feeling like he'd been left out in the desert sun for days. He'd been incredibly thirsty, but pain free as he recalled.

"I don't think so," he said finally, hopping on his bare foot to remove the other sock now. "But we'll check with someone."

Nicole nodded absently. Her gaze had shifted to his groin, her eyes widening at the sight of him.

Jake finished pulling off the second sock, tossed it aside and stepped forward to crawl onto the bed, his hands and knees on either side of her body as he moved up the bed until he was directly over her. Looking down into her precious face, he said solemnly, "Nicole, I promise that no matter what happens, I'll never hurt you like Rodolfo did."

"Rodolfo who?"

Jake blinked in surprise and peered into her eyes, relaxing when he saw the laughter there. He opened his mouth, but whatever he'd been going to say, died on a hiss as her hand closed around his erection.

"Jake?" she whispered.

"Yes?" he got out through ground teeth as her hand moved over him.

"Please, shut up and make love to me now."

"God I love you," he growled and lowered his mouth to claim hers even as he shifted out of her hold to claim her body. He did love this woman, Jake acknowledged as Nicole moaned and arched into his thrusts. The grim future he'd envisioned since waking up to find himself an immortal suddenly rolled out before him a much brighter, happier one . . . and much longer too.

In fact, it seemed now like his being stabbed had been a gift. Jake never would have been turned by Vincent, and then wouldn't have run away and met Nicole without it. He'd have worked out his sunset years as the daytime VP at V.A. Inc., a bitter old mortal, resenting everyone around him. But now? Now he had Nicole, and she was everything he could have ever wanted. The future looked bright, and he was one hell of a lucky vampire.

Want more Lynsay Sands?
Keep reading to check out
her classic historical

The Switch

Available December 2013
from Avon Books

Lord Radcliffe drew his horse to a halt and stared at the spectacle being played out before him. A young lad in the clothes of the gentry was standing under the front window of an inn, staring up the skirts of a girl hanging out of a second-floor window. The lad seemed to be speaking to the lass as he tried to grab at her feet, but Radcliffe was too far away to hear what was being said.

Deciding that they were probably trying to run out on their bill, Radcliffe started to urge his horse on to the stables, not really caring enough to get involved. But at that moment, the girl pushed herself off the ledge to dangle from her arms. Radcliffe slowed and stopped again, amused. The boy caught the girl's ankles to keep her from slamming into the building, then stepped under her to offer his aid the rest of the way down.

Unable to see what she was doing, the girl stepped on the lad's wig with one foot, setting it askew.

She nearly lost her grip and tumbled backward to the ground when the obviously irate youth jerked her foot from his head to his shoulder. He then directed the other foot with about as much care.

Radcliffe chuckled under his breath as the woman suddenly dropped to sit on the boy's shoulders. Her skirts fell over the lad's head as she did, blinding him, and the shift in position unbalanced him enough so that he stumbled backward, then to the side as he fought to push the skirt out of his view. At this point, the woman clutched at his hair for balance, forgetting it was a wig. It lifted from his head with her hands, and her upper body swung backward. The lad, already off-balance, tumbled backward with her. They both hit the ground with soft thuds, hidden briefly in the shadow of the inn.

"**D**amn," Charlie muttered, staring up at the treetops above them until a pitiful moan from Beth stirred the cool night air. Sitting up, Charlie surveyed the prone girl with a worried frown. "Are you all right?"

Elizabeth sighed at the question. Her moan had been one of chagrin, but the concerned face suddenly leaning over her own told her that it had been misconstrued.

"Fine," she said dryly. She sat up to brush grass and dirt off of her dress.

Charlie started to help, but Beth waved the attempt away.

"Your wig is gone," she pointed out.

Sitting back, Charlie searched the shadows for the errant wig, then slapped it irritably against one leg to remove the grass clinging to it before slamming it back in place. "Is it straight?"

Beth glanced up long enough to nod, then struggled to her feet.

"Well. That wasn't so bad," Charlie murmured cheerfully, standing and moving to snatch up the bags they had thrown out the window before descending themselves.

Beth turned sharply, mouth open to give her own opinion of the debacle, but caught the twinkle of laughter in the coal black eyes that were so like her own. She relaxed, grinning back. "A ride in the park," she agreed dryly.

Laughing softly, Charlie handed her a bag, took the other one, and led the way to the stables.

"Is he unconscious?" Beth murmured as they entered the tottering old building and spied the stable lad slumped in a corner against a bale of hay. The bottle they had given him was still clasped to his chest.

"Seems to be. You did put the sleeping powder in there, did you not?"

Beth nodded silently, but held her breath as her twin carefully approached the boy, then lifted his head and let it drop back to his chest. He didn't even stir.

Shrugging, Charlie stepped back. "Out like a drunken sot."

Her breath rushing out in relief, Beth moved quickly along the stalls until she found the one where her mount had been settled for the night. Murmuring soothingly, she stepped inside to set about quickly saddling him while Charlie did the same for the mount in the next stall.

Several moments later, Beth was aware at once when her twin suddenly stiffened. Going still herself, she glanced up and about, her heart nearly freezing in her chest at the sight of a figure in the shadows by the door. Charlie tossed her a warning look, then affected the accent of the servant class and asked, "Some'ing I can do fer ye, m'lord?"

One eyebrow rising at the boy's accent, Radcliffe smiled slightly. "It is very bad manners to sneak out without paying one's bill. And stealing horses is a crime."

Charlie stiffened, eyes shooting to Beth's face. The girl was as pale as the moon, her expression panicked as their gazes met.

Radcliffe noted the silent exchange and wished for better lighting in the stables. He'd bet a lot of money that the girl was a beauty. His eyes were straining to make out her features in the darkness when the lad spoke up again.

"We are not stealing. The horses are ours."

The false accent was gone, he noted absently, glancing at the boy. Obviously gentry, as he had suspected. "And your bill?"

"Taken care of."

Radcliffe raised one doubting eyebrow. "Then why not leave by the door like most people?" he asked, noting the couple again exchanging glances.

Charlie was trying to decide just what to tell the snoopy hitch in their plans when Beth suddenly moved out of the stall and into the stream of moonlight coming through the stable doors.

Noting the look of appreciation that immediately entered the stranger's eyes, Charlie peered at the girl now too, curious to know what the man found so attractive. Beth was pretty enough. Straight nose, good teeth. Her eyes were her best feature, large and blue-black, while her hair was an unremarkable brown. All of which described Charlie as well. Not surprising, since they were twins. But it was doubtful that the man had noticed that fact yet.

"We were forced to leave through the windows to escape my uncle," the girl said.

Radcliffe arched an eyebrow. "Why would you need to escape your uncle?"

Noting yet another exchange of glances between the young couple, Radcliffe smiled wryly. "Or need I ask?"

"I beg your pardon?" she murmured uncertainly.

"You need not explain. 'Tis obvious you are about to head for Gretna Green."

"Gretna Green?"

Charlie could have kicked Beth for her look of astonishment. If the saying were true that everyone loved a lover, they might have had a better chance of the man not interfering in their escape plans. He'd obviously thought they were eloping. Instead of leaving him with that mistaken impression, however, Beth gestured toward Charlie.

"Charlie is my twin—"

"Charles," Charlie corrected quickly, stepping forward to join her in the light.

Beth blinked, then nodded slowly. "Aye. Charles is my twin brother."

Radcliffe's eyebrows shot up as he looked the boy over. Except for the white wig, the two were identical. Well, of course there were the obvious physical differences. Where the girl's chest was

ample, the boy's was not. After his initial surprise
had passed, Radcliffe's eyes narrowed with some
suspicion. "Why would the two of you need to flee
your uncle in the dead of night?"

"Our parents died four years ago," the lad answered this time. "Our uncle took over our care.
He has done his best to run the family estates into
the ground, and now wishes to replenish his coffers by selling Beth off into marriage. To Lord Carland."

Radcliffe stiffened at that name, shocked. Carland was a brutal bastard. He had been through
three wives already. The first had died in child-
birth. It was said that a beating had sent her into
labor, and may have had something to do with her
death as well. The second wife had killed herself.
The third had plunged to her death down the stairs
of the family's country estate. There was much
speculation as to whether she had had some assistance from her husband in that plunge.

Whatever the case, not one of his wives had
lasted a year, and no one would even consider allowing their daughter to marry the bastard now.
But from this pair's description, their uncle was
more concerned with his coffers than his kin. Were
they telling the truth?

"What are your names?" he asked abruptly.

There was a pause as the two exchanged glances
once again.

"Charles and Elizabeth Westerly."

Radcliffe searched his memory briefly, then
nodded as he recalled having heard of Nora and
Robert Westerly. Happy couple. They'd had twins,
though he had thought they were girls. The family

members had spent most of their time on their country estate and hadn't cared much for town life. The parents had died four years ago in a carriage accident. Robert's brother Henry Westerly had supposedly taken over the care of the twins and the running of the estates. There had been some rumors of late that he was running through the money quickly in gambling, and from what the boy had just said, he had, and intended to make it up by selling his niece into a marriage that would likely result in her death.

Radcliffe wasn't at all surprised to hear that Carland was willing to pay for a bride. The man needed an heir, else his estate would be left to some distant nephew. His gaze slid over the girl and he sighed. She was a delicate little creature. Other than her over-endowed chest, she was thin to the point of frailty everywhere else. He did not think she would last a month with Carland.

"Where are you going?" he asked abruptly, gesturing impatiently when the boy stiffened at the question, suspicion tightening his mouth. "I am not going to tell on you. I would not wish to see your lovely sister in Carland's hands either. She would be dead in a week."

There was no doubting his sincerity. There was loathing in the man's eyes even as he said Carland's name. Still, Charlie hesitated to tell him the truth, that they were going to stay with their cousin Ralphy, a relative on their mother's side that Uncle Henry did not know existed. Lies were the only alternative. Oddly enough, the plan that came tripping out wasn't half-bad.

"London."

Radcliffe's eyebrows rose yet again. "Relatives there?"

"No."

"It takes money to live in London."

Charlie grinned. "Uncle Henry went through our father's family fortune, but our mother turned her fortune into jewels years ago. She left them to us in her will."

"And your uncle did not try to cash them in or—"

"He would have if he could have found them," the lad interrupted smugly. "But he couldn't. Mother and Father hid them years ago, in case of an emergency. Other than our parents, only Elizabeth and I knew where they were, and we conveniently forgot to mention that they had told us."

Radcliffe's mouth quirked at that; then he sobered. "He will find you in London."

"Eventually," Charlie agreed. "But by then Beth will be married off to someone in the ton."

"And you?"

"I shall be living well off of investments made once I have sold my share of the jewels," Charlie lied nonchalantly.

"You intend to give your sister a season by selling some of the jewels?"

The boy nodded.

Radcliffe frowned. "If you give her a season, your uncle shall hear about it and know where to find you."

"As I said, eventually, but he will not look in London first. He shall head back to the family estates, then check with relatives on my father's side."

"Why would he not look in London first?"

"Because that is where he was taking us. He

would hardly think we had run off in the middle of the night to beat him there."

Radcliffe nodded at the sense in those words. Even Beth looked impressed with the reasoning, and Charlie grimaced at her slightly. She was supposed to already know of this plan. If she was not careful, Radcliffe would see it for the lie it was.

"What of Carland?" Radcliffe asked.

Charlie glanced toward the man. "Carland does not go to London. Most of the ton refuses him admittance. My uncle was taking us to London to purchase a trousseau for Beth, then we were to continue on to Carland's estates."

It was a sound plan for the most part, Radcliffe decided. What the boy lacked in brawn, he more than made up for in brains, it seemed. However, there were weak points in every plan and this one was no exception. For instance, if they planned on living off of a treasure of jewels, they obviously had the jewels with them. Probably in the bags, he decided, remembering the way they had carried them: one each, two-handed, as if they were heavy. All it took was a highway robbery to turn them into paupers at their uncle's mercy again, and he would guess the foolish boy was unarmed. Aside from that, there were all sorts of complications that could arise in London. Theft, of course, or a jeweler could cheat them if they went to the wrong one. And that was only the start of it.

Radcliffe tried to shrug away his growing concern for the pair, but it would not vanish. He would have to help them, he supposed, but couldn't for the life of him figure out why he felt the compulsion. His gaze rested on the girl briefly, but he mentally shook his head. No, it was not that he was enamored especially of this girl. Oddly enough, he suspected he was going to do it because of the boy. There was a certain stiffness to the lad that spoke of fear, pride and courage all mixed in together as he stood protectively by his sister. He was taking a lot on himself to rescue her, trying very hard to be a man, though Radcliffe doubted that the pair was more than fifteen or sixteen.

"You had best finish saddling up. Time is passing. You will wish to be far and away from here come the morning." With that, the man turned and left the stables.

"Do you think he will tell?" Beth asked anxiously as they listened to his fading footsteps.

Shrugging, Charlie walked back into the stall to finish saddling the mount. "It does not matter. It might be good if he does, since the plan I gave him was a lie. But mount up quickly anyway. If he wakes everyone up, I do not wish to be here."

Nodding, Beth hurried back to her mount, then giggled nervously. "Where did you come up with those lies?"

"They were not all lies," Charlie pointed out grimly, and Beth's smile faded.

"No. The part about Uncle Henry losing all and trying to get it back through marriage was true enough. But I am not to marry Carland. I am to marry Seguin. Why—"

"He would hardly be sympathetic to the fact that you are being married off to a fat old goat," Charlie pointed out dryly. "That happens every day. Carland is another kettle of fish altogether."

"Aye. Besides, it was not really much of a lie,

was it? After all, Uncle Henry was selling *you* in marriage to Carland," Beth murmured quietly, her gaze moving over her twin sister. She still found it a little startling to see her in men's clothes. Especially with her breasts bound so tight they seemed nonexistent. She wondered suddenly if it hurt Charlie to have them all squashed up like that.

It had been Charlie's idea to dress as a man. A brother and sister traveling alone would not be noticed. Twin sisters traveling alone would have. She supposed they could have traveled as two boys, but Charlie had not mentioned the suggestion, and truth to tell, Beth had not even thought of it until now. Besides, twin brothers might have been just as memorable as twin sisters. Nay, she decided. 'Twas better this way. She as herself, and Charlie masquerading as her brother.

It was just the adventurous sort of thing Charlie liked to do. She was the braver, wilder of the two. Beth wasn't very adventurous at all. She was the sedate one. Well behaved, obedient, well mannered, she did what was expected. Until she'd found out about Seguin. But she probably would have obediently married the great cow if not for Charlie. Still, Charlie simply couldn't marry Carland. As the stranger had said, she'd be dead in a month, or in goal for killing him in self-defense. That's why Charlie had decided to run away to Cousin Ralph to seek protection. And where Charlie went, Beth followed. They were twins, after all. They'd never been separated in all their twenty years, or not as far as Beth could remember.

"All set?"

Beth glanced up at her sister's question and

nodded as she hooked the bag with her half of their mother's jewels onto the saddle.

"Good. Let us go." Charlie led her horse out of his stall and Beth followed suit, trailing her out of the stable. The pair walked their horses silently around the inn. Beth was staring at the darkened windows, wondering where the stranger had gone, when Charlie suddenly slowed and cursed. Glancing forward, she noted the man standing by a horse on the lane in front of the inn. "What do you think he is doing?"

Charlie was silent for a moment, then sighed. "I suppose we shall have to ask to find out."

Radcliffe smiled to himself as the pair approached. The girl wasn't bothering to hide her anxiety and confusion about his presence. The boy was hiding both staunchly behind a stiff exterior.

"I have decided to travel with you to London," he announced when they stopped before him, then nearly laughed at their blank expressions. They obviously hadn't thought to be so lucky. Deciding to give them a moment to recapture their thoughts so that they could thank him properly, he continued, "It is a three-day journey from here to London. The way is littered with highwaymen and perils of every nature. Since I am headed that way anyway, I thought to avail you of my protection."

Charlie glanced at Beth's nonplussed expression, her own face stiff with fury. Why the devil hadn't she considered that the oaf might decide to join them? Why did he even want to? The jolthead was going to ruin everything. She did not for one moment think that he really wanted to help. So, what was he after? she wondered. The answer came to her almost immediately. It wasn't that hard to figure out, really. She should not have mentioned the jewels. He must have realized that they carried them with them and most likely, he intended to rob them somewhere down the road.

Straightening her shoulders, she glared at him coldly and announced, "Your offer is kind, I am sure, but I am quite capable of protecting my sister."

Radcliffe frowned at the boy's reaction, then realized that he had pinched his male pride. The pride of young men was a most fragile thing, and while Radcliffe normally would have done his most to protect such tender feelings, now was not the time for it. Not when the boy's pride might very well see him and his sister dead. "You are not even carrying a weapon, lad," he pointed out sternly. "If I had been a thief, I could have killed you both and taken your jewels in the stables."

Charlie blinked, wondering if the man had read her thoughts as regarding his motives, then shrugged such worries aside. She had more important concerns. Such as finding some way to refuse his offer and avoid raising his suspicions at the same time. "Who are you?"

Radcliffe blinked. "What?"

"Your name, sirrah?"

He stiffened at the insulting address, then arched one eyebrow rather superciliously and reached into his pocket to withdraw a small card which he presented to Charlie.

Stepping forward, she took the card and frowned

as she read the name out loud. "Lord Jeremy William Richards. The earl of Radcliffe." She looked up at him. "Lord Radcliffe."

He gave an ironic little bow, then relaxed as he saw the recognition on their faces and the way the brother and sister exchanged glances again. "You know the name."

"You knew our father," Charlie countered.

"I never met him," Radcliffe corrected. "But we did correspond on occasion. We were partners in several ventures."

Charlie nodded solemnly and did not correct Radcliffe's polite phrasing. *Partners* was a bit of an ambitious word to use for the investors who threw in with Radcliffe. The man was a genius, according to what her father had always told her. He had the Midas touch. Any investment he made paid back in at least triplicate. Everyone knew this and everyone wished to invest with him, but he was a choosy fellow. Very few people were invited to invest with him, and if one was not invited, one did not invest. As for it being a partnership, there really was none. The investors often had no idea where their money went, and fewer still really cared so long as it paid off. Radcliffe did all the thinking in the investments; those who he invited along simply rode on the coattails of his genius.

She turned the card over in her hand thoughtfully. Lord Radcliffe would hardly need the jewels they carried. While they were a small fortune, they were nothing compared to the wealth he enjoyed. "Why would you trouble yourself to help us?"

Radcliffe raised an eyebrow at the blunt question. "As I said before, you are not even carrying a weapon, lad. But, if I am right, you *are* carrying your mother's jewels." He grinned when Charlie stiffened. "As I thought. One highwayman and the two of you are paupers at your uncle's mercy."

Charlie winced considering that prospect, and Radcliffe's expression softened. "I am headed that way anyway. I see no harm in offering my company as a deterrent to thieves."

Charlie hesitated a moment, then grabbed Beth's hand and urged her a safe distance away, dragging their horses behind them.

"What are we going to do?" Beth hissed as Charlie stopped and faced her.

"We go with him."

"What? But—"

"He is right, Beth. We could be robbed on the road. I did not think of taking a pistol." Sighing, she shrugged. "He is protection. It is one thing to go to Ralphy with our inheritance. It would be quite another to show up penniless."

"But he is heading the wrong way," Beth pointed out after a hesitation.

"I know." Charlie thought for a moment, then grinned suddenly. "That might be to our advantage, though. As I pointed out earlier, our uncle will hardly look in London, or even in that direction for us." A soft laugh slipped from her lips. "We shall go that way with Radcliffe; then when he stops to rest, I shall steal his pistol and we will head for Ralphy's."

Beth looked uncertain. "But, Charlie, he is offering to help. I cannot like the idea of stealing his pistol as repayment. He—"

"I shall leave him one of Mother's bracelets. That

should pay for the pistol three times over." Her gaze slid back to the man in question. "He must have been on the road most of the day and this evening. He shall probably stop at the next inn, or the one after. There we will make our escape. And that will give us most of the night to travel."